Turning for Home

Alex & Alexander: Book Five

Natalie Keller Reinert

CW01335727

Natalie Keller Reinert

Also By Natalie Keller Reinert

The Florida Equestrians Collection

The Eventing Series

The Alex & Alexander Series

The Grabbing Mane Series

The Show Barn Blues Series

The Sea Horse Ranch Series

The Briar Hill Farm Series

The Project Horse: A Florida Equestrian Novel

The Hidden Horses of New York: A Novel

Sweet, Small Town Romance

The Catoctin Creek Series

Learn more at nataliekreinert.com

Chapter One

"HEY ALEX, THAT HORSE still running?"

"Stick around, I think he gonna win the last race!"

"Yeah, too bad you entered him in the eighth, huh?"

I smiled congenially to our hecklers and then, with a display of the ladylike elegance I am known for, flipped Eddie and Mikey the finger. The railbirds guffawed and went back to their hard work holding up the backstretch rail. They had the last few races to lose yet.

"Don't listen to them," I told Tiger, who was most manifestly *not* still running, but who was prancing along beside me, every inch The Tiger Prince and seeming to have absolutely no idea that he'd just run forty lengths behind the winner of the bottom-most allowance race Tampa Bay Downs had to offer. "You're just having a bad patch, that's all."

Tiger eyeballed a candy wrapper alongside the horse-path, considered it for a moment, and then gave in to his deepest, naughtiest desires: he snorted at the wrapper and spooked hard. Since the candy wrapper was to his right, that meant he spooked to his left—directly into me. I grunted as his rock-hard shoulder collided with my (much smaller, lighter, weaker) shoulder, then gave him a solid *whack* with the knotted end of the leather lead shank, right on his big handsome hindquarters, knocking sand out of his hide with the impact. "Brat!"

Tiger leapt forward, hit the nose chain and came to a screeching halt, snorted once again, shook his head, and finally subsided, contenting himself by returning to his high-stepping jig. He was the picture of a racehorse in fullest bloom of youth and energy.

He was six years old and sliding downhill fast. Speed had deserted Tiger, and all he had left was hubris. Of *that,* his reserves were endless.

I kicked at a seashell dotting the horse-path and sighed.

The fact was, Eddie and Mikey Tipton, the brother-trainer-wonder-duo who considered themselves the backside comedy troupe, hadn't been calling out any jokes I hadn't heard before. I'd even told that joke more than a few times. When horses run that bad, that's just what racetrack people say, then we shake our heads to one another, once the unlucky trainer is out of earshot, and wonder what they're going to do with that slow-ass horse of theirs. Turn it out, drop it in class, give it away, breed it...well, that last one wasn't an option for Tiger.

The racetrack rail along our left gave way to short-cropped grass as we slowly walked into the stable area. Low green barns ran in tidy rows; horses peered over their stall webbings to see their compatriots returning from the eighth race. A man leaned over the railing of his barn, feed buckets in hand. "Sorry about the race, Alex," he called. "Maybe next time, huh?"

"Thanks, J.T.," I replied, with what I hoped looked like a smile. J.T. was a good guy. He waved, turned back under the stable banner that read *Speed To Burn Racing Stable,* and got on with evening feeding.

We turned into the shed-row of our own barn, Tiger dancing beside me, and Alexander turned from his perusal of some other horse hidden within a stall, some other horse to distract him from ours.

My eyes met his and he smiled ruefully.

"Surprised he's not still running," Alexander said lightly.

I walked on past him without a word.

I just didn't have the joke in me this time.

"Alex?"

I paused and looked back, pulling up Tiger. The horse blew hot air on my wrist and shook his head impatiently. Standing still was not in his post-race agenda, and he knew it. Time to walk the shed-row, pausing for a sip of water every second turn. Time to make faces at that filly at the north corner that hated him so much, she had to bare her teeth and take a chunk out of the wall every time she saw him. Time to spook and rear every time he passed the Monster in the Muck Pit, just like nearly every other horse in the barn. "What? I have a hot horse here."

Alexander spread his hands in a consoling gesture that just looked helpless instead. But his blue eyes were kind, which I appreciated—I would have expected at least *some* impatience from Mr. Never Forget This Is A Business. Empathy would be a welcome improvement. "Look—I know it was bad. But no one is talking about it. At least you have that. Did you hear about those horses in the Everglades?"

Oh Lord, yes. I nodded stiffly; it wasn't a story I felt up to talking about right now. I'd been in the paddock, saddling Tiger for his race, when the Everglades story broke. An outrider scrolling on his phone while waiting for the post parade had found some headline on Twitter—three horses, three *Thoroughbreds*, had been found abandoned and starving, wandering somewhere in the Everglades, in a piney upland, I figured, where a little bit of grass would push through the sand. Most of the non-natives were busy asking how a horse could be wandering around in a swamp for any length of time. The Everglades were way more than water and alligators. Not that it mattered. This was going to be a major scandal, and bad for all of us in the racing game. As it should be. Until the rotten apples were sorted out, most of America seemed content to throw out the whole bushel—Alexander and I included. Maybe, at least, they could prosecute this particular apple. "Any more news on it? Whose horses they were, maybe? They have to find whoever dumped them and throw the book at them."

"None. But I just wanted you to know—*that's* the gossip all over the track. If you were going to throw a clunker, this was the race to do it in. No one's going to be talking about you tonight."

"Thanks," I sighed, and clucked to Tiger to walk on. He squealed and danced next to me, his hooves throwing up a cloud of dust to glitter in the golden light of late afternoon. "I don't even know why I'm walking you out," I told him. "I don't even know how you're hot from that little canter around the track. You big embarrassing dummy. Don't you know I have a name to maintain? How am I going to lift my head around here?" But Alexander was right—with a fresh abuse scandal breaking upon the racing community, my worst showing yet from Tampa's winter meet would go unnoticed. That was a mercy, anyway. It hadn't been a wonderful winter so far, not for me.

"I almost wish I was back in Saratoga," I went on, and Tiger jogged beside me, his ears flicking between the shed-row ahead and my familiar voice. We'd been together for how long now? The years went by in a blur of foaling seasons, hot summers, wet autumns, with every morning bringing the same chores. And except for leaving him behind for last summer, when I went racing in Saratoga, we'd spent time together nearly every day. Tiger was more pet than racehorse to Alexander and me, and I was even worse about it than Alexander was.

I galloped Tiger, I saddled Tiger in the paddock, I caught Tiger after the race. I kept Tiger at home with me between races. He'd been an anchor in a dangerous time for me, when my world was stormy and I felt adrift from everything I had ever loved. I had a special place in my heart for my wicked colt, Personal Best, who lived up to his name in every way as the best horse I had ever bred, foaled, and trained; I had a special attachment to my foolish filly Luna Park, who had been on the road to ruin when I claimed her and gave her a re-education.

But when Alexander had proposed that we run our good horses at Gulfstream over the winter, and went so far as to say they ought to be stabled at a South Florida training center for easy access to the track, I'd given the go-ahead. I'd kissed P.B. and Luna good-bye, along with Virtue and Vice and Shearwater. I'd kept Tiger, though. You couldn't expect me to give up all my pets at once.

Bathed, cooled out, and legs done up in alcohol wraps, Tiger attacked his hay-net with all the viciousness of a real tiger, leaning over the stall webbing and tearing at the green ball of hay with tooth and muscle and temper. I leaned against the rail of the shed-row and watched him. Alexander leaned against the office door and watched me. I ignored him with the pointed air I'd perfected over the years. I didn't want to talk about it.

But as usual, Alexander wanted to define when we'd have the discussion. "You know it's time, Alex."

"It was a bad race."

"It was an embarrassment."

I ground my teeth. Tiger wrenched hay from his net with long yellow teeth. They weren't the teeth of a young horse anymore. Racehorses started their careers with little nubbins, barely grown out of their milk teeth. They left their careers when they were literally long in the tooth...the lucky ones, anyway...

"Can I at least have a cup of coffee before we talk about this?"

"That I can do." Alexander stepped back and waved his arm towards the office door. "Come into my castle, madam."

The office-slash-tack-room was half the size of our big comfortable office in the training barn back at Cotswold, and into that half we'd had to squeeze a saddle rack, heaped with saddle towels and girths and one perfect little exercise saddle, as precious as a child's toy, for the handful of horses we had sent down from Cotswold for the winter race meeting. One corner was occupied by steel trash cans, their lids held down by bungee-cords to discourage crafty raccoons, and a small mountain of feed supplement buckets . My gaze flickered over their familiar labels: joint lubricants, immune boosters, hoof builders, vitamins, electrolytes, even powdered garlic to ward away mosquitoes and biting flies. Our horses got nothing but the best, but I hadn't taken a multi-vitamin since I was a kid.

Wedged into the opposite corner, commanding a small view of the shed-row and the hot-walking machine beyond, was a thrift-store desk, a rusting filing cabinet topped with a dusty coffeemaker, and a small television of impressive vintage. On the floor, a small refrigerator groaned its way through the warm winter afternoon. I opened it now and pulled out a little carton of vanilla creamer. If I was going to have to listen to how badly my horse was racing, I was going to spoil myself with some decadent coffee.

Alexander eyed the creamer but didn't say anything; he didn't believe in spoiling good coffee with flavors and syrups. He set out two mugs with the farm logo on them, chipped and battered, the words *Cotswold Farms* in strong white Roman letters striding across a green field, and when he poured, he supportively left enough room in mine for a healthy dose of creamer.

I practically turned the coffee white as milk.

He looked at me, eyebrows raised.

"I've had a rough afternoon," I explained, and took a long draft of sweet milky indulgence. "You're lucky I'm not demanding an ice cream sundae right now."

Alexander grinned. "That sounds good, actually."

"There's a Friday's right down the street."

"Maybe later. Let's talk about this right now."

"It isn't as if he couldn't have done better in the race." I dove right in, fortifying myself with a gulp of sugar masquerading as coffee. "He's been training perfectly well. He went out there with two excellent works on paper. He was almost the favorite."

Alexander put on a pair of reading glasses, the better to peer at me over the lenses with. They were a rather recent accessory which he enjoyed balancing precariously at the end of his nose for this very purpose. It gave him a fussy, headmaster-ish look, which he loved. It made him feel very wise. I had a feeling he was starting to believe I knew a bit too much for his comfort. He needed to do his wise old owl bit if he was going to continue to feel superior to me, and feeling superior to everyone was part of Alexander's personality. It was one of the things I liked best about him. I wouldn't have him any other way, even if he made me crazy nearly all the time. In the spirit of fairness, of course, I repaid the favor in spades.

"Alex, he ran forty lengths behind the winner," Alexander began in a measured, *let's be reasonable here* sort of tone. "I think that we have discussed this eventuality and come to the only reasonable conclusion."

"I'm just saying he loafed. He wasn't trying. I'm not saying anything else." I didn't actually know what I was saying. It was all nonsense. But I was desperate not to face this. I couldn't run him in a claimer without risking losing him—and he'd shown today that he wasn't going to win at the allowance level. All I really knew was that Tiger was going to have to leave the training barn, and I didn't know where he would go.

Still, I wasn't going to lose him without a fight.

"I wish he hadn't ended with such a bad race," I went on stubbornly. "It's a terrible way to end his career. He was a good solid runner. He deserves a better send-off than that."

Alexander sighed, as Alexander sighed so often. It was his sigh that reminded me I could be a real trial to him, but he loved me anyway, or that he loved me because of it, who knew? He was just as insane as I was, in the end. We were in the racing game, weren't we? Filling our lives with horses, day in and day out? That didn't say much for our good sense. He ran his finger along the rim of his coffee mug, making the cheap ceramic squeak. "You can hardly keep him in training only to run one more lackluster race. And if you drop him in class we stand to lose him."

Well, that wasn't a possibility for one second. *No one* was ever going to put a claim tag on that horse's halter. We'd worked too hard to find him. He was *ours*—end of story. Alexander knew that as well as I did. He was just mouthing empty threats now. "He'll *never* go in a claiming race," I said pointlessly, simply for the sake of saying the words aloud, making sure they were still true.

"Well, there you have it. He isn't an allowance horse anymore," Alexander went on dourly. "And there's nowhere else for him to go. If he can't win in Tampa—"

"I know." Then he couldn't win anywhere—not anywhere in Florida, anyway. Not anywhere legal and sanctioned by the state. Gulfstream Park, with its richer purses and tougher competition, was beyond his reach now.

"We'll take him home and turn him out for a little while. Then you can call Lucy Knapp and ask her to take him into training once he gets bored. She can hang on to him for six months, see what kind of career he might have ahead of him, or you can take him back for a pony. Come on, Alex. It's for the best. I don't want to see him go either, but I don't know where we'd put him. And you want to see him working, don't you? You don't want to see him fat and wasted in a pasture."

"Of course." I tried to think of excuses. "We have a big farm, though, we ought to be able to find somewhere to stick one little gelding."

"Well, we can, for a little while, anyway. But long-term? He can't stay in the training barn, the broodmares will beat him up, *he'll* beat up the yearlings, and he doesn't belong in the stallion barn."

I was quiet, running my finger around the rim of my own coffee mug, wondering why the stallion barn was out. It seemed like the perfect place to stick one little gelding who didn't have a job right now. There were four empty stalls up there, just gathering cobwebs, growing dank and moldy, wasted space we hardly noticed in a barn I rarely went near.

But Alexander held the stallion barn, and our two stallions, firmly under his own power. If he said that Tiger wasn't welcome up there, that was the end of it.

Now Alexander took a breath and made his proclamation, fingers laced together, the image of a reasonable man, a good husband, a sensible horse trainer. "Lucy can bring him along as a riding horse. We'll keep close tabs on him. We'll visit him and make sure he's happy. Once she's finished with him, we can decided the next step. If you want to keep him to ride, you can board him with her. Or we can find someone close by who can ride him, and lease him out."

I rubbed at my forehead. This wasn't supposed to happen. A barn without Tiger—I didn't want it, didn't even want to *think* about it. I'd given up Luna, I'd given up Personal Best—I saw them on trips south to check on their works, and run them in races, but that wasn't the same as having them in the barn. Now my Tiger had to go? "I never thought we'd let him go," I said reproachfully. "I thought you felt the same."

"Of course we won't let him go. I know he is our pet, and obviously we would never sell him. But he needs a job, and we'll be all right without him. There's hardly a lack of horses in the barn." Alexander's voice was gentle and reasonable, which for some reason made everything seem all the more upsetting. "You've barely gotten to know the new two-year-olds. There's bound to be a new pet in the bunch. You find one every year. Last year it was Personal Best, remember?"

"And now he's in Miami," I sniffed. "And so is Luna. That's not helpful. If I lose my favorite every year, I'm just going to stop getting attached."

Alexander shook his head, looking amused. "Oh, Alex, if only. But you'll get attached to someone new. It's in your nature. And then you can cry about him next year, too. It's your way. It's emotionally exhausting, yes, but it's just the way you are." He held up his hands and smiled as if there was nothing he could do about me, despite all his best efforts. I was unfixable.

"They're *all* dull this year," I sniffed, ignoring his teasing. "I don't know what we did wrong, or if there was something in the water or what, but not one of these babies has the personality of a banana."

Alexander gravely considered the potential personality of a banana. "Well," he said finally. "At least they'll be easy."

He had a point. Personality usually meant brains, and brains usually meant trouble. Young horses who thought too much got ideas in their heads that were not easily removed, ideas about who was in charge, the rider or the horse. Tiger was an excellent example of this. Tiger asked himself, and me, this question every single morning.

I sipped at my coffee, which had taken on the approximate taste and consistency of a truck-stop latte, and leaned back in the chair. I could see my reflection in the mirror tilted against the wall behind Alexander, resting crookedly on the dusty filing cabinet. I frowned at myself. I was thin this winter, from constant riding and farm work, and my shoulder-length blonde hair was in an untidy pony-tail that seemed to accentuate my cheekbones and chin. It wasn't really flattering. Alexander told me to eat more. But I'd been anxious constantly since the string of horses had gone to south Florida, and all I'd wanted to do was work. I'd even gone back to galloping a few horses every morning, instead of watching the sets go by from the back of a pony. When I was galloping, I wasn't thinking about anything but that horse, in that moment. It was a relief to let everything else slip away for a few minutes, and just concentrate on the sound of hoofbeats rumbling and tack jingling, to communicate to the young horse how to change his leads in the turns and how to match his strides with his work-partner.

I had to admit I'd been spending an inordinate amount of time on Tiger. Tiger, the horse who lost. I'd been so excited over his last two works. What a morning glory he'd turned out to be in the end! The loss could hardly have been more painful. Forty lengths was bad enough. Forty lengths was practically in the next race, all racetrack jokes aside. Forty lengths was a sign you might consider a new career for *yourself*, never mind your horse. But when you considered who had won that race, and with what sort of horse, it got a thousand times worse.

Mary Archer had looked like the cat that got the cream, too. I could practically hear her purring as she accepted the memorial plaque that had accompanied the race. Behind her, the horse she had won with, some Nobody by No One out of Nothing Much, had looked around the winner's circle with wild eyes. As well he should have, since it was the first time the five-year-old gelding had ever seen the inside of one. That horse blew up the board and busted a few pick-six millionaires that day. Mary Archer had looked over at me, as I sponged water over my sweaty horse's poll, and gave me a squint-eyed glare, as if I were something she'd scraped from the bottom of her shoe.

So had the press.

And the horsemen around the barns. And the bettors. And basically everyone in the world.

Tiger had been the second-favorite, you see.

Today hadn't been my best day.

Then, the gossip had hit, and Miss Mary Quite Contrary had disappeared very quickly. Back to the barns, back to her truck? Amongst the clusters of horsemen repeating the unbelievable news that had just come out of south Florida, Mary was absent. Conspicuously so, it seemed to me. But maybe that was just because of our ongoing feud. Maybe it didn't mean anything at all.

"I guess I just didn't want to believe he was so done. I knew he was slowing down, but I didn't know it would be so terrible."

"It was terrible," Alexander agreed promptly. "It was an embarrassment. It was a kick in the balls. But that's racing. It's nothing personal—he just let you know he was done, in the most public way possible." He picked up his coffee, took a sip, then quickly put down his cup as if he'd suddenly had a revelation. "Is this just about Tiger, or are you upset about Mary Archer beating you?"

I slumped in my chair. *Caught.* "A little," I admitted. "But look at the streak she's on, and with all these horses right off the claim. She's jumping them in class and they're all winning and no one is questioning that even a little bit? All this and she's training for *Littlefield*, Alexander! Horses no one else in town would touch with a ten-foot pole. That horse that beat Tiger hadn't even run at that level before, let alone put his nose in front. That's not a little nuts? And she was nowhere to be seen once the word broke about those abandoned horses. I don't know how many bad schemes one person can be in on, but I've only seen her in the worst of company, and you know it." The bush track at Otter Creek came to mind. Mary didn't worry much about social conventions, or which side of pari-mutuel law she was on.

Alexander looked around to see if anyone was listening. "Maybe this isn't a public conversation," he suggested in a reproving tone.

"Fine." He was probably right. At the races, you never knew when you were alone and when there was someone just outside the door, loitering and listening. Secrets were worth good money here.

"But whether her horses are legitimate or not, Tiger didn't get beat by a nose. He got beat by forty lengths. That's got nothing to do with the winner."

I sighed. I knew that. I *did.* But it didn't make things any better. I was still losing a horse, and I'd still seen him get beat by the woman who had tried her best to make me look like an idiot in Saratoga, and followed that up by being my only rival for a classless claimer who needed a safe retirement. I'd done all right at Saratoga despite her, and Christmasfordee would soon be safely installed in

Lucy Knapp's training barn, where she would learn to be a sport-horse, but Mary was always back for more, a thorn in my side, pointing out my every mistake.

"I guess that's it then." I brushed at my tingling eyes. "This dusty barn!"

Alexander took my hand and rubbed his thumb against my palm. "We get so attached," he teased. "We really are awful at this business."

I had to smile at that, and at Alexander, and at us, two trainers with horses running and winning all over Florida, a breeding and training farm recognized the world over, and the softest damn hearts in the game. "At least we don't have a guilty conscience keeping us up at night," I said lightly. "Not everyone in this business can say that. Sure, we get our feelings hurt, but our horses are healthy and safe and happy."

Alexander nodded. "You're right about that, love." He reached across the desk and took my hand. His calloused grip was soft on mine, but I could feel the power there, the sinews and tendons and muscles and hard bone beneath leathery warm flesh. We were strong, I thought. We were mighty, and we would not let a little thing like retiring a horse bring us down. We'd provide for Tiger as we had provided for every other horse who had been entrusted to our care. We were the good guys, and even if I'd been a dismal failure as a trainer today, my day would come. Simple karma said so —karma and hard, hard work.

Alexander's phone suddenly buzzed, bouncing across the desk like an angry bee, and we both jumped. He let go of my hand to pick up the phone, and I put it back into my lap, feeling anxious, even a little cold, without his comforting touch.

Goodness, I was just all kinds of a girl tonight, wasn't I. Time to toughen up and remember who I was. I smiled at Alexander as I got up and headed back into the shed-row to find something to do. There was always something to be done. That might be the best thing about working with horses.

Chapter Two

W HATEVER WORK THERE WAS to be done, I really couldn't find it. The feeding was done, the shed-row was raked, the horses were watered and settled in for the night, the grooms were gone home. I gazed off down the shed-row. Just a short distance away, slanting winter sunlight sparkled on the white rail of the backstretch. It was almost post time for the last race; in a few moments a field of horses would go thundering by, and the slumbering backside would awaken for one thrilling moment as horses hurried to their stall doors to look out and see the excitement, and then just as quickly as the galloping herd had arrived, they would be gone, and it would be nothing but the usual sounds of a resting barn for the remainder of the evening and night —the munching of hay, the scratching of manes on door-frames, the thumping of hooves as a horse rolled too close to the wall, the occasional *I'm here, are you there?* whinnies of anxious horses making sure that they hadn't suddenly been left all alone. The frogs would peep when the sun went down, and the crickets would sing from the drains and the wash-racks, and the whip-poor-wills would call their names from the nearby pine barrens.

But we'd hear it all from Ocala, not Tampa, because we were going home tonight. That was what I liked best about Tampa, besides its good surface and unpretentious atmosphere—we could ship in and out so very easily. We all slept better in our own beds, horses and humans alike.

There was a sudden *bang* from behind me, and a few horses neighed in alarm. I jumped and turned sharply, and saw Tiger leaning over his webbing, yanking triumphantly at the hay-net he'd finally pulled down from the door-frame, taking a few inches of wood with it. He appeared to be intent on dragging it into his stall. "You are seriously messed up," I told him, but he ignored me, concentrating on trying to get a good grip on the cotton rope with his teeth. "Tiger was just a name, not a life-choice suggestion."

I was still watching him struggle with his prey when Kerri strolled into the barn, jingling the truck keys in one hand. "You almost done or—" She stopped short at the sight of Tiger the Vicious Jungle Creature and his dead hay-net. "So he finally did it. Dude, you killed the hay-net!"

"I guess the wood around the stall door was rotten."

"Don't downplay his moment of triumph. Tiger, buddy, you did it! After all those years, you taught that old hay-net who was boss!" Kerri applauded, to the dismay of the spooky three-year-old in the next stall. The colt snorted and disappeared into his stall with a rattle of hooves.

Tiger ignored Kerri and the silly colt next door with equal aplomb. He slid the hay-net a little further into his stall, then stepped back to confront the problem of getting it out from under his webbing. You could practically see the wheels turning. Tiger was a scary-clever horse.

"Are you just going to let him drag that into his stall so he can get all tangled up in the netting and learn his lesson? Because he'll break all four legs and his neck before he learns anything from this. You know how stubborn he's gotten."

Alexander came out of of the tack room, his face stony. "He learned that from Alex."

Uh-oh, I thought. That must not have been a good phone call. Sensitive, empathetic Alexander had disappeared, and I didn't like the look of what had replaced him. "What did I do?" I asked warily.

"You talk too much," Alexander retorted. "Especially when people of good sense tell you to keep your mouth shut."

"Where is this coming from?" I was astonished by his tone, especially when not five minutes ago he'd been trying to make me feel better, but I was more than up to the challenge of getting good and pissed off in five seconds or less. "I hope you have a really good reason for talking to me like this," I snapped.

Kerri busied herself yanking the hay-net away from a furious Tiger, who went sulking to the back of his stall after she shooed him away from his prize.

"I have a bloody *great* reason. You've landed us in hot water with that magazine article you did, Miss Responsible Retirement." Alexander hurled the false title at me like sharp stones. "They've traced one of those Everglades horses back to us, but not a word would have been said if you hadn't been posing like the Mother Teresa of horse racing. Instead I've just been warned that at least one news van is parked at the farm gate. We're staying here tonight."

The Everglades horses? Connected to us? I felt light-headed with horror and started to babble. "How could there have been one of ours? We were just there last week. No one has said anything!" *Oh God,* what horse of ours could it have been? *Oh God,* was it the one who had died? *Oh God, oh God, oh God.* I thought of Luna, I thought of Personal Best, of Shearwater, of Virtue and Vice—it couldn't have been anyone of them, though, they hadn't been starved, they were safe at the training center—

"Not one of our horses, although the news will tell it differently." Alexander's voice was thin with his own brand of ice-cold rage, but his eyes were fiery. "Someone has deciphered the tattoo on one of them and it turns out he was in our barn for breaking as a long yearling. Market Affair. A bay gelding, five years old, with a star and a snip and two white hind legs. By Lost Wager and out of some Marquetry mare, I've forgotten her name. Ring any bells?"

I chewed my lip, thinking back. Dozens and dozens of horses had come and gone in the years I'd been at Cotswold. A five-year-old who had been a long yearling—that would have put him on the farm back when I was a gallop girl, before I'd held any sort of power at the farm. I tried to picture a weather-worn collar, with the name of the sire and dam and foaling year engraved in brass, bobbing through a mop of black mane as I jogged some youngster through the pastures in a nose-to-tail line of baby racehorses. I tried to imagine picking out two white hind hooves, worrying over seedy toe in rain-softened pale hoof walls; I tried to picture pulling a bridle over a little yearling face, the browband brushing the white spot on the nose and the white star between the eyes as I slipped it up and over the fuzzy brown ears.

"It could have been anyone," I began, and *then* I remembered, the images washing over me like a cold wave. A nippy little colt with a big dynamic trot that made my repressed dressage intuition hum and sing, a habit of opening his mouth for the bit and then clamping down and refusing to let it go after a ride, an overwhelming desire to lie down in mud puddles that had once ended with me leaping from his back as his knees buckled into the mire for a forbidden roll. "Oh *no.*" I trembled and suddenly felt weak-kneed and queasy, horror roiling in my belly and clouding my vision. I put out a hand to steady myself, gripping the rough railing of the shed-row with everything I had.

"So you remember him." Alexander's voice was grim. "He *was* on our farm."

I gulped, found my voice again. "I remember."

Kerri finished rigging up the hay-net, threw away the rotted wood that had been tangled in the knot, and sidled up alongside me. "You okay?"

I shook my head, my jaw tight, thinking of that sweet little colt left abandoned in the Everglades with two other Thoroughbreds, his skin pulled drum-tight over his ribs and hips and shoulders, his eyes bewildered and his heart broken by a cruelty he could never have deserved.

Kerri put an arm around my shoulders and looked at Alexander. "But why the news van? I mean, this is terrible, but it's hardly the first case of abuse, especially in south Florida. They're all crazy down there, far as I can see."

"The problem is that someone phoned the local media and told them that the horse is connected with Cotswold Farms, and that Alex has been held up as a model of responsible racehorse retirement in the equestrian world." Alexander sighed. "And now she is going to be held up as a hypocrite. Everyone—the news media, the animal rights activists, they'll be looking for someone to blame—and they'll find Alex has made herself an easy target."

Kerri's arm stiffened around my shoulders. "How can that be?"

"How *can* that be?" I echoed, my mind still swirling with horrible images of that sweet little colt I had started under saddle. "I never did anything to cause this! And he did so well. He trained beautifully. He got a good price at the April sale, as I recall. I think he breezed in a little over ten."

"It's not about his training," Alexander said. "It's about the fact that he was with us at all. They're going to pounce on someone who talks such a good game about retirement, but allows a horse to end up in such dire straits. The perfect poster child for anti-racing organizations, because they can point and say that even the good guys are really bad."

None of this was making any sense. "How can that be my fault? I was only an exercise rider back then, and you didn't even own him! He was a consignment!"

"It *isn't* your fault and no one in the business would think it was your fault—but since you had to get into that magazine chattering on about how you keep track of the Cotswold horses and everyone's calling you a model breeder and horsewoman and the essence of change, anyone anti-racing is going to try and use the media's total lack of knowledge about the racing business to crucify you." Alexander shook his head in exasperation. "And it's going to be very bad for business. Wait until Wallace hears about this. Dammit. He's going to flip his lid. That one's lost for sure."

Then, as if he couldn't take another moment of my presence, Alexander stomped off, his Italian race-day loafers coated in dust from the shed-row, in search of solace from heaven-knew-where. The clubhouse bar, maybe. The man who had held my hand and reassured me that I was going to successfully retire my favorite child had utterly disappeared. I watched him go, then turned to Kerri. "Um, who is Wallace?"

She shrugged. "How should I know?"

I sighed and stepped out from the embrace of her arm. Her comfort felt heavy and overbearing to me now; I needed to *act.* I couldn't sit and wait for the news reporters to figure out I was at the track still, or be kept away from *my* farm by their mere presence. Tiger watched me intently, his eyes burning with some inner flame that should have signified his competitive nature but really just meant he wanted some grain to go with his hay. He felt the same way, though. He wanted to be *moving,* all the time. Never standing around, waiting to be given permission.

"Oh well...some potential client we just lost, probably," I said dismissively, to close the subject without looking too out of the loop in front of Kerri. But even that didn't make much sense—we didn't take on many clients. We concentrated on our own horses. It was a decision we'd made a few years ago and we'd stuck with it. Along with the few outside owners we took on, things had been working just fine. So why would Alexander be courting new clients? And why wouldn't he tell me?

I shook my head. That didn't matter right now. We had to *move.* I picked up the wash bucket left outside Tiger's stall. "Let's get ready to pack this crazy horse up and get out of here."

"Alexander said we were staying here tonight."

"Well, he's welcome to, if he's going to stay in a mood. But I'm going home. No one's telling me I can't drive in my gate and sleep in my own bed, and Tiger doesn't need to stay at the races a second longer than necessary."

Kerri looked at him thoughtfully, his big eyes, his flared nostrils, his pricked ears. He was the picture of a fit racehorse, bursting with run, anyone could see it. The racetrack atmosphere had him sky-high on endorphins and self-satisfaction. "So he's retired?"

"As of today." I pushed down the hurt those words caused me and resolved to concentrate on the future. He hadn't made a champion racehorse, but there were other championships out there for horses to win. Yesterday couldn't matter—yesterday was Market Affair as a two-year-old, and sending my Saratoga string to south Florida, and now it was going to be Tiger's racing career as well. *Tomorrow* was all that mattered, I resolved. Whatever was coming next—I'd focus all of my energy on that.

We got busy putting the day's gear back into the green-enameled tack trunk. The wash bucket, filled with sponge, sweat scraper, and liniment, went into one corner; the neatly folded cooler into another. The bottles of Show Sheen and shampoo and fly spray were wedged against a little wooden box that rattled with spare horse shoes. The scissors and spare bandage tape were put into the grooming tote alongside combs and brushes, and the grooming tote was placed gently on top of the rest of the trunk's contents. I closed the lid, its bandage slots empty now that Tiger was all wrapped up like a Christmas present, and Kerri and I each picked up one brass handle and marched it out to the horse trailer where it waited, two barns away, in the parking area.

My fingers fumbled as I pulled the little tack room key out of my pocket and it bounced away into the gravel somewhere beneath the trailer. Cursing, I set down my end of the tack trunk and dove after it. I stood back up scarcely a minute later with stone dust on my khaki slacks and Mary Archer grinning down at me.

Kerri stood off to one side, her side of the tack trunk still hefted against her shin, looking at me nervously. "Thanks for the warning," I said dryly, not bothering to greet Mary. The other woman laughed in a coarse, smoky voice; she made no pretensions about our relationship.

Kerri only blushed; she had always been afraid of confrontation with the rough-edged Appalachian trainer. But I knew now that Mary Archer was all venom and no fangs. She could sling dirt with the best of them, but she'd never been any real threat to me—even when she was spreading gossip about me all over the backside, all she'd ever really done was hurt my feelings. My horses hadn't suffered, so what difference did it make in the long run?

After I'd seen her run for the hills at the Otter Creek bush track, and get one-upped by the Rodeo Queens in their big hats and stiletto heels down in Miami, I was starting to think gossip was the only weapon she actually had.

But Mary Archer just went on grinning her big toothy smile, the one she saved for *gotcha* moments just like this. "Just wanted to say hello to my favorite do-gooder. How's business these days, Alex? Ready for a big breeding season with those fancy stallions of yours?"

My eyebrows came together before I could guard my expression. What on earth could *that* mean? "I guess so," I answered, trying to keep the suspicion from my voice. "Not breeding a lot this year. Keeping things simple."

"Oh, was that the plan?" she asked archly. "I coulda sworn you were plannin' on rampin' things *up* this spring."

"Nope." I turned my back to her and unlocked the tack room door, my mind racing as I tried to catch up with her veiled words. What on earth was she getting at? We had only two stallions, and neither of them were by any means fancy. They were barely practical, at this stage in the game. We wouldn't have a big stallion on the farm until Personal Best retired, assuming he went as far as we hoped.

"Well, that's good then. You won't be disappointed this way."

"Disappointed? No, don't think so." I reached past her for my end of the tack trunk, and nodded at Kerri to help me lift it up into the tack room.

"Think Alexander might see it different," Mary called, rocking back on her heels. "Think he had somethin' maybe he hadn't told you yet. Might not matter now, though."

I stayed in the tack room, busying myself with moving jackets on hangers. There was a hot flush on my cheeks despite my best intentions to ignore her barbed tongue. *Was* there something he wasn't telling me? Was this something to do with that mysterious Wallace character?

Why would Mary Archer know more about my farm's business than me?

Ridiculous. She didn't know a thing. I carefully ran the zipper up a few monogrammed jackets, pretending they were in danger of falling from their hangers. If I ignored her, she would leave. Like a dog begging for scraps, if she didn't get anything, she'd move on to the next table.

Kerri, following my lead, climbed up into the sleeping quarters and made a great show of fixing the sheets and pillows. Mary poked her head inside, and her voice echoed in the small space.

"This looks comfy. Might wanna use it. Cuz I wouldn't go home tonight, Miss Do-Gooder."

"What?" I turned around, slippery satin jackets sliding to the floor.

"You heard me. I wouldn't go home. Unless you figure any publicity's good publicity. You're about to get real famous on the evening news. I think if you leave now you might make the eleven o'clock broadcast." Her malicious grin was unbearable, and I immediately knew without a doubt that she was the one who had called the local news.

Kerri realized it too. "Mary, why would you do this? We've never done *anything* to you."

"Oh no?" Mary eyed Kerri skeptically. "Well, maybe you haven't, child, but your boss has done *plenty*. She's interferin', she's connivin', and she's got a lip on her. Thinks she can get away with anything she wants cuz she married money. Well guess what —" Mary turned her beady eyes back on me, squinting at me through a thousand wrinkles. "Your fast little mouth has finally caught up to you." With that, Mary's head disappeared from the tack room door.

Kerri jumped down from the sleeping area and poked her head out. "She's heading around to the frontside," she reported after a moment. "What was she talking about?"

I didn't answer at first. I slipped the fallen jackets back on their hangers and arranged them carefully on the metal bar. I straightened Alexander's wide-brimmed oilskin hat he'd brought back from Australia, and the small collection of baseball caps on the rack above. I fixed the blinds on the window so that they hung perfectly even. I had leaned down and started to pick up bits of hay and straw from the berber carpeting when Kerri finally gave up on getting a straight answer from me.

"There's no point in talking to you when you're like this," she sighed, and I heard her footsteps thump on the metal step outside, before she left me all alone.

Finally, the solitude I'd been waiting for since Alexander had announced I was a target. I sat down heavily, letting the flakes of straw slip from my fingers, and leaned back against the wall. I meant to think about Tiger and his future; I meant to begin planning, for real this time, the next chapter of his life. It was more important than whatever cryptic B.S. Mary had been trying to get me to pay attention to. She was nothing, I reminded myself. Nothing. Whatever silliness she'd stirred up, well that would pass. It had to. In the meantime, Tiger was what was important.

Still, when I closed my eyes to picture my dark handsome ex-racehorse, all I saw was the field of broodmares back at the farm, as I'd seen it this morning, driving towards Tampa. The mares swishing their tails across bellies swollen with pregnancy, moving heavily through the brown-green winter pasture, their expressions content and their actions unhurried. The older mares had the quiet knowing that comes from years spent in their most natural of functions; the younger ones were eager to please and followed in the matrons' footsteps. They had all been athletes once; their lives were given over to making new athletes now.

They wouldn't all be successful at that job, not every year, not with every foal. There were two foals already in the pasture, the earliest of early January foals, and it was impossible to know if lightning would strike and new racehorses would emerge from those spindly-legged little babies snoozing in the grass, or if they'd fail at the vocation they'd been born and bred for, and have to seek gainful employment and kind owners in another discipline. If they'd be another Personal Best, or if they'd be another Market Affair—who could say? Or, I thought sadly, they could be another Tiger. Fast, but not fast enough. All careers came to an end, and when the breeding shed wasn't an option...only luck could save a horse then.

Every foal born was a roll of the dice, and we were gaming with lives.

Chapter Three

A LEXANDER STILL HADN'T COME back by the time I'd pulled the trailer around to the loading dock. I pretended I didn't care, and threw open the trailer door anyway. Kerri led Tiger, still bright-eyed and bushy-tailed as if he'd never run a race (and the fact was, he really hadn't), up the gravel ramp and settled him into one of the trailer stalls. Naturally he was unconcerned with the loading business and was only interested in the hay-net already tied up inside, so much so he nearly dragged her into the corner where it was hanging. If Tiger could have spoken up and told us what he wanted as his next career, I'm sure it would have been "professional hay-eater."

If that was a viable career path, I'm sure he would have been top-notch.

As it was, I thought, checking the door latches and trailer hitch with a thoroughness that bordered on paranoia, it was hard to say what he was going to be good at. His temper had become legendary around the barn over the past year—he wasn't *mean,* but he was too clever by half. He had "a sense of humor," as horse-people will say when they like a naughty horse that they probably shouldn't. He took peoples' hats without their knowledge and buried them under dirty straw bedding; he threw saddle towels under the hooves of horses walking the shed-row to initiate explosive spooks that he could settle back and watch with clear amusement; he had progressed from gently nibbling his handler's neck and shoulders during a curry-comb session to tearing shirts and drawing blood with what was less a love-nip and more a coltish provocation. And then, of course, there was his behavior under saddle—the rearing and spinning, the roguish baiting of lead-ponies, the occasional dropped shoulder and spin maneuver that had gotten me off more than once.

"He's basically turned into a big bully," I reflected.

Kerri pulled on her seat belt. "Who? Tiger?"

"Yeah."

"He's an asshole," she agreed amiably. "But I like him for some reason."

"He's smart. Every time he does something, you're reminded of how smart he is. It's different than when a horse does nasty things out of spite. He's not malicious, he's just..." I turned on the truck, trying to think of what it could be. What was Tiger trying to tell us, when he was being a big pain-in-the-ass teenager?

"He's bored," Kerri suggested.

"You think?"

"He's been running in circles for a really long time."

"That's true." I put the truck in gear and the diesel engine rumbled reassuringly. I did love the sound of a diesel truck. It was the redneck in me. Every horsewoman's got a little, no matter how urban or sophisticated she might have started out. We started to creep along the bumpy road towards the frontside.

In the trailer behind, Tiger kicked the walls with a rhythmic *bang-bang-bang*. I knew from experience that he wasn't going to stop until we were out on Race Track Road. I suspected he only kicked to show off to the other horses that he was leaving for the countryside and his very own paddock while they were stuck in their stalls, with only their dwindling hay-nets and dirty old Jolly Balls to amuse them. *"Such* an asshole," I muttered, shaking my head, and Kerri laughed.

As we approached the clubhouse parking lot, I slowed the truck and peered at the cars that were left over after the day's card. "Do you see Alexander's car?"

Kerri leaned out of the window. "I think that's it up by the very front," she said after a moment. "The black Audi?"

"There are like ten black Audis."

"The one that belongs to your husband, if that narrows it down? The one that is parked in your driveway and that you see every day and sometimes also drive places in?"

"Shut up." I stopped the truck altogether and craned my neck to see over Kerri's head. "I guess that could be his. He got here pretty early."

Bang-bang-bang! "Goddammit, Tiger."

"Why's he hanging out on the frontside still? That's not like him." Alexander was more social than I was, but he still preferred the solitude of home to any sort of crowd, especially after a race-day. *Especially* after a poor race-day like this one.

"He thinks we're staying in town tonight." I sat back down and touched the gas pedal gently. "He doesn't even know we're leaving." And I turned the truck onto Race Track Road, cutting off a few cars for the hell of it. Time to go home. He'd call when he realized I wasn't back at the barn, and I'd ignore the call, and he'd be mad at me tonight, and then tomorrow he'd come home and see that there hadn't been any reason to worry about going home as planned, and everything would blow right over.

It had to.

Tampa and Ocala are neighbors, but not near ones. Kerri had dozed off, head against the window, and I was nearly through a Super Mega Giant Gulp full of Diet Coke from the truck stop before we exited the interstate for the last time and drove west, cutting through the dark country night with our retired racehorse in tow. I was tired, although the caffeine was keeping my eyes open and my hands on the wheel, and the thought of putting Tiger in his stall, straightening his wraps, and giving him another few flakes of hay was just about all the work I could face before I crept into the house, took a shower, and finally found my bed. Hell, with Alexander gone for the night, maybe I'd just skip the shower.

Kerri stirred and woke as we rattled over Marion County's less-than-pristine roads. "We almost home?"

"Five minutes. You going home tonight? You can crash in the guest room if you want." The guest room was more of a storage room where we threw all the things we did not want to think about, like a broken vacuum cleaner and several dozen cases of an equine dietary supplement some company had sent to us as a promotion, without mentioning that horses on it tested positive after races. (Luckily, someone else made that mistake before we did.) But behind all this there was a bed, anyway, with sheets on it and everything, and that was all anyone needed, right? "I think the sheets got washed since last time you stayed." Maybe.

Kerri stretched and yawned. "Tempting. I'll let you know after we get Tiger unloaded."

We turned onto our own road and the engine rose in pitch as the truck climbed the first in a succession of high hills between us and the farm. Cotswold sat in the most rolling section of Marion County, and the hills were like mountains to me. It seemed like the truck felt the same way, especially with a trailer to haul. I was looking down at the RPMs, wondering if I ought to change gears, when Kerri straightened in her seat and said "What's all that light?"

The truck crested the hill and several tall towers, lit with spotlights and capped with satellite dishes, appeared in the distance. We blinked at them for a second, and then the truck was plunging back down the hillside and the towers disappeared. Only the glow of artificial lights remained, its source hidden below the hill ahead, but its gleam unmistakably foreign on a county road lined with expansive horse farms and secluded houses.

"I don't know," I lied. *I've just been warned that at least one news van is parked at the farm gate,* Alexander had growled.

"Those were spotlights." I could feel Kerri's eyes on me in the dark truck. "And satellites. Those were news vans. Mary wasn't lying. They *do* want to put you on the eleven o'clock news."

The engine coughed as we began to roll up the next hill and I realized I'd let my foot drift up from the pedal. I floored it, and the diesel roared back to life, carrying us back towards another view of the battlefield ahead. As we hit the crest of the hill, just a quarter mile left between us and the farm's driveway, the spotlights' white glow was nearly blinding. Beneath the dome of light, there they were: the showy news vans, their satellite dishes reaching towards the stars, ready to broadcast my homecoming to the world. I could picture the reporters slicking back their hair and straightening their jackets every time a truck appeared on the country road, ready for the one that would hold the rogue horse trainer they were waiting for, the one whose horse had been abandoned in the Everglades.

"Don't stop," Kerri said urgently. "Keep driving."

"Where to?" We were almost to the driveway, and I was letting the truck coast now, losing speed without jerking Tiger around by braking. My turn signal was on; so were my high-beams. I left those on, because blinding the news crew seemed like the least I could do with all the trouble they were about to cause me.

"Someone else's place. Lucy Knapp's place."

"She's all the way out in Williston! No way."

"Margaret's place. She's just down the road."

"Margaret goes to bed at eight thirty every night. It's an hour past her bedtime. She'd be furious, and anyway, I bet her gate is locked. Come on, Kerri. We can deal with these pricks." I took a deep breath and summoned all the bravado that I could muster. The news vans loomed up. They were parked along the verge before the driveway. Just three—the local Gainesville and Ocala stations, no one from Orlando or Tampa, thank goodness. *This is a non-story,* I reminded myself. *And this just proves it.*

I pulled the truck into the driveway with the same care for my horse and my rig as always, my eyes on the rear-view mirrors to make sure that the trailer followed along without taking down the mailbox or ending up in the culvert. I wasn't looking ahead, and I was concentrating so hard that Kerri's short scream barely registered. I glanced over at her to see what made her yelp, and that was when my truck hit the reporter.

Chapter Four

THERE WAS A MOMENT of perfect silence. Then all hell broke loose.

Kerri was screaming, the reporter was screaming, the other assorted reporters and drivers and producers and whatever other people who work in the news business were screaming. Tiger was outraged at the way the trailer had come to a sudden, jarring halt when I'd realized the truck had knocked down a human, and was kicking the trailer walls with abandon.

I sat very still and stared straight ahead for what felt like a lifetime, but was probably only a few seconds. My foot was against the floor, the brake pedal down as far as it could go. I hadn't put the truck into park, a realization I came to hours later, thinking about how much worse things could have gone.

The reporter got up, clutching her elbow, and looked at me with loathing. Her neat little skirt and suit jacket were smudged with dirt from the asphalt; her careful helmet of blonde hair was standing up on one side as if she'd just gotten out of bed. She rubbed at her elbow and then bent down and picked something up. Her microphone. She advanced on the driver's side door as if she still meant to attempt an interview with me, even if I *had* just tried to run her down.

(I hadn't.)

Bang bang bang!

We both looked around for the source of the gunfire. The reporter included. Kerri was the first to figure it out.

"Tiger," she whispered, her voice gone ragged from screaming. "Kicking."

"God*dammit,*" I snapped, and I threw the truck into park (thank heaven for habits), popped the door open, and hopped out. The reporter jumped back as if I was going to finish the job with my fists, but I ignored her. I had more pressing issues than some small-town reporter who wanted to put me on the eleven o'clock news. Who the hell was even awake at that time anyway? This was a farm town! Everyone I knew was fast asleep, only a few hours away from their alarm clock. This chick was delusional if she thought anyone had ever seen her face on TV.

But that was just inconsequential stuff, floating through my mind while I made for the horse trailer. I stepped up onto the wheel-well and pulled down the drop-down window. Behind the steel bars, Tiger's bright eyes were on mine immediately, wide and angry at the delay in his trip. He kicked again, his hind hooves connecting with the trailer wall with a resounding crash. I slapped the bars with my open hand, and he jumped back, startled.

"You knock that off," I hissed. *"You rotten bastard."*

"So that's how you talk to your horses?" The reporter was right behind me, her voice horrified.

"When they're busy trying to get themselves hurt and acting like they have no manners," I ground out, not bothering to turn around. Tiger turned in a quick circle, the trailer rocking with his movement, and put his nose up to the bars again, snuffling at my palm. I stuck my finger in and gave his muzzle a little tickle, and he wiggled his upper lip in response. "Stupid jackass," I told him affectionately. "No breaking yourself. We'll be at the barn in a minute."

I jumped down from the wheel-well and the reporter had her microphone in my face immediately. "Lisa Roberts, Action News Nine. We'd like to hear how you respond to reports that one of your horses was found abandoned in the Everglades."

"And I'd like to get *this* horse back to the barn before he injures himself." I brushed at some sand in the microphone's foam cover. "Sorry about knocking down your toy here. But I have to go."

Lisa Roberts, Action News Nine, narrowed her eyes and got snippy. "You know, for a person who just ran me over, you don't have nearly the moral high ground you might think."

"If I'd run you over, you wouldn't *still* be in my way right now," I pointed out, and shoved past her. Behind me, Tiger kicked again. *"Knock it off, you stupid brat! I won't have it!"*

Lisa Roberts, Action News Nine, wasn't impressed by my elegant logic or my eloquent words. She followed closely, pressing on with her demands for a useful quote. "You're accused of owning a horse who has ended up abandoned and half-starved. What do you have to say to that?"

"Who is accusing me? You?" I reached the truck door and jumped back in. Kerri was studiously ignoring another station's reporter, who practically had his nose against the glass of the passenger window, entreating her to open up about her boss's disturbing pattern of abuse and lies. Her cheeks were bright red, but her gaze never wavered from the wrought iron horse decorating the front gates, tantalizingly close.

"Sources tell us that the horse in question was trained here at Cotswold Farm."

"I didn't own the horse." I slammed my door shut to signal an end to the conversation, but Lisa Roberts Action News Nine actually slapped her free hand against the window and started shouting just as loud as the reporter on the other side of the truck.

"Ms Whitehall, some people are saying that you have set yourself up as a champion of responsible racehorse retirement even as you are allowing horses once in your care to end up in deplorable situations—"

I put the truck back in gear and gently touched the gas pedal. I would have loved to screech off and leave the perfume of melting rubber in their smug faces, but Tiger's safety came first, no matter what they thought of me and my attitude towards my horses. Besides, truck tires were expensive. The truck crawled slowly forward, and neither reporter, to their credit, chose to throw themselves beneath the truck or allow their toes to be run over by the tires in some sort of bid for a newsworthy report to send to their studio. Instead, they stepped back and watched sullenly, their cameras following our stately progression to the farm gate. I watched them to make sure no one was following, then reached up and clicked the gate opener. By the time we reached the big black gate, it had slid back on its wheels, admitting us.

I kept driving after we passed through the gate, trusting that it would close with the reporters on the correct side. Kerri looked back nervously. "Aren't you afraid they might follow us?"

"I wish they would," I replied calmly. "I could call the police then."

"How are you so calm?" Kerri's voice cracked dangerously. "That was *insane*. And you *hit* that woman. Oh my God, Alex, you could have killed her. Then *they'd* be calling the police. That guy was banging on my window and saying he was going to—"

"She got in front of my truck and it bumped into her. She was totally in the wrong. Any sheriff would agree with me. The last time the sheriff's department argued in favor of a pedestrian, we still had horses and buggies on the streets. And it's *my* driveway, besides."

"But you're acting like nothing happened."

"How else should I act?"

"You should be a little freaked out, that you knocked down a TV news reporter with your truck. Just a little."

I looked in the rearview mirror. The lights and vans were still there, but the gate had closed with all of the reporters on the other side. The driveway curved sinuously and the trees behind gathered thickly, blocking them from sight. I fastened my eyes on the driveway ahead and sighed. "Kerri," I began, "of course I am freaked out. But there was no way I was going to let any of them see that. That's what they want. They want me rattled and saying any little thing that comes to mind. Then they'd edit it all to get the quotes that they want. They'd have me saying that horses die every day and there's no protecting them and I'm not responsible for every horse that ever set foot on this property, and they'd put that on TV and it would get picked up by PETA and be a national scandal. Is that what you want?"

"No, of course not. I just..."

"What?"

"Let's just say I'm really glad you're the one that has to deal with them," Kerri said ruefully. "Because I don't think I could hold my composure as well as you. Or at all."

"Well, they think I'm a soulless witch already," I sighed. "So I guess in a way, I gave them what they want."

Kerri considered this in silence, and I watched the headlights lead the way through the driveway, picking out the live oaks and fenceposts, the eyes of passing armadillos and creeping barn cats, the phantom shadows of grazing Thoroughbreds in the broodmare pasture. I looked up the hill towards the house as we passed its turn-off, but of course the windows were dark. Alexander was in Tampa, or he was driving home after me; there was no telling what he'd decided to do about me once he'd gone back to the barn and found that his wife and his racehorse had flown. He'd be mad.

Let him be mad, I thought. I'd dealt with the media in my own way.

By running over someone? My husband would not be impressed.

In the trailer, Tiger kicked the walls. I resolved to turn my mind to the important things: horses.

Kerri was too rattled to stay the night with someone as clearly insane as me, so once we pulled Tiger off the trailer and had him set for the night in the training barn stall he had called home for years, I told her to head on home. Farm work was the ultimate relaxation, though. After filling water buckets and a hay-net, she

TURNING FOR HOME   43

was composed enough to wave goodnight cheerfully as she climbed into her little car.

"Won't you be worried about running over a reporter?" I teased, and she smirked and said she'd call the police if they got in her way, and ask for the sheriff's permission before flattening anyone. Just to be sure.

"Always thinking ahead." I watched the red tail-lights go bouncing down the lane, glad she could laugh at the incident at the gate. For me, the enormity of it was just beginning to catch up. Accosted at my own farm gate by television reporters, expected to take the blame for this poor horse I hadn't seen since he was a colt, a horse that hadn't even belonged to me...Mary had done her job telling tales very well, once again, and someone could have gotten seriously injured.

I could have killed someone, with just a tap on the gas pedal, and be spending the night in jail. Maybe quite a few nights. I turned back to the half-lit training barn, to the alert eyes watching me from the stall doors. All of my responsibilities...I couldn't do them any good from prison.

Mary had gotten inside my head, too. Or maybe it wasn't just her and her nasty little smile. It was Market Affair that was haunting me now. He had just put a face on the horror that had been haunting Florida for a few years now. The truth was, scandals like this were nothing new, and it would be yesterday's story to all but a few passionate souls in just a few days. South Florida had more than its share of horrific horse abuse cases. Horses were found abandoned, dead, even *butchered,* their carcasses dumped in the swamps or found tied to trees, locked in stalls or wandering highways. It was unbearably sad when it happened, and it was infuriating, too, because there were people in my business doing this. Maybe people that I saw at the races, or at the sales. Maybe someone, although I could scarcely believe it might be true, that I'd had a cup of coffee with one morning, leaning on the rail and watching works, or killing time in the track kitchen.

To actually *know* one of these horses, to picture him in this state...that hit home. Hard.

I was tired, and I wanted to go to bed, but I knew my brain wasn't ready for that. So I set off along the driveway, leaving the truck and trailer by the training barn. That could be dealt with in the morning. Now, I needed a walk, to think about the horses that were in my possession, the horses that I *was* responsible for, and would be for as long as they lived, in some degree or another.

It wasn't the handful of racehorses in their little paddocks outside the training barn that I stopped to contemplate. I went on, down the driveway, to see the next generation.

By now the winter-brown grass was wet with dew, and a north wind that tasted of fog and cold rain was sighing through the live oaks, sending little spirals of dripping leaves all around me. One landed on my face like an icy tear; I swiped it off and wiped my palm on my dirty slacks. A few steps more, my boots glistening with the damp, and I was leaning against the black-painted top board of a wire mesh fence, gazing down the gentle slope of the broodmare pasture. The scent of creosote was sharp in my nose; this fence had been painted recently. My eyes roved the dark field, searching, and then the clouds parted to show them to me.

There they were in the moonlight, a dozen mares clustered close together, some grazing, some napping. Stretched out in the grass a few small shapes: the early foals, our pair of January babies, fast asleep in the cool Florida night.

There was a rustle from above me, somewhere up in the ancient oak trees, and then a great horned owl called out: *Hoo-hoo-HOO-hoo, Hoo-hoo-HOO-hooo!* The trumpeting call was loud enough to make me jump, more like a recording amplified from a loudspeaker than a sound any living animal could have made, and I hoped the new litter of barn kittens were locked in a feed room for the night. The owls of north Florida were no joke—they'd been known to fly away with rabbits, cats, even at least one (smallish) Jack Russell Terrier.

Despite our orderly pastures, our black-board fences, our meticulous barns, our measured racetracks, I supposed Ocala was still a wild place at heart. As our well-trained racehorses were born wild, kicking and quivering and full of run, on these chilly winter nights.

A sleeping foal startled at the whoop of the owl, his head shooting up from the ground where it was pillowed on soft Ocala sand. The white blaze on his face shone like a luminous gem in the moonlight—it was Crow's foal, a tiny little brother to my big-hearted Shearwater. He nickered, a tiny, tremulous sound, thin in the foggy-wet air, and his mother neighed in return, her deep voice rumbling across the field. There was an ensuing chorus of whinnies and whickers, nickers and neighs, as all the dozing horses awoke and immediately sought verbal confirmation that everyone was right where they had left them. A few sharp neighs from the training barn, on the other side of the farm, pierced the night air, and then it was still again.

Satisfied that the herd was all around him, Crow's foal went back to sleep. The other foal got up and headed for her dam, in dire need of a quick snack.

I laid my cheek against the dark wood of the top rail, breathing in its creosote smell, and watched them. They would only be so little for a little while; soon Crow's foal would be sleeping in a bed of straw, not sand, and he would be poking his white-blazed face over a webbing in a racetrack shed-row, not peering up sleepily at the laughing moon.

Where were they all going to go? Was the world big enough for them?

Little lives I was responsible for, whole existences that were dreamed into life and coaxed into being because I and my associates had wanted them to happen. But I wasn't a deity. I was a breeder.

It had been a bad day for news. I could recognize that. I could blame my nerves and worry on everything that had happened today: the poor race, the racetrack gossip, Alexander's temper, Mary Archer's venomous attack, the reporters at the gate. They'd all made for one sucker punch after another. I was dizzy with it all.

A gray mare shook her head; her silver mane flew out in a parabola from her arching neck, catching sparkles in the moonlight. She hadn't foaled yet, and her midsection was round as a barrel, skin stretched tight to accommodate the little life form inside of her. Not so little—the foal in there, nearly due, would be a couple hundred pounds of muscle and bone and sinew when he finally greeted the world.

Another horse in a crowded world.

Today every horseman at the track had been buzzing about the horrific news from south Florida. Every one of those abandoned horses had had tattoos inside their upper lips. Every one had raced at Calder the previous meet. Their trainer would be known. But maybe their trainer had left the state; it wouldn't be the first time horses had been dumped and the trainer had dashed. Maybe he had signed papers selling them to a dealer who could not now be found; maybe the state would not file abuse charges, maybe nothing would ever come of this but more bad press for horse racing. The only certainty was that charities would have to plea for the thousands of dollars it would take to rehabilitate and retrain the horses for new lives. We'd send money, even if it looked like a gesture of guilt. Of course we would, but that wouldn't fix the problem.

If the entire backside had turned out carrying torches and demanding a lynch mob gather to march on Miami and find the bastard responsible for dumping these poor horses straight out of their coddled racetrack life and into a wilderness unsuitable for any animal that could neither swim nor fly, I wouldn't have been out here staring at my babies, wondering what their futures would bring. I would have been hoisting a torch with the rest of them.

So why was the mob, such as it was, coming after *me?* Maybe Alexander had been right to mock me, maybe he was right to sneer and say I'd set myself up as, what was it? *The Mother Teresa of horse racing.* Maybe the things I'd said to the reporter had been too smug for my fellows in the business, trainers and breeders and owners who had never really liked that up-jumped gallop girl Alex Whitehall much anyway, marching around the paddock at Saratoga and Tampa and Gulfstream like she owned the place. Maybe, maybe, maybe. I didn't know. I'd just been honest. I was responsible for my retirees, and I said so.

As of today, I had one more retiree to plan for.

Accountants would say that I couldn't keep them all; common sense knew this to be true. They'd leave. Some would be runners, some would not. They wouldn't be mine. It shouldn't really matter.

The filly pulled away from her dam and reared up, playfully swatting at the mare's back with her little button-hooves. The mare shook her head at her foal, ears flattened—*go play with your friends, leave me alone.* The filly took the hint and trotted away, looking for someone her own age to bother. She found her sleeping friend and gave the colt a few taps with a foreleg; the sleeping colt jumped up, squealing, and took off across the silver pasture, the trouble-maker in hot pursuit.

They were fast *now,* anyway.

I was going to take care of all of them, no matter how hard. I promised it to them right there, by the light of the moon.

But the moon has always had a mocking smile and I knew, I knew.

It wasn't a promise I could keep.

Chapter Five

D OWN THE SHED-ROW, TIGER kicked.

Alexander swung down from Betsy's saddle and dropped the mare's split reins on the ground. "Stand," he commanded, and Betsy stood. Then he looked at me, with a gaze that demanded answers. *What are you going to do about Tiger?* his furious blue eyes were blazing. It was the same questions over and over. When was I going to send him to a trainer and get him out of this racing barn? Would it be before or after he injured himself kicking the walls—or just plain made us all crazy?

When you have been with one person day in and day out, for years, you get pretty good at mental telepathy. It makes it harder to ignore the things you just don't want to hear.

Of course, sometimes he just shouts them at you until it's impossible not to hear. As was the case when he called my phone at midnight the night after Tiger's race, and I foolishly decided to pick it up. Well, the wine had made it seem like a good idea. I'd told him all about how I'd nearly run over a reporter with the truck and he'd told me all about what an immature irresponsible silly girl I was. And then we both said a few more unrepeatable things and then I told him that I was plenty old enough to make my own decisions and anyway, no one had actually *died,* and then I fell asleep with the phone tucked under my ear When I got up a few hours later, the imprint of the phone red upon my cheek, he was in the kitchen, making coffee as if nothing had happened. He hadn't quite forgiven me, but we were getting along just fine.

Until it became clear that I didn't have a plan beyond bringing Tiger home.

Down the shed-row, Tiger kicked.

I dropped my eyes and studied the black and brown strands of Parker's mane, lying soft and disciplined beneath my knuckles.

Alexander stomped off into the office, probably in search of more coffee. I hoped the grooms had remembered not to let the coffee pot sit empty again. Last week, a new groom had tipped the last few drops of coffee into his mug, then set the glass carafe back down on the burner without adding more water and setting it to brew again. It would have been bad enough if Alexander had come back from watching a set of horses train and found that someone hadn't bothered to make more coffee. It had been an outright disaster when he found that the pot had cracked on the burner. He'd sent the errant groom out for a box of coffee from Starbucks and made him pay for it with his own money.

I'd suggested that someone just run over to the broodmare barn and steal the coffee-pot from that barn's feed room, but Alexander was too caffeine-deprived to see sense. I had to admit, the extra jolt from the Starbucks coffee had been a welcome surprise. The second half of the morning went by at lightning-speed, and we were all done with training twenty minutes early. I hadn't even felt compelled to take a nap afterwards, and the disgraced groom seemed pretty content with his punishment, too. Sometimes, things turned out much better than one could have ever expected. Maybe it would be luck if the coffee-pot *had* been neglected again this morning. I could use a little jet fuel this morning. Sleep had been hard to come by last night.

Down the shed-row, Tiger kicked.

I got down from Parker's back, easing myself gently from the saddle and onto the clay of the shed-row a little more slowly than I might have done in front of Alexander. My knees hurt me more and more these days. I'd galloped two racehorses earlier, mature campaigners who were coming to the end of lay-offs and nearly ready to head back to the track, and now I felt like my left knee might come apart at the joint. I was going to have to lengthen my stirrups again, I thought, and if I kept lengthening them I wouldn't be able to breeze properly anymore. You couldn't get a workout from a racehorse if you were riding with a dressage leg on them. There was too much motion there, too much churning from those pistons of legs once they hit racing speed. The only way was to be balanced above the withers, crouched there with knees bent in an acute angle.

I grimaced at the thought and made extra-certain that I didn't walk with a limp as I pulled the reins over Parker's curiously pricked ears and draped them over the shed-row rail. Parker needed a little more specificity in his ground-tie than Betsy required. If I dropped the reins, he'd go straight back to his stall when I dismounted, which was cute when we were done with work, but we were still in the middle of training hours and I'd like for him to stay where I left him.

A groom sidled past with a newly-minted two-year-old who raised his hackles at the sight of Parker. The old Thoroughbred pinned his ears and gave the baby a side-eyed glare that sent the little brat into a prancing jig in his eagerness to get away. The groom laughed. I laughed. Parker snorted a snort that could have been a laugh.

Down the shed-row, Tiger kicked.

In the office, Alexander was pouring tar-black coffee into his tumbler. He held up the pot as I came in. "A refill, my dear?"

His voice was stony.

I was in trouble.

"Yes, please," I said tonelessly and handed him my own tumbler. He gave the cold stuff within a healthy splash.

"You didn't drink much of this."

"My stomach is all knotted up this morning."

He looked at me, pale eyebrows knitting together in his tanned forehead. "You're going to do it today?"

"I have to, don't I?"

"Well, I think that's your decision, you know that."

Down the shed-row, Tiger kicked.

"It's his decision," I said glumly. "He's going to hurt himself."

"So where will you take him?"

"I'll talk to Lucy." I accepted the coffee and took a sip. It was hot and inky and bitter and delicious, but it was doing my nervous tummy no favors. I set it down again. "We'll have to pay her, since she won't get a commission for selling him afterwards."

"But what comes afterwards? When he's a show horse, but not for sale? What are we going to do with him? Have you considered the next step?"

"We'll pay someone to show him." It was the right thing to do. Tiger deserved a career.

"He won't be in the barn anymore." A gentle warning, to be sure this was the bed I wanted to lie down in.

"No." I let the word hang there in the chill morning air.

He'd be gone. We'd had Tiger here for so long, it was nearly impossible to imagine the training barn without him.

Alexander settled down into the cracked leather chair behind the office desk and swung idly from side to side, regarding me with a bemused expression. "Did we ever plan for this, even for a minute?"

I threw myself down in the other chair and surreptitiously stretched out my sore knee. "Plan for what?"

"For his retirement. For a gelding that we bought out of sentimentality. We knew he'd be done racing someday, sooner or later, and then we'd have to find a new job for him. Any other horse, we'd sell. We knew we wouldn't sell Tiger. Did we ever stop to consider what we'd do with him after retirement?"

"I guess we thought he'd be a pony."

"He could still be a pony. He just needs some time and some seasoning with other horses."

"No," I said stubbornly. In my mind, I knew Alexander was right—Tiger could be tamed, turned into a pony like Parker and Betsy. Both were growing older, both could use the break that a third pony could provide. But in my sentimental, stubborn heart, I didn't want Tiger to be just another pony. I wanted him to win accolades, I wanted him to shine bright for his athleticism and his talent and his wondrous brain. I knew that a good pony was worth his weight in gold—but who would ever see him, buried here in the training barn, dragging around fractious yearlings and escorting stronger, better racehorses than he had ever been?

I wanted more for my Tiger.

"I'll find a rider for him," I suggested. "We'll send him to a show barn."

"If he's good enough," Alexander added.

"He's good enough," I said.

Down the shed-row, Tiger kicked.

"You don't have to do it now," Alexander said. "If you aren't ready to part with him."

"What?" *Where else could he go?*

"There's a few empty stalls in the yearling barn. He could go over there at night, someone could bring him over to the paddock after training hours." Alexander drummed his fingers on the table. "You're going to lay him off for...how long? Six weeks? Two months?"

"At least two months." He needed time off to be a horse before Lucy started him into a new training program. Keeping him here for a lay-off wasn't a bad idea, if we had somewhere to put him. Lucy had individual turn-out, but it was limited—he'd only be able to go out for a few hours a day, unless he somehow managed to stop being an idiot around other horses and could go out in the larger fields with her more sensible geldings. I wasn't sure *that* was ever going to happen. He'd been alone, with no companions but Parker, for such a long time.

This way, too, he wouldn't be leaving. Not right away, anyway. I could keep my horse around just a little while longer.

I smiled. It was the best news in five days, since the last race, since the Market Affair story broke and washed over me like tsunami. "Okay, let's do it."

Down the shed-row, Tiger kicked.

"Right now."

Chapter Six

TIGER WENT TO THE yearling barn that evening with a spring in his step, and watched me walk away with a hurt look in his eyes—or so I imagined. The yearlings stayed in all night during the winter, so that they couldn't get themselves into trouble with no one around for hours on end. He looked with disdain at the youngsters in the stalls around him and then rushed his stall door, whinnying into the red-tinged evening. I might have been worried enough to call the whole thing off, had he not gone back to his hay almost immediately, tearing off a bite and rushing back to the door so that he had a snack to keep him company while he stared me down.

Incorrigible Tiger. I wanted to hide behind a tree and watch to see how long it took before he settled to his hay (I gave him maybe three minutes), but I had an actual, social commitment tonight. A fundraiser for some Thoroughbred charity at the Ocala Hilton. It was pretty good timing, actually...I just hated going to fundraisers. I wasn't a dress and chit-chat kind of girl.

I had more on my mind than Tiger and finding something nice to wear, just so that I could hide in a corner with a glass of wine all evening. I took a distracted shower, forgetting to put conditioner in my hair the first time, and then a second distracted shower, forgetting to rinse the conditioner *out*. By the third shower I was pretty sure I was not mentally fit to be in public. I flung myself on the bed, wrapped up in a white towel, and looked at the ceiling.

Finally, Alexander, dressed in jacket and tie and ready to go, came upstairs and asked me what all the sighing was about, why I wasn't dressed, etc. It was the invitation I'd been waiting for, and yet I couldn't seem to put my worries into any sort of suitable frame. So I just blurted out the best summation of it all that I could manage.

"Where do you think they'll all *go*, Alexander?"

The question had been gnawing at me all evening, worrying away at my conscience while my body went through the motions —driving the golf cart around the farm, checking the mares, helping with turn-out, filling water buckets. I had felt the bags of six pregnant mares and checked the cool hard tendons of four young colts, but I hadn't truly *seen* a single horse that I had handled all afternoon.

All I could see was the white star, the quizzical eye, the bushy forelock of Market Affair. Not as he'd been here, a bright-eyed colt with his whole career ahead of him, but as he was in the horrible photo.

The photo had been arriving steadily as email attachments, as tweets, as Facebook posts, since around noon. It had gotten so bad that I'd had to turn off all the notifications on my phone, made my Twitter account private, deactivated my Facebook account. There were too many abusive posts to even keep up with reporting to admins, so I just let the flood bubble over while my phone languished unused in my jacket pocket. It had to end sometime.

In the meantime, I'd seen the picture.

Just once would have been enough. Now I knew what Market Affair looked like, or what he'd looked like at nine AM this morning. While I'd been sitting easily on Parker, sipping at my coffee and watching a set of promising two-year-olds gallop around the training track, Market Affair had been about to receive his first hoof trimming in months. After weeks wandering in the south Florida wilderness, his hooves were so soft and rotted that he was having trouble standing on pavement. In the photo, he was posed in front of a barn, his overgrown fore-hooves pushed pitifully out in front of his body so that he could bear more of his weight on his heels than on his tender toes. He was bald across his rump and back from rain rot, shaggy across his abdomen and neck from malnutrition, and everywhere his bones protruded from drum-tight skin. He was the picture of misery.

Lucky for me, every photo came with a custom caption.

You did this! Have you no shame?

Yull go to hell for wat you did to this pore horse!!!

So this is what Responsible Racehorse Retirement looks like to Alex Whitehall?

#StopHorseRacingNow look what they do to their slow horses

I waited for Alexander to ease my mind. He'd say something thoughtful and philosophical and reassuring, and I would feel much better.

Alexander did not answer my question. He looked stern instead. I am sure this was the easiest course of action.

"Get dressed, Alex. We should have left ten minutes ago."

"I don't have anything nice to wear. Can I wear jeans?"

"Of course you can't wear jeans." Alexander fixed me with an exasperated look. "You're acting like a ten-year-old."

I flung open the closet doors so hard that the right one came out of the metal runner, swung wide, and slapped the wall. I jumped back to avoid getting hit. Alexander glowered at me.

It wasn't the first time I'd broken the closet door. I only kept my going-out clothes in the closet, after all, and I was never in a good mood when he made me put them on. Going-out clothes usually meant, as they did tonight, some annoying fundraiser that I had to smile through, covering up my yawns with a program or a glass of wine, wishing I was on the couch in my flannel pajamas watching reruns of *Modern Family*.

I observed my meager supply of sundresses without pleasure. "I don't have anything for cold weather."

"It's fifty-five degrees out there. It's hardly *snowing*. Put on a sweater." Alexander unknotted and re-knotted his tie and studied himself in the bathroom mirror, turning a little to check the symmetry of his work.

It was very easy for men, they wore coats and pants to everything. I rummaged through my dresses and pulled out a brown dress that I'd had since high school. It was rather worn and had a spot near the hem, but no one was going to be looking at my knees, anyway. I shrugged myself into it, popped my arms through the cap sleeves, and noted the way my biceps strained the fabric. I hadn't had nice arms like this in high school. All the dressage and jumping in the world couldn't build up biceps like galloping racehorses.

Alexander frowned at me in the mirror. "That dress has a spot on the hem."

How on earth could he see that? "No one will see it."

"I can see it from here."

I knew he didn't need those spectacles. He just liked to balance them on the end of his nose. "Well, what would you suggest? I have three other dresses." They were all basically the same: cotton patterned sundresses, sleeveless or nearly so, scooped neckline, knee-length, hardly glamorous. They were meant to be worn with flip flops. "Or I could wear my paddock clothes." I had nice slacks and blouses for running horses, but all of them were marked around the hems with permanent mud stains from being worn around the barn and wading through the deep sand and clay of the racetrack.

"Alex, when are you going to grow up and buy a nice outfit? We have these parties all the time and you never look presentable at any of them."

"We haven't been to one of these parties since last spring," I argued.

"We need to go to more of them." Alexander poked at his pale blonde hair with a comb, layering the strands into neat damp rows that would puff up into their usual disarray once they dried. "We need to be out in the local society a bit more if we're going to stand our stallions with any measure of success. It isn't just about their racing records, you know. It's about relationships. There will be ten good stallions with stakes records standing freshman seasons next spring. After the nicking is done, mare owners be looking to see who their friends are."

"Sounds like these friends will be looking for bargains," I huffed, wriggling into a yellow dress that was a carbon copy of the brown one. It had a delicate pattern of white daisies scattered across it in a way that I did not hate, which was saying something. "Sounds like half-off stud fees and comped mare boarding." The friends and family discount. "I can't think about stallions and breeding right now, Alexander. I'm too worried about the horses we've already made to deal with the possibilities of all the horses we're *going* to make."

Alexander came back into the bedroom and put his hands on my shoulders. I studied his tie, the stripes of yellow and blue, until he tipped up my chin with one callused finger and made me look him in the eye. I gave him a mutinous glare. His own eyes were quiet and content. Alexander, as always, was a man who was exactly where he wanted to be, doing exactly what he wanted to do. I wished I could be so steadfast and confident in my decisions. Someday, I promised myself, I would be as rock-solid as my ridiculously self-assured husband. In a few decades. I'd catch up.

"Listen to me," he said gently. "You are going through a rough patch with all this retirement nonsense. But *you're* in the right here. Not them. So don't let them get to you."

I smiled weakly and brushed a hand across my eyes. They were burning a bit. Allergies. In January. Right. "I'm trying. But it's hard to see the community turn against me like this."

"It's the Antis, Alex. Anti-this, anti-that. It's the animal rights fanatics that want to set all the horses and dogs and cats free. You can't listen to people like that. You can't let them get in your head. I know I gave out to you about that interview, but still—you were right. You stand for everything good in racing, you know that?

Look at your principles: your horses get turn-out, your horses get time off to be horses, your horses are retired sound and sent on to second careers. You're doing everything right—Alex, of *course* people are going to hate you. Certain racehorse people because you're going to cost them money in the long run; animal rights activists because you are proving them wrong every single day."

Now my eyes were more than burning; they were spilling over. I fell forward into Alexander and his arms closed around me, strong and warm and oh-so-reassuring. He held me there while I indulged in a good cry, soaking the front of his shirt, overcome with his reassuring words. I could handle *anything*, I thought, as soon I was done crying I'd be right on it. I was doing all the right things. Alexander was right—I was making people on both sides of the aisle nervous. I was changing the status quo, one horse at a time. I was a pioneer! An advocate! Why on earth was I still crying? I used his soft oxford shirt to mop up my tears. He had more, he could change.

Then, when I was finished at last, he gave me a little push towards the bathroom while dropping a soft kiss on my head. "Now please, go get *ready*."

Chapter Seven

I WAS CHARMING.

Okay, I wasn't the belle of the ball, nor the life of the party. I was Alex, after all, shy of strangers and happier in a barn than in a ballroom at the local Hilton, twenty years younger than most of the so-called "young people" in the room, with the exception of a few upstart trainers who had been making names for themselves at Tampa this winter. The realm of breeding racehorses, though, that belonged to the senior members of the racing community, and they made me downright uncomfortable. I still felt, after five years here, that my presence at Alexander's side amused them.

Tonight I was feeling a little more chipper than usual, thanks to my newfound role as the great innovator of horse racing, the harbinger of change, the mover of mountains, the despised of the status quo. I slipped on an argyle sweater of Alexander's over my sundress because I knew it looked like I'd gotten dressed in a vintage store and it would be a marked difference from the silks and paisleys that the other ladies would be wearing, and every time I found myself without someone to talk to, I simply made my way through the crowded little ballroom with a glass of champagne, a determined look on my face, as if I was going somewhere very important.

Usually I was: the table with all the cheese on it, for example, was *very* important. Then someone would waltz up and start a conversation with me, and I would be spared the uncomfortable wallflower feeling I had at most of these events. I talked with a lot of the Rodeo Queens, since we had worked together to claim a mare for a Christmas make-a-wish back in December, and they all wanted to relive the glorious heady moments when they'd descended to the winner's circle while I was still trying to figure out what the heck was going on. The fact that I wasn't in on the scheme at all didn't deter them from congratulating me on such a wonderful surprise.

"And how is dear Christmasfordee?" Tracy Apogee was asking, her silver cross trembling on her astonishing bosom. She reached out a boney hand bedazzled with turquoise and silver rings and plucked a square of cheese from the plate at her side. I watched her deftly put the cheese in her mouth without stabbing herself in the face with her inch-long talons and admired her dexterity. Fifty-five and a barrel racing champion, Tracy Apogee had a flair for the dramatic that was in perfect opposition with my desire to disappear into the woodwork, but I was finding out that she was awfully nice despite all the feathers and Native American affectations.

"She's fine. Out with our other open mares, enjoying some pasture time before she goes for training. She likes to eat entire salt blocks, so that's a thing. The vet ran bloodwork and couldn't find anything weird."

"I had a dog who ate salt blocks," Tracy reminisced. "When he licked you, if you had any cuts, it burned. He was practically made of salt."

"That's crazy." I was seized with a desire to know more about the salt-eating dog, and to eat more cheese. I put down my empty champagne glass and went for a wedge of white cheese speckled with cranberries. "What breed was he?"

"He was half Catahoula hound and half—" Tracy trailed off and her gaze became fixed on a point just beyond my left shoulder.

I turned very slowly, expecting Alexander to be doing something ridiculous, like holding a wine glass over my head and pretending he was going to pour it all over me. Of course, he would never do that. I was wearing his sweater.

But it wasn't Alexander. There was a woman there, standing just inches away, a woman with her face twisted in rage, a woman in sweatpants and sweatshirt stained with farm work, a woman who had most obviously not come to the fundraiser for champagne and cheese and smalltalk about racehorses or salt-eating dogs, and in her hand, her fingers clenching the edges so tightly that it was crinkling within her grip, was the photo of Market Affair.

I took a step backward and collided with the cheese table. I heard a metallic *clink* as my champagne glass toppled and hit the cheese platter. *Thank God it didn't shatter,* I thought, as if that would have created any more of a scene than Tracy Apogee's startled shriek, echoing around the high ceiling of the ballroom. I could feel the silence descend over the room of gossiping horse trainers and breeders, and I knew all eyes were on me.

Especially hers.

Her lips spat out my name with a vicious hatred. "Alex *Whitehall,* you lying bitch. Whaddya think happens to them once you've used them up and passed them on? This is what happens. *This!*" She pushed the photo towards my face and I leaned away backwards, trapped against the banquet table, its folding legs quivering beneath my assault. Market Affair was in my face again, his defeated gaze directed towards the ground, his devastated hooves turning up like elven slippers, his gaunt body and ruined coat living reminders of what could happen to *any* of my horses once I let them go—

"Where d'ya think they all go when you're done with 'em?"

I should have been stepping around her, pushing down her trembling hand, looking around for security, a frown of calm displeasure on my dignified face for the audience, slack-jawed and astonished, that surrounded the two of us.

Instead I looked at Market Affair, and tears welled up in my eyes for the second time that night, and guilt was written across my face for all the world to see. Or, at least, for my accuser to see, and that was plenty enough for a crazy person.

She crumpled the photo and dropped it on the carpet at my feet. Then she turned her back on me. She was a wide, short, waddling little woman, lank brown hair falling in kitchen-sink curls over sagging shoulders, ankles wobbly over dirty sneakers the color of horse manure. People got out of her way, no one wanted to touch her, even for the sake of security—was there no security? A mall cop, for crying out loud, to shove into the ballroom and take her by the wrists and haul her out of here and make a lot of empty threats about what would happen if she ever came here and accosted hotel guests again?

Apparently not. She pushed open the heavy metal door at the end of the ballroom, the one with the sign that said *Do Not Open — Emergency Exit Only — Alarm Will Sound* and the door's alarm started shrieking and it blended oddly with the excited wasp's buzz of chatter that was sweeping over the ballroom about the trailer-trash redneck who had just silenced that upstart Alex Whitehall.

Alexander's hand was suddenly there, on my back, hard as iron, and he was propelling me through the open path through the crowd left by the woman. I went where his hand dictated, walking on numb feet, past curious men, past women clutching their pearls. *He wants to catch her,* I thought. *He wants to chase her down, make her apologize, admits she's a liar and I did nothing wrong, absolve me for myself if no one else.* But when we got outside into the biting cold Ocala night, the traffic on 200 buzzing by, she had already disappeared into the dark parking lots that surrounded the hotel.

Alexander's hand propelled me directly to our car, and into the passenger seat, and he closed the door once I was secured there.

I looked out the window as he drove in silence, the country mixture of rusted trailer and imposing mansion flashing by behind the pastures and riding rings. Was she out there in one of those trailers, in one of those barns, laughing to herself that she'd done what none of the letter-writers and the tweeters and the emailers had managed—she'd gotten in Alex's face and made Alex cry? She must feel amazing right now. She must feel like a heroine.

While I was left, once again, with that question: where did they all go?

For all my record-keeping and barn checks and "this horse has a home" stamps on the Jockey Club papers of every Thoroughbred we sold, how could I ever protect them once they were out of my hands? Horses disappeared. People did what they wanted with their property, and for some reason abandonment and auction houses were somehow easier options than a phone call to a breeder, asking them to send a truck for a horse before they ran out of grain.

That wasn't my fault. I knew that.

But their existence—their very existence—*that* was my fault. The children I had brought into this world, and then set adrift, to live or to die, to prosper or to suffer, to be the property of fickle, unpredictable, mercenary humans—they were my fault.

We drove up the lane and I saw the mares in foal, and the light in the barn where the night watchman sat over the ones heavy and ready to lie down in the straw and bring their colts and fillies into the world, and bit back a groan.

In the house, Alexander went to the kitchen and began pouring things. I heard the clink of glasses, the rumble of the ice maker, the heavy sound of some bottle raised and returned to its shelf. I sank into the couch and slipped off my silly little Payless flats and pulled a racehorse-patterned throw around my shoulders. *He's bringing me more wine, and I need it,* I thought, but when Alexander reappeared in the living room it was with two tumblers of the brown stuff.

I guess he thought he'd better bring the big guns to deal with this particular attack of Alex-hysteria. It was a shame I was so predictable.

Lowered onto the couch beside me, glasses set gently on racehorse-emblazoned coasters before us, Alexander tucked one of my cold hands into his and gave it a squeeze. His hands were big, engulfing my own sturdy fists, and tanned and spotted and hard as any good farmer's hands must be. I traced the curves of old scars with my eyes, the hook-shaped ridge of white around his thumb knuckle, the mark of a rein buckle as a horse being led to the starting gate had wrenched free from his grasp, years ago in England, where there were no ponies to escort horses onto the track. The puckering scar at the back of his index finger, where a half-mad colt had tried to take off his finger but only closed his teeth on skin. The fissures that ran along each fingertip like canyons, the mark of hay and straw tearing at the skin in cold dry air, making winter a special torture for those of us who toiled outdoors.

My fingers were hidden within his grasp, but I knew they looked much the same. Tan and freckled, scarred and cracked, sinewy and tough. I'd never had a manicure in my life, and if I went into a salon now, the entire staff would surely burst into tears. If you prized soft, elegant fingers, and polished perfect nails, then my hands were a horror, an atrocity, a victim of long-lost war.

I only valued horses, and every callous and every scar was a badge of honor earned in my fight to keep horses happy, healthy, well-trained, fit, desirable.

A horse that was desirable was never in danger, never wanted for a home, after all.

Alexander started to speak, changed his mind, reached forward and picked up the cut glass tumbler before him, studying its flashing rainbows in the soft yellow light of the table-lamps. He took a slow sip, savored, then another. And thus fortified, he turned to face me, forehead wrinkled, blue eyes concerned.

"You can't let one crazy person torpedo your entire life, Alex."

I furrowed up my own brow. This wasn't exactly clear. Chiding, or sympathetic? What was it going to be tonight, Alexander? *"One* crazy person? You think that old bat is behind all of this?"

"Of course not. I think Mary Archer is behind all this, to be perfectly candid. I think she fed the story to the Antis and they lapped it up. But I also think you're lapping it up, too, and that's my problem."

Mary Archer didn't care where the horses went when she was done with them. But she knew that I did, like thousands of other horsepeople out there. We cared. She told them that I didn't, and she was wrong. Right now, it was all that I could think about.

"Are you saying that it isn't a valid question, though? Where *do* they all go? If you and I were to die tomorrow, the horses would go to a sale, right? Who protects them then?" My voice was rising, and I could feel my face flushing, the blood stealing across my cheeks to burn at the corners of my eyes and the tips of my ears. All those luckless horses I had willed into this world— "Their lives are in my hands. The lives I made. Shouldn't I look at what we're doing and evaluate and make sure I'm doing the right thing?"

Alexander's lips had grown narrower throughout my impassioned speech, and he was now looking at me with much the same expression that crept across his face when he was watching an unsound horse jog on hard ground. Trying to find the problem at its source. Was it the anti-racing activists, he was wondering. Was it the state Market Affair had been found in that had truly set me off? Was it simply the annual exhaustion that came riding on exhilaration's coat tails every spring, as the new foals simultaneously delighted us and sapped every last bit of strength and sense from our bones and brains?

It was all of that, I thought. But most of all, it was me. I was the problem. I had done this to myself, painting myself neatly into a corner, smiling at an earnest young reporter over a latte at Starbucks, conscious of the red light on her iPhone's recording app as the device was set gently onto the table between us. She had nodded and she had encouraged elaboration and the iPhone drank up all of my silly notions and grand ideals. Then, once I had explained my ambitions to keep all of the horses Alexander and I bred and trained sound and happy for life, she had thanked me and taken the phone and driven home and cobbled together a rosy picture of another earnest young woman much like herself, determined to change the world of horse racing completely. She'd gotten *that* from the caffeinated babble I'd spilled into the silently listening phone. Alex the picture of Responsible Retirement, the visionary of a racing industry free of culls and abuse and abandonment, the spokeswoman for a new age of horsemen and horsewomen who took pride in all the talents of their horses, whether they had speed or not.

I'd read it in the pages of *New Equestrian* and I'd believed it.

I didn't know if that was better or worse than the fact that other people had, too.

The *New Equestrian* article went unremarked upon along the backside, probably because the magazine was aimed at English show riders, and most of the horse racing community held themselves steadfastly apart from those show people. Granted, it could be disorienting, after a day spent in the pursuit of speed and purse money, to converse with people equally passionate about five-stride lines and fifty-cent ribbons. But truly, we all wanted and needed the same things: healthy horses, sound horses, safe horses. The difference in our performance goals shouldn't present such an insurmountable gap between us.

Plenty of show horses went lame and disappeared without a trace as well. They bucked off the wrong kid and got bundled off to auction without name or papers. Even responsible retirement was a burden we shared across the disciplines, although to hear some people tell it, every racehorse died horribly in a slaughterhouse, and every show horse died fat and happy under their favorite apple tree, aged thirty-five, with friends and family in loving attendance.

Even if only a small percentage of *New Equestrian*'s readership believed such gaps in treatment existed, though, I had wanted them to know that racehorses could have happy endings too. So I'd talked and talked about my success stories and best practices, about my training partnership with Lucy Knapp, about my files with last-known addresses and phone numbers of people who had purchased retired horses from us.

What I didn't mention, because it had never been asked and because I'd been too caught up in the moment, in my own importance as the self-appointed ambassador of change, was that it didn't always work. That horses still disappeared, that cell phone numbers changed and farms closed and fortunes turned for the worst. That some people valued a horse's life above the price of rubies, and some did not. So when readers looked up from my bold words in *New Equestrian* and saw my name attached to

Market Affair, they couldn't know what part, if any, of my interview had been a lie—so they could safely assume all of it was.

Of course I could have told them the truth in the beginning: that I'd hit dead ends before, had to accept that a horse I'd once known was out there on his own now, but before Market Affair, I'd never actually seen the disappearing horse re-apparate...not that he'd been on my tracking list, but even so. I'd known what *could* happen, but living with the photographic evidence that it absolutely *had* happened was something that I didn't know how to live with.

"I let him down," I whispered. "He slipped through the cracks. Who else could end up like this? What about those babies down in the training barn? The yearlings? The coming foals? And what about all the horses I've sold over the years? What's happening to them?"

"This was a freak occurrence. This is not the norm." Alexander's voice was steady. He spoke a with conviction I envied. "Most horses live very normal lives. Alex, you know this. You see them every day. In people's yards, on hobby farms, at boarding stables. Just because they're not tripping any alarms by showing under their racing names doesn't mean that the worst has happened. And most of the ones who *do* show get their names changed anyway." He handed me my own tumbler of whiskey, the ice clinking musically against the glass, and waited while I took one sip, and then another. He nodded, satisfied that it would soon settle my nerves. "I know it's all been a shock," he went on. "And what happened tonight was unfortunate, but maybe not isolated. What you need is some time on the farm. Out of the public eye."

I had been taking a third sip of the whiskey, but this gently-delivered command in the guise of advice made me choke on the mouthful. I put down the glass. "Stay on the farm? What about the racehorses?"

"I can handle the racehorses," Alexander said patiently. "I am sure you can trust them to me. I think it's time for you to lay low and let this blow over. Any time you spend in public is just going to open you up to attacks like the woman tonight—to say nothing of questions and scrutiny that I don't think you want any part of."

I faced Alexander sullenly. My mulish nature was asserting itself, wiping away the insecurity I'd been feeling just moments before. Now he was telling me I couldn't even watch my own horses train? Or, worse, I couldn't run them myself? "The Mizner is next weekend," I said icily. "Are you telling me to sit it out while you run Personal Best?" That couldn't be the case. P.B. was *mine*. Alexander would *never*—

"That's precisely what I'm saying. And any other races we might be dropping horses into over the next few weeks, or however long it takes for some new scandal to pop up and take you out of the spotlight. The Mizner is a graded stakes race and there will be Derby hopefuls in it. There will be press. And you're in no fit state to be talking to the press. They'll ask you leading questions and manipulate every word that comes out of your mouth until you're all turned around again, just like you were tonight." Alexander's voice had grown cool as he issued his commands. Now he softened it again. "Alex, this is for your safety as well as the horses. Do you want to attract protestors to the stables or to the track? There's no shortage of crazies, especially in Miami."

He was right. Damn him, he was right.

I didn't want to face it yet, though.

I got up and left the room, walking purposefully through the house, stopping at the front door to pull on my muddy Wellingtons, hopping from one foot to the other as I shoved my bare feet into the resistant boots, then flung open the green door and threw myself out into the night. It was late, and the high moon was wreathed in a blue glow of ice crystals. The goosebumps rose on my bare arms, but I went down the porch steps anyway, awkward and loud in the rubber boots, and across the dewy grass of our scruffy patch of front lawn, down towards the dark line of the pasture fence. I could see the girls out there, the moonlight silvery on their bay and chestnut and gray backs, the colt and the filly dark sleepers in the grass nearby. Heads lifted and ears pricked as I tramped through the grass, and a lilting whinny echoed through the little valley.

I was nearly at the fence and starting to wonder what the plan was—the fence was built of no-climb wire, topped with a flat black-painted board, and couldn't be scaled—when Alexander, who was taller and faster and quieter and more rational than I was, placed a hand on my shoulder.

"When are you going to stop running away?"

I had been steeling myself to do just that. But he always knew. The longer I let the weight of his hand sink in, the more his touch became all the warmth and comfort in the world to me.

I just didn't want it. I wanted to rage at him, I wanted to shout that he was taking my horses away, I wanted to accuse him of jumping at the chance to take his old power back after he'd let me take over as their trainer last year.

But I knew better. I knew that we were partners. I knew deep down, in my most rational of hearts, that he was doing everything out of consideration for me.

So, I stood still.

I wasn't running away.

"I'm not," I said instead, like a child.

"You always run away," Alexander chided. He turned me around to face him, to show me that he meant no insult, only concern. His eyes sparkled with silver glints in the moonlight. "You're half-horse yourself. You think you solve all your problems by just running faster." Alexander stooped and placed a gentle kiss on my forehead. I sniffled, throat suddenly tight. "This time," he went on, fingertip at my chin, "You will just have to stop and wait it out."

"I can't be still," I admitted. " I don't know how." If I wasn't training racehorses, what was I doing? The farm chores and the morning works and the broodmares seemed to fade into little distractions. The frequent trips to check on my horses in south Florida and in Tampa were what truly made me feel like a trainer.

"It's easier than you think. You just need a project. Or you can think of it as a vacation. You like those."

I did like vacations. Until I got so keyed up and excited about all the work I was going to do and goals I was going to make as soon as I got back home that I became restless and anxious for the vacation to end. I usually lasted five days.

This was going to take longer than five days. "What kind of project?" Maybe he had something in mind.

Alexander only shrugged. "With enough time sitting idle, something will come to you. Now come back inside. The ice is watering down that nice whiskey."

I accepted the arm he held out and we made the trudge back up to the house, leaving the mares and foals to their silvery pasture. There would be frost on this grass in the morning, I thought. Whiskey was probably exactly what I needed. My nerves had gotten the best of me tonight, and now I was cold through.

I tightened my grip on Alexander's arm, thankful for such a strong anchor to cling to.

Chapter Eight

MORNING TRAINING HAD LOST its luster.

With my favorites at the training center near Miami, and Tiger in the yearling barn until after training hours, wondering what had happened to his life, the morning rides felt utterly bereft of any passion. I felt like I was just dealing with a succession of forgettable young horses who would pass out of my care and into some other trainer's barn without ever making much of an impression on my life. Of course, that was a typically dramatic Alex response. A few days ago, they'd all had their own charms for me—personalities and quirks and mannerisms. If I didn't love them the way that I loved my own string, my P.B. and my Luna and my Virtue and my Shearwater, well, that was partially because I hardly knew them. After all, I rarely rode babies, and half the new two-year-olds in the barn were client horses anyway. They were here to learn to be racehorses and prep for the rapidly approaching two-year-old in training sales.

But partially, too, it was because I was shutting myself away from them, haunted by the futures that I feared they were galloping headlong towards along with their daily gate lessons and their weekly fast works.

I felt that if I let myself fall in love with any of them, I wouldn't be able to let them go. It was probably true. When I fell in love with a horse, I fell hard—witness Tiger, witness Personal Best, witness Luna Park. But that had been different—all of those horses had held something special and indefinable for my heart from the get-go. It was easy and getting easier, as the years went by and the horses came and went, to ride and train and condition relatively emotionlessly. To take the logical, rational approach to training and selling horses. While that was as it should be—Alexander considered this essential for one to run racehorses as a business—it wasn't compelling for me in the way that riding a horse I truly loved and connected with was. One gallop on Tiger was enough to energize me through five uninspiring sets on client horses.

Without that passion for a horse invigorating my brain, the mornings dragged. Now, without even my semi-weekly visits to south Florida to look forward to, the days congealed into a meaningless clump of hours divided between sitting in the saddle, holding mares' halters, helping scrub foals' bottoms, mixing feed, and throwing hay.

By the third morning after the fundraiser party that had gone so wrong, I was ready to go back to bed after the second set. I would have, too, but Alexander wanted me to ride a big, burly colt in the third set, a strong two-year-old who either needed a diet or a gelding. His neck and shoulders bulged with beefcake muscle, and his jowls already seemed to be widening in stud-horse fashion. I had suggested that the colt's owner had lied and sent us a late-summer colt who was actually three on January first, not two.

Alexander suspected (possibly more rationally) that he'd been subjected to haphazard hormone doping to get a big yearling for the sales ring, and the pigeons were coming home to roost. Either way, Alexander thought the horse had a lot of promise if he would stop gaining muscle long enough to grow the bone he needed to support his own hulking weight, and wanted my first-hand opinion of how the horse moved before he consulted with the owner about a little turn-out time.

I took a look at the big colt, looming like a bull over little burros in the stalls on either side of him, and decided that this was not the sort of vacation I liked. "Can't Juan ride him?" Juan was a tough guy. He actually liked riding this brute. "Just tell him what to be feeling for."

The colt neighed as a filly sashayed past, a stallion's rumble already echoing in his massive chest. The filly, so close to childhood it would have been pedophilia if he'd gotten anywhere near her, broke forward nervously, her eyes wide as the hot walker tried to settle her down again. The colt bounced up and down behind his stall webbing, watching the panicky filly with excited eyes. He blew hard through his nostrils and took a restless turn of his stall before shoving at the webbing again, but by now she was making her escape, dragging the hot walker down the shed-row. I didn't blame her.

"He's a thug," I said in disgust. "He doesn't need time to mature, he needs cut."

"You're probably right," Alexander said regretfully. "But he's from the last crop of Serengeti Sun, and the owner is keen to make a stud out of him someday."

"Pity the fillies," I sighed. "And me." But he wasn't so terrible under saddle, from what I'd seen, just easily distracted, especially by the ladies. Oh, and once he had his blood up, he'd pull your arms out before he'd slow down, so that was fun. "Put him in an elevator bit," I told the groom loitering outside the stall. "I'm not going water-skiing today."

A quarter-hour later, mounted on the giant colt, I felt a little better about the ride to come. I trusted myself on horseback—so many ways to directly influence what the horse was going to do net. Seat, legs, hands—I had all those tools at my disposal, and I knew how to use them. On the ground, I had only my hands and my voice—not much of a fight if a horse really wanted to defy me. I settled my boots into the stirrups just a little deeper home than usual, toes and knees turned in. The equitation of security. I gathered my reins, looping the ends of the long racing reins into a firm knot that made for a nice handle in case of emergency. The colt circled in the straw, restless to get out, but I did all my safety checks before I let him go anywhere, right down to leaning over and tugging the girth up an extra hole. Then I nodded at Miguel to step out of the doorway. He checked for traffic, found the shed-row free of oncoming baby racehorses, and waved us on out.

The big colt hopped eagerly out of his stall, jigging sideways as soon as his hooves hit the churned up clay-and-sand of the shed-row. I had been compelled to lay my cheek against his cresty neck as we went through the stall door, but as soon as I straightened up, I sat down in the saddle and gave his spine a little reminder that there was a human on top, and one that expected obedience, besides. He subsided down to a walk, or close enough, straightening out and stepping out in something just shy of a nervous jig as we rounded the corner. I allowed it. I hated to start a ride with a fight.

We caught up with the rest of the set on the other side of the barn—five colts, no fillies, by design. But even without hormones to inflame my would-be Casanova, there was a tautness to his body that I didn't like. We filed out of the barn and onto the gravel horse-path, and he was already rooting at the bit, asking to be allowed to lead the set.

"You can't always be the leader," I told him, and his black-tipped ears flicked back to catch the sound of my voice. "Sometimes you're going to get dirt in your face. As long as you pass them before the wire, it doesn't matter."

He snorted, blowing so hard that he spooked a flight of mourning doves from a nearby live oak. They quickly evaporated into the thick layer of fog that was resting like a blanket over Ocala, but he used them as an excuse to dance sideways on the path. By the time I had straightened him out, his nose was brushing the rump of the dark gray colt ahead, and said colt's ears had swept back. He shook his head, hunched his back, and gave a little crow-hop, which got the message across to my colt loud and clear. The cowardly monster showed his true colors, backing right off.

"Uh-huh," I told him, after I'd waved an apology to the scowling Richard, turning back to see why I was crowding his horse. "You're nothing but a big fat bully. You can dish it but you can't take it."

Chastened for the moment, the big colt just lumbered on, but he was far from calm. I could see a sheen of sweat darkening the taut muscles of his bullish neck despite the cool morning. He was hyped up and looking for trouble. I prayed to the racing gods that he wouldn't find any this morning.

But trouble will always find a racehorse.

We were cantering along the far turn. All was quiet. The horses were going easily, the colt had settled into a nice pace as the outside partner in the first pair. It was a spot I liked for him because he needed a little extra ground on the turns; those long ungainly legs needed all the room they could get. He would never thread his way up the rail and sneak in on the turn for home, but he could swing wide and make a drive, if he had the stamina and the endurance to run just a little further than every other horse in the race. "It's like galloping a stork," I commented to Juan, who was galloping on my inside with a neat little chestnut colt who took his work very seriously. Juan laughed and tipped his whip at me. He could afford to break his focus—his little colt had his head down and his ears back and was working like a professional.

Juan still only had one hand on the reins when it happened. I know, because I was looking right at him, at his grinning white teeth, at his right hand in the air, using his whip to point at me. I wasn't looking forward, to the track ahead, nor off to the right, towards the foggy pasture next door where our elderly neighbors had long grazed black Angus cattle as they and their parents and their grandparents had done since before the Thoroughbred colonists came south to found their new nation of horse country.

I wasn't looking, but my big colt was. What he saw emerging from the curling mist sent him lunging towards the inside rail like a car losing a tire.

The chaos was immediate. I saw Juan's smile turn into a grimace of panic, growing closer and closer until it was gone—disappearing from my view as my colt slammed into his chestnut and sent the little horse tumbling heels over head. I had a death-grip on the reins, but I'd lost my left stirrup when his outside shoulder dropped away from me and sent me swinging to the right, and when the impact with the chestnut colt nearly sent my horse to his knees, I found myself high on his neck, gripping leather and rubber and mane with everything I had. There were other horses streaming across the track, and the fallen colt waving his legs in the air, and I didn't want to be down in the dirt and in the way of all those erratic hooves, whatever happened. But I didn't know where everyone was, and I was turning my head to the left, to look back and see where the other four horses had ended up, when suddenly my own colt's neck was rising before me, and just as I realized that we were jumping the inner rail and hedge, and dug my knees in for grip, something big and heavy slammed into my colt's hindquarters and he fell out of the air, an ungraceful Pegasus falling to earth, and landed face-first just beyond the hedge, and as the ground rushed towards me I realized we were flipping over.

My fingers opened and I let go of everything and shoved away, as hard as I could.

Time has a way of stopping when you're in the middle of a bad fall. You have time to think—*Oh, those hooves will land near my face,* or—*If I land on my hand I will break my wrist,* or—most significantly—*This is going to hurt.* You have plenty of time to think and to imagine and to dread. But you do not have time to act. Not usually, anyway. You are only waiting for the inevitable.

I don't know how I managed to shove away from the colt as he twisted through the air, his jump arrested in mid-flight at the moment his hindquarters were swept from beneath him. I didn't have a destination in mind, either. My body must have reacted independently, on its own agenda, not willing to be slowed down by my molasses-in-winter brain, working its slow comprehension through the pain it was about to experience. An alarm bell was ringing deep within some ancient self-preservation instinct, and it instantly pulled the trigger on the evacuation procedure when it became apparent that my horse and I would be switching places before we landed on the other side of the fence.

When I hit the ground at last, time and brain functions resumed their previously scheduled programming, and I did what I always did before I'd even managed to suck a mouthful of air into my gasping lungs—I rolled myself into a ball and braced for impact from above. The ground shook when his massive hindquarters hit the ground next to me, and I squinted open one eye, hazarding a glance—and I would have sighed with relief if I'd had any breath left to do it with. The colt had fallen away from me, his legs falling to the left, where he couldn't kick me as he scrambled and flailed to get back to his feet—

Except that he wasn't scrambling to his feet. I lay still for a second, then another, my cheek pressed against the dew-damp grass, and watched that big barrel of an abdomen. It rounded hugely where the ground pushed his barrel up, before narrowing delicately where the girth of the saddle crossed just behind his forelegs. And it wasn't moving.

I looked at his head then, stirring myself to get up, pressing an elbow and then a hand into the ground to get a better view, and then I knew.

There was a rumble of hooves on the racetrack, hidden from me by the hedge, and then Alexander was leaning over just as far as he could without tumbling from his own saddle. His eyes fell first on the colt, and widened. I saw the panic streak across his face before he saw me, sitting upright, uncrushed. His tanned cheeks were white. "Are you hurt?"

Oh, I was hurt all right. Every bit of me hurt. But I was a connoisseur of hurts, knowledgeable of all the finer points of aches, twinges, bruises, stabbing pains, and the peculiar delicacy of electricity firing through nerve pain. What injuries I had sustained this morning was more of the epsom-salts-soaks-for-days variety than the hospital variety. I sat up the rest of the way, cautiously, and found that everything still worked tolerably well.

"I'm okay," I croaked, still missing lungs full of air. "But him..."

"Broken neck," Alexander said grimly. "The old fall-over-the-rail trick. I wish they wouldn't do this. I heard the Martins lost a good one this way last week. They say he died twice—he panicked, hit the rail, flipped over, and the vet found a broken neck *and* a heart attack."

The last crop of Serengeti Sun, I remembered, and I'd wanted to geld him. I stood up, wobbly on my tingling feet, and made my way over to the sprawling mountain of horse. His head had plowed into the dirt before his momentum flipped him over. Turned to one side, blood on his teeth and dirt on his face, he was no smaller than he had been five minutes before, galloping on the track. He was not diminished by death. He'd been a beautiful horse, for all his faults of temperament and clearly overactive pituitary gland. This was a loss, no doubt about it. Not just of life, but of blood. He could've been a star. He could've sired stars. He could've made more beautiful horses, fast and feckless.

I sighed, my lungs working again at last, and leaned down to unbuckle the girth from my saddle. I slung the little exercise saddle over my hip. The rest of the tack I left to be picked up later. It was a long walk back to the barn.

Evening came with more than its usual share of aches. I wanted nothing more than to slip away, run a bath, and sink down to my chin in hot fragrant bubbles, but just as I was psyching myself up to get off the couch and go upstairs, Alexander came into the living room looking harried, and I knew I'd left my escape too late. I got up anyway and collected the whiskey and glasses from the kitchen. He'd just spent an hour on the phone with the dead colt's owner, and I could see he needed the same sort of medicine I had required after the fundraiser affair.

He took the tumbler almost greedily from my hand and had knocked back a healthy gulp before I'd even sat back down on the couch. Then he smiled at me rather sheepishly, blue eyes twinkling like a naughty boy's. "Thanks, love," he said weakly. "He wasn't exactly a happy customer."

"No, of course not. But this happens. He's been in the biz long enough to know that." As Alexander had said that morning, crashing the inner rail wasn't an unknown accident amongst young horses. Horses could, and did, flip on fences and break their necks. It happened in training accidents with racehorses, but it also happened in horse shows, events, and steeplechases. I'd even seen a particularly stupid mare do it over a metal pasture gate when I was a kid. She really didn't like being the last one brought in for dinner, but she was also a terrible jumper. I used to watch horses cross that spot for months afterward, waiting to see if she haunted the spot where she'd died, but no one leaped about in the Dead-Horse Patch manner, so that was one more fairy tale Enid Bagnold had told me.

"Yes, but, this was an exceptional prospect," Alexander said regretfully. "On paper alone, of course. He could have gotten some okay stud fees based on that sire alone, even if he never raced. And then—there's the fact that you were riding him."

"Oh." Because of me? I thought about this, holding a spicy swallow of scotch in my mouth until my eyes started to water. It slid down my throat, burning hot, and beat a warm trail through my middle section. Almost as good as a bath. "Because I should have been able to prevent it since I'm a trainer and more experienced? Because listen, I told you, no one saw those horses coming in the next pasture. They came out of nowhere. And no one saw where they went." It had been discovered, through a rehashing of everyone's recollections of the incident, that the colt was spooked hard by the sight of two horses galloping in the neighboring pasture, coming down the fence-line towards us. The field that had previously only housed placidly grazing black cattle had suddenly erupted into a training track, and the colt had panicked and turned left to get away from them.

Who had decided to gallop horses in that field? It was a puzzle. The elderly couple, who occasionally would drive the pasture in an aged SUV, checking the fence, neither owned racehorses nor aspired to own racehorses. I'd spoken to them once or twice—the husband was old-time cattle people, a Florida cracker, who said that as soon as he'd stopped rounding up cattle on the thousands of acres of his old ranch, he'd plunked his ass in a nice comfortable truck seat and never looked back. Horses had been a vehicle and a chore to him, not a grand passion. I couldn't imagine him buying a racehorse for a minute, even if it was just an investment.

No, someone else was using that land now. Some foolish dreamer, probably, who thought they could condition a racehorse on uneven pasture land. What they'd save in not paying stall rental at a training center, they'd spend in buckets of poultice and time off work. But Ocala had never lacked for people more frugal than sensible, and horse racing attracted the penny-wise and pound-foolish members of society like flies to honey.

"The problem is that right now nobody trusts you."

I stopped musing about the mystery neighbors. "What now?"

Alexander studied his glass, looking pained. "This whole thing with the Everglades horses, with the protestors, that article, the lady at the banquet—people are talking, Alex. People are questioning your judgement."

"Not *our* people. Not racehorse people." Racehorse people understood that it was all being blown out of proportion, through misleading headlines and manipulative articles. They had to.

"Some of them, too." Alexander's voice was sympathetic. The cloying sweetness of his tone, so unlike his usual dry drawl, scared me more than the actual words. If Alexander thought that I needed comforting over something that wasn't even worrying me, he really did think that things were dire. I pulled my legs up beneath me, squeezed my toes together, wrapped my arms around a pillow, but it couldn't ward away the chill creeping through me.

"I've heard a little," Alexander went on. "Mind you, I don't think you're the talk of the town. It's not that. It's a few people who think you are a black eye the sport doesn't need right now, and what makes it worse is that you were paraded as some sort of champion before this. And the magazine story rubbed a few people the wrong way—maybe they have guilty consciences—and so they're using this story as an opportunity to show that you're no saint and they have nothing to be guilty about."

"I never said I was a saint," I choked out. "I only said the truth. I said that racing needed a strong retirement structure to do right by our horses and then I explained everything that I do—that *we* do, to protect our horses—" I stopped and took a breath. Alexander was shaking his head gently, and I knew why. The magazine story was old news, water under the bridge, over and done with. I'd pissed people off with it, plain and simple. I'd said they weren't good enough. I'd said they didn't care enough about their horses. Whether that was true or whether they were simply thoughtless, cutting corners where they shouldn't have been, didn't matter. They were insulted. I'd said too much and I'd said it too smugly for the tastes of many, many people in the business.

I should have been quieter. I should have kept my mouth shut. I should have just worried about my own horses. But how could I, when there were so many horses out there that no one else was worrying about?

But it was all said now. "So who's at the bottom of it? Who started this?" I asked, but I had an idea.

Alexander took a sip of whiskey. "Do you have to ask?"

Mary.

"I called her a name *one time...*"

"Not very professional, calling people names."

"Not very professional, telling the world I dump horses!"

"She has a few friends," Alexander went on. "Renee Adams, from what I hear. Some more, mainly some of the lower-level trainers who have time to gossip."

"Isn't Renee the one who made her old claimer into a show jumper? I'd think she'd be on my team. She knows what these horses can do besides run. The others think they're worthless as soon as they can't find the winner's circle."

"She is," Alexander agreed. "But depending on how far on the other side of the fence some of them might be, they might think you just plain lied through the whole interview. That's what the animal rights people are saying, anyway."

"We had coffee together at the Breeders' Cup party last fall," I said blankly. "And talked about her horse show record being better than her win record. How great off-track Thoroughbreds are at everything. And now she thinks I made it all up?"

"A lot of people do. The anti-racing people do. And maybe she didn't think the crack about her horse show record was so funny."

Well. But to be fair, she'd brought it up. "But they don't even know me..." A feeling of desperation washed over me. I had thought I'd be safe amongst my own people. I had thought they'd close the ranks and protect me as one of their own. "Goddammit, Alexander, how long do I have to be in this business before I'm accepted?" I set down the glass with a bang that made him wince— that was good crystal. "Yes, I showed horses when I was a girl. Yes, I *am a girl*. Yes, I married into the business. But for God's sake, I'm a stakes-winning trainer with good horses and I don't deserve to be treated like a spy!"

"Well, then you shouldn't be talking to magazines like *New Equestrian* about what racing needs to change. You should be speaking to *Thoroughbred Monthly.* Don't go airing racing's dirty laundry to the horse show people."

I looked at him coldly. "Is that what you think?"

"It's not what I think," he said mildly. "It's what they think."

I sat back and chuckled to myself. "Oh, Alexander." He lifted an eyebrow at me. "You were right. All those times you told me I really ought to make some friends? Now everyone that might have been on my side is just waiting for me to cut my own throat and get out of their way." I shoved myself up from the couch. "And now, enough of this. I hit the ground today. I need a hot, hot bath."

Alexander poured another glass of whiskey and waved it in my direction. "I'll be up shortly," he said. "I just have to rethink my stallion plans...again."

I didn't know what that meant. It reminded me of something else Mary had said—God, that woman said a lot, didn't she?— something about big plans for our breeding program. I gave Alexander an absent kiss and went up the stairs, fingers trailing the banister's smooth wood, wondering if he had planned to stand the big colt at stud *here* at Cotswold.

Chapter Nine

MAYBE I HADN'T SPENT my years in Ocala making friends in the racing community, but at least I had Kerri. Still my assistant in name if not in reality, since she spent most of her time in the broodmare barn now that I was exiled from the racetrack, and really, before that. Kerri had been my assistant in Saratoga and Tampa and Gulfstream, and she'd been wonderful and committed and completely priceless...but now I was starting to wonder if her heart was really with the mares and foals.

If that was the case, I really couldn't blame her. I just missed her when she was sequestered on the hillside with her ladies and babies while I wrestled the older horses down in the training barn.

I wasn't in much of a wrestling mood today. All of the horses looked like more trouble than I wanted to deal with. And the riders in the training barn, well...none of them seemed in the mood to talk to me...or listen to me...or look at me...or acknowledge my presence in any way, shape, or form. It wasn't exactly the confidence-booster one wanted after a near-death experience. I stuck to Parker, and when Alexander asked me if I wanted to gallop anyone, I said no. I couldn't imagine the dead silence out there on the track, somehow smothering the rumble of hooves and the jingling and squeaking of tack, while every rider gave me the silent treatment.

So instead, I bowed out of following the last few sets, citing my aching shoulders from yesterday's fall (not a lie, by the way), and jogged Parker up the driveway to the broodmare barn. There were a few mares turning restlessly in their stalls, awaiting a mid-morning vet visit. The rest were outside, and they tossed their heads and flattened their ears at Parker as we passed their herd. Parker minded his own business. He was a wise old gelding. He knew better than to mess with a herd of hormonal mares.

The wheelbarrows were already heaped with manure and straw when I turned Parker into the center aisle of the barn. A broodmare, open and in season and ready for a man, neighed a throaty welcome to my diminutive gelding. He whinnied a high-pitched response that made me roll my eyes, but the mare (who was, frankly, desperate) decided she was into it and hollered back. The others joined in, and the morning's peace was shattered for a few minutes by trumpeting horses, all competing to be heard.

Kerri emerged from a stall with a pitchfork in hand. She looked annoyed. "You had to set them off," she grumbled. "They only just recovered from the trauma of turn-out time."

"I'm sorry." I made my voice contrite, although I wanted to laugh at her dark mood. She'd learned those from me, little Miss Chipper. "I wanted a visit. I haven't seen you in forever."

"You saw me two days ago."

"Ages ago," I persisted. "We used to work together all day. Now it's just me and Alexander and all those riders who are pissed at me about yesterday."

Kerri leaned her pitchfork against the cinderblock wall and weaved her way around the wheelbarrow. She waited until her hand was on Parker's warm neck to ask, in a hushed tone, "Are you okay?"

"My shoulders ache," I said, wondering what all the whispering was about. Then I glanced up and saw that the other two grooms were peeking through the stall doors. I frowned.

"No, I mean...are you *okay?*"

"What's going on?"

"I heard..." Kerri paused and bit her lip.

"What did you hear?"

"That you're going through some sort of crisis," she burst out. The words came in a rush. "That you rode so badly yesterday you caused the accident that killed that colt. That Alexander is pulling you out of the training barn until you get it together, and that the wagering board is thinking of pulling your license over the horse abuse scandal." She sighed and shook her head. "I didn't believe any of it, but then you rode up here in the middle of training, so..."

I shook my head, incredulous. "That colt wasn't my fault, for starters. Didn't anyone mention the galloping horses next door? Or did we decide those are phantasms brought on by my breakdown, and they never really happened? Despite the fact that I wasn't even the one who saw them. It was Richard and Michelle who saw them. And the wagering board thing is just plain made-up. I'm not even under investigation."

"I did hear about the horses coming up the fenceline," Kerri admitted. "Richard says you should have seen them. He said everyone saw them and you were the only one caught off guard, and that you couldn't control your horse, so you caused the accident."

"Oh really? That's not what I heard. I didn't hear Juan piping up that he saw them."

"That's because you were talking to Juan instead of paying attention to the track."

I had been. But that was hardly unusual. "Maybe *Ricky* can't manage to ride the easiest horse in the barn and still carry on a conversation, but I'm capable of doing both. I think that the colt saw the horses coming before anyone else did. He panicked, plain and simple. I don't think anyone could have stopped him from spooking so hard."

"Juan says he started pulling up his horse just before your horse cut him off. He said he saw them, but you didn't react at all."

My mouth fell open. Bald-faced lies, really, from the best rider in my barn? Kerri gazed up at me, her face full of concern, and went on.

"He said that ever since the bad press, you've been distracted. Kind of half-here."

She believed them.

I narrowed my eyes at her, and she stepped back, her hands leaving Parker's neck. He nosed after her, wanting more attention, but I'd had enough.

How *dare* she believe them? How *dare* she sit and listen to them gossip about me, and believe their nonsense? What sort of friend was she? "Did you defend me at all? Did you tell them there's no way in hell I would let anything in my personal life affect my riding?"

Kerri shook her head. "I don't ever say anything when they gossip. What do you want me to do? I *work* with these people. While you're having breakfast with Alexander, we're eating tacos in the tack room. They talk, I hear them."

"You could have breakfast with us."

"I can't be the teacher's pet if I want to have anyone to talk to here. It's a long day when no one talks to you."

I'd certainly figured *that* one out this morning. "So that's what being my friend means? It makes you the teacher's pet?"

"A little bit, yeah. Of course it does! You're the boss, Alex. You're my friend, of course—but you're the boss, too. Your employees are going to talk about you. That's the way it works. If I'm always telling them to shut up about you, they'll just do it somewhere else—and they won't talk to me at all."

I reined back hard, thinking only that I needed to be away from her, *now*. Parker picked up his head and backed up a few steps, chewing at the bit uncomfortably. Kerri stepped away, too, her jaw set and angry. I'd upset the horse and the human equally, and I should have felt bad about it. The horse, at least. All I could think was that if Kerri wouldn't stand up for me, maybe I didn't have the friend I'd thought after all. Maybe she'd gone back to the broodmare barn because she didn't want to work with me constantly anymore. Maybe I'd read way more into our relationship than what was actually there. I wasn't a person who had friends. I wouldn't know.

Relaxing my hands to settle Parker's hurt feelings, I wheeled the pony around with a touch of the reins to his neck. "Tell your friends that *Superman* couldn't have stopped that colt," I said as we went, without looking back. "And then find someone else to gossip about. I don't pay people to talk shit about me." I rode out of the barn, heels pressed to Parker's side, before Kerri could reply. Maybe she didn't have a reply. Maybe she shrugged and went back to her work, picking up the pitchfork and returning to mucking out the broodmare stalls. Maybe she thought *Thank goodness that's over.*

All the way back to the training barn, I rehearsed the tale I would bring to Alexander, the *you won't believe this* and the *they have some nerve* and the *I thought we were friends.* The last line made my eyes sting, hot and furious, but I blinked the damp away and wiped my cheeks and dried my hands in Parker's mane. I wasn't a child, and this wasn't a barn spat between teenagers. This was work, and we would all do well to remember it. I should have been making friends and allies in the business a long time ago.

Well, now I would. Where, and how, that was something I'd worry about another day. The important thing was to stay tough and resolved in front of my staff. So they thought I was having a breakdown? So they thought I wasn't paying attention and causing accidents? And just who the hell were they? How dare they doubt my ability? I was their boss—if they didn't like it they could go ride for someone else.

I was prepared to vent it all to Alexander and then give the cold shoulder to everyone in the barn. But when I rode into the shed-row, I found the place in chaos.

Juan was shouting at Ricky, who was covered in dirt from head to toe. Luz, one of the more capable grooms, was holding the reins of a trembling colt, still fully tacked in saddle and bridle, while Alexander bent to pick up a foreleg. But every time his hand got close, the colt jumped backwards, legs churning dangerously.

Nearby, the other riders stood and made suggestions, peanut gallery style. "Grab his ear, Luz!" "Gotta trank him first!" "Lip chain's all you need!"

I hopped down from Parker's saddle and let the pony walk off to his stall alone while I sprang into action. One thing you could say for the equestrian life, there's never any time to sit around brooding about hurt feelings. Something was always breaking, someone was always getting hurt, the world was always turning and turning as fast as it could, hoping it could fling us off and be free.

The sore colt was diagnosed with a contusion on his fetlock, sustained after he and Juan's mount had a collision on the track. They'd been spooked, Ricky said, and his colt veered into Juan's. Just like yesterday, but with less fatal results. The neighbor horses had been at it again, galloping out of the fog like ghosts and disappearing again just as mysteriously. Ricky had seen them this time, and Juan—hell, everyone had. No one apologized to me for claiming that I was cracked in the head for blaming strange horses on yesterday's accident. Of course not—they didn't know that I had heard about their gossip. Today's gossip wouldn't be about me, I figured, it would be about who the hell was running those horses up our fence-line every morning.

Now the colt had been poulticed and wrapped and the grooms were raking the shed-row. The horses were pulling at their hay-nets, the riders were joking over tacos in the tack room, its green-painted steel door slid closed against the chilly morning air. Another day of training had come to a close. Nothing left to do now but find some breakfast and then go up to the broodmare barn for the vet visit. Something I was in no hurry to attend today. I walked the shed-row, leaving a row of boot-prints in the raked clay, to make sure that everyone had cleaned up their grain and had water in their buckets. The fog was swirling through the barn rafters, covering everything it touched with damp and cold, and I shivered.

I shrugged into an extra hoodie I'd left hanging on a peg in the center aisle, shoved my hands into the pockets, and immediately removed them again with handfuls of old hay. I guessed I'd been helping with hay-nets the last time I'd needed two sweaters. "This is a damned cold January," I said, and Alexander grunted a reply that might have been a denial or an affirmation.

He was upset, of course. We had a serious situation on our hands. Some unknown trainer galloping horses next to our training track, two injuries, one catastrophic, in two days. And yet I had a guilty little sense of relief rubbing shoulders with my worry. Now that Ricky had lost control of his horse, I couldn't be blamed for yesterday's accident.. Sure, Ricky wasn't the world's greatest exercise rider, but he'd stayed on top yesterday, something that I hadn't managed. Today, he was the one in the dirt. This was more than Alex losing her focus.

Not that anyone was going to acknowledge that fact out loud, but just knowing it made me feel slightly better about life in general.

Still, someone had to figure out who was running those horses, and if they were doing it on purpose. Suppose they were timing their gallops to match up to ours? It sure looked that way.

"This is suspicious," I said, sidling up to Alexander as he leaned on the shed-row rail and stared out into the gray fog. "This whole thing with the horses next door. Very suspicious."

Alexander shook his head. "No it's not." Of course. He didn't *want* it to be suspicious, so it wasn't. "You're looking for conspiracies now."

"Why would I want a conspiracy? Wouldn't I rather this just be chance?"

"It *is* just chance," he said instead of answering me.

"Of course. Two horses galloping up our fence-line at the same time that our horses are rounding the turn into the backstretch. Were these the same horses?"

"One's a gray, one's darker—bay, maybe, or liver chestnut."

"So it's the same horses."

"Or they have two grays. And it was a different time of morning."

"There are only two horses, and they're holding them at the top of the field until they hear our horses coming around the turn," I suggested.

"That's very elaborate. And who is doing this?"

"The same people that sent me two hundred emails in the past three days informing me that I was a hypocritical horse killer? Even though the horse that I didn't own, didn't actually die? I found out who's at the bottom of this, did I tell you?" I kicked at the footboard that held the clay in place, stopping the expensive footing from sliding out into the bahia grass and sand outside. "Citizens Against Slave Horses. CASH."

"That's their *name?* You're not serious."

"Oh, I'm serious. That's who is leading the charge now. They have pre-written emails on their website and their Facebook page. And they're taking credit for sending that woman to scream at me at the banquet. Take a look." I thumbed through my phone and showed Alexander their Facebook page. He scanned the vicious posts and his face sagged.

"This is terrible."

"I thought it was terrible when it was just emails. But there are physical threats in these emails, and now look what's started happening just a day after they started arriving. Horses out of nowhere, staged to scare our horses—"

Alexander interrupted. "You've gotten threats against the horses or the farm or—?"

"Just against me, personally." I looked out over the paddocks. The wind was picking up and the fog was starting to thin at last. I could see the black boards of the nearest paddock, where Tiger would be turned out once the grooms were finished up with the morning clean-up. "But so far they've only managed to hurt horses." My sore shoulders didn't count.

Alexander leaned his head against a support column and sighed. We stood in silence for a few minutes, watching the paddocks and trees slowly come into focus. It might just be a pretty day after all, I thought. The sun could even make an appearance and warm us up a bit. Behind us, the grooms hung up the long-toothed shed-row rakes with a clatter of metal. The sliding door to the tack room rumbled open, and there was a buzz of conversation, a staccato burst of laughter, released from the party within; then it was closed again and the training barn was draped in the silence peculiar to horse barns: a quiet made up of teeth pulling at hay-nets, shifting hooves rustling through straw, the occasional snort. It was never perfectly silent in a barn, but to our ears, the stillness was complete.

"If it was deliberate, and it is this group...who do you think is behind it all? Who's the ringleader?"

I shrugged, but I was happy that he was at least listening to me. "It could be anyone in the world. Plenty of people have a bone to pick with racing."

Alexander shook his head. "It's not CASH, though. You're forgetting, those are *racehorses* running down the fence-line. If they're really being used against us, it's racehorse people using them. There's no way a radical group like this would team up with a racehorse trainer."

"So someone who doesn't like me in the racing business. That list is still pretty long. I'm not winning any popularity contests. *You're* pretty well-liked, though. Maybe they're hoping you'll get fed up with my bad image and the trouble I bring to the barn and you'll kick me out."

"And what, marry one of their spinster daughters? This isn't a Victorian murder mystery, Alex. But—as you say—someone who doesn't like you *personally*..."

I chewed my lip. The conversation was kind of a downer. It's one thing to know you're an outsider. It's another thing entirely to consider that there's someone who dislikes you enough to attempt bodily harm. "You think it's her?"

"It could be."

"Mary bloody Archer," I said bitterly. What had started with a few traded insults and one crazed man-eater colt had turned into a rivalry that was reaching Dick Francis proportions. "She doesn't have to get me killed, either. All she has to do is make me sound like an even bigger idiot than I already do. And from what Kerri said earlier, she's already succeeded."

"What do you mean? No—wait." Alexander hushed me and we were quiet while Luz went strolling by, whistling and swinging a chain shank.

She waggled her fingers at us as she passed. "I go to get Tiger now," she explained.

"Thank you, Luz," I said. "I appreciate you taking on the extra job."

"I like him. But he crazy boy yesterday!" she laughed. "He go straight up—*wooo!* And I say, 'you get down crazy boy,' and give him a yank, and down he come, but he dance all the way to outside." She paused and put a hand on her hip. "You need to ride him, Alex. He need calming down. He need hard work."

"I know, Luz. But he's supposed to have some downtime to just be a horse after all his hard work racing."

Luz shook her head, still grinning. "If you say so, Alex. But I think he bored. He missing work. I go get him now." She gave another wave and went marching down the driveway, her dirty sneakers crunching on the gravel. I watched her go, my mind slipping over to Tiger's attitude problem for a moment. Was he only going to get worse, instead of better, with this lay-off?

"What's the story, Alex?"

"What?" I turned back to Alexander, who was looking at me with an impatient expression.

"*What* did Kerri say?"

"Oh." From one distressing subject back to the other one. I flipped back with ease; what's a little more trouble? "Kerri wanted to know how I could let my attention slip so badly. Apparently the riders were all talking about the accident and blamed me for it. Saying that I wasn't paying attention because I'm so upset about the bad press and everything. And you *know* they went gossiping all over town once they got off work. By now all of Ocala will be hearing some telephone version of this."

"They'll have a different story to tell tonight, though. That the same thing happened two days in a row and you weren't there the second time. How can they blame you for this one? It's terrible that it happened, but I think it clears you, too."

I didn't mention that I thought so, too. "Not causing an accident isn't going to be enough get me out of this. I need someone on my side. Or I have to do something that's going to make a difference."

"You could sponsor a retired horse in training," Alexander rubbed his chin in thought. "Or a Thoroughbred show? A class? Maybe Lucy knows someone putting one together."

"Throwing money at the problem."

"Well, you have some. If you're short on allies, at least you can buy some good press."

He had a point, but having money in the bank was one of the things people *didn't* like about me. I wished it would be easy to get a little press for retiring Tiger after that clunker of a race, but we already retired all of our horses, so that was hardly news. Throwing money at a retirement charity 1 when we already spent plenty retiring our horses didn't make a ton of sense either. "Writing a check just looks like guilt, and I don't want to look guilty like that," I argued. "Just sending the money to pay Market Affair's vet bills makes me look guilty. I want to do something that stands apart. Something real."

We looked at each other. Neither of us, I knew, had any idea what I wanted.

Finally I shrugged, followed by an involuntary little shiver. "It's too chilly for me out here. Let's go back to the house." I pushed off from the shed-row railing and started for the golf cart.

"Alex," Alexander said, not moving. "What if you rode Tiger?"

I stopped and looked back at him. His tweed cap was beaded with moisture, his breath was white in the cold air, and I knew he was feeling the chill as much as I was, but his face had brightened as if the greatest idea in the world had lit him up from the inside. I hadn't the faintest idea what that might be. "What? I can't ride Tiger for months. He's had no lay-off at all."

"But just look at him." Alexander's gaze flicked past me and he nodded. I turned just as I heard the hooves crunching on the gravel.

Coming through the thinning fog like a racehorse going to the post, Tiger pranced alongside Luz, who was swinging the leather shank carelessly in her hands, ignoring the Thoroughbred's antics. He was swishing his tail, arching his neck, his forelegs and hocks rising up in a *piaffe*, then pushing forward in a lunge of power when she got ahead of him and gave the lead a yank to hurry him along. He'd lurch forward, hit the chain over his nose and skid to a prancing halt, and then the whole process began all over again. He clearly thought he was one of the rare dark bay Lippizanners. Or a racehorse.

Luz shook her head at him and laughed. "You a big dumb horse," I heard her tell him, her voice carrying through the fog. "But someday, somebody gonna get on you and make you work hard. Then we see how bad you act for me." She swung open the paddock gate and Tiger threw himself through the gap, spinning around to face her so quickly that dirt went flying through the air. I heard the clods hit the ground with a series of damp thuds. Luz pulled the gate closed behind her, carefully unbuckled the chain from the halter while Tiger stood rigid, every muscle tensed, and then she jumped backwards, swinging the lead shank at his shoulder while she went.

The lead never touched Tiger's shoulder, nor even his hindquarters. By the time she had leapt behind the gate, the horse had spun around and exploded into a gallop, not even bothering to kick out as he went. All of his energy and focus was dedicated to running as fast as he could, and as he lapped the little paddock, sod flying up from his hooves, I realized that Tiger was working just as hard as he could, at the only job he knew. Then my eyes began to sting, watching him like that. Seven years old, and he'd done the same thing every day for four years. Of course being turned out in a field every day was confusing the hell out of him. Of course he was bursting out of his skin with nerves and boredom. I wiped at a hot tear before it could make its way down my cheek and give me away.

Naturally, Alexander always knew best. "You ride him, Alex," he repeated. "Skip the lay-off. Skip sending him away. You ride him. You both need it."

Luz looked up as she came trudging up the gravel path towards us. She grinned. "You see that crazy horse? What I tell you? Every day he the same. When he last race? Two weeks ago? He still want to go."

"He didn't want to go in his last race!" I stretched my mouth into what I hoped was a smile and forced a laugh.

Luz just chuckled, shaking her head, and went past us into the barn. When she had disappeared back inside the warm tack room, Alexander pushed himself off the shed-row rail and came around the doorpost to join me on the driveway. His calloused hand found mine and squeezed it tight. "You have an ally, Alex," he said gently. "And you have a purpose. You have me, and you have a horse who needs a job. I don't think you could pick a better time to spend extra time on the farm." He looked up at the dark bay horse who was still cantering around his field, his sides heaving and his ears pricked. "You're needed here."

Chapter Ten

I WASN'T CONVINCED SO easily.

There were a thousand reasons why Tiger shouldn't be pulled out of a post-racing lay-off so soon, and at least a thousand more why even if he was, I wasn't the trainer to start riding him. For one thing, I was his exercise rider.

"Then he'll already be more attuned to you," Alexander argued.

What about the fact that I hadn't reschooled a racehorse in more than six years? I barely remembered what to do.

Alexander just laughed at that one. I tightened my fingers on the golf cart's steering wheel and told myself he was wrong. This was all going to blow over soon, after all. I wouldn't be on house arrest forever. I might be missing Personal Best in the Mizner Stakes next weekend, but I wasn't about to miss Luna's next race. I'd been aiming her for an allowance debut at Gulfstream with the hopes of getting her into an overnight stake. She had been training like a monster at long last. When I'd last seen her two weeks ago, I'd given her three peppermints, told the exercise rider to let her go for five furlongs, and then stepped back and watched the jaws all around me drop as she smoked every other horse on the track.

Then she came back and nosed at my pocket until I handed over the rest of my peppermints. That was my sweet girl! I missed her.

Now that she was sitting on a win, I was determined that I would be the one to walk her to the paddock, saddle her up, and hand her off to the pony rider. I *had* to be.

Thoughts full of my chestnut filly and my chestnut colt, I had just started to swing the golf cart up the driveway to the house when Alexander put his hand on my arm. "Let's go up to the stallion barn."

I shrugged and kept the golf cart on the main drive, and we went rattling past the yearling barn turn-off and the sparkling dew-drop field where the young horses were out grazing, swishing their short tails. Ahead, the stallion barn stood alone on its hill, pleasantly symmetrical: a small square box within a square box made of six small square paddocks. Four of those paddocks were empty.

The stallion barn was the one place on the farm that I didn't visit daily. I rarely came up here without a mare to breed—the stallions were unquestionably Alexander's horses. They'd been retired from racing to stallion duty long before I came on the scene. He went up every day while I was fussing over a yearling or attending a vet visit in the broodmare barn, to chat with the two old men who had helped him build up Cotswold Farm: stately, aging Thoroughbred stallions named Virtuous and Cotswold Ramble.

When we pulled up to the barn, Alexander went inside and stood for a moment, looking around him as if he'd never been there before. There was a faraway look to his eyes that kept me sitting in the golf cart, giving him a minute. Then I decided I had a wifely duty to show support, or something like that. He was being weird and nostalgic—most unusual behavior for Alexander, who always kept his gaze facing firmly forward. I was the one who wasted time on *what ifs* and *do you remembers*.

I came up behind him and touched his shoulder. "What are you looking for?" I asked gently, wondering if the answer would be physical and simple (most likely with Alexander) or existential and philosophical (a worrisome development for him if I'd ever heard of one).

He sighed and reached out, knocking aside some cobwebs from the bars on the nearest stall door. The stall was dark and uninhabited, the clay floor swept clean and dry, the shutter on the window closed up tight. There were a few bags of shavings leaning against the wall, and a blue plastic barrel storing heaven knew what. Surely there had once been a horse in this stall, but not in my time here. "I wish there were more horses up here, that's all," he said, ending with another wistful sigh.

I nodded, glancing around at the empty stable. The six-stall barn was nothing fancy—it was one of the first barns built on the property, raised before prosperity and success had expanded the farm into the training center it was today, and so it was no showpiece. The big farms in Ocala housed their stallions in massive stalls, with rubber-paved boulevards for aisles, lit by chandeliers and ornamented with brass fittings. Framed win photos decorated the walls, so that broodmares could see their swain's past triumphs as they were led into the padded chamber of the breeding shed.

Cotswold's stallion barn was a nice-enough center-aisle design, with a concrete aisle, twelve-by-twelve stalls, and bars on the stall fronts so that horses could see into the aisle. There were sliding doors, and automatic waterers, and a wash-rack, and a tack and feed room. A breeding shed had been built behind the barn, large enough for a mare and stallion to have an assignation without any of the grooms getting crushed against a wall when things got exciting. And that was pretty much it. It looked like an old hunter barn. It was nice enough, as I said—much like the two Cotswold stallions, who were also nice enough.

The view was what made the stallion barn impressive. Looking down the short dark tunnel of the aisle, the paddocks with their neat lines of black-board fencing dropped away in a gradual slope that showed off the spectacular spread of Ocala's farms below. Our stallions might have been living with an unimpressive floor plan inside, but they had one hell of a view from their patio.

"Has anyone been in the apartment upstairs lately?" Alexander asked, looking at the cobwebs draping the staircase next to the front entry. We both gazed up at the dark windows that looked down upon the barn aisle. In theory, a full-time stallion manager would live up there and always be able to look down on his charges when they were inside for the night. But we'd never had one, certainly not in my time on the farm. We'd never had enough horses up here to justify it. Two stallions didn't get their own groom. One of the yearling grooms came up and took care of the boys after the yearlings were fed. Once they were turned out for the day, if there was no breeding in the books, they were left alone until supper time.

This year, there was virtually no breeding on the books, besides our own mares. It hadn't bothered me much, but I knew Alexander was a little disappointed. Or maybe a lot disappointed. Mary Archer's words about a busy breeding season shouldered their way into my mind. What was he plotting?

"Alex? Do you know?"

"I think the apartment was cleaned out in the autumn." Seasons got cloudy in my brain. I was usually wondering what time of year it was anyway. Florida can do that to you. "I'm pretty sure we had it done when we had the other dorms done. Oh! That's right. One of the cleaning ladies said it was full of spiders and had a panic attack. They almost called an ambulance for her."

Alexander took a step towards the stairs.

I took a step back.

Doris hadn't been faking that panic attack. She'd seen things. Terrible things. Ocala spider things.

Alexander shook his head and turned away, walking down the aisle instead.

Thank God. I wasn't going anywhere near an empty old barn apartment full of spiders. If I went up those stairs and found an apartment full of giant spiders, I'd burn this entire barn down and move the stallions to the training barn.

Spiders were not my thing.

Definitely not Ocala's signature spiders, which are as big as tarantulas and twice as fast, and just love hanging out everywhere you don't want them to be, like in between your shower curtain and the liner, or on the ceiling of your bedroom, waiting for you to wake up in the middle of the night, open your eyes, see them watching you from a shaft of sparkling moonlight, and never fall asleep again.

I shook my head to rid it of visions of spiders festooning the walls of the empty rooms over my head and looked for Alexander, who had wandered off. There he was at the end of the aisle, standing with his hands in his pockets, silhouetted elegantly as he gazed out over the sunlit valley. In the two paddocks immediately in front of us, his stallions grazed. Virtuous lifted up his dark head and watched us, grass dangling from the sides of his mouth. Cotswold Ramble just went on grazing. With his plain bay coat roughed out for winter and his big, Roman-nosed head buried in grass, he looked rather unfortunately like a plow horse. The sight was less than inspirational. But they had both been good runners, and they had both been solid mid-list Florida stallions.

Still, no one had lined up to fill Ramble's book in his freshman year, some eight years ago, and Virtuous had been a freshman so long ago that it didn't really bear thinking about. They had never been the "it" stallions, but they had sired plenty of good runners, who ran their races and stayed sound. If only *that* was fashionable.

I put my hand on Alexander's back. "They're good boys," I offered, not really sure where his head was at. "You should be proud of them."

Ramble hadn't had a winner outside the claiming ranks in two years, and Virtuous's golden years had come and gone before I had ever arrived on Cotswold. Virtue and Vice was the brightest star he had ever sired, and we were still waiting for Virtue to truly mature and show us what we suspected he could do. They weren't great stallions, it was true. But they were *good* stallions. It was just that a good stallion cannot have a good career without the mares to back it up. We had too few to support them, and the good stakes mares weren't coming here. They were going to the stallions with big stakes careers. The A-listers.

Alexander chuckled, but it was a rather mirthless sound. I curled my arm around his side and leaned into him, feeling his disappointment in his empty barn, his unsung stallions. I supposed that being in Australia for the breeding season last year had been tough on him. Seeing his brother's massive operation, one of the largest in the Southern Hemisphere, and then coming back to Ocala, where these two old boys were grazing towards their retirement, while all the top stock in our training barns seemed to come from bloodstock sales or other farm's stallions...it must have stung, and the sting hadn't left all these months later.

"Did you know," I said, trying to turn his head. "I heard Len Robinson say you're going to end up in the Hall of Fame some day, based on your whole career. He said it just last week at Mason's Farrier Supply. He didn't know I was in the room."

"I want to fill up this barn," he said gravely, cutting over my prattle. "I want six stallions, and everyone in Ocala trying to get into their books."

I was startled into silence. Alexander rarely talked about building up the breeding business. We usually discussed how to get *fewer* horses on the property, not more. Quality over quantity, yes, but not quality *and* quantity. I supposed that if he meant to bring home one of the racing string, say Virtue perhaps, and stand him here next year, we could limit the stud book, and build up demand that way...he could be on to something. There were favors to call in, and we could buy a few mares to get some good looking yearlings to send to the sales. We could easily hire a stud groom and extra staff for the breeding season next year...I ran over potential candidates in my head. Luz certainly didn't mind studdish antics, although it was a little unusual to have a female head stud groom... eyebrows would raise amongst the good old boys...

Alexander turned and looked around the dark barn again. "Let's get this place cleaned up. We'll start as we mean to go on. We have all of the breeding season ahead of us. Anything could happen."

"Are you...are you going to *buy* stallions?" I doubted we could afford to start buying up successful racehorses, and the very idea of starting a syndication was exhausting. *That's all you, Alexander.* I didn't want any more stress in my life, and shareholders and lawyers would be ten times as obnoxious as everyday owners.

Alexander brushed a thumb over a dusty nameplate, glinting dully on the closed door of an empty stall. *Heaven's Silence.* The Roman letters glinted in the mid-morning sunlight, streaming in from the eastern end of the aisle. "Good horse," Alexander said thoughtfully. "I bred him myself, in England. When they say they'll put me in the Hall of Fame, this is the horse they are thinking of. But I'm not done yet." He turned and looked at me, and his face was determined, as if he'd finally made up his mind after a long struggle. "I have a few ideas for this season. Something might change, you never know. But either way, we'll be ready for the Cotswold boys when they come home, Alex. Our own stallions. Idle Hour, Shearwater, Virtue and Vice, Personal Best. I'm going to test them out there, and then they're going to stud right here, with the race record to prove that they're worth it. There's a stall for each of them. And if we need more room, we'll build it."

I nodded and tried to muster up the enthusiasm I knew he expected from such a grand proclamation, but inside I was hurt. *I'm going to test them out there.*

I'm.

Not *we're.*

Alexander really *doesn't want me at the races any more.* I bit my lip and said nothing, letting him go on building his imaginary empire.

Alexander was walking about the aisle, running his fingers through layers of dust, clucking and shaking his head at the state of the empty stalls, the unswept feed room. It all would have been cleaned up next week, I thought irritably. Before the breeding sheds opened. It wasn't as if we were showing Ocala the face of a farm that had given up with our dusty barn and our neglected equipment.

But of course, that wasn't what I was upset about. I tried to bite back the words, but my temper simmered over, as it always did. "You're really not going to let me go back to Gulfstream," I said tightly.

He didn't look at me, just went on inspecting the barn aisle. "I can't *let* you do anything, Alex," he joked, a slight smile on his face.

"You know what I mean. You don't want me there. It's not temporary. You want your name on those wins. You want people congratulating *you* when P.B. wins the Mizner, and then you want the magazines talking about *you* when he starts to rack up points for the Derby. That's what this is about." I was shaking with anger, my head spinning with outrage. I put a hand back on the stall door behind me, the one with the stall plate that read *Heaven's Silence.* Alexander's champion, the horse he had bred and broke and trained himself. All himself. I'd wanted that for myself. "Personal Best was *always* mine, from the day he was born—"

"This is about your safety, Alex. The stallions have nothing to do with it," Alexander interrupted. He turned and faced me from across the aisle, his eyebrows raised in surprise, and I could see that he had never expected me to be so upset by his announcement. He hadn't heard the proud possession in his words. "Keeping you away from the races is about people making threats against your life because of a hate-filled media campaign. Why would you make it me versus you? What other ally do you have, my love?"

I opened my mouth and closed it again. What could I say? My only ally...and here I was picking fights with him over the words he chose in a spur of the moment speech. My eyes were suddenly hot and stinging, and I swiped hard at them with the sleeve of my hoodie. "I'm sorry—"

"It's fine."

"I'm sorry, Alexander." My heart was aching now, just as it had been filled with black rage seconds before. I was having more mood swings than a mare in foal these days. "I'm just so overwhelmed with...with all the crazy."

He opened his arms, and I walked into them and placed my head against his chest. He folded me within his grasp, and when he spoke, his voice rumbled against my ear. "Crazy is the name of the game, my love. All I ask is that you lie low and let this particular crazy run its course. You have a little retirement work to do now."

⤜⤛⤚⤙ ⤐⤑⤒⤓

I had retirement work to do. So Alexander said, and it made a lot of sense. Retiring a horse myself, maybe calling some press to let them know what I was up to...not a bad idea. But it still seemed so unorthodox to ride Tiger without the usual lay-off period. It flew in the face of every training principle I'd ever been taught—except for one: *every horse is different.*

There was no doubt that Tiger was not like other horses. So I went out to ask him what he thought.

In the mid-morning's sudden new sunlight, blinding yellow and chipper as if it had been there all along and we'd simply made the fog up, I drove back out to the paddock by the training barn and leaned over the fence. But the dark bay horse, who once would have come trotting to the fence nickering a greeting, just gave me the cold shoulder, ignoring me in favor of ripping at the grass with his characteristic vigor.

It wasn't the answer I'd been hoping for.

Maybe he *did* want to go back to work, and he was showing me how irritated he was with my lack of attention. Maybe this was how he told me he didn't think it was funny, the way I'd stopped riding him every day, the way he'd been booted out of the training barn and had to live with those stupid yearlings (sorry yearlings, his words, not mine). Tiger in exile, bored and blaming me, swishing his tail over his haunches though there were no flies to brush away, just to let me know what he thought of me. Tiger walking his stall in the yearling barn, whinnying to his old friends in the training barn, destroying the bedding and making twice the work for the grooms. Tiger the demon, acting like a maniac when Luz led him over for turn-out and took him back again at night.

Maybe *that* was his answer—screw you, lady, I'm not ready for the retirement pants yet. I could buy that. I could see Tiger's point in that—he'd gone from the favorite child to forgotten in five days flat, and he wasn't about to just get used to it.

So fine, maybe the ninety-day lay-off wasn't going to fly for Tiger. Not every horse was the same, right? If he needed to be in work to be happy, well, then, I could arrange that. But then, I could ask him one more time, in a different language, just to be sure—I stuck my hand in my pocket and crackled some candy wrappers left in there. If he wanted attention, if he wanted to come back to the barn and get tacked up and go to work, wouldn't he hear those wrappers and make the connection? I couldn't remember the last time I hadn't given him a peppermint after a gallop.

But he just went on grazing, taking short, vicious bites from the browning grass, ripping up dirty roots from the soft ground and brushing his mouthful from side to side to knock the sand from them. He was as ferocious to grass as he was to hay-nets. Tiger approached everything he did in life with vigor that often crossed the line to aggression. Look at how seriously he had taken competition as the years went by—even the ponies weren't safe from him anymore. Every horse he saw was there to take attention away from *him,* and that he could not countenance.

It must have been heartbreaking for him when he went for his final run and the speed just was not there. To trail all those horses... the ego-bruising he must have taken that day made my own pale in comparison.

He needed another chance at being a star, I thought. He had so much competitive energy burning within. He'd make a hell of a jumper, with that attitude, taking it all out on the course, flinging himself at the jumps with brash confidence. I was looking at him now with the sort of hungry appreciation for a racehorse's sport potential that I'd had when I was a teenager, looking for slow horses with nice movement and intelligent eyes. Something I'd shrugged off along with riding jackets and black hunt caps years ago.

But now I could see it again—the trainer's vision of a changed horse. Turn that heavy neck upside-down, losing the thick pad of muscle developed while the racehorse ran against the bit, and relocating it to the crest, to rise up beneath a braided mane. Lower the head, lift the spine, and develop a top-line that would streamline the hindquarters into a graceful slope from croup to delicately lifted tail. Add an inch or two of height and a full hand of movie-star presence as he learned to move from behind and carry himself with pride.

With all that energy and muscle and outright aggression—if aggression was the right word, for what he had was less violent than that implied, more a hybrid characteristic made up of dynamic athleticism and an overbearing need to win, to be the best of everything (*Thoroughbred*. That was the word for that characteristic.)—with all that *Thoroughbred* contained between hands and seat, like a rocket fueled and ready for launch the moment the rider signaled ignition—well, what *couldn't* he do? What jump couldn't he jump, what movement couldn't he make?

I was starry-eyed with his bright future.

"You could be the best," I breathed to the rough-grazing, tail-swishing, hoof-stamping horse in the paddock. "You couldn't have been the best of racehorses—we always knew you were just a good runner, a workhorse, someone who could bring home a check, and that's nothing to sneeze at, bud—but if you could jump? If you were trained properly? If you loved it? What couldn't you do?"

Tiger looked up at me at last, his ears dark silhouettes against the electric-blue sky.

I was a teenager in love. A child in a dream. I sighed like a moonstruck high school sophomore who has just discovered Shakespeare's sonnets and read far too much into them. Standards set impossibly high, I waited for him in a breathless state of anticipation that could only end in disappointment.

Until I closed my fist on those candy wrappers once more.

The crackling sound of thin stiff plastic made its impression on Tiger this time, perhaps because he was actually paying attention to me now. He shook his head, as if making up his mind at last, and then began to amble across the paddock towards me in an unhurried stride.

Chapter Eleven

"SO LET'S SAY I were to ride Tiger. *Where* would I ride him?" I settled down at the breakfast table with a cup of coffee, the tenth or twelfth or twentieth of the day; I'd lost count. Outside the tall windows, the winter sun was streaming across the hillsides and illuminating the mares and foals in the broodmare pasture. I could see the vet's truck bouncing along the drive. I'd forgotten to join Kerri and the broodmare grooms to help out with the visit. She'd manage just fine without me. Probably preferred it that way.

"You could use his paddock for a while. And then we'll sort it out if you need more than that." Alexander was placid and happy with his decision; he sipped at his coffee and flipped through his issue of *The Blood-Horse* without any real concern. He paused at an advertisement for a stallion standing his freshman year at a farm just down the road, and frowned over the copy for a moment. Then he was back. "Or you can hack him out in the fields to start, just like we do with the yearlings. You don't know if he was started like that. I sincerely doubt that he was, considering who his connections were when we bought him. They weren't exactly the most sympathetic of trainers."

Since that particularly charming ex-trainer of Tiger's had boasted that one of the best ways to prep a horse for a race was to shut both his stall doors and keep him completely penned up and isolated from society for days, until he was going out of his head with energy...no, sympathetic his past trainers were not. The easy pasture rides that our babies went on every morning for their first month or two of training weren't exactly an industry standard, either, but they were enjoyable, and taught the horses to look forward to riding as a pleasant diversion. Since Tiger needed to learn that there was more to life than running headlong in a circle, jogging the fence-lines around the property *could* be very good for him. A nice hour every morning, while the broodmares and yearlings were inside eating their breakfasts...

Which somehow I would have to accomplish during training hours, when everything else was already going on. I needed to be out on Parker or galloping a problem horse, not gallivanting through the fields with Tiger like a teenager on summer vacation. It was a nice idea, but terribly impractical.

"When am I going to find the time to do this? Especially on days when you're in south Florida? I have training, I have the broodmares and yearlings to keep on top of, I have a full day's work as it is."

Alexander sighed. "It's a shame we haven't any staff and you have to do all the work and don't even have time to ride a horse every day. Alex, this is our slowest year yet. We have no more than ten foals coming. We are sending half the two-year-olds to the spring sales. The stud books are wide open. For once, you have all the time you could want. Why not use it to enjoy yourself? Go play with your horse. Don't even call it work."

"But it's not what I do anymore." I had no idea how to explain what was stopping me here. I wasn't sure what it was myself. Out there in the paddock, I had handed Tiger the one loose peppermint I'd had left and I had *known* that we had a brilliant future together. Driving back to the house, looking out across the racehorse training center where I had centered my career, all my hopes and dreams, the future as a trainer, I was afraid that it was a huge step backwards, towards a job I wasn't sure I even knew how to *do* anymore. "I know you think this will make me look great when I turn out a gorgeous new show horse, but I haven't done this work in years. I'll screw it up. I'll screw Tiger up. And then things will just look worse than ever."

He went back to studying the ad for the new stallion. I craned my neck to see what was bothering him so. Lots of flowery italics. *Fairwinds Farm was proud to present Avenging for his freshman year. Millionaire winner of two Grade 1 stakes races, three Grade 2, Florida Stallion Stakes winner. From dam of champions, etc., etc.* The usual hype for a horse who had run a few nice races, retired after his three-year-old year, and was untested as a sire, but had the bloodlines to do great things...if bloodlines played out the way one hoped. There was no way to tell if he'd sire champions or duds, but he'd get the ladies this spring. Pinhookers went gaga for foals from freshman sires, so breeders lined up for these young stallions, got their mares in foal, then sold the colts and fillies as yearlings to the pinhookers. The pinhookers trained them up, and sold them at two-year-old in training sales. *Then* the wealthy owners stepped up to buy the first-borns of a horse they remembered from the Derby trail or the Breeders' Cup three years before.

It was all about name recognition, really, I supposed. Especially if the money in the room wasn't really coming from a horseman's wallet. As a general rule, I didn't think any of it was good for the breed, and Alexander had always agreed.

Yet Alexander had been looking at these ads quite a lot of late.

I wondered again what he'd meant when he said something could change before the breeding season was over. None of our good horses were anywhere near retirement, unless there was a lameness. God forbid. Knock on wood. If they did retire, they weren't anywhere near this sort of freshman sire hyperbole that Alexander seemed to want to build up for them.

But I didn't ask. I had enough going on.

I left the table.

Upstairs, I changed out of my dirty jeans and pulled on a clean pair. *The* clean pair, the ones I called my going-to-town jeans. The one pair I hadn't ridden in, staining the inner calves black from rubbing against a horse's sides. I decided that I would pay a visit to Lucy Knapp at her training farm, and for that I was going to look presentable—if only to make myself feel more like a professional adult person than usual. Lucy and I would chat about Tiger, and she would agree that he needed more time off, and that it would be silly for me to try and retrain him when I had been exclusively riding racehorses for the past six years. Obviously I would be giving Tiger all the wrong cues, confusing him, making things worse. We would come to the conclusion that the original plan was still the best plan—Tiger would continue to be turned out for three to six months, and then when she had room for him during the summer, he'd come to her farm for training.

It was all going to turn out for the best.

Although it didn't sound very exciting.

"I'm going to Lucy's," I said when Alexander came into the bedroom, looking inquisitive. "To talk about Tiger. Figure out a game plan." As if I didn't already have one settled in my head.

Alexander nodded. "Good idea." He glanced out the window, where sunlight was pouring in as if the morning's cold fog had never happened. "It's going to storm this afternoon," he announced gravely. "Big cold front coming, you know."

"Thank you, Mr. Weather Channel."

"I just mean, don't be gone too long. You don't want to get caught on the road if there's a big storm rolling through."

I smiled at him, unreasonably touched. "I'll be careful."

Chapter Twelve

I DROVE THE HALF hour out to Lucy Knapp's farm with the radio loud and my windows down, soaking up the cool winter air. I was full of confidence—Lucy would solve the Tiger problem for me. She had always handled our retirees. She had always had room for a Cotswold horse. She would see the correct answers immediately, maybe even have a better idea for how to work out my little P.R. problem without trying to retrain a horse myself.

Once Tiger was dealt with, I'd be free to deal with Alexander's little power play, maybe even take a few public swings at the rabble saying I was responsible for Market Affair. Maybe I'd roll up my sleeves and do a little rabble-rousing myself. I wasn't exactly a person who spoke in public, or even in mixed company at small dinner parties, though, so that part of things looked a little cloudy. I was sure it would all work out.

I saw Lucy as soon as I pulled into her barn's little parking lot. She was riding in the ring just beyond the barn, clearly trying to beat the dark wall of cloud that was hanging ominously in the northwest sky, threatening to end our few sunny hours today. The cold front Alexander had mentioned was getting closer; the DJ on the radio station had cut in with word of a tornado watch for our part of the peninsula. Another nasty winter cold front, spinning up cyclones and leaving us shivering afterwards.

Strictly speaking, neither of us should have been out with the heavy weather threatening. Lucy should have been helping her grooms pull in the jumps and pulling tarps over the shavings bin. I should have stayed closer to home so that I wouldn't be out on the roads when the weather grew dangerous. But we were both hard-headed women, typical horse-people, and sometimes we just did what we wanted and damn the consequences.

I parked the car by the barn and left the keys in the ignition. Jenny, Lucy's barn manager, came to the entrance of the barn aisle to see who the visitor was. I just threw her a casual wave hello to spare her the trouble of tolerating me—Jenny wasn't a racing fan, although she was professionally nice to me anyway—and then turned for the riding ring beyond the barn, where Lucy was cantering a leggy bay horse in tight circles between a scattering of brightly-painted show jumps.

As I approached, she swung the horse into a collected canter, keeping its haunches deep beneath its body, and turned the horse expertly in a tiny fifteen-meter circle before popping, with only a few strides' warning time, over a vertical bar at least three and a half feet tall. The horse lifted her knees to her chin and cleared the fence in a back-breaking bascule, arching her spine perfectly from nose to tail.

It was an impressive sight. I halted in my tracks without realizing it, watching the horse flip her tail on landing and skillfully swap leads before cantering away to the right, still in tautly held collection, and then Lucy turned the horse in another tiny circle and took the fence again from the opposite direction.

After another beautiful bascule, Lucy stopped her seat's motion three strides after the fence, sitting deep in the saddle, and lifted her hands slightly. Instantly, the bay horse came to a tire-screeching halt, four legs balanced perfectly, and held a statue-worthy pose for a long moment. I stood still and watched the expert performance, entranced, until finally Lucy looked over and saw me.

She smiled immediately, and, dropping the reins onto the horse's sweaty neck, waved a gloved hand. "Alex!" she called, letting the mare walk towards me with her ears pricked in anticipation of potential treats. "Just the person I want to see."

"Really? What did I do now?" Besides make the local news for abandoning horses in the Everglades? I leaned on the fence and watched her mount, a splendid bay mare, approach with a gorgeous swaying gait. She was like a very tall and very athletic leopard. "This is some bronc," I joked as they grew closer.

"Mohegan is the comfort of my old age," Lucy said with a wink. "The last horse in the barn that can perform a dressage test without terrifying the judge and taking out the arena chains."

"Everything's that bad? Tough winter." The last time I'd been out, in the fall, she'd been happy about her improving client base. She'd been getting close to having a barn full of mature show horses, instead of a barn full of babies and problems. For a little while, *my* silly racehorses had been her only headaches, but I'd heard that she'd been getting a few more Thoroughbreds lately. Maybe someone had been sending her their un-broke warmbloods again; once a breeder had sent her a half-dozen five-year-old Hanoverians who had never been so much as stabled since they were weaned. That had been a frazzled Lucy. "Hanoverian-nightmare-bad?"

"Not quite that bad," she admitted with a rueful laugh. "You love to remind me of that! I never should have taken those horses. But it's close. I have nine off-track Thoroughbred in there and all of them have borderline personality disorders. Their owners, too. Three came from the Western Oaks sale, so you can guess what sort of animal they are."

"Yeesh, that's always bad news." Western Oaks, which was even further west of here, out in some *real* hillbilly country, was a fairly grand name for a dusty collection of cattle pens that hosted a monthly livestock auction. Every third Thursday evening you could drive out there and fill your trailer with goats, chickens, stolen tack, and traumatized, half-starved horses. Plenty of which were Thoroughbreds, abandoned or dumped when they failed to make money at the track, their papers thrown away and their lip tattoos blurred by age to a blue smear beyond recognition. Some of those horses had been bred on million-dollar farms not thirty minutes away, and they'd go to slaughter or to live in ramshackle sandy corrals behind rusty mobile homes, dwindling away to skin and bone, without their breeders ever realizing what had happened to them...

...Or end up in the Everglades, or running in tight circles at bush tracks, I reflected. I'd learned a lot over the past few weeks, none of it anything I'd really wanted to know, about Where Slow Horses Can Go.

"Yeah, *yikes* is right. One of them I won't even get on. He flips over when you put your foot in the stirrup. I have to have Teddy Wilkins out to get on him and see if he can be fixed. Otherwise. . ."

She shook her head. "Pasture pet. Hopefully with a forever home, so he won't kill someone by accident down the road."

"Why would the owner even bring you a horse like that? That's not what you do." Mohegan thrust her nose at me and I ran my fingertips down its velvet softness. "They should've taken it to Teddy in the first place." Teddy Wilkins, an Ocala fixture, took in the truly dangerous horses and taught them the facts of life. There wasn't a trainer in Ocala who didn't have his number in their phone.

Lucy groaned. "Because Baby's Mummy is afraid Teddy Wilkins will hurt sweet Baby. Luckily, Mummy doesn't know he makes house calls." She picked up the reins again and walked Mohegan in a small circle. "Thank God there's only one that serious. But I have seriously seen my farm turned into a rooming-house for emotionally disturbed Thoroughbreds, Alex. And I blame you."

"Me! Come on, Luce. . . How is it my fault?"

"You talk me up too much to your little trainer cohorts, and they call every time one of their horses trips, wondering if I can take it off their hands. And that interview you did with *New Equestrian*...Oh, Lucy Knapp is such a whiz with our retirees. Oh Lucy Knapp just *understands* Thoroughbreds. Oh that Lucy Knapp and her walking on water! Hallelujah! She's come to save racehorses! She's a savior! She's a goddess! She's a goddamn slow racehorse whisperer! You get me in that magazine and poof...my life is over." Lucy waved a hand in the air to somehow indicate that she had died and evaporated into thin air.

"Are you done?"

"I think so, yes. Since you're clearly not going to apologize for turning my life into an equine insane asylum."

"So can we talk about important things now?"

"Meaning...?"

"My problems."

Lucy went on circling the mare. "Oh, of course! The main attraction. Alex, tell me all your problems. I do hope they're racehorse problems."

"Are there any other kind?" I grinned.

"These days?" Lucy could only shake her head. Mohegan did the same, spattering me with foamy saliva. "I heard about that colt from your farm. Too bad."

"He was a sweetheart. But he was a consignment for the two-year-old sales that year...he never belonged to the farm. And I was just an exercise rider then." What was I blathering about? Explaining myself as if she thought I was guilty? But I couldn't help but feel defensive, even to a friend. Who knew what she really thought of me now?

Luckily, Lucy was well-used to the insanity of the equestrian community. She chuckled instead of chiding. "Oh, you don't need to explain any of it to me. How could it be your fault? You never had a thing to do with this—it's just the anti-racing maniacs looking for someone to take the blame, and you're an easy target because you're their worst nightmare—a racing trainer who actually has a *good* reputation. They don't want anyone to know people like you exist. Whatever. We'll just keep on doing what we do, and let this blow over."

A gust of wind blew down the solid panel of one of the brightly colored jumps just then, and Mohegan jumped.

"Speaking of blowing over..."

Lucy clapped one hand on her neck to reassure the big mare. "Let's do what we do inside the barn, yeah?"

Jenny took Mohegan's reins as we entered the barn, and Lucy steered me into the office. "I need a Diet Coke," she sighed, heading straight for the refrigerator. I eyed the old fridge's main decoration: a long whiteboard magnet with the day's to-do list scrawled on it.

"Lucy, this list has fifteen horses on it."

She handed me a can of soda and pulled out one for herself. "This is what I'm saying. I only hope once the equestrian world realizes I'm in cahoots with Alex Whitehall, Racehorse Murderer, I won't get so much business and I can take a freaking vacation."

"I didn't *murder* anyone. I just abandoned a horse in the Everglades to be eaten by crocodiles. Get it right."

Lucy laughed and sucked down half her Diet Coke. "You're an evil witch, either way."

I laughed too, but it was hollow. "The real witch is Mary Archer and her little gang, spreading gossip. I didn't think she could touch me with words, but this time I was wrong. I know she called the news on me."

"And the news is gone. You threaten to kill one little reporter, it's amazing the way they disappear."

I grinned at the memory. Kerri shrieking, the look of shock on the reporters' faces when I knocked down one of their own... Accidental, sure, but still satisfying in retrospect. "That part didn't even make the eleven o'clock news, though. In fact, none of it did. Maybe I did scare them." Although a few mainstream equestrian websites had picked up on the fact that Market Affair had once spent time in the care of Cotswold Farm, now co-owned by noted retirement advocate Alex Whitehall (their words, not mine), the local TV stations had opted not to air any footage they'd obtained the night that the story broke. I didn't know why—maybe someone at the station had racehorse connections and had put a stop to the story once they realized how ridiculous it was. With them gone, it was just the CASH death threats. The story *had* to be blowing over, right?

"Death threats, huh?" Lucy looked appreciative when I told her about the emails. "You *are* moving on up in the world. To think I knew you back when."

"I figure most of them wanted everyone in the racehorse business dead already, they just didn't have my name on their list yet. I'm not exactly famous. It's bittersweet, really. I thought I'd make the PETA hit-list by training a Derby winner. And here Personal Best doesn't even have the points to go to Churchill Downs."

Lucy laughed and threw herself down in a battered rolling chair. "Plus it's not even PETA. It's some radical offshoot. Oh Alex, you're such a nut. And despite all that, you'll be famous for your training yet, I'm sure of it. Great training doesn't come to a girl overnight. You have years ahead of you. Take a seat now and let's talk about your *real* problems."

I explained, through much Diet Coke, about my Tiger troubles. "So I guess," I summed up, "my best-case scenario would be to get him going as a jumper or an event horse, then send him to a trainer who will compete him, take him through the upper levels.

Assuming he can get there." I squirmed in the metal folding chair. "Can he get there?"

"Hell, I don't know. I've never seen him, remember? I don't have time to watch racing. But is this really what you want? I thought this horse was like your pet. Your's and Alexander's both, actually. Didn't you go to New York to get him because he was related to another horse you had?"

Red Erin, I thought. He was Red Erin's half-brother. A lifetime ago, when Alexander and I had just gotten together, when I was galloping racehorses every morning and questioning the purpose in everything I did, when I was still trying to figure out what I wanted to be when I grew up. I'd been wondering if there was a life for me with less heartache, where horses like Red Erin didn't get a hold on my heart and then die. Then, we'd seen Tiger on TV, and knew we had to have him.

From that trip I'd learned that there was no life for people like us but this one, breaking our hearts regularly in some fresh way. "Yeah," I said simply. "I went to New York."

Some things were still too raw and close to the heart to talk about, even with close friends.

"Why aren't you keeping him for yourself?"

"I explained, he's too aggressive to be a pony—"

"Not to be a *pony,* Alex." Lucy put down her empty soda can and reached for another. "Look, don't pull that racehorse trainer nonsense where you act like anything outside of racing is some enigma you know nothing about. I mean a show horse for *you,* Alex. Or even just a fun horse to ride. Don't you miss just riding for the sake of riding? Or working on your equitation, or jumping

a course? You could do all that with Tiger, and you wouldn't have
to send him away to some other trainer's barn."

A riding horse. Everyone wanted me to have a riding horse now.

My childhood riding event horses seemed a thousand years ago
now. When was the last time I'd even been in an English saddle?
Last summer, I remembered, when I gave Luna a basic dressage
background in order to give her a working set of brakes.

Oh, it had felt so good. Dangerously good.

If Alexander thought I should keep Tiger for myself, that didn't
mean a whole lot. He still might just be trying to placate me and
keep me from hopping in the car and driving off to Gulfstream. If
Lucy agreed, that was another thing entirely.

But who had time for a pleasure horse? Not the owner of a
Thoroughbred breeding and racing stable, that was for sure. I was
in the saddle all morning as things stood already. I had the horses in
south Florida, too, and what if Personal Best *did* make up the
points he needed to get into the Derby? I'd *have* to go to
Kentucky, and then on to Saratoga for the summer...he couldn't
possibly stop me from that...so how would I have a riding horse?
As lovely as it sounded...no. "I wouldn't be able to do it," I said
regretfully. "I wouldn't have the time to ride him. I don't see any
way around it. I have to have someone else do it."

Lucy shook her head. "That's a shame," she said. "Because I
don't have time to ride him, either."

What? Aw, come on Luce—for me! You gotta do me this
favor!"

"I don't have time! You see my schedule. How do you think I
can fit *sixteen* horses into a day? Are you crazy? Do it yourself,
Alex. You know how to ride. Throw a dressage saddle on Tiger

and teach him to carry himself. I'll lend you a French link snaffle if you need one. He can't lean on that as hard as he can a regular loose-ring. Really comes in handy with the racehorses."

I chewed at my lip. A part of me wanted this very badly. Of course I did! I loved riding Tiger! But...what if I just loved *galloping* Tiger? I hadn't shown a horse in years. Take a racehorse fresh off the track and retrain him to do something I myself hadn't done since I was a teenager? Please. She had to be out of her mind. Everyone was out of their minds. I was the only sane person left. I opened my mouth to say so, but Lucy spoke up first.

She leaned back in her chair and regarding me with a lazy smile. "Alex, you don't want to give up this horse. And you don't want to send him to some big-name trainer, either. You're just afraid you can't do right by him yourself. You're afraid you're going to let him down."

Chapter Thirteen

"WELL, WHAT DID SHE say?"

"She said she wouldn't take him, and I should do it."

"Poor you, forced to ride your own horse. Are you upset?"

"No...no...it's fine, really." I swerved around a squirrel that was determined to end its furry life under the wheels of my truck. "Whoops, that was close. I'm sure you guys are all right about everything, as per usual—"

What was close? Where are you? Pay attention to the road." Alexander's voice through the truck speakers was somehow more British, more imperious, more demanding than in real life. "I don't like this damn Bluetooth. It's more distracting than they say. Wait until you come home to talk to me."

"It was just a squirrel. Relax."

"So you say. I'm hanging up now. Be careful."

I looked at my phone on the passenger seat. The screen went dark. Well, I was half an hour from home. Half an hour alone with my thoughts, something I had been trying to avoid. Now I would have to come to the same conclusion everyone else already had.

Lucy was very convincing; it was one of her more annoying characteristics. It helped her sell horses, which I liked, since I sent her so many retirees to train and sell on. It helped her train horses, too, or so I figured. You had to be *very* convincing with some of these horses, when they wanted to gallop and you wanted them to learn a medium walk or something similarly mundane and boring.

And so she had found it a simple matter to convince me that I was only so hellbent on sending Tiger to a new trainer for his retraining work because I was so disappointed in *myself*—in my own failure to make him a racehorse worth his salt. "In all fairness, he was a winning allowance horse, which is no mean accomplishment," she'd reasoned. "But you wanted more for him, didn't you? You wanted at least a stakes win for him before he retired. You wanted to prove that you were able to do more for him than his old trainer. And maybe he was supposed to be the champion that you had thought your old horse—what was his name? Saltpeter, that's it. He was supposed to be a champion in the place of Saltpeter."

"That's not it," I'd said feebly, because that *was* it, and I hadn't known it before she said it, and I found the whole situation alarming. "And it doesn't have anything to do with Saltpeter, that was a long time ago, that's water under the bridge—"

"*Some* trainers might be over the death of a young horse that they loved," Lucy cut in. "But not you."

Of course she was right. I still thought about Saltpeter, often in the middle of the night, wide awake and staring at the ceiling, at that special hour that seemed reserved for waking up and thinking over every bad decision you'd ever made, and every regret you'd ever harbored. I still thought about Red Erin, too, and how desperately Alexander and I had mourned him. I thought about every horse I'd ever lost, and there were more than a few, but the soulmate horses, the ones that really clicked with you, those were the ones that continued to gnaw at your heart, years after they were gone and the rest of the world had forgotten them.

I never wanted *anyone* to forget Tiger, I realized now. *That* was my motivation and my fear. I didn't want his name to fade away the way the others' had. I didn't want him to disappear like the others who hadn't been fast enough for the record books. No one would ever remember Red Erin, and Saltpeter who had never even gone to the races, never even had a lip tattoo or a gate card or a published work, no one but us. Unless I did something about it now, no one would ever remember The Tiger Prince, an allowance horse who managed to bring home a few purses in New York and Florida before he vanished into obscurity.

So I'd sat quietly while she'd nodded vigorously and worked her way through another Diet Coke and explained all the ways in which I was going to start Tiger as a riding horse. "And once you've gotten him going nicely at all three gaits, relaxed and starting to stretch into the bridle, you can add in a few little fences, just for fun, and see how he likes it. And you'll know real quick if he has a nice jump, or if he's just falling over the fences. Then you'll know if you're aiming for dressage or a jumping career for him. Does he have the gaits for dressage?"

"He does." I'd pictured his big floating trot, his long swinging stride, his sloping shoulder and matching croup that made his conformation so pleasantly symmetrical. "But he's so impatient, I don't know if he can stand the discipline."

"Maybe he's an event horse," Lucy suggested. "The jumping and the fitness work will cut into the tedium of the dressage. I know a girl, Jules Thornton—she's got a real nice hand with the OTTBs, and she exclusively events. If I'm still too busy in a few months and you want someone else to take a look at how he's going, I'll give you her number. But you have to start him first. This is *your* battle."

Now I slowed the truck as I passed a field full of cross-country fences. There was a triangular jump made of logs close to the road, a hanging log between two trees further away, and in the distance I could see a water complex, the jump down into the water looming like a cliff. I hadn't evented in years. I wondered if I still had the nerve to do it on *any* horse, let alone on a cheeky bastard like Tiger. What would it be like galloping Tiger in a huge open field? Probably like riding a runaway rocket-ship. I had to be honest with myself—if I was going to do this, I was going to have to allow an enormous amount of time.

So there it was. I had pretty much decided that I was going to do this.

I pulled off to the side of the road and studied the cross-country field a little more closely. Besides the water complex and the hanging logs and the hog's back, there were plenty of other obstacles to send a galloping horse hurtling towards, if you were so inclined or possibly had a death wish. There was a treacherous-looking ditch-and-wall at the bottom of a gentle slope, a massive coop at the top of a rather steep hill, and that more innocent-looking earthen bank in the center of a flat stretch would probably trick a few horses into hopping onto the top of it rather than jumping all the way over it. I was considering the way the fences would ride, tackling them in my head, when the sunlight suddenly vanished and the field was cloaked in gloom. There was a rumble of thunder that shook the land beneath the truck, and the dashboard vibrated with a plastic rattling sound.

My phone, on the seat beside me, started chirping with weather alerts.

Alexander was standing in the farm driveway, his unbuttoned Barbour overcoat flapping in the gusting wind, looking with an expression of amazement at the northwestern sky, which was rapidly turning a particularly threatening shade of gray. When I pulled in from the county road he turned slowly, saw me, and lifted a white handful of mail in the air. A massive gale was on its way, and Alexander had decided to take a stroll down for the post.

I stopped the truck next to him and he climbed in. "I wish you'd take the little car," he grumbled as he settled himself. "This monster is a gas-guzzler."

"No one takes me seriously in the little car," I replied unrepentantly. "This is Ocala. A girl needs a truck. And don't change the subject with me. Why are you wandering around in your raincoat like a mad housewife? Didn't you notice the world's about to end?"

The sun was gone, and the white ripple of clouds signaling the gust front was rapidly approaching in the rear-view mirror as I gunned the engine. A gust of wind slammed into the truck and physically shoved it to one side. A tire dipped into a hole alongside the driveway. I pulled the wheel straight again and the truck lurched back onto the pavement. "It's like a hurricane out here."

Alexander peered at the trees, massive oaks along the perimeter fence that were swaying in the gusts. It wasn't exactly fun to drive through; branches were crashing down and twigs and leaves were pelting the truck like hailstones. I drove much faster than usual, rushing through the trees and into the pastures on either side of the drive, which were conspicuously empty of life. "I had everyone that could be brought in, brought in," he said. "If we lose one of those trees that could mean a whole section of fence goes too."

"Good plan." Chasing loose horses was no way to spend a wet afternoon. I hit the brake to turn up the hill to the house, but Alexander shook his head.

"Let's just drive around and check," he said. "We have a few moments more."

I looked into the rearview mirror, at the ominous fleece of white clouds hanging low over the trees in the distance. They glowed brightly against the pitch-dark storm behind them. *Just a few moments.*

But I nodded anyway and followed the gravel drive as it curved left around the base of the hill, and then swung the wheel at the next turn-off and climbed the small slope up to the broodmare barn. The pastures glowed eerily in the otherworldly light, the afternoon's low sun filtering through the encroaching layer of cloud in disconcerting shades of jade and emerald. But at least they were empty pastures.

I pulled right up to the barn's center aisle and we peered in. Manny and Martina waved from their folding chairs in front of the feed room, where they were sitting in a small ocean of convenience store wrappers. Kerri poked her head out of the feed room and waved. "All good!" she shouted, cupping her hands so that we'd hear her through the truck windows. So I wouldn't have to get out and ask her, I figured. So we wouldn't have to bother with the discomfort of a conversation.

Manny reached for a bag of chips and gave us a cheerful wave of his own. He must have come up from the training barn to help the girls get the broodmares in. They were short-handed today, but Manny was always up to help out Martina. He offered her the chips chivalrously.

"A feast for the storm," I observed drily, turning away from the junk food debris.

"Well, they got the mares in." Alexander shrugged. "They'll clean it up. Yearlings?"

I nodded and circled around the barn. The yearlings were on the other side of the farm, far from reminders of their mothers. I drove back down the slope to the main drive, turned left, and sped past the training barn. The paddocks out front were empty. Tiger must be back in the yearling barn, his outdoor time cut short. I waved out the window to the boys in the shed-row entrance, drinking from Big Gulps and watching the clouds.

The yearling barn, where our babies went after weaning in the fall and stayed until they moved to the training barn a year later, was a neat white structure with half-walls all the way around as well as between the stalls; white-painted chain link completed the upper halves of the walls. Nervous babies could always see their friends, but couldn't climb or jump out. It was a lovely little set-up, but I wished we had found a way to add shutters, because the wind-driven rain was going to make for some wet stalls—and a wet Tiger.

I made a slow circle around the barn, its snowy walls flickering weirdly in the shifting green storm-light. We waved to Luz and Erica, who were drinking coffee in the aisle in much the same relaxed positions as the grooms in the other barns. Luz pointed to Tiger, who was pricking his ears at our truck from an end stall, and waggled a finger around her head to let me know that he was still crazy. I waved to Tiger as well. I'd deal with his crazy later.

"It looks like everyone laid in provisions before the storm," I said as I pulled back onto the main drive. "Someone must have made a convenience store run before they had to bring the horses in."

"Well, they had plenty of warning. I told them back at one o'clock to have everyone in by three. The weather radio said that's when the storm would hit Reddick."

There was a sudden flash of lightning. I looked at the dashboard clock: 3:07. "Damn. They're good."

Alexander chuckled. "So that's everyone under shelter but us. Let's head back to the house and you can tell me all about Tiger's new life. And where you're going to allow him to spend it."

I smiled. "About that..."

"Yes?"

"You win. His new life is with me."

So it was decided, once and for all.

I would stay home at the farm, oversee the breeding season, light as it would be, and the training barn, though it would be nearly empty in a few more weeks, and ride Tiger every day. Alexander could continue with his plan to go to Miami without me, something which I never would have countenanced before, and he could make decisions about the racehorses' training and race entries without consulting me.

It was hard to take, even though I knew it was the smartest course. Staying low. Staying out of the limelight. Trying hard to be forgotten. After I'd fought so hard to be recognized as a trainer in my own right. After my break-out summer at Saratoga. After my first fall training horses in Florida. After all that, I was handing the horses back to him and taking on a retired racehorse to train for the show-ring.

I felt like I'd done something wrong. I wasn't just back-pedaling here. I'd done a complete U-turn.

Or perhaps a change of direction across the center of the ring, in horse-training terminology.

I went down to the training barn after we'd hashed it all out, the sky still rumbling with the remnants of the afternoon's storm. The horses had all gone back out and were grazing in their wet paddocks, tails slapping at the constant mosquitoes. Tiger looked at me from the center of the paddock as I approached, his ears pricked with interest. In the next paddock over, Parker whinnied gently, hoping for carrots. A few other horses followed his lead, and their neighs carried through the damp air, crossing the paddocks and the training track beyond, alerting a few horses on the neighboring farm. But it was Tiger I'd come to see, and my pockets were empty of peppermints.

He'd really gotten too nippy for hand-feeding anyway.

Now he came over to the fence and leaned over, lipping eagerly at my hands, my shirt-sleeves, my hair. If it could get into his mouth to be gnawed and investigated and spit out again, dripping wet and slimy, Tiger wanted to know about it. He was mouthy as a colt, aggressive as a stallion, and as beautiful as he had ever been.

I ran my hand along his muscled neck, beneath the fall of mane, and wondered how deep the temperament problems truly went. Surely with a little more time turned out, with some of his muscle gone to fat and some of his competitiveness gone to grass-gourmet, he'd recover his old sweetness. Even now, nothing he did—he was pulling at my shirt collar, he was stomping the ground in frustration when I pushed him away—was done with cruelty or bad temper. It was done with mischievousness, and an excess of energy and high spirits, and a brain that wasn't being exercised fully. He was too smart to be a racehorse, I thought. Just as Kerri had said, he'd been running in circles for a long time, and he had tired of chasing his own tail.

"I'm going to have to find something challenging for you," I told him, and he waggled his ears at me and snorted. *That* for your challenges, he seemed to be saying. I ran my hand quickly up his face, rubbing at the tiny spot between his eyes, roughing up his thick black forelock before he could shake me off. But instead of pulling away, as he had begun to do lately, he pushed his head down so that I could scratch between his ears. The thick bush of forelock there hid a hard ridge of bone; just behind that, the unprotected junction of spine and skull that was one of a horse's most vulnerable secrets. Not every horse would let human hands touch them here. Tiger put his head down and all but begged me to give his poll a good hard scratch.

So I leaned over the fence and I did just that, ignoring the mosquitoes whining in my ears, as the sun sank into an orange mist in the west, and the thunderclouds grumbled and darkened in the east, and the night frogs were already peeping when he decided he had had enough and went back to his lonesome grazing.

Chapter Fourteen

THREE WINTER DAYS IN Florida can feature the weather of three different seasons. On the evening after the storm front, it was cold and windy, and the grass sparkled with frost that night. I lay awake in the moonlight, listening to the music of drumming hooves on frozen mud, as the yearlings frolicked in the unusual cold.

The next day was bitter-cold and clear, the yellow sun blazing away without sharing a bit of warmth. I helped the grooms break ice in the water buckets and glowered at that false sun, my soaking wet hands blue and pinched. When I washed them under warm water, my fingers burned and stung. I bit my lip and tried not to be dramatic about it. I knew people handled horses up north all winter long in temperatures far worse than this; even Alexander was happy to trot out horror stories about the cold and the wet of English winters on the family farm. But that wasn't my life. I was a Floridian, and my hands were so cold they hurt.

It was traumatic for me.

Don't laugh.

On the third day it was warmer at last. No frost on the grass, no ice in the water troughs. The fog had rolled in through the hills, and moisture dripped from the diamond mesh of the fences. But it wasn't so cold, so what was a little fog? I smiled as I slipped into Parker's saddle and rode him out of his stall, ducking my head beneath the stall door frame, and came up next to Alexander and Betsy, just outside the training barn.

Alexander took in my lack of chaps and safety vest. "No babies today?"

"We have a full house today." It was a rare pleasure when all the riders showed up, but today they had, and Juan had even brought along a friend who needed work. We'd be done in record time, and I didn't have to do anything but sit on Parker and look pretty. Or so Juan had told me when he introduced his friend, who was already wearing his skull cap when he jumped out of Juan's little pickup. I stretched my arms up in the air, the reins loose on Parker's neck, and groaned as my spine popped. "I'm going to try and take a little break. My body could use it."

"I do wish you'd stop beating yourself up," Alexander said drolly. "If you age anymore beyond your years I'm going to have to find a younger wife."

"You should be so lucky." I leaned over and smacked his shoulder. He made a face and rubbed his arm. "*Your* extreme old age is the concern here."

"Betsy, do you hear how she wrongs me?" Betsy, evidently fast asleep, flicked an ear in his direction and then resumed her nap, shifting her weight from one hind leg to the other. Alexander heaved a theatrical sigh. "Even my steadfast mare deserts me in my hour of need."

"Am I the steadfast mare, or Betsy?"

He grinned.

It was a good morning, or so it seemed. The first set went out and behaved themselves prettily. Amazing to think that they were growing up. The two-year-old races would start showing up on race cards before we knew it, and I could almost envision a few of the babies being ready to head to the track for their first published works, their gate cards, their tattoos, and then their first starts. They flicked their short little tails, only reaching down to their hocks, and nipped and played with one another on the way to the racetrack, but they put their heads down and worked on the track, and then came back huffing and puffing, their breath white in the cool dawn, their eyes focused and serious. *Racehorses.*

The second set was going nicely as well, though I was watching these horses more carefully. There was one silly filly who looked at every little shadow on every little clod of dirt, and she was fully capable of turning the three pairs of working horses into a scattering flock of startled hens. I put her in the back and on the inside, where she didn't have much to look at besides the heaving hindquarters of the horse in front of her, but still I was worried that she'd see something—a bug, a lizard—and launch a tremendous spook that would knock the composure and concentration out of every other horse on the track.

"Did we ever figure out who had moved in next door?" Alexander was looking beyond the horses, who were cantering away from us, moving easily down to the first turn. His gaze was set beyond the backstretch, where the neighbor's big back pasture was wreathed in morning fog.

"No, never." But things were getting more serious. Yesterday, what looked suspiciously like a make-shift training track had been dug up from the good grazing. No rails had gone up, but there was no mistaking the oval, nearly as long as ours, though not as wide. The sand had been harrowed, as well, with a track conditioner that dug deep into the sand and worked the heavier, more solid stuff to the surface.

"Hmmm. What does that look like to you?" Alexander pointed. Just then, Parker and Betsy both picked up their heads and pricked their ears, as if they had seen Alexander's gesture.

I squinted through the half-light. The sun was trying to lift above the tree-line, tinting the fog a yellowish-gray, and all I could see was the dark shapes of a few lone palms that stood in the field. And then I saw the motion, just a glimpse through a swirl of cloud before it was gone again. "Was that a horse?"

Alexander picked up Betsy's reins. "I really hope not."

I looked back down the track at our babies. They were rounding the turn now, coming onto the backstretch. I knew that the riders' heads would be down, their concentration on getting the youngsters to change back to their outside leads as they left the turn. They wouldn't be ready if any new horses suddenly appeared, bursting from the fog like ghosts—

—And then there they were, two horses, galloping flat out, the sound of their drumming hooves flowing through the wet air and washing over us, whizzing along the fence-line of the pasture, and our horses broke like a tide against a sea-wall at the sight of those strange horses coming at them, horses where there had been no horses before, enemy horses, demon horses. I was kicking Parker forward alongside Alexander and Betsy, but they were shocked too, and tried to turn their heads to head back to the barn. I dug my spurs into Parker's sides, my hands held high to block his big strong neck from fighting me, and then we were charging forward to catch the babies as they came back towards the turn in a ragged bunch, some riderless, tails flagged, heads high.

I turned my head as we galloped, looking for the horses that had appeared next door with such suddenness, but they were already gone, disappeared back into the fog.

In the fourth set, two more horses appeared. The fog was thinning and I saw the white face of a chestnut flashing in the weak light. Different horses from the first two. So there were at least four.

This time, a filly spooked hard—well, she was a stupid one— and Juan was almost unseated. He rode back to the gap afterwards with a hard look on his face. "You need to find this person and give them a hard time, or I gonna go over there and do it for you," he growled at Alexander, and Alexander only nodded. What could he do? It wasn't illegal to gallop racehorses next to someone else's track. The only thing that we could do was be prepared. The riders over there weren't having any issues; clearly they expected to see horses come out of the fog, since they could *see* that they were riding alongside another training track. We had been caught off-guard, and the results had been tragic. Now we just had to manage as best we could.

"We have to be ready for them, Juan," I said. "They're not breaking any laws."

Juan gave me a dark look and rode on without replying.

The perfect morning was spoiled, but let's be honest—perfect mornings almost always are. We got on with it. After I checked legs and left the horses to their lunch hay, I slipped into the golf cart driver's seat and waited for Alexander to climb in beside me. He did so with a sigh and groan, as if life were immeasurably hard. Juan had taken him aside after training was finished; I supposed he'd gone at him again about the new neighbors. After all that, he'd been on his phone for another half an hour, while I was going from stall to stall to run my hands down legs, with his face like a thundercloud the whole time. I didn't know who he could be talking to, or what about, that was putting him in such a foul mood. But I was so frightened that it might be some fresh nonsense that I had caused, I didn't dare ask.

"It's going to clear up today," I declared prophetically, pointing at a patch of blue sky that appeared for a scant moment before the clouds filled in again. "Warm and sunny, that's all I ask for." Weather was always useful for changing the subject, right?

Alexander grunted. He had the Gulfstream condition book in his hand and was flipping pages back and forth, wavering between two races. I knew he was thinking of running Luna and I was trying very hard to put it out of my head. The thought of her being led to the paddock without my hand on the lead-shank was positively painful. I pointed at Tiger for a diversion, as he was out in his paddock, pulling at the brown grass with his usual viciousness. "Look how nice he looks this morning! I think he's starting to put on some weight, lose that greyhound look."

Alexander glanced over at Tiger. The horse picked up his head and gazed back, dark eyes inscrutable. His dignity was somewhat compromised by the stalks of grass sticking out of his mouth on either side. He watched the golf cart with the pair of humans he knew best rattling by, and then he squealed, twisted his body in a corkscrew, and exploded across the paddock in a record-beating gallop. If he'd broken from the gate like that just once, I thought, he could have made the leap to stakes horse quite easily.

He threw the brakes on at the corner of the fence, uprooted grass and black sand sailing through the air, and watched us drive away, his head high and his nostrils dilated. Alexander turned in his seat to look at the horse. "You going to ride that bastard or what?"

I swallowed. It wasn't exactly my first choice to get on a horse who seemed to have spent his two weeks of retirement working on his bucking form, no. But I had told everyone I was going to ride Tiger myself. Even Kerri knew—and approved!—so I had pretty much painted myself into a corner. "I thought maybe next week," I hedged. "On the calendar it said an owner coming to look at Ramble this afternoon at three o'clock..."

"I can handle that," Alexander said crisply. "It's John DeSoto and he has a good mare to bring to Virtuous. He'll expect to see me personally."

In other words, this guy John DeSoto was going to bring a mare to Alexander's stallion because Alexander had asked him to, or called in a favor. He must be some old friend of Alexander's. I knew the name vaguely, from fundraisers and sales catalogs and racing programs. Most of Virtuous's business this year was coming from similar circumstances—personal favors to Alexander. Hopefully someone would owe him enough that he'd have to bring over a good mare, a big mare, not just whatever open maiden he had sitting out in a pasture. We'd had enough winless maidens come to Virtuous over the past few years to fill the training barn, and their foals had been as unimpressive as their dams. You're supposed to breed like to like and hope for the best, not no-good to nice and hope for a miracle.

I glanced down the slope of the broodmare pasture as we drove past. There were three foals in the field now, a colt and two fillies. One was Virtuous's—a chestnut filly with dark spectacles that belied her future as a steel gray. Her dam was Surfrider, which made her a half to Virtue and Vice. She already had the solid, sturdy legs of a turf horse. Virtue had been winning—an allowance here, an restricted stake there. If Virtue made it as a stakes horse, and this filly did the same some day...the connections were there. Maybe Virtue and this filly would be Virtuous's redemption. Maybe he still had a shot at being a desirable Florida stallion. Maybe, if Alexander would just be patient, we could breed our own instead of bringing in outsiders. If that was his plan. I still hadn't asked.

"So you'll ride him this afternoon?"

"Huh?" I had been lost in contemplation. Imagining the race career of a week-old filly, now there's a mistake! I pulled up in front of the garage and put the golf cart into park. "What now?"

"You'll take out Tiger this afternoon. If you need a field, have the grooms bring in the yearlings early. They can do some mane-pulling."

They'd just *love* that. But if I was riding, I didn't have to sedate babies and yank their manes into submission. Even a bucking bronco was more fun than *that*. "Okay, I'll ride him. But first, coffee."

So much coffee.

While we sat at the breakfast table, sipping strong black coffee and flipping the pages of old racing magazines, the tall windows we faced slowly filled up with light. By the time the antique clock in the front hall had worked its laborious grinding way to chiming the noon hour, the fog had completely burned away at last, leaving behind one of those cerulean blue skies that was so deep and clear that all proportion was drained from the landscape. While summer skies were crowded with puffy clouds and mountainous thunderstorms that seemed to float bare inches above the treetops, these empty expanses of blue that dominated the winter season were dizzyingly high. Everything seemed to shrink beneath that vast emptiness, retreating from the eye as if a camera was forever slowly panning out.

I had never cared for these featureless skies, preferring the tumult and wild beauty of summer storms, but I had to admit it was better than fog. Energizing, even. I had been contemplating the problem of the neighbors, and now I stood up so quickly that the table trembled and Alexander put down his copy of *Florida Horse*.

"You're going to ride right now?" He was pleased.

"Not yet," I said. "First, I'm going to find out who is next door."

"How are you going to do that?" We had never been next door. There was no house visible from the road; massive old live oaks and a dense thicket of underbrush hid the property from view, and the dark driveway that tunneled through the oaks disappeared over a rise before any buildings showed themselves.

But there was a mailbox, and the mail delivery was right around noon. Right around now. I had a very good excuse to drive down to the road and park my truck there. No one who knew us would think anything of it if they happened to drive by, and the neighbor's mailbox was just down the road...

"I'm going to look at their mail," I decided. "I'll wait in our driveway until the mail lady goes by, and then I'll just sneak a peak at whatever they get."

"I think that's illegal," Alexander said mildly.

"It's the perfect crime," I replied, pulling on my paddock boots and zipping up the fronts. "No one gets hurt, no one's the wiser."

>>>⟩   ⟨⟨⟨⟨

I took the truck instead of the golf cart. That way, I could zip right down the road to raid the neighbor's mailbox after the mail lady's car disappeared around the next bend. Plus, I'd be less recognizable. If someone I knew saw me sitting in the golf cart, they were liable to stop and try to have a chat, and I might miss my chance to get to the mail before the neighbors did. In the truck, I could have been anyone—Alexander, a groom, Kerri.

The black gate swung closed behind the truck and I parked right there in the center of the driveway, where the concrete bridged the drainage ditch that ran alongside the county highway. It was just about the same spot where I'd hit the news reporter almost three weeks ago. I remembered how panicked Kerri had been, the way she had looked at me as if I was a crazy person, and wondered if that was when she had started to actually question my judgement, wonder whether or not I was losing it.

"Well, now I'm sitting in a truck waiting for the opportunity to spy on my neighbor's mail, Kerri, so you might be right," I said aloud, hopping out of the truck. I checked the farm's big black mailbox, large enough to comfortably house fat sales catalogs and the weird things horse-people and farmers sometimes sent and received via unsuspecting postal workers, like envelopes full of hair for DNA testing, or samples of horse-friendly paving stones. Since a day didn't go by where the farm didn't receive a small mountain of mail—bills, invoices, stallion show announcements, real estate agents seeking listings, Jockey Club correspondence, horse show fliers, incentive fund applications, tack catalogs, racing magazines, donation requests for fundraisers, thank you cards for donations to fundraisers, offers for free samples of synthetic racetrack footing— the empty mailbox was a sure tip-off that I hadn't yet missed the mail. I clambered back into the truck, turned on NPR, and waited.

And dozed off.

I sat up very quickly when there was a *rap-rap-rap* on the driver's side window.

I blinked confusedly at the person just outside—a round, red face with frizzy henna-colored hair and faded blue eyes was grinning at me. I realized she was the mail lady. I'd never seen her out of her station wagon before.

"Ma'am!" she shouted, in an accent so Appalachian it could strip paint off a wall. *"Ma'am, I have mail for you!"*

I furrowed my brow—wasn't that why we had a mailbox in the first place?—and hit the window button to lower it, a procedure which was carried out very slowly and with lots of squealing and complaints, like any good farm truck that has been subjected to too much hay and dust in its time. "Can't you put it in the box? I'm waiting for something." *For you to leave.*

"No, ma'am," the mail lady said emphatically. "This here's a big load a'mail. You want, I can throw it in the truck bed here."

"That's fine, thanks." I sat back weakly, still groggy from the cat-nap, and waited as she stumped back to her station wagon, the "mail carrier" placard sitting dusty on the dashboard. Mail carrier, that was the word. Not mail lady...

She emerged from the rear hatch of the station wagon with a massive canvas mailbag, hoisted it in her arms like the week's garbage going to the curb, and duck-waddled back to the truck. The bag was lumpy, with hard corners pressing against the canvas from within. Envelopes? A nervous flutter wavered in my stomach as an idea of what those envelopes might contain popped into my brain.

The mail lady—I mean mail carrier—grunted as she flung the sack into the truck bed. "Woo!" she hooted, rubbing her hands together. "That's some special delivery! Lemme just get the reg'lar mail for ya now."

She made the trip between truck and wagon again and presented me with a more reasonable selection of mail. Then she grinned again. "Pop'lar gal, huh?" The southern breeze tugged at the tight curls of her fading orange hair. "Now I gotta git join'. Late today." She raised a paw in farewell.

"Wait!" I blurted. We had a funny kinship now, this mail carrier and me. Maybe she could just *tell* me. "Who lives next door?"

The mail carrier cocked her head. "Now honey, ya don't know yer own neighbors? Although I guess they did just move in. I can't give out names, though. You'll just have to drive over and say howdy."

I nodded, disappointed but not terribly surprised. "I'll do that," I promised, while thinking *not a chance in Hell.* "Thank you."

I realized that now it wouldn't be noticeable or surprising if she happened to catch me driving up the neighbor's lane, so there was that. I resolved to wait longer before I went over there, in case she suspected my game and doubled back. I wouldn't want to be caught with my arm halfway up the mailbox when she went cruising by again.

When she'd been gone a good ten minutes I made my move, throwing the truck into gear and easing out onto the county road. I passed a quarter mile of black board fence and a thick shield of old-growth oak trees before the next driveway appeared, a ribbon of rutted gravel cut through the trees and spit out through the brown grass and dry ditch to meet the road in a small canyon of potholes. The truck banged down onto the driveway as I turned, and I bounced on the seat, nearly rapping my head against the window. "That's why you should always wear your seatbelt," I reminded myself. Then I put the truck in park and looked around carefully. The highway was deserted.

I leaned down from the truck window and eased open the rusty old mailbox, and found—

Nothing.

Hmm. This would be an embarrassing story to carry home to Alexander.

I closed the mailbox and frowned.

Sadly, there was only one Plan B, and that just didn't bear thinking about: driving up the driveway and seeing for myself what lay behind that hilltop. If I'd thought it was going to be the nice old cracker I'd met while he drove along his fences, I would've gone up without hesitation. But I didn't. The cattle were gone, and he didn't give a fig about horses or horse racing. Someone else lived here now, and driving up overgrown country lanes to spy on strangers wasn't a great idea. At least, not in north Florida. Supposing the new tenants were survivalist gun enthusiasts. They'd hardly feel out of place in Ocala, even if all these paved roads and grocery stores were probably a little urban for their tastes. Hell, my old farrier had instructed me on the finer points of tinfoil hat construction, concerned that the mind-reading CIA satellites were going to steal all my training secrets. He was clearly certifiable, and *he* had owned five nice mares and a Florida Stallion Stakes winner. That is to say, he fit in beautifully, crazy as one of those loons on some Discovery Channel reality show, but with racehorses like any good Ocala citizen.

Add the potential for crazy survivalist with firepower to the conviction I held that whoever was lurking on the other side of that ridge was actively trying to kill me, or at least ruin my business, and you had a non-starter of an idea. I shook my head and threw the truck back into reverse. I'd have to figure out who was living there some other way. Going up for a visit just wasn't in the cards.

I backed onto the road and swung back into my own driveway, throwing one regretful glance towards the distant farm lane I'd left behind before pulling through my own gate.

I saw a truck easing down the ridge, sunlight glinting on its windshield as it emerged from the thick forest.

I slammed on the brakes and sat still, heart pounding, watching the truck. Which way would it turn? Would they be heading to town? They'd have to drive right past me to get there. I could get a glimpse. Maybe there'd be a farm name on the truck's door...

I squinted as the truck crept down from the tree-line, bouncing over potholes. There were letters on it, all right. In just a second, they'd come into view...

I blinked.

It was *our* truck.

It was one of the farm trucks. The logo on the side was the same one I saw every day on letterhead, on coffee mugs, on tack trunks. There was no mistaking it.

Or, as the truck came closer, that slim profile, that pixie haircut...

I turned away and accelerated through the open gate, irrationally hoping that she wouldn't see me. I didn't want to know that she was involved. I didn't want to know that she'd lost faith in me so completely. Whoever she had believed, whatever she'd heard or read or witnessed that could make her believe I was a liar, a horse-dumper, a mess on the verge of a breakdown—let that be on her. I had been prepared for Mary Archer. I wasn't ready for this.

Chapter Fifteen

K ERRI CAUGHT UP WITH me before I even reached the
turn-off to the house. I shook my head no when she flashed
the farm truck's headlights, entreating me to stop, but when I
turned towards the house and she immediately followed, I knew I
had no choice but to get out and listen to her side of the story. I
wasn't taking this to the house. Alexander already thought I was
completely overreacting to the entire situation with Kerri and the
farm staff. I wasn't about to have a dramatic girl-fight in front of
him.

So I climbed out of the truck, and so did Kerri, and for a few
moments we just faced each other in the bright winter sunlight, the
breeze tugging at my ponytail and riffling through her bangs.

Neither of us wanted to, but it was Kerri who spoke first.

"I know who it is."

I hadn't expected *that*. "You mean, you're part of this whole
scheme," I corrected, but even I could hear the uncertainty
trickling into my voice. "I shouldn't be surprised, after the way
you talked to me in the barn the other morning," I went on boldly,

determined to hang on to my anger. What else did I have these days?

"Part of this *scheme?*" To my complete shock, Kerri burst out laughing. She had to lean against the truck's hood for support, she was laughing so hard. It was really annoying. "God, you really are a paranoid mess, you know that?" she gasped. "Of course it's not me. And it's not even a scheme. But the new neighbor *is* exactly who you would expect. It's Mary."

Now I was the one clutching the truck hood for stability. I mean, of course. I just *knew* it all along, didn't I? But I didn't want it to be true. That proved all my worst fears were true. I was her target. She was trying to bring me down. She was determined to destroy our business and my good name—*huh. Wait.* I tried to get hold of my own insane thoughts. Kerri might be right, I might be a paranoid mess. "Are you sure?" I asked with what I thought was a reasonable and believable tone of incredulousness.

"Pretty sure. Your very own nemesis!" Kerri smiled brightly. "You're like a super-hero!"

"Can someone please explain what I did to deserve a nemesis?"

Kerri just laughed and shook her head at me.

"And, in all seriousness, doesn't this seem like taking things a little too far? Couldn't she just enjoy watching my career implode from a distance? She has to move in next door and—what? Scare my horses? That's just a coincidence? Wait—did you talk to her?"

Kerri shook her head again. "Just a groom. He told me she's got six horses over there. Apparently she owns them all and couldn't get stalls at Littlefield, so she had to rent her own place."

"Dennis wouldn't give his own trainer a couple stalls?"

"I guess Littlefield is full. And he's had to beg for every extra stall he's gotten this season at the track. The barn's on a hot streak and he has clients coming out of his ears. It's not that crazy, if you look at it that way. He's too big for his own place, and Mary's horses are just competing for the same purses that his horses are."

"Yeah." I looked across the pastures to the distant training track, nearly hidden by the gentle sweeps of the Ocala hills. A quarter pole stood above one rise, cheerful red and white stripes sparkling in the clear air. "But what's crazy is that she's next to us, and that she's galloping horses right next to our track." I swallowed. I didn't want to believe it was intentional, I really didn't, but it was so hard not to. *"Please* tell me there's a rational reason for this."

"Surprisingly enough...there is. The groom said that's the only flat piece of land in the whole property. But still—honestly? I think it's really suspicious that she set up shop right next door. I mean, I'm sure it's renting cheap because there's nothing there. A six-stall pony barn, no aisle, no tack room. A mobile home from the seventies that's basically rotting. An old pole barn full of cow shit. I don't think the last tenants lived there, but damn they had a lot of cows."

"They didn't. They just grazed cattle there. The old guy didn't like horses. That's how I knew it wasn't him."

"Well, there are cow pies everywhere." Kerri put her hands in her hoodie pockets and leaned back against the truck. "Hard as rocks. The groom said if you trip over it while it's frozen you'll break your foot. The place is a mess."

"I hope none of the horses trip on them," I said, my concern for delicate equine legs an automatic response. Nemesis or not, I didn't want anyone's horses getting hurt. Although we'd had our share of accidents from this little neighborhood kerfuffle. *Mary bloody Archer,* I thought. *This is getting old.* I turned my face up towards the sun, closed my eyes, and let the warm light press through my eyelids, crimson red on my retinas. "Do you want to come to the house? Tell Alexander? Then he can tell us there is absolutely no reason to believe that Mary is actively attempting to ruin my reputation and/or kill me."

Kerri shook her head. "Tempting, but I have to turn a couple mares out once I'm sure they're awake. The vet took cultures on the open mares and no one wanted to cooperate so they all got cocktails. I think we'll be able to breed Silly on the next cycle, though. Finally. And then I need to wash tail-wraps and mix evening feed. But come up if you can and we can talk about it."

I nodded, even though I was supposed to go ride Tiger next. There were a lot of warring emotions here—crazy with worry over Mary, dizzy with relief that Kerri was on my team after all. I wanted to spend the afternoon working with her, just chatting and being silly the way we had done in Saratoga. I wished she'd come back to work in the training barn. She said she wasn't needed there, but I could have found something for her to do. There was always something to do in a barn. "Are you staying in the broodmare barn?"

"Like—long-term?"

I nodded.

"You have plenty of help in the training barn, so...you know..."

"Last year all you wanted was to work in the training barn. If you want to be down there, you can be. Of course." *Don't have gone back to the broodmares because you were tired of working with me.* I smiled what I hoped was a winning smile, but it was probably just desperate.

Kerri shrugged. "I guess I just didn't want to miss the babies this spring." She looked around as if searching for the right answer in the dry grass along the road. Nothing presented itself but a small brown lizard, racing his way towards the sizzling heat of a black-painted fence post. I waited.

Finally, she met my eyes again. "Maybe we'll go on the road together again next summer. That would be fun."

I nodded and smiled again and left it at that. But I doubted there'd be any girl-trainer road trips this summer. If Alexander took Personal Best into Derby territory, he wasn't going to be in a hurry to give the horses back to me. I'd better start choosing which of our handful of two-year-olds I wanted for myself this fall. If I had to sit out the spring, at least I could be ready to come back ready to win in the fall. Hell, maybe by then, Kerri would be ready to come play my side-kick again.

Kerri got back in the farm truck and backed it down the drive to the barn lane. I started to do the same, then noticed something in the bed of the truck. I stood up on my tip-toes to investigate—the mail bag. I'd forgotten all about it.

I stared at the unwanted cargo for a moment, the bulging canvas bag bristling with bumps and points like some kind of poisonous prickly fruit. I had a feeling I knew what was inside, and I didn't want anyone else to know about it.

I bit my lip and looked back up at the house, trying to see through the dark windows. With the sun glaring down, it was impossible to tell if Alexander was still sitting in the breakfast room, if he was peering through the window and wondering what on earth I was doing out in the driveway. I decided to chance it. I'd go to the office in the garage and see for myself what was waiting for me in that bag.

Maybe it wouldn't be that bad.

By the tenth letter, I had stopped reading the words. They were all the same, and I'd read them before. It was the form letter that CASH had sent out last week and that had been emailed *en masse* to me and several racing websites.

The words were hateful, and inflammatory, and libelous, and just about enough to make me forget every worry and every hope I'd had warring within on this tempestuous winter morning.

Last week, the web editor of *The Thoroughbred Project* had actually emailed me after he'd received about two hundred of these emails. He'd assured me that he knew the accusations were false and that I'd never owned Market Affair, and he posted a column on his website about the whole situation.

But a horse racing website was about as credible to an anti-horse racing activist as Fox News was to a liberal Democrat. I'd sat through enough political discussions with my father to know that much. Nothing that *The Thoroughbred Project* could post would ever reach the eyes, hearts, or minds of the angry online activists hitting copy, paste, and send on these vicious emails. The threats in them made Mary's couple of horses galloping by each morning shrink into small annoyances, like finding mice had gotten at the feed bags before they'd all been emptied into storage bins. I was warned not to go to the track, not to get into my car, not to go to the feed store...

"Or what?" I said aloud, flicking the corner of one bent envelope. "Or you'll blow up my car? You'll shoot me like a sniper? Bunch of cowardly hags."

I threw the small pile of letters I'd opened back into the mail-bag with all their little friends and leaned back in the desk chair, the springs squeaking in protest. "God," I said aloud, and then, "God*dammit.*" This was going too far. Things were getting too crazy. Now, 1 thought, now I could see the truth of Alexander's fears for my safety. Giant bags full of hate mail, all coordinated by one radical animal rights group, felt like a declaration of war. Open season on Alex. As if they'd actually do anything. Writing a letter, sending an email, using words provided by another person's hand —yeah, that was pretty different from putting an explosive under someone's car.

And yet...bad things happened. I felt the slightest bit nervous, and that made me even angrier.

"What utter *shit,*" I muttered, and kicked the offending bag.

People making assumptions and listening to other people's unfounded accusations, that was what really made this so infuriating. They ought to see this office, I thought. They ought to see what I really do, in my non-existent spare time—well, it was non-existent before I got put on house arrest, anyway. I spun my chair around and surveyed the filing cabinets lining the office's back wall. From rusty with age to shiny and new, they were full of horse records, some decades-old. Alexander never threw away anything, and I'd learned all of my business skills from him. The last filing cabinet on the left, under the poster for the 1998 Kentucky Derby —won by Real Quiet, a Florida-bred—belonged to me and my retirees. That was where I went now.

The drawer squeaked open and there they were, names and foaling years written on tabs, dozens of them. Retirees.

I riffled through the folders, pulling out files at random and opening them, noting the last check-in dates. The oldest one was ten months old—due for a check-in in another two months. The horse, a five-year-old homebred gelding we had raced lightly at three and four before sending to Lucy for retraining, was competing in the low jumpers with a doting owner down in Tampa. He'd never won us more than a few hundred dollars. He'd cost us tens of thousands in upkeep and training over the years. But that money spent was *our* choice, as breeders. A commitment we had signed up for the moment we bred his dam. We'd made him. We'd brought him into the world. He was our responsibility from birth to death, or until we found him a new owner who was willing and able to shoulder that responsibility for us. Even then, I wanted to keep tabs on him. Maybe Forever Homes weren't a real thing, but safety nets were. I owed him that much.

He was one of mine.

Not everyone saw breeding horses that way, but it was part of my personal religion. Hell, it was *all* of it. Was there anything I believed in more deeply than my responsibility towards these horses?

That's why this attack hurt, even if Alexander and Kerri and Lucy and even Richie from *The Thoroughbred Project* all assured me that it was the work of scoundrels and hate-mongers. Because people preferred a scandal to a triumph, preferred to believe in bad before good, and these clueless emailers and letter writers who didn't have five minutes to research some cause they saw on Facebook before they got outraged and clicked *share,* these people were bound to convince even more people, bring more equestrians and animal-lovers around to their cause, if they kept making all this noise, more noise than the people who might have defended me could ever make with their plain, boring facts.

One thing was obvious—it was getting worse, and I had to defend myself. But I wasn't sure how to do that when I was locked down at the farm.

I looked around me at the filing cabinets, thinking of the horses and their stories contained within. If I was a writer, I could write their stories down, send them to a magazine or post them on a website. But that didn't seem like enough. It seemed like too little, too late—and too quiet and unassuming, besides. *So you think I'm a horse-murderer? Well here's a little blog post saying I'm not.*

The office phone rang, startlingly loud. I slammed the filing cabinet shut and went back to the desk, where I regarded the phone without pleasure; it wasn't usually my thing to answer it, but the secretary was off today and Alexander always got on my case if I didn't do my fair share of picking it up. The phone didn't care about my apprehensions and went on ringing shrilly, so I sighed and picked up the receiver. "Cotswold Farms, Alex speaking," I recited in a monotone, thinking that playing with Tiger was probably exactly what I needed, and if I'd gone straight to the barn to ride him, I wouldn't be stuck on the phone now.

"Alexis Whitehall?" It was a female voice, sharp and Southern and laced with cigarettes, not unlike Mary Archer's. I dropped my gaze to the caller ID on the phone's display, but there was no number listed. *Blocked.* Oh, that was very reassuring.

"Yes..." I said cautiously.

"We're watching you, Alexis Whitehall," the voice snapped. "Everyone here at CASH knows what's going on with you and your horses. This Market horse was just the tip of the iceberg, and we know it. You'll be found out, and you'll be brought down. We're demanding that you lose your trainer's license and owner's license. You better enjoy your horses while you're allowed to have them, because your little racket is almost over."

My mouth had dropped open during this little speech, which took slightly longer to speak than the printed page can reasonably describe, due to her slow Southern accent, but even so there was a long silence before I figured out how to use my brain to make words again. I wasn't good on the phone. "I don't know what you're talking about," I stammered finally, which probably was not the most coherent defense I could have come up with.

"Oh, you know," she said mockingly. "And now you are looking for somewhere to dump another horse that can't run for you! Where is The Tiger Prince, Alexis? He hasn't had a published work in three weeks! And after that terrible run in Tampa! What have you done with him, Alexis? Have you dumped him too? Did you run him through some sale and wash your hands of him, Alexis? Did you? *Did you? Did you?*"

I jumped up from the chair, fist clenching the phone receiver, face hot and red. "First off, stop calling me Alexis. If you were really so aware of my every move, you'd probably know I haven't been called Alexis since the first grade. Second off, I happen to be retraining The Tiger Prince myself. Third, who the hell are you? If you know my name, I deserve to know yours."

When she spoke again, her tone was more subdued. "This is Cassidy," she admitted. "And I speak for thousands of concerned horse owners at CASH who don't want to see another horse die because of your two-faced lies!"

"Wow, that is harsh, since none of my horses have died and I have never lied." I sat back down, feeling a little more in my element. She was just some stupid redneck. I could handle stupid. Stupid was easy. "It would probably be much easier for you to win this game if you had any, you know, actual *facts* to back up your stories."

"What about Sunny Virtue?"

Just like that, I was thrown off my game.

"Who?" I couldn't think of a horse by that name. Although the *Virtue* part was a little troubling. There were plenty of horses with *Virtue* in their name who had started out at Cotswold, though a sizable proportion of those had left as fertilized embryos. Virtuous might not be fashionable, but he had seen his share of ladies.

"Sunny Virtue," Cassidy repeated, her tone razor-sharp. "Seven years old, last ran at Fort Erie two months ago, finished twenty-two lengths behind in a twenty-five-hundred dollar claimer, vanned off the track, hasn't been seen since." She was reading the words, her southern drawl dissolving into a staccato reciting of industry jargon I could tell she didn't really understand. "He was bred by Cotswold Farms."

Bred by the farm? I'd never even heard of him. "I can do some research on that," I offered. "But he wasn't here when I came here. I've only been here five or six years, you have to understand. Even if he was born and trained here, he was gone by the time I started working here. And at a guess, I'd say he went to a sale and was never run by the farm."

"So you admit that once they're gone, they're not your problem anymore?"

"I didn't say that!"

"This was your farm's horse and now you're telling me you don't even know his name. You are running a racehorse factory over there, just like the rest of them, *Alex.* You are a symbol of a rotten industry that has reached the end of its usefulness, and you are going *down.*"

Before I could breathe a word in my defense, Cassidy from CASH had ended the call.

"Well," I said aloud, to the desk and the filing cabinets and Real Quiet and the win photos hung on the wall, "that was unpleasant."

Sunny Virtue...

I got up and walked down the row of filing cabinets. If Sunny Virtue was seven and had been born here, the evidence would be in one of these drawers. My eyes scanned the labels. Top drawer, fifth filing cabinet against the wall, there it was—the label for his foaling year.

The drawer groaned as I opened it, and I stood on my toes to flip through the hand-written labels on the manila folders. Ah! *Virtuous Foals 20 —.*

I pulled out the folder and riffled through the sheets within, detailing the live foal reports of the more than forty foals Virtuous had sired that year. I didn't have the broodmare's name, and none of the foal reports included the foal's eventual registered name. It was possible that Alexander hadn't even named the colt. If he'd sent him to a yearling or two-year-old in training sale...

The words *Sunny Susan* caught my eyes and I paused, pulling out the typed sheet.

Virtuous — Sunny Susan, February 14th, colt. An early foal, product of some careful planning by Alexander and his then-broodmare manager. I ran my finger down the page, searching for the foal's owner. If he hadn't been bred and owned by Alexander, none of this could even be pinned on us. If the broodmare belonged to a client...

Broodmare Owner: Kevin Wallace. Foal Share with Cotswold.

Just below that, scrawled in pencil: *Wallace buy-out, full ownership of foal, June 14th.* There was a bill of sale, notarized by Ida from the general store up the road, paper-clipped to the page. The mare and foal's transportation report were the next paper in the file, noting that they had both left the farm on a Sallee van a week after the buy-out, thus ending the Cotswold—Sunny Virtue connection.

I smiled and nodded, tapping the words. "Kevin Wallace, expect a call from your new friend Miss Cassidy, assuming she's doing her research properly. This one's on you."

I stowed the files again, shoved the squeaking cabinet drawer shut, and settled back down in the leather comfort of the desk chair. I needed a change, I thought. I needed to think about something completely different, to clear my head.

There was only one sure way to clear my head after *this* mess, and that was to take a ride.

I opened a desk drawer and pulled out a leather-bound black notebook I'd been saving for the right moment. It was a fancy little blank book, a notion I'd picked up at Barnes & Noble in town one day, killing time before a doctor's appointment. I hadn't needed it, but who doesn't want a nice notebook lying around the office? Now I knew what to do with it.

I plucked a nice ink-pen from the farm mug on the desk and opened the notebook to its creamy first page. I touched the pen to my lips and thought —what would I do with a retired racehorse on the first day of training? I went back to my teenage days, remembering the lawless auction finds I had turned into solid show horse citizens of the world. Every horse was different, but, I supposed, every horse really could be started the exact same way, no matter what he already knew or thought to be right. The pen hovered over the page, then I began to write, in smooth black strokes.

Day One, Round Pen.

Chapter Sixteen

D *AY ONE, ROUND PEN.*
    "Here we go, buddy..." I closed the door of the round pen and led Tiger to the center of the ring.

It was a little round pen, no more than fifty feet across, with high wooden walls all around to discourage distractions and peeking. The perimeter was rutted with the hooves of many young horses; the center was a hump of dark sand, packed flat from boots turning as someone—Juan, myself, whoever was working the babies that day—followed the movements of young horses. We started our babies in here, usually long yearlings, although now and then a client sent a two-year-old or even, heaven forbid, a three-year-old, who hadn't been backed yet. The walls kept their attention locked on us, the Gods in the center of the ring. The horses learned to read our voices and body language in order to know when to move forward, when to halt, when to change directions.

The young horses learned that in here, the human was the head of the family, the boss mare, the herd stallion. They took those lessons with them once they graduated from the round pen and went on to shed-rows, pasture rides, and finally the training track.

Well, now Tiger would learn it all over again, and he'd take it with him to the riding arena. Once I found one for us—I hadn't quite figured that part out yet. A boarding stable might be our only option, once we had worked out his jollies in the round pen and done some stretching work in the paddocks. It wouldn't be my first choice, but a boarding stable would have arenas with good footing, and jumps—how else would I find out if he liked jumping? (I suspected that he would.)

But I was resolved to have him behaving like a gentleman before I tried to take him to a boarding stable, and for that, I was going to have to round-pen him until he remembered that I wasn't just his galloping buddy—I was his boss.

I unsnapped the lead-shank from his halter, looped it around my hand, and gave the trailing ends a friendly shake in his direction. "Go on, get!" I said encouragingly.

And Tiger *got,* with all the panache of a prize bronco. With a tremendous snort, he flung himself away from me, grunted, twisted, and bucked high in the air. I gasped and ducked, just missing his flying hooves, though not the flying dirt. I was still spitting sand out of my mouth when Tiger got to the round pen wall, plunged to a halt, and whipped around to face me, his head high and his tail flagged. He flared red nostrils at me and snorted again, as if to ask me what the hell I was playing at.

"What the hell are *you* playing at?" I snapped. "Trying to take my head off? Get up, get *up!*" I punctuated my shout with another wave of the lead-shank.

Tiger pinned his ears and shook his head. *A warning*, I realized. *He* was telling *me* what was going to happen next. Well, damn. He'd gotten more pig-headed and snotty than I'd realized. Love is blind. I considered my next move while he gazed at me with challenging eyes. Then I bent down, picked up a handful of sand, and pelted it right at him.

Tiger leapt away from the onslaught and picked up a sharp gallop along the circumference of the round pen, his outside hooves slamming against the boards as he went. His ears were pinned so flat I could barely see them through flying forelock and mane, but one finally flicked in my direction when I shouted "that's right, get up now, *get up get up get up!*"

He increased his speed, going dangerously fast now in the tight confines of the pen, but I kept him going because I figured as long as he was galloping hard he couldn't make a sudden left-hand turn and charge me. From the way he'd been looking at me when I first tried to get him moving, the idea had definitely crossed his mind. Whether he'd thought it would make for an excellent game or he'd truly been angry at me for bringing him to the round pen after three weeks of downtime, I couldn't say. But I wasn't going to give him any chances.

Instead I turned quickly as he barreled around the ring, making sure my outside shoulder was always pushing him forwards, as if I was standing just behind him instead of walking a tiny circle at the center of the round pen. I kept my eye on his, a forceful *go away* glare, so that he would not make any mistake about my demand that he move, move, *move*.

"Keep it up now," I growled when he started to falter, turning his head a little towards me as if to head back to the center. "Get up now." I shook the lead again and the sand flew from his hooves as he lurched forward.

Three weeks hadn't been much time off, I had to admit. I watched him barrel around the pen with an athleticism that was dismaying, to say the least. He was still too muscled, still awfully fit. His last race would be as fresh in his mind as if he'd run it yesterday.

I twirled around and Tiger found himself galloping right towards my forbidding shoulder, my waving lead-rope, and my angry glare. He stopped short, sand flying from his hooves, and then spun around and took off the other way. "Good boy," I called, impressed. Some horses just kept going when you first tried to teach them to change directions, and you practically had to leap in front of them with a buggy whip before they figured out that they were supposed to turn around.

I wasn't keen on jumping in front of Tiger in his present mood.

I kept him galloping until the veins were popping from his neck and the sweat was starting to darken his flanks and drip down his shoulders, swapping directions every few minutes to keep his mind on the task. Then I stopped moving and turned away, letting him come down from the gallop at his own pace. His steps quickened at first, as if he was nervous that I was playing some new trick on him, and I felt a little bad—it wasn't nice to make your own best friend distrustful of you like that. But we had to re-establish the rules, I reminded myself. Lucy had repeated that several times. It wouldn't be pretty, not at first, but it had to be done.

It took Tiger fifteen minutes to get up the nerve to approach me. I kept my back to him and my eyes on the ground, watching the ants wander through the sand on their ant-journeys. The sun came out from behind a layer of heavy clouds that had been aimlessly rolling through the sky and beat down on me; sweat trickled down my back. I listened to Tiger move restlessly around the round pen, snorting at the high walls, at his own deep hoof prints in the sand, at me, incomprehensibly ignoring him.

Then, at last, he came up behind me and stood still. I waited, hopeful that he'd reach out and touch me, but after a few minutes I realized that was too much to ask from the first session. I turned around and reached out to touch his lovely face, and Tiger lowered his head so that I could rub his poll.

"Good boy," I told him, scratching his sweaty head. "Such a good boy." I thought about what I'd write in the training journal later on: *resistant at first, good at body language, gave in after fifteen minutes but didn't touch me.*

Better than expected.

Chapter Seventeen

"THANKS WALLACE. NO, NO, you are absolutely right. Of course. Well, let's talk again very soon. There's no rush, as you say."

Alexander put down his cell phone and looked at it with a decent amount of rage.

"Alexander?" I was prying off my riding boots at the front door, pulling with all my might against the bootjack. I had thought it would be fun to try using my old dress boots from before I started galloping racehorses, without considering how very different my calf muscles were these days. If I ever got these boots off, I was going to take them straight to Quarter Pole for zippers and an elastic gusset to be added. *If* I ever got them off. "Who was that?"

"No one," he said, with an admirable attempt at absent-mindedness.

"No one you want to tell me about," I panted, and my right boot came off with such force that I nearly took out my front teeth with my knee. "Christ almighty these boots are tight."

Alexander got up, but not without putting the lock-screen on his phone. "Sit on the couch and I'll pull that one off you."

"You'll go flying backwards when it comes off," I warned, but I went over to the couch anyway, leaving the other boot to lay limply on the tiles of the entry and think about what it had done.

Alexander took hold of the heel of the boot. "Now pull," he instructed.

I pulled back. "Who was on the phone?" I asked between tugs. My heel slid up slightly and the pressure on my ankle was eye-watering. I grunted and tugged harder.

"Nosey tonight, aren't you?"

"I'm trying to take my mind off the loss of my foot due to poor blood circulation," I explained. "Since I'm losing the feeling in my toes and all."

"You have to pull harder," he instructed. "Don't worry, I'll cut the boot away before the foot has to go."

"These are Vogels! They were custom-made for me! You can't cut these off!"

"Custom-made for sixteen-year-old you. It might be time for new boots."

I considered the thought of new custom dressage boots with deep pleasure, before realizing that Alexander was just distracting me so I'd stop asking him who Wallace was. Usually I let him conduct his business without bothering too much about it, but for some reason I really wanted to know about this one. Wallace... Wallace...where had I heard that name? I should really start taking something for my memory. Last week it had taken me ten minutes to remember the dam's name of one of the client horses. In front of the client. Alexander had not been amused.

"Almost there..." He pulled and my foot slipped slowly upwards and I closed my eyes and grimaced and the boot came free

—

Alexander went stumbling backwards, dress boot in hand, and I sat forward in excitement. "Wallace is the person you were talking to before Tiger's last race! You guys are in on some business deal together. You have to tell me now, I guessed."

"Did we agree this was a guessing game?" Alexander put the boot neatly next to its companion that I had left sprawling on the floor.

"You're right, it's a business partnership. Silly me. Now you really have to tell me." I peeled away my sweaty boot socks. "Or suffer a boot sock to the face."

Alexander sat in the easy chair farthest away from me and my socks. "It's like dealing with a twelve-year-old sometimes," he grumbled.

"Ain't easy being a cradle-robber," I agreed cheerfully. "Now tell me—Wallace?"

"He owns March Hare," Alexander said reluctantly. "And he's looking for a Florida farm to stand him at stud when he retires."

I dropped my socks, astonished. "March Hare! Didn't he win the Florida Derby last year? And the Sunshine Millions Classic?"

Alexander nodded. "Four years old and pointed at the Breeders' Cup this fall. But if he doesn't make it—and there's every chance he won't, as he's been having abscess problems—Wallace doesn't have a farm of his own. And he's a Florida-bred with plenty of good nicking to every broodmare in Marion County, so there's no reason to send him to Kentucky. Or so I've been trying to convince Kevin."

"Kevin?"

"Kevin Wallace. He's the majority owner of March Hare Syndicate. The final say is his. They're all having a hell of a time trying to agree between Florida and Kentucky, and I think I have him on my side now."

Kevin Wallace. Wait... The hot excitement in my veins slowly chilled to ice. "Have you done business with him before?"

Alexander nodded. "A while ago. He bought out the one foal we did a share on, then sent it on to another trainer for finishing. That was before you came along," he added generously, "and took the training center to the next level. My last training foreman wasn't anywhere near as effective as you."

I remembered. Joey Berman had been an alcoholic who managed to hide his addictions from an overworked, overextended Alexander with an expertise that did not extend to his ability to start, train, and condition young racehorses. I counted myself lucky Alexander hadn't known an addict was running his training barn when he hired me. That had given me the chance to move up and take over the barn, a break I might not have had otherwise. Then, of course, the business had grown so explosively that we'd both been completely run ragged. Now that we only took on a few select clients, and saved the rest of our stalls, and our time, for our own home-breds, poorly thought-out partnerships like the one with Sunny Virtue need never occur again. We could keep an eye on all of our horses now.

But as for this Wallace guy...he'd already had one strike with us, in my book. Why give him a second chance? I had to admit, having March Hare would be a huge coup...but what would we be giving up in order to do business with this guy? Someone who Alexander had clearly already had a falling-out with in the past?

I had to put a stop to this right now. Which wasn't going to be easy, considering how sold Alexander was on getting a big stallion for the farm. Once I told him about Sunny Virtue, though, things might change. Maybe the threat of bad publicity would be enough to end this budding partnership before things got out of hand.

"I got a call about the foal he bought out from you. From the CASH people."

Alexander looked up sharply. "CASH people? What the hell are you talking about?"

"A horse at Fort Erie that's dropped off the map after some bad races. Seven years old. They traced him to me. Well, to the farm. He was by Virtuous. I looked him up—there was a colt by Virtuous out of Sunny Susan that matches his age, who was a foal-share with a Kevin Wallace. Pretty obvious it's the same guy. Dropped the horse into bottom-level claimers instead of retiring him...you want to do business with him again?"

Alexander shrugged. "Seven years sounds about right. What of it? Why shouldn't we try again? Both of us are in better financial situations now. Obviously he is, if he has a horse like March Hare in his stable. This could be very good for us. Let me worry about my past business relationships, Alex. I have first-hand knowledge of him, which you do not. I'm sure you'll find him perfectly agreeable." With that, he reached for his iPad as if the conversation was over.

Don't you dare blow me off. I bit back a short reply and took a deep breath, opting for continued calm instead. A raised voice would get me nowhere. I was going to have to convince Alexander that something he wanted very, very much was simply not going to work. That required a seriously cool head. "Alexander, if he's somehow involved with a broke-down claimer that CASH decides to publicize, that's going to look very bad for us. Especially if we find ourselves in business with him again. Don't you think?"

Alexander glared at me from over his reading glasses, and even from across the living room I could feel the iciness in his gaze. I found myself pressing back against the sofa pillows to get away from it. What was all this animosity? Was he blaming me for all of this trouble? The implied accusation cut deep. Wasn't he the one in the wrong here, if anyone was? *I wasn't involved with either of these horses. These are* your *mistakes.*

But when he spoke, his words were clipped, only his frosty tone betraying his deeper anger. "I won't be coerced by some anxious housewives with an Internet connection and the spare time to research slow horses. If they were worth my time at all they'd be able to see that we never owned the damn horse. Whatever Wallace did with him is none of my concern. March Hare, and getting a good roster up in the stallion barn now, that *is* my concern. You worry about the broodmares and the foals we have, and play with Tiger, and stay out of the rest until this nonsense has blown over. I'm not going to lose business because your racehorse retirement god-hood is coming to an end." He went back to his iPad and began flicking things about without missing a beat, as if he hadn't just rebuked me like an unruly child.

Or washed his hands of my problems as if they only mattered to him in a purely financial manner.

Well, fine. I would fix this on my own. There were more things to tell him—about Mary Archer renting the farm next door, about the bag of hate mail, even about starting Tiger and what a disaster/triumph that had been. It had been a very long day, I thought wearily. Had all that happened just today?

I didn't have the energy to talk about it all, especially since we had already begun the evening on a sour note.

I quietly got up and left the living room, balled-up boot socks in my hand, and found myself a bottle of red wine from the rack above the fridge. I tossed the sweaty socks on the kitchen table, letting them roll to Alexander's accustomed place and appreciating the timely insult, then dug around in the silverware drawer for the corkscrew. When the cork had been sufficiently mangled and liberated from the bottleneck, I tipped the bottle to my lips and took a long, pleasant swig.

The over-sweet flavors washed over my tongue and flooded down my throat, sweeping away the lump left there by Alexander's callous words. I put the bottle down and wiped my face with the dirty back of my hand, unheedful of the mud I was probably smearing on my chin and cheeks. Then I considered the glasses in the cabinet above my head before reaching up for a decent-sized tumbler, a galloping horse etched on its side in ghostly white, and pouring myself a healthy helping.

"You need to sit for a minute," I told the dark red wine once it was poured. "I might be an ignorant child, but I know that wine needs to breathe." I opened the fridge door and took out a chunk of gouda cheese, its golden warmth nestled within a red wax wrapping, and disappeared into the pantry for a box of the English water crackers that Alexander preferred.

I laid it all out on the marble counter: the cheese and the crackers and the tumbler of wine, and I considered it for a moment. When I had come here five years ago, I'd never had any of these things.

Gouda or water crackers or wine of any color—if I had ever thought about them for a moment, and I hadn't, I would have probably said they were for older people, wiser people, richer people. I had been a child running away from home, with nothing but a saddle and a dream, and it hadn't even been the right kind of saddle.

I'd made the dream come true, easier than some other people had done, for sure, but in other ways, maybe it had all happened too fast. Maybe too much had been given to me, when I should have had to claw and grasp and fight for it. Maybe I wouldn't have been such an easy target; maybe the community would have been quicker to draw ranks and defend me.

"Those that can't, are first to tear down those who can." My grandmother had told me that, when I was little and crying over some criticism of my riding, a missed lead or trotting on the wrong diagonal in a short stirrups class.

Cassidy Whomever-She-Was had outed herself as the ringleader of the Anti-Alex campaign from CASH. But I was willing to bet her reasons were more personal than just some overzealous love of the horse. No one would chase me around on such flimsy accusations unless they were desperately snatching at straws, looking for some way to bring me down.

Well, I had a computer and I had basic Google skills.

I could figure out who Cassidy was and why she had such a problem with me, easy as pie.

The wine and cheese would help, too.

On my way out of the kitchen, plate of crackers and cheese in one hand and tumbler of wine in the other, I paused, looked back at the wine bottle, and then doubled back. I tucked the half-empty bottle under my arm.

Sleuthing was thirsty work.

Chapter Eighteen

"SO, WHO WAS SHE?"

I grunted as the mare slammed me against the wall, her big anvil of a head nearly crashing into my nose, and gave her a resounding slap with the end of the shank. "Could this wait?" I panted. "Like, until after this foal comes?"

"This is a maiden mare," Kerri said reasonably, safe in the barn aisle, with a wooden door between her and Princess Zelda, who was not at all happy with the current state of affairs. "The foal might not come until tomorrow night. And I want to know about all of your cyber-stalking. Are you going to drive to her house and leave a dead squirrel on her porch?"

"That would be weird, so no." Zelda groaned and flung up her head at the pulse of another contraction and commenced dragging me around the foaling stall again, shambling through the knee-deep straw. "And wouldn't she just assume her cat had brought her a present? Why a squirrel? Why would you even think of that?"

"It would be very symbolic," Kerri explained, apparently unaware that she was insane.

I didn't ask of what. Sometimes Kerri's ideas defied logic. *"Whoa,* Zelda, *give* me a *minute—"* I unsnapped the lead and ducked away from the pain-addled mare. "I can't chase her around all afternoon. I still have Tiger to work today, if she ever drops this damn foal." I leaned against the stall door and watched the big bay mare pace the stall. She was young and still lean from her racing days, with only her great bulging belly to give away that she had been retired for a year and was about to give birth to what we hoped would be the first of many foals.

At five years old, Zelda was the veteran of thirty races and had seen the inside of a winner's circle eight times, but the next fifteen years of her life would be spent between pasture and deep-bedded straw, the changing seasons punctuated by yearly foals and a visit to whatever loverboy was residing in the little stallion barn on top of the hill. It would be a fairly peaceful life after the hustle and bustle of the racetrack, but at this moment, she found it nothing short of terrifying.

"It's hard with the good racemares," I said as Zelda pawed at the straw, throwing bedding through the air. "They don't know how to give in and just let things happen."

"Save the philosophy," Kerri groaned. "And *tell me.*"

"It's boring," I warned.

"Tell me!"

"Okay." I slipped out of the stall and slid the latch home as the rampaging mare went barreling past me. Her hip knocked against her water bucket and water went flying everywhere, including on her hindquarters, and she squealed and kicked out. I narrowly missed losing my head, but that was normal around here. "So here's the deal. Cassidy Lehigh lives down near Jupiter. Kind of close to West Palm, but her farm is no fancy show barn. It's basically a falling-down ranch."

"Typical Florida barn, got it," Kerri grinned.

"Yeah, you know the type. Half walls, sheet metal roof, perfectly serviceable, but Wellington it ain't. Or—" I waved an arm around the aisle of the comfortable broodmare barn, "—Cotswold Farm. And Cassidy has been training Thoroughbreds to event, but she doesn't get really far. Most of them go Novice level and then she sells them for a couple grand. She hates racing with a passion, thinks it ruins good horses, but she loves Thoroughbreds…maybe because they're cheap for her to get and show? I don't know."

"So she's not the greatest Thoroughbred advocate."

"Well, I mean—that's fine. But judging from how active she is on the horsey forums, Cassidy wants to be famous. And she hasn't managed it from her training skills yet, so she's going for another route."

"Tearing you apart?"

"Being an advocate," I corrected. "Although the tearing me apart factors into it. It's publicity, as far as I can tell, for the horse show she's putting on. The South Florida Thoroughbred Makeover."

Kerri laughed. In the foaling stall, Zelda pricked her ears and whinnied at the sound. We both watched her for a moment. "She's nuts," Kerri announced.

"The horse or Cassidy Lehigh?"

"Well…Cassidy Lehigh might be on to something. The makeover competitions are getting pretty popular, I think. She's putting one on down here?"

I nodded. "Near Gulfstream at the county equestrian center. Mid-April. For retired racehorses who last raced in the past twelve months, with no other show records. I guess the idea is they should all have been on lay-off since they left the track, without any additional training. Level the playing field."

"When's the closing date?"

"Oh, I don't know. Hey—is her tail wrap slipping?"

"How dare you? My wraps never slip. And why don't you know? You need to get on this right away."

"Why?" The tail wrap was definitely slipping. I unlatched the stall door again and started to slip through.

"Because you and Tiger have to win it."

I had to hand it to Kerri, the idea was so brilliant and so perfect and obvious that I stood stock still in the doorway for a minute, imagining the joy and glory of winning a Thoroughbred competition, making my Tiger a star at last and putting down this Cassidy Lehigh with one bold stroke, and I didn't even get mad when Zelda slashed her tail and slapped me right across the face with a thousand stinging strands of hair. I was dreaming of bringing down my enemy and giving Tiger the accolades I had always wanted for him in one fell swoop, and the dreaming was sweet indeed.

Of course, it was only a dream. Aiming for a horse show less than three months away, with a horse who had been racing just a month before? Insanity. I wouldn't ever do anything so irresponsible in real life. It was bad enough that I was already starting Tiger back into training. I reassured myself that he was already looking brighter and happier after that first day's work; this morning he hadn't even run away from Luz when she'd turned him out, just stepped away from the paddock gate like a gentleman. That was nice to see.

But I was curious anyway, and I resolved to look up the Thoroughbred Makeover closing date and classes later that night, once Zelda's foal was out, up, and nursing. What harm could it do? Maybe I'd missed mention of another one, later in the year. Maybe there was one this fall that we could enter. By fall Tiger ought to be a well-adjusted member of show horse society, I figured. Or at least trot around an arena without killing anyone.

Unfortunately, I didn't get the chance to look things up until *late* that night, and by then I wished I was dreaming in truth, asleep and dreaming to be exact. Princess Zelda, true to maiden mare form, managed to hang onto the foal for hours and hours, all through the long afternoon. The sun had disappeared below the hills and the sky had gone from golden and pink to a luminous deep blue before she finally stopped her pacing, arched her back, and cocked her tail. Her body was steaming with sweat and her nostrils were pink-rimmed with exertion, but I clapped her on her wet neck and told her she was a good girl as her water broke and poured into the straw. "You got this. Next stop, motherhood."

Of course she didn't have this. She was still a maiden who had no idea what was going on. She didn't want to lie down to have the foal, and Kerri had to come and take her by the halter after some anxious moments in which the delicate little hooves were nearly smashed against a wall as she took careless turns around the stall with a baby trying to be birthed just under her tail. Alexander had come by then, bearing pizza and beer (we weren't allowed to have beer until after we'd gotten the foal out, so it was sort of an incentive to look forward to), and he rolled up his sleeves and came into the stall with me to help tug the newest member of the family into the Ocala night. We had one of the broodmare grooms, Erica, stay late after feeding, sending Martina, home to feed her children. Erica was unmarried and had no children, an ideal state for a groom in foaling season. But it was her first year and this was her first maiden mare, so Alexander and I took the wheel while she hovered nearby, watching everything with wide eyes and an expression halfway between horror and wonder.

The foal was halfway out when Zelda decided her legs couldn't hold her up for another moment and went crashing to the ground knees first. The foal slid out another three inches as we jumped back to avoid her flailing hooves and I dove into the straw to stop its head from slamming into the ground beneath the bedding. Alexander was on his belly beside me. "Time to draw out the hips," he grunted. "Got a leg?"

"Got it. Three...two...*one...*" We tugged with all our might every time we saw the mare pushing, pulling along with the contractions. I winced when I saw the foal's hips were a tad wider than what the mare's body had counted on. "Gonna need stitches," I panted.

"Tomorrow," Alexander agreed. "After the swelling goes down. Ah—*pull!*"

There's no position harder in the world to exert all your strength and energy than flat on your stomach, tugging on the slippery leg of a foal that doesn't want to join the outside world. My shoulders were screaming by the time he came slithering out, feathery hooves pushing against the amniotic sac, soaking the straw beneath us with blood and fluid. But oh God, what a beauty, what a dark little beauty he was. Alexander busied himself clearing the sac and I was free to let my eyes rove over the wet heaving sides, the ribs pressing through the damp foal fuzz, the long legs with their great boney joints. Two white stockings that ran up the inside of impossibly long hind legs; two dark black forelegs that lightened to mahogany by the time they ran into massive shoulders. A tender seahorse head with blinking dark eyes and a white blaze that would show the way down the homestretch, a beacon for others to follow but never to pass. "Oh God, what a beauty," I whispered aloud, and Alexander smiled, and Kerri nodded, and Erica, who was still young and tender-hearted, sniffed noisily.

Now Zelda realized she was a mother, and went lurching up hastily, nearly trampling the gorgeous young prince. The cord broke and there was blood and Kerri was snapping at the mare to knock off her stupid tricks and Erica was being sent for the iodine left just outside the stall door to treat the foal's brand-new belly button, and the havoc of birthing foals was back in full swing.

I was tired when I made it back to the house, but the pile of mail waiting on the kitchen table woke me up. There was a mountain of envelopes there, every one of them addressed to me, every one of them so slim they couldn't contain more than one folded sheet of paper. I supposed that was a mercy, and sat down to confirm my suspicions. I slid on calloused finger, still smudged with sweat and horsehair and blood and other various body fluids, under the envelope's flap and tore the paper open.

The letter that fell out was another form letter, no doubt written by CASH. I skimmed through the diatribe, which suggested that I crawl back into the swamps where I had come from instead of dumping my unwanted horses there, and which indicated that my comeuppance was approaching when the mainstream media took up their cause and crucified me for the horse murderer I was, and then pushed back from the table, face thoughtful.

Alexander came in just then. He saw the pile of letters and the single opened one discarded beside its siblings. "Fan mail?" he asked with a wry smile.

"Something like that." I started past him, giving him an absent kiss on the cheek as I went.

"You have somewhere to be? I was going to heat up some dinner."

"I'll be right back," I promised. "I just need to look something up."

Upstairs, my computer took its sweet time loading up. I stripped out of my filthy foaling clothes with one eye on the screen, waiting for the beach ball to stop its annoying spinning. Finally, down to my underwear and in dire need of a shower, the laptop announced it was ready and willing with a triumphant little trumpet sound, and I threw myself across the bed to do a quick search.

South Florida Thoroughbred Makeover, coming late Spring. "Well, that was easy," I muttered, clicking through the participant guidelines. I found the closing date and whistled softly. Two days left. "Skin of your teeth, Alex." If I did it. Which I wouldn't. Of course.

Alexander was in the doorway then, arms folded. "You didn't invite me to the pajama party."

"Do you see me wearing pajamas?" I laughed and closed the laptop. "I just needed to check something. I'm ready for supper now." The pizza had been a very long time ago.

"It's in the oven," Alexander said, looking me over. "I think we have time for a shower."

"Too tired," I sighed, flinging a hand over my eyes and lolling on the bed. "I must sleep in my filth, for I cannot make the walk to the bathroom."

"Oh, I don't think so," he rumbled, and with a leer he stooped and picked me up, throwing me over his shoulder.

I always had been rather lightweight.

Somehow, in all the fuss, I'd forgot to tell Alexander about our delightful new neighbor, Mary Archer, until the next morning. Alexander listened gravely to my story while we rode out to the training track. He waited until I was done. He did not interrupt. Then he said:

"Alex, my dear, I'm starting to think you'd benefit from a vacation away from horses altogether."

I stuck my tongue out at him. "I knew you wouldn't believe me."

"Oh, I believe you. I believe everything you said except that there is a conspiracy against you being led by Mary, and that she rented the place next door solely to make your life more difficult. Mary rented that farm because it is centrally located but ridiculously cheap, so she gets the benefit of a Millionaire Mile address to show to prospective owners on paper. Which will work for her for as long as they are willing to be *absentee* owners. If anyone takes it in their heads to visit, well, I don't think they'll like what they see. But if the groom told Kerri that's the only flat piece of land on the property, that's where she has to gallop. We're all better prepared and know to watch for the horses, and we'll just have to be vigilant."

"Alexander, a horse *died.*"

"In a terrible training accident. Not murdered."

I gave up that tack. Alexander was no fool, and he'd seen racing rivals do insane things. I'd heard his old stories of ringers, of drugged horses, of fixed races. Galloping horses in a field? Hard to prove the criminality in that one. Even Rational Alex, making a rare appearance, had to admit that.

But I didn't ride anyone on the track that morning. I sat decorously on Parker and watched the sets go by, and commented when the Icarus filly didn't change leads three times in a row, and suggested to Alexander that the Viewliner colt needed some time off to grow. "His ass is six inches higher than his withers," is how I put it, and when we got back to the barn, following the steaming young horses, I dismounted and wrote "turn-out" under his name on the tack room whiteboard. One more out of rotation. With the eight horses headed to the first of the sales in two weeks, things were going to get quiet around here. We might have to let a rider go.

Besides me.

Alexander didn't say anything when I got through the morning without trying to get a ride in a set, but I could tell that he approved. He gave me a dry kiss on the cheek as I stripped Parker's tack, and I made a mental note to slip lip balm into his jacket pocket.

"Will you ride Tiger today?"

I nodded. "I put him in the round pen yesterday—no, two days ago." Yesterday had been a blur with Zelda's extended foaling adventure. I pulled the saddle and blanket off Parker's back, flipping the girth over top of it, and heaved the pile of tack out of the pony's stall. "But I didn't get on him."

Alexander was pleased. "Glad that you two are going to get moving on this. Clearly, turn-out wasn't right for him. He's a horse that needs a job." He followed me and we filed out of the stall, leaving Parker to his hay-net. "I'm going to south Florida tomorrow," he added conversationally.

I bit my lip and waited until I'd gotten into the tack room, placed the saddle on its stand, and hung up Parker's bridle on its hook. Then, I took a Diet Coke out of the refrigerator, pushing aside a bottle of penicillin, several syringes of encephalitis vaccine, and a jar of pickles in order to reach it. "We need more Diet Coke," I said carelessly, and flipped the can lid open. I took a long sip, facing him, waiting for him to go on. *Tell me I'll be missed.* That was all I wanted right now—to know that *he* knew that I ought to be there. That I was wasted here. That I belonged at the races.

"Alex..." Alexander stood in the doorway, heedless to the grooms and riders who needed to get in and out of the tack room but didn't want to bother what was clearly another domestic dispute between the bosses. I saw Manny peek in, bridles over his shoulder, and I started to tell Alexander that he was disrupting the morning routine, but then I heard the cheerful *honk-honk* of the Taco Lady's minivan heralding the arrival of brunch, and everyone dumped their tack on the ground and went out to see what her coolers held today. The Taco Lady waited for no groom; she had dozens of barns to visit. What timing! "Alex, you know I'd take you with me if I could. But it's like we've talked about. I don't want you in front of all the media down there, to say nothing of the activists. It's not like here, you'll have a whole lot of city people who don't know a thing about horses and they've been *told* you abuse horses and they'll make trouble. You know this."

I did know this, and it had been decided already, and I had agreed.

I smiled mutely and pushed past Alexander to retrieve a bucket of water cooling in the center aisle, and then back again to snatch up a bar of saddle soap and a sponge. I went to work scrubbing Parker's bridle, dirty foam rising up and dripping to the concrete floor below. A chorus of whinnies was going up from the shed-row outside, so someone had opened the feed room door, probably in search of someplace to eat while Alexander and I went on frightening everyone away from the tack room. I heard Tiger's high-pitched neigh sounding distantly from his paddock. Luz had brought him over early today. He would get a nibble of lunch, just a taste, so that he wouldn't fuss at being skipped over while the training barn ate, but not so much that he'd gain weight or build up even more excess energy than he already had. He was in the waiting room right now, not a racehorse, not a show horse, just being told to stay put and wait, and suddenly I knew just how disconcerting and disorienting that must be for him. With Alexander, however wisely, barring me from the racetrack, after I had finally thought I'd found my place there, and being told to go back to training a retired racehorse instead—I got it. *I get it, Tiger. I get you now.*

I found myself laughing.

"Alex?" Now I was worrying him.

I wiped the foam off of the bridle. "Nothing," I chuckled. "I have plenty of work to keep me busy here. Foals. Maiden mares, always a party. Two-year-olds to ship to the sales grounds in two weeks that need to be prettied up and on their best behavior. Tiger. February is packed. I can keep myself occupied."

"We are also fully staffed," Alexander reminded me. "Perhaps over-staffed. Don't let the other work crowd out Tiger. Build up your good name again—do it with Tiger."

Alexander was leaning over my computer when I came out of the shower later, dripping water all over the carpet. "What are you looking at?" I asked, and he whipped around with a guilty face like a toddler caught in the pantry. "What did you do?"

"Nothing," he said. He closed the laptop.

"Alexander, what did you do?"

He went to the bedroom door, opened it, and disappeared into the dark hallway. I sighed and went after him.

The printer was humming away in the upstairs study, industriously printing off a few pages of something that Alexander was evidently very keen to get his hands on before I did. He plucked them off the tray as soon as the printer spat them out and held them up above my head. Annoyed, I let the towel drop and snatched with both hands, finally grasping one page. I yanked it from his hand.

Alexander smiled nervously. "Now don't be mad—"

I looked at the entry form in my hand. My name was on it, and so was Tiger's. That was our address, and that was our credit card information. I glared at Alexander. "What. Did. You. Do."

He shrugged and smiled beatifically, as if no one could ever be mad at such a charming fellow. "I thought it would be something fun for you to work towards."

"A horse show in like three months? On a horse who raced three weeks ago? Are you crazy?" I felt a little faint.

"If you can't manage it, you can always just scratch," Alexander said reasonably. "But if you *do* manage it, well, this way you aren't missing out because you didn't want to enter."

"I can't scratch, Alexander." I handed the entry form back to him and shook my head. "The person running this is the person behind the CASH bullshit. The person running this is going to tell the whole world if I can't get my horse ready for her little show."

Chapter Nineteen

T HERE WASN'T A GOOD way to tell Tiger that we
couldn't screw this up now.

Especially when he'd just dumped me in the mud.

Still, I had to try. "Tiger," I called from the puddle where I had
landed. "Tiger, it's really important to Mummy's career that we get
this right, or the rabble might just get what they want and run me
out of the horse business."

Tiger, who after sunfishing and bucking and twisting on the
pretense that he had heard a horse in some nearby pasture
galloping, was too busy inspecting the high walls of the round pen
to bother responding.

I sighed and got up, shaking the dirty water from my jacket and
brushing the dark mud from my breeches. This was what I got for
shooting for the stars. A dirty bum and the potential to look even
worse in front of my detractors than I already did.

Tiger saw me heading in his direction, swished his tail, and
promptly trotted off, his hooves buffeting the round pen walls.

"I get it," I sighed. "You don't want to work. You've been
telling me that all week." I went back to the center of the round

pen to kick at the dirt and think.

Day One had come and gone seven days ago. In the meantime, in between foaling out Zelda and two other mares, breezing an older horse coming off a lay-off for Alexander to take to South Florida on his next trip, and waving goodbye to Alexander and the older horse while they went down to run Shearwater in a minor stakes race, I'd had five more rides to describe in the little training notebook.

Day One might have gone better than expected, but Day Two had *not* followed in its footsteps. It took Tiger thirty minutes to meet me in the center of the round pen and end our session with a little snuggle-time.

On Day Three he simply ran around the pen whinnying, trying to look out over the high walls, because he heard the yearlings galloping in their pasture. This went on for twenty minutes before I finally gave up.

On Day Four he caved after about twenty minutes and I took the opportunity to mount up and ride, and then he reminded me of how strong his neck was after years of galloping heavy on the bit. The speed he managed to reach in the tiny round pen was truly frightening. We were not on the racetrack anymore, but I was apparently the only one who noticed.

On Day Five, we achieved a nice quiet trot around the pen, with halts in the center and changes of direction that weren't the ugliest things in the world, and I reminded *him* that he was fully capable of carrying his own head and indeed was expected to if we weren't galloping. I was sufficiently pleased to give him a day off after that.

So here we were today, Day Six, and he had decided that if he could put his head down without my hands on his mouth, he might as well take that opportunity to just put his head between his forelegs and buck.

I guess he hadn't needed that day off.

It shouldn't have been this hard, I thought, while the horse prowled restlessly around the pen, snorting at the walls that shut out the world around him. I'd been riding this horse for years, granted in a different saddle and with different expectations, but still—was it so much to say, 'Okay Tiger, now instead of trotting and galloping around a racetrack, you're going to trot and change directions in the round pen?'

"Should we just go back to the racetrack and try it there?" I asked, and Tiger flipped one ear in my direction, as if the idea caught his fancy.

That wouldn't be the right move, though. Back on the racetrack, he'd known exactly what to do for years—and he wouldn't understand why I was telling him to change everything. He needed a new environment. The pasture idea had been thrown out. I had no interest in taking this beast out and trotting around the vast reaches of the yearling pasture. Tiger was still way too much horse, too fit and too full of himself, to be shown such freedom. He needed walls and containment, not open frontier.

We needed an arena.

We needed a boarding stable—as awful as that sounded.

I'd always had to board my horses as a kid. I was a suburban kid, and even though five-year-old Alex had argued with conviction that we had plenty of grass for a pony, and I'd do all the clean-up required, ten-year-old Alex grasped that a quarter-acre plot wasn't space for a pony *or* a horse. So it had been a boarding stable life, with all the politics and petty wars that went on in such places. Put five or ten or twenty tween girls in one place and see how well they all get along. Then make them incredibly competitive and horse-proud.

Then back away slowly.

We fought like alley cats, and in between fights we built and betrayed alliances with one another so often that a dedicated historian couldn't have kept them all straight.

Then there that nervous feeling when you were sitting in the backseat of your parents' car, driving up the barn lane—the fear that something might have happened to your horse while you were away. Maybe he had gotten kicked and no one had noticed when they brought him in from the field that morning. Maybe he hadn't cleaned up his hay and was standing dejectedly in one corner of his stall with the beginnings of a bellyache that could end up a life-threatening colic. I'd never been good at trusting my possessions to others, and that went trebly for my horse, even when I was just a kid.

I was pretty sure I wouldn't handle it well as an adult, either. I was having trouble just allowing my racehorses out of my sight, even with Alexander checking them regularly and an assistant trainer that he trusted implicitly. I'd cheerfully sworn off boarding stables after I'd become a resident at Cotswold Farm and seen how sweet it was to have your horses under your own watchful eyes night and day. Now I had the wrong sort of farm for my horse. Wouldn't you know it?

Tiger came to a reluctant halt and watched me as I walked over to take his reins. "You're a nerd," I told him, and he blew his red-rimmed nostrils at me in response. "But you're *my* nerd. What am I going to do if I'm always worrying about you somewhere else? It was one thing to send you to Lucy. She's better at horsekeeping than I am. But how am I going to find someone else I trust as much as Lucy?"

Tiger didn't have any answers. He never did. His only response to anything at all was to run, and that answer wasn't left to him anymore. So, it was all up to me.

>>>>> <<<<<

Kerri, however, had a few answers of her own. She'd been bouncing around the Ocala-area barns for a while before she came to Cotswold. She had a relevant response to every single trainer I suggested. With Kerri perched on a tack trunk, I sat at the desk in the training barn office and looked up local boarding stables. I ran my finger down a list of hunter/jumper barns and listened to her one-sentence reviews.

"Stay away from Driver's, he's a maniac and thinks drugs are the answer to everything."

"Monica Parsons is nice if you like having your tack borrowed when you're not there."

"Jilly Hopkins? She hates Thoroughbreds. She wouldn't even consider Tiger."

"Oak Ridge Farm is great if you like ten-year-old girls in pigtails bouncing around on ponies."

"Jessica Ryder is moonlighting in adult movies."

I paused, finger still on the farm listing. "That's not necessarily a strike against the farm, you know. If she wants to be in porn that's her business."

"She does the filming at the barn," Kerri went on. "It's a series of movies called *Ryder's Up.*"

I considered the remaining stables on the list without much hope. I was sure each of them had something desperately wrong with them, according to Kerri. Since Kerri and I tended to hate the same things, I trusted her judgement. It was one of the reasons we got along so well. "This list is about tapped out," I sighed. "Is it possible there's someone in Ocala that hasn't made your hit list?"

"In hunter/jumpers? No." Kerri had a bag of potato chips she'd unearthed from some secret tack room stash, and she began eating them, one at a time, with great ceremony while she considered the stables she had known. "In eventing, maybe. That's where you should be looking. They love Thoroughbreds."

"I know. I grew up eventing, remember? But I don't know all these new people who moved in since I started racing." The eventing barns in Ocala seemed to have grown by the hundreds since my teenage years. Trainers flocked to the warm weather and the year-round eventing. I sighed. "And I haven't talked to my old trainer in years, so I can't ask *her*. I don't even know if she's still riding."

Kerri shook her head at me. "You shouldn't lose touch with people so easily," she said sagely. "Out of sight, out of mind—that's you in a nutshell."

"Save the lecture and help me figure this out. Or I'll send Martina home and leave you all the broodmare stalls to do alone." Six pregnant mares and seven foals sharing stalls with their dams all night made for some wicked messes. All that wet straw they left behind was *heavy*.

"Okay, okay." Kerri ate a few chips and affected a pose of deep thought. "I got it," she said after a minute. "Get on the web and type in *Roundtree Farm*."

"Are the people nice there?"

"Sometimes. Why not. Type it in."

I shook my head and typed the letters into the search bar. My pinkie pounded the *enter* key. Then I waited.

And waited.

And waited.

"What the hell is with the internet connection in this barn?" I roared, waving my hands around.

Kerri laughed so hard she had to put down her potato chips. "That sentence," she cackled, gasping to catch her breath. "I'm sure no one has ever had to say that before ever. You have the most first world problems ever, Miss Alex ma'am."

I ignored my disrespectful assistant and glowered at the computer screen. But it turned out it wasn't the internet connection so much as the horrendously designed Roundtree Farm website. The entire background appeared to be a massively oversized image. The original was probably very nice, and so high-resolution that it could have been printed as a wall poster, but in this particular case all a viewer got a glimpse of was flared nostrils, wide eyes, a foamy mouth open around the bit, veins standing out on a muscular neck, and water droplets flying through the air. It was a time capsule website. The copyright year was 2002.

"Someone's way too proud they ran around Rolex," I observed as the photo finished loading, revealing that it was the front half of a horse leaping down into the Head of the Lake at Kentucky Horse Park. "Who is this person?"

"Elsie Carter," Kerri said. "She's nuts, but she's very good. She did Rolex back in the nineties."

"I've never heard of her." I squinted as words revealed themselves, nearly impossible to read against the backdrop of the leaping horse. "Do I really want nuts?"

"Nice-nuts, not mean-nuts," Kerri clarified. "Like us."

I struggled to read the description on the screen. Full-service boarding facility, dressage arena, jumping arena, cross-country jumps, center-aisle barn. Best feed and hay, owner lives on site. All of the high-end farm amenities were covered, but it was the bold print towards the bottom that interested me. *No Princesses — No Drama.*

I guffawed, and Kerri smiled delightedly. "You see? She's nuts, but in a good way."

"No princesses! I love it! So you're telling me this will be a drama-free boarding stable?"

"Oh, hell no. You'll find a boarding stable full of unicorns before you'll find one that's drama-free. But it's better than most, and Elsie doesn't much care what you do with your horse. She's not going to be standing around judging you. She has her own horses to ride. I rode someone's horse there a few years ago and it was the most drama-free barn on the planet. I loved it. But I never had enough money to board there."

"It's expensive?"

"The nice barns always are. And this place has it all. You need the right barn if you're going to get him ready to show in a few months. A barn with other riders, jumps, a little bit of bustle..."

She was right about that. Taking Tiger to his first horse show had to be carefully planned, or he'd think it was just another ship-in to the races. Boarding him at a show barn with a little hustle and bustle could help him get over his brain's connection between busy stables and racing.

A barn owner who minded her own business while her boarders were bouncing around in the arena was another plus. I wasn't itching to get my terrible equitation dissected by some frowning hunter/jumper or dressage trainer while I was busy trying to get Tiger to act more like a gentleman and less like a rampaging bronco. It was going to be bad enough having other boarders around to see how my riding position had devolved after years of defensive chair-seat posture (for the babies) and hunched-over posture (for the galloping). "You call her for me," I suggested.

Kerri folded over the top of her potato chip bag and hopped down from the tack trunk. "I'll do you one better," she said. "I'll take you to meet her."

Chapter Twenty

ROUNDTREE STABLES TURNED OUT to be just a
few minutes away, down a winding road that wrapped
through rolling pastures studded with live oaks and criss-crossed
with dark brown fencing, the kind of countryside that made real
estate agents salivate at the prospect of relocating here so that they
could specialize in equestrian properties. I even saw a few people I
knew along the way, out driving around their properties or
heading into town or, in one case, checking their mail from the
comfort of a golf cart, a Jack Russell terrier wagging his stump of a
tail from the passenger seat. I waved and Kerri honked the truck
horn whenever there weren't any horses around, which wasn't
often. There were horses everywhere. That was the whole point of
Ocala, if you asked me, or Kerri, or any of the folks we saw along
the way.

When she slowed the truck at last, it wasn't for a big brick-
paved driveway with a sparkling fountain marking the farm
entrance, or a cast-iron gate with the farm logo filigreed in loops
and curls in the center. It wasn't even paved. Kerri turned off the
country road onto a rutted grassy track that led off into a

hammock of ancient oaks, their overreaching branches so thick the driveway seemed to be disappear into the gloom despite an outwardly sunny day. The entire atmosphere was very haunted house.

I looked out at the rusty mailbox on its leaning wooden post as we went past. There was no name or number on the mailbox.

"Kerri," I said lightly, "There are easier ways to murder me."

She laughed. "I told you Elsie didn't care what anybody thought. Don't worry, the barn's great."

I looked into the jungle of oaks and palms pressing close to the truck windows on either side. "And how do you know her again?"

"I rode a friend's horse there."

"How many times?"

"Like...six or seven times."

"How long ago?"

"Dunno...three years ago?"

"And you've never been back?"

"It's fine." Kerri glanced at me and smiled. "Really. It's a nice barn. My friend isn't there anymore, though."

"What happened to her?"

"She stopped paying her board and Elsie had to kick her out. There was a padlock on the stall door and everything. It was a mess."

A tree branch slapped against the windshield of the car.

"She doesn't associate you with this friend, right?"

"No, no, we got along great. Everything's *fine.*"

I hoped so. The way this driveway was looking, I wouldn't be surprised if it ended up in a clearing just big enough for a rusty shack, complete with a shotgun-bearing crazy woman ready to send us on our way.

The kind of place I'd always suspected Mary Archer had come from. Thinking about Mary Archer did not give me any confidence at all.

When the driveway finally widened into a clearing, Kerri gave me a told-you-so grin, but I was too busy admiring the little farm to feel too annoyed. I looked back and forth, taking it all in. "This is lovely," I breathed. "Damn, Kerri, this is a hidden gem for sure."

Roundtree Farm was small, no more than twenty acres, at a guess, and yet at first glance it had everything a boarder could want for their horse. For their *show* horse—it was definitely different than any sort of racing stable. A center-aisle barn with ten windows sat before us—real, open, unbarred windows, with horses poking their heads out and blinking curiously to see who was driving the unfamiliar truck. Even from a distance, I could see that each horse had a neatly pulled mane and groomed coat.

Just behind the barn, a tiny little fieldstone cottage, a relic of the Cracker era, gleamed yellow and white against the green pines along the back property line. Off to the right of the barn, a patchwork of paddocks was scattered over the gentle hills, each one connected by cross-country fences: coops and fieldstone walls and two-rail fence sections.

Within the paddocks, jumps had been cleverly set up wherever nature could support them. There was a hanging log set between two oak trees, a water complex in the hollow of two hills, an Irish bank atop a small ridge, and dozens of other little fences scattered everywhere.

Hard to our right was a dressage ring and a jumping ring, as the website promised. A winding stream made its way through the paddocks and widened into a shimmering little pool, dancing with cattails, near the barn.

All around the property, sheltering it from the neighboring farms, the oak trees and pines grew thick and full. It was a tiny little haven, hidden from prying eyes and the roar of traffic, where a girl could just get away from the rest of the world and enjoy a little time with her horse.

Oh, and use all of the jumps and the dressage arena to train hard, of course.

"It's a miniature horse park," I said, shaking my head in disbelief. "Absolutely amazing use of space."

"Awesome, right?" Kerri pulled the truck up beside the handful of other cars alongside the barn. "Let's go see if Elsie's in the barn. That's her truck over there." A venerable old Ford dually sat at the far end of the parking area, its dark blue body gleaming under the wintry sun. I spotted a few stickers on the back window, including a Trakehner breed logo. I frowned. *That's not encouraging.* The warmblood community was rarely fond of Thoroughbreds, and especially not those Thoroughbreds fresh off the track.

Well, it was too late to turn back now, and Kerri had sworn the owner wouldn't mind Thoroughbreds. I squared my shoulders and followed her swinging pony-tail out of the short-cropped grass of the parking lot.

As soon as I walked into the central aisle of the barn, I found myself blinking in the dim half-light. I wasn't in love with the center-aisle barn as a general rule—as a racetracker I'd grown used to the open walls and back-to-back stalls of the shed-row style barn, and I liked the breezes and sunlight shed-rows afforded the horses. I did have to admit, though, that this barn was a lot warmer than mine was right now. I wondered if it was cooler in the summer. It was certainly *darker*. There were a few translucent panels in the steel roof, but what it really needed was for someone to just switch on the lights.

The stall fronts were barred—again, a very traditional sort of show barn set-up, with little square openings in one corner for a feed scoop to slip through. A few horses pushed their noses through the feed doors as we walked by, whickering their hellos. Kerri paused by the second horse down the aisle, who shoved his big dark nose into her palm, fluttering his nostrils against her skin. "This is Legacy," she said before planting a kiss on the white snip between his flaring nostrils. "A school horse. I rode him once with my friend. He dumped me in the water, yes he did, yes *he did*." Her voice descended into baby-talk. "Legacy's a bad pony, yes him is!"

Legacy seemed content to rest his nose in Kerri's palm, breathing her in. He didn't seem like a bad pony, but water jumps can make good horses do crazy things. I remembered that much from my eventing days.

"Oh, I hear we have visitors out there!"

I looked up the aisle and saw a small woman coming out of what must have been a tack room in the middle of the barn. Kerri waved. "Hello Elsie! It's Kerri! And I brought my boss Alex!"

"Ah, Kerri, where have you been? I have not seen you in so many months." Her accent was slightly foreign, as if she had spent time overseas. It wouldn't be too unusual for a successful trainer, though. Our influences were very European.

"Or years. I went to school, and now I work at Cotswold Farm, for Alex Whitehall. You know who she is, don't you?"

"Alex? I have heard of Alex Whitehall, but I am thinking it was not your Alex?" The woman walked up, her features slowly becoming clear in the gloom of the unlit barn. I wished she'd flip on the lights already.

She walked right up to us and stopped beneath the faint glow from a translucent panel in the roof above, so that I could get a decent look at her tiny frame, her sharp features, her shining boots and dark olive breeches. She wore a polo shirt, neatly tucked in beneath a brass-studded leather belt; her hair was gray and closely cropped around her head; her tanned skin was wrinkled and she wore no makeup. This was one of the old guard, then. I knew her type from my childhood. I extended a hand and waited to be judged.

Elsie's hands remained behind her back for a beat while she studied me—my short ponytail, my Cotswold polo shirt with a green horse kiss just above my left breast, my dirty jeans, my scuffed paddock boots—and then she gave me a short nod and offered me her own hand. I grasped the calloused little hand and received a lesson in just how strong a grip could be. Elsie was kind of terrifying.

She was also kind of inspiring. *I wouldn't mind being this scary when I'm old.*

"You are the one they say abandons the horses?" Elsie's accent was odd, rather stilted, as if she had been born in New England but then spent most of her life amongst a variety of Europeans, Australians, and possibly a Russian or three, and took the most interesting parts of each language for her own use. "The one they say leaves the horses in the swamps."

Play nicely. "Yes, they say I do," I said with a rueful smile. "But I don't abandon horses. It's all false. Exaggerations and lies."

She considered me a moment longer, narrowing her eyes. Then she decided. "That is good to know," she said, and took her hand back before mine was crumbled to dust in her grasp. "I read your story in the magazine. You say you retire all your horses and have a model retirement program. I admired that. I was disappointed it might not be true. I am happy to know it is."

"It's all a smear campaign," Kerri broke in. "They were looking for a scapegoat, and Mary Archer gave them one."

"Mary Archer?" Elsie looked sharply at Kerri. "She's involved with this?"

"You know Mary Archer?" I asked, but no one paid me any mind.

"We've had a few run-ins with her," Kerri said. "She hates Alex like poison."

"She *is* poison," Elsie declared. "Any horse she has had, is poisoned. She is no good."

I decided I liked Elsie quite a lot.

We toured the farm inside and out, from the big freezers that could hold ten bags of grain and were impossible for a horse to open, to the cross-country course set in the paddocks, clambering over the coops and stone walls set between the fences. A few boarders showed up to ride their horses as the afternoon shadows grew long, and Elsie nodded gravely at each of them as they rode out to the arenas, their horses impeccably turned out in white polo wraps, white saddle pads, and shining leather tack.

We watched as one of Elsie's students took her horse around the show-jumping course, hopping through a three-foot-six course with aplomb. Her horse, a block-headed bay with a roached mane that made his head seem even bigger, never missed a spot, never missed a lead, and halted perfectly after a round twenty-meter circle at the end.

"Fantastic," I sighed, letting out the breath I'd been holding. I couldn't ride like that, not a chance. That door had closed a long time ago.

"They are good," Elsie allowed. "I may let her go Preliminary in a few more months."

"Alex, you rode Prelim, didn't you?"

I shook my head at Kerri. "Nothing so grand. I was always on green horses. They were usually sold before I got anywhere."

"Well then," Elsie said crisply, "You should be doing just fine with this new retiree of yours."

"I'm not, though. That's the whole point."

Elsie nodded, her eyes still on her student in the arena. "A change of scenery will do him good. Who knows, maybe if you keep this one, you'll be on the way to Preliminary yourself."

My eyes followed the rider and her bay horse as they took a gymnastic combination, jumping a one-stride, a bounce, and then three long strides to a big spread of an oxer. It was a taxing series of fences, requiring the horse to expand and contract his body like an accordion. The hammer-headed bay moved like a leopard, the picture of grace and athleticism, and the girl on his back barely seemed to move. They made the difficult jump sequence look as effortless as water flowing down a channel.

I could scarcely remember the last time I'd jumped a horse over a fence, or had the occasion to sit so quietly and beautifully in the saddle. I shook my head ruefully, remembering the collection of motley off-track Thoroughbreds and auction bargains I'd grown up riding. It was possible that I'd *never* had the opportunity to present such a picture of perfect equitation. I'd probably always been hunch-backed and chair-seated, on the defensive, ready for anything that day's bronco might throw my way.

The woman on horseback took her horse in one final circle, the bay collected into a taut bundle of muscle, profile vertical to the ground, hindquarters reaching nearly to his girth. Then, she sat still and straight and tall, and the horse dropped to a perfectly square halt. She sat like a statue atop his back, as if they were posing for their monument in the National Mall.

I sighed.

I couldn't ride like that if I trained for ten years. My muscles wouldn't know how to hold themselves so tall and proud. They'd be waiting for the horse to drop the pretense and act the fool. They'd be screaming at me to get into a defensive mode and protect myself.

It was silly to feel this jealous—I could stick to tough horses and I didn't have to look good doing it.

Riding like that wouldn't do me any good when I was taking a racehorse out for a two minute lick.

But, damn, it was sure was beautiful.

I heard laughter and realized that I had been missing a conversation between Elsie and Kerri. I stepped a little closer and smiled, as if I'd been in on the joke. Elsie smiled back at me and went on with her story. "I said to her, my dear, I don't care if that horse was sired by a hammerhead *shark,* you can't pass up that kind of talent! And so she bought him, but she had the last laugh when she named him."

Kerri guffawed.

"What's his name?" I asked, giving up any pretense that I'd heard the whole story.

"Jaws," Kerri laughed. "Just *Jaws.* She shows him under that and everything. He has some fancy German name but this girl's like, who cares. I like her already."

"Jaws isn't that crazy a name when you ride around on a horse named The Tiger Prince."

Kerri went on laughing. "Everyone who names horses is insane," she snorted. "You included."

"I didn't name him!"

Elsie harrumphed for attention. She was ready to get on with business.

"Bring your horse here, dear," she said firmly. "I think we need a Tiger Prince around here. And I would not mind kicking dirt in the eye of that Mary Archer." She smiled charmingly, but I saw the steel in her eyes.

I have a new ally.

Chapter Twenty-one

I T WAS STRANGE TO drive to another farm after the morning training was done.

Almost as strange as it had been to settle into the boarding stable's tack room, to put my old jumping saddle and some bins of grooming supplies I'd cobbled together from the training barn into a locker, to snap a lock on the closed doors and look around at the other lockers, wondering what sort of tack they held.

Almost as strange as it had been to walk away from Tiger's stall while he ate hay within, already accustomed to eating hay from a pile on the floor instead of from a hay-net hanging from his open stall door, and leave him to the care of strange grooms I didn't know.

Almost as strange as it had been to see his empty stall in the yearling barn, the straw swept out and the buckets removed. A stall stripped clean and left bare—that was the sure sign of a horse that was gone for good. It was what you saw when a horse was sold, or a horse died. It was haunting and lonely, and it made me wince every time I passed it.

Now I was going to see him, and work him, while I was still in a riding sort of mood. Looking for distractions, I'd done some riding during morning training this week, and I'd been on three already this morning. Nothing too crazy, just well-behaved two-year-olds who had already been in training for six months. They were well on their way towards adulthood. They knew how to gallop, how to change their leads (mostly), how to stand in the starting gate without having a panic attack.

(And no one had jumped out of their skins when Mary Archer's horses galloped by in the opposing direction. It was becoming routine, another part of the morning. Those neighbor horses over there, doing the same job we were doing, what of it?—that was how our horses were starting to reason. It was enough to make me stop thinking that she'd moved there just to do me wrong and make my life miserable. After all, there were easier ways for her to do me wrong and make my life miserable, without engaging in real estate transactions and setting up a new training barn.)

If it was strange to drive to another farm, it was stranger still to walk into the barn and see new faces there. Not just new faces— different faces in every way from what I was used to. There were so many other *women,* women in breeches and tall boots or half-chaps, women in bright polo shirts and carrying grooming boxes and jumping saddles, a woman with the buckle of her hard hat dangling below her chin while she fastened up the throat latch on a massive warmblood, as he stood patiently in a set of cross-ties. Women everywhere, because just as males dominated the racing scene, females dominated the showing scene. The estrogen in the barn might have been palpable; I felt nervous, like I was walking into a broodmare pasture at breakfast time. It would be all hooves and teeth until they decided to accept me as one of their own.

I paused in the doorway as the faces turned and saw me, feeling my own face heat up and turn red like a film of a tomato ripening in fast-forward. I felt like I had tumbled back in time, to my teenage years, and it was not a good feeling. I was skulking into the boarding stable hoping none of the mean girls had seen me. My teenage years had not been my glory years, unlike some. I had no wish to revisit them.

It was too late to run away and hide—they'd all seen me. Horses and people alike. The warmblood in the cross-ties pricked his ears and nickered, as if he thought he knew me from somewhere else. He would be embarrassed in a minute when I got closer and he realized he'd been saying hello to the wrong person. Well, at least someone had said *something*.

I picked up my faltering strides and went on into the barn, forcing a smile onto my face, cursing Tiger for his inability to just settle down and work at home. I had my own lovely farm where I didn't have to face any of my social anxiety. Why did he have to drag me back to the drama of my youth?

"Hello!" the woman with the dangling hard-hat buckle said brightly. "You must be the new girl!"

That was me. I was the New Girl. Lucky me! "I'm Alex," I said, not nearly as brightly. The words barely came out, actually. I cleared my throat and tried again, meeting with some moderate success. At least she understood me this time.

"Alex...Whitehall, right?" She came forward to meet me, ducking under the horse's cross-tie, and put out a deerskin-gloved hand, the hide so delicate that she could buckle a bridle while wearing them.

I took the supple deerskin in my own hand and obligingly smiled back at her, studying her all the while. She was tall and thin and young and pretty, with a sweeping golden pony-tail curling around her shoulder, and teeth that were too straight and white to be true. Young and beautiful, was she rich too? I hazarded a side-eyed glance at the horse standing at her shoulder and figured she'd have to be. That was not a cheap piece of horseflesh, and the bridle on his handsome head was marked with the metal stamp of Stubben. The big dark bay stood quietly in the cross-ties, but his gaze was attentive, his eyes intelligent. He was the sort of horse that didn't miss much, and obviously cost a fortune.

"I'm Jean Martin," she said cheerfully, flashing those white teeth at me again. Her teeth had probably cost a fortune, too, I reflected. "We're so glad you're here." She glanced over at the stall, where Tiger was impatiently running his nose up and down the stalls bars, demanding my attention. "And your—uh—*horse.*"

I cocked my head, my smile faltering. Did I read her tone correctly? Was that a snide note there? The warmblood nodded his head vigorously, swinging the cross-ties, and we both took a step away. Mine was backwards. Her's was forwards. I felt like I was already in retreat. "Thanks so much," I replied, just a hint of questioning in my voice. *Are you really implying my Thoroughbred isn't good enough?* "I hope he's been a good boy."

Jean laughed. "Oh, well, racehorses are always a trial, aren't they?"

"What's he doing wrong?" I asked quickly, hackles rising at the deliberate insult. I'd been nice, hadn't I? I'd been perfectly nice!

Jean just shook her head, her smile still sparkling, though it perhaps stretched a bit tightly at the corners. "Oh, of course he's fine. We just don't get too many Thoroughbreds here. You know, since we mainly show. We have a few eventers, but these days, since Elsie doesn't compete any more, we mainly stick to hunters and jumpers. And of course we mainly have warmbloods for that."

"I didn't realize Elsie didn't compete anymore." Somehow none of this had been conveyed to me during the barn tour. Kerri had implied that this was an eventing barn and eventing barns, it seemed, were one of the few places in the riding and showing world where Thoroughbreds were still welcome. Plus there were cross-country jumps everywhere. Plus there was the student who was getting ready to go Prelim...

"Heavens no," Jean tinkled. "She's getting up there, you know. She still does some teaching but not much riding anymore. I ride the farm horses, show and sell, you know. Elsie only rides her own horse—and he's a Trakehner, imported from Germany...she rides him Prix St. Georges. Isn't that something! At her age! She used to ride Thoroughbreds too, when she was younger...but of course she wants a quieter, more well-behaved sort of horse now. And it's paid off. Not many women riding at her level in their senior years, you know?"

I murmured something to convey how deeply impressed I was with Elsie's golden years of riding, while valiantly trying to cover up my disappointment. A hunter/jumper barn, with this princess running around flashing those fake smiles? That's not what I had signed up for at all. I was nearly twitching with my need to get away from the lovely plastic-featured Jean and slip into the security and privacy of Tiger's stall, and I'd only been here five minutes. I had to survive multiple *months* of this character, to get Tiger to the Thoroughbred Makeover?

And what was I going to do with him after that? Take him back to Cotswold and let him dissolve into a maniac again?

I gave my head a little shake to straighten out my thoughts again. Anything after the Thoroughbred Makeover didn't matter yet. Only what came before. "I'm sure you'd like to get out there and ride," I began, trying to slip past Jean and make my escape.

Unfortunately, it seemed Elsie had appointed Jean to make sure I was comfortable as a boarder at Roundtree. "Let's just make sure you know everybody first!" she announced, and took me by the arm. I bit back a sigh and allowed her to steer me towards the center of the barn, where a few cross-ties were set back alongside the tack rooms and office.

Jean's first order of business was to introduce me to the other boarders who were there in the middle of the day—Kelly, Maggie, Chrissy, and Melody. If I hadn't expected to encounter other boarders at eleven o'clock on a Thursday morning, I tried not to let it on, while secretly I wondered what *their* husbands were doing for a living. I supposed they could all be married to racehorse trainers, too. I didn't ask, instead trying for a joke with those matching names. People just loved jokes. They'd think I was funny and we'd all get on famously.

"Nice to meet you, Kelly, Maggie, Chrissy, Melody." I turned to Jean. "I'm surprised *you* don't go by Jeanie."

Crickets.

Jean just looked a little confused, as did Maggie, Chrissy, and Melody, but then Kelly snorted with laughter. I threw her a grateful smile.

"My husband said the same thing once," Kelly laughed. She was round and middle-aged, her short brown hair run through with gray. "I told him to hush up making fun of our names, because we're a beautiful poem when we ride together. *He* said the best poems don't rhyme. Men. If it isn't on the golf course, it doesn't mean a thing to him. You married?"

Not a racetrack wife, then. But I liked her rougher style; Jean's ice-cold beauty and precise speech was making me so jumpy I wasn't sure I'd be able to buckle on Tiger's halter right now. "I am, and my husband would say the exact same thing," I agreed.

"Oh, haha, that's very funny," Jean said out of the blue, and Kelly and I both turned very slowly to look at her. Jean remained oblivious. She was ready to move on. "Let's go over the arena rules!" she announced cheerfully, and took me off to point out the arenas' finer points and explain that we rode left-rein to left-rein, and riding lessons took precedence in the jumping arena, and faster horses should stay to the inside. The usual. The things we learned in the kindergarten of riding lessons.

"It seems pretty straight-forward," I said when she was done. "Like the other barns I've ridden at. I've been riding since I was a kid," I added, so that she understood I wasn't going to flub up all the normal courtesies riders paid one another, just because I was some racetrack hick. "I evented and—"

"But your horse is *very* green, isn't he?" Jean interrupted. "I hope you won't be having any trouble with him. If he's bad-tempered, you might want to ride him when the arena's empty. Just because so many of us are preparing for shows, and we wouldn't benefit from having a worked-up horse while we're training."

I blinked. "Of course. He's green, but he's not bad." *That's only half a lie.* "I won't get in anyone's way."

"I'm sure we'd all appreciate that." Jean gazed out over the arena. "This is a small farm, but we have big careers ahead of us. I'm showing Marcelle in the High Jumpers all through HITS, and hoping to get into our first Grand Prix class by the end of the festival. He's a very talented jumper. Elsie says he's got the most potential she's ever seen. Did you know she trained in Germany and France? And competed internationally? She knows what she's talking about."

I muttered that I had, although the truth was that while I knew very little about Elsie, I was finding I was loathe to let Jean think she knew a single thing more than I did. The teenage rival instinct was strong.

We went back to the barn so that Jean could take out Marcelle to school in the jumping arena. She was nice enough as she took her horse's halter and cross-ties off, and her smile, as she expressed hope once again that Tiger and I would not disturb them in their schooling, was sweet as sugar.

I went into Tiger's stall, where my retired racehorse was blissfully crunching through a pile of hay, and buried my face in his neck.

Which, I thought a little later, pulling strands of mane from my sweater, was exactly what I had done when I was a kid, once the mean girls were through with me.

Fortunately, though, Tiger seemed happy, and that was all that mattered.

Or so I kept telling myself, as I avoided doing anything that involved leaving his stall, including fetching his grooming kit and getting him cleaned up for a ride.

I waited until Jean had warmed up Marcelle and was taking him around the jumping course before I even bothered tacking up Tiger. He'd never been cross-tied, so I looped his lead-rope in a quick-release knot around one of the stall bars, and groomed him in his stall. If the other women bustling around the barn thought that was weird, none of them said so. I saw a horse walk by once, his hooves clopping on the concrete aisle, but Tiger's stall was near the end and the cross-ties and tack room were in the middle of the barn, so I was largely left alone. I had plenty of free time to imagine all the things they might be whispering about me, of course.

Tiger was content to be tacked in his stall, as he'd been groomed and saddled and doctored in his stall for his entire life anyway, and by the time I had my hard hat buckled and my vest zipped up, he was nearly asleep, dozing against the slack in his rope. I had to give his head a little wiggle to lift it up before I could put the bridle on. "I like this version of Tiger," I whispered, fastening up the noseband and throat-latch. "Could this carry out to the arena as well?" There was no round pen here, and he didn't know how to lunge. I was going to have to mount up cold, hoping that the foundation work back at my own farm was good enough.

I took a deep breath, said a little prayer to the horse gods, and slid Tiger's door open. He followed me into the aisle with an eager step, ready for adventure.

Everyone seemed to have gone out to the arena by now. The barn was deserted except for a groom sitting on a hay bale, working her way through a Subway sandwich. I paused as we came up to her, and she politely put down her sandwich and smiled at me. She looked like she was about sixteen, tan and pony-tailed and basically a younger version of me. "I like your horse," she said. Her southern accent twanged like a banjo.

"Thank you!" That was the first time anyone here had complimented Tiger, and it made me feel warm inside. Behind me, Tiger commenced rubbing his face on my shoulder, as if to make sure the groom didn't make the mistake of thinking he was polite or anything. I shoved him off. "I'm Alex," I added.

"Tanya." She held out a dirty hand and I shook it with my own dirty hand.

"You're not one of the *ee's,*" I said, grinning, and she looked mystified. "Your name doesn't end in ee," I explained hastily, lest she think I was insane. "Like Kelly, or Elsie, like everyone else—" I pointed out the end of the barn aisle to the arena, where the women were riding in companionable little pairs.

Tanya figured it out. "Oh, that's right. You're not the only one's noticed that. Elsie thinks it's funny, the two girls that run her barn, me and Jean..."

"Jean helps run the barn?" Somehow I'd missed that.

"Barn manager," Tanya said, nodding. "And show rider. Elsie doesn't show much anymore. Jean goes to the shows, rides the sales horses. I stay here and clean up after everyone."

"Ah." That explained Jean's propriety air.

"She's very good," Tanya went on. "But stuck up, if you don't mind my saying so."

"I don't. So, do you ride?"

"Yup! I'm Elsie's working student. Going to be an eventer someday. Just jumping Novice right now, but Elsie might let me move up next fall." Tanya looked delighted at the thought. She grinned. "My parents both ride Western. They think I'm crazy, but I'm going to show them. Jean thinks I'm crazy too, because she thinks I ought to be show-jumping like her. But I like a good gallop."

"Good for you. Galloping is where it's at, but showing your parents is pretty awesome too." I got Tanya's ambition and the way it was colored a little with proving her loved ones wrong. There wasn't anything mean-spirited about that. Showing my parents I wasn't crazy and could make it in the racing game had been a big motivator for me, too.

And look at me now, ma and pa! Standing in a boarding stable, about to go out and ride in a dressage arena, just like you wanted. Life was very confusing sometimes.

Tiger, bored of waiting through an interminable Girl Conversation, suddenly gave me another massive head-butt, which nearly sent me flying into Tanya and her hay bale. Tanya carefully moved her Subway sandwich to one side, reminding me that she probably didn't enjoy much of a lunch break with someone like Jean in charge. Time to let her get back to that sub.

"I better be going. Enjoy your lunch!" I wrestled Tiger's head around, pulled my breeches up where he'd pushed them down over my hip bone, and dragged him out to the dressage arena's in-gate. The arena was regulation-size and complete with its dressage letters marked around the edges, but it had a full-size three-board fence around it, not just a little white plastic chain like you had at the horse shows. For *that,* I was grateful. I wasn't sure Tiger would recognize the boundaries presented by a tiny chain four inches off the ground. He'd barely recognized the boundary presented by a six-foot solid pine wall, back in the round pen.

I paused by the gate, looking around, and spotted a wooden mounting block nearby. I was grateful for that, too. Long accustomed to getting a leg-up, I still wasn't steady on mounting Tiger from the ground, and I didn't really trust him to stand still while I made the attempt. He was already pulling his head around, looking this way and that, fascinated by the other horses in the jumping arena, by the leaping Marcelle and the quietly trotting and cantering workmates. It wouldn't do for me to mess up my mounting and be swinging around from the side of the saddle in front of all those riders—and Jean.

"You've been here three days," I told Tiger quietly, leading him up to the mounting block. "Plenty of time to get used to seeing the other horses out here. And now all you have to do is be nice and let me get on and take you for a little walk. That's it! Can you do that without embarrassing me?"

By now, Tiger had seen the mounting block and decided that it was something he could do without. He snorted his way up to the scary wooden stairs-to-nowhere, blowing his nostrils alongside it, then lifting his head and turning up his lip in a flehmen face. I sighed and let him do his thing, even though the giggles I could hear from the jumping arena had to be directed at us.

After a minute or two of inspection, Tiger consented to stand alongside the mounting block, although he still cocked his head so that he could keep a wary eye on it. *You never can tell with mounting blocks*, he was thinking. I maneuvered myself over to the steps, praying he wouldn't take off while I had such a tenuous grasp on the reins, and climbed up.

Tiger sidestepped away and turned so that he was facing me.

"Goddammit, Tiger," I told him, and he snorted again, his ears pricked as he waited for me to do something normal, like get off the weird stairs-to-nowhere and take him someplace for a gallop. He was probably wondering where the track was at this crazy place.

I hopped down and walked him in a circle around the mounting block. "Now stand," I said firmly when I had him positioned once again next to the block, and climbed up again. I reached out a toe towards the stirrup...

...Tiger sidestepped away and buried his muzzle in my chest.

"God*dammit,* Tiger!"

I led him up the mounting block again and didn't even get my foot in the air before he had swung around and was blinking at me innocently.

"Goddammit, Tiger," I sighed.

We tried once more, and this time Tiger waited until my foot was in the stirrup to swing his haunches around to face me. It was go-time.

With a lot of luck and very little grace, I found myself in the saddle even as Tiger spun around in a hard circle, trying to figure out what on earth I was doing. By the time I had my right foot in the stirrup, he had accepted that I was mounted up and was ready for business. What he didn't notice was that I was holding the reins, one-handed, at the buckle. No problem for Tiger: he took off at a brisk canter, head held high, heading away from the deserted dressage arena and directly towards the hustle and bustle of the jumping arena, where Marcelle was still leaping around the course, the perfect Jean sitting chilly in the saddle.

Chapter Twenty-two

WHEN TIGER BURST INTO a canter, I *shouldn't* have been thrown wildly off-balance. After all, riding horses that bolt from halt to gallop is kind of my thing. Problem was, I still wasn't used to the broad expanse of the jumping saddle, which seemed to do more to mask my horse's movements than anything else. In an exercise saddle, I always felt like I was practically riding bareback, and it was very hard for a horse to surprise me when I could feel every twitch of every muscle. The jumping saddle, with all its flaps and pads and blocks, gave Tiger a real edge when it came to throwing surprise moves.

I have to admit, and this pains me, that I flailed like a beginner when Tiger took off. I fell backwards against the cantle, my legs shooting out wildly in front of me, and it wasn't until I got my heels down and used the stirrups as leverage that I was able to reach forward with my right hand and grasp the reins just at Tiger's withers. I slid my left hand forward from the buckle until it met my other hand, then dropped them both to his rising and falling withers and sank the weight of my upper body onto my fists.

Instantly I was up above Tiger in a familiar spot, the modified two-point position of the exercise rider. Once he felt me there, he moved into a bigger and bolder gallop, pushing his mouth down hard against the bit, confident that I'd hold him there and let him counterbalance, confident that he was doing the right thing.

I'd be lying if I said I didn't want to just stay there in that moment, in that stride, because it felt so perfect and right. It was where Tiger and I had always had our meeting of the minds, where we felt most at home. It was our happy place, that balanced gallop. Feeling it again, I didn't want to give it all up and learn something new. I wanted everything to stay the same. I knew that Tiger felt the same.

That was when I heard Jean's angry shout, and realized how rapidly we were coming up on the jumping arena, and how astonished the horses inside were by the sight of the new horse galloping towards them.

Shocked into action, I stood straight up and reined back as hard as I could, my boots jammed against the stirrups, my hands high, and Tiger opened his mouth and shook his head and tried to dig down against me for a little bucking action, but I was the more determined of the two of us. Mortification can be a compelling motivator. Tiger wasn't embarrassed; quite the opposite, *he* felt like a million bucks, and so he was gracious in defeat, dropping down to a choppy trot and then a bouncy walk just as we came up to the arena.

It was a quick recovery, but not quick enough. In the arena, Jean was out of the saddle, picking up one of Marcelle's hooves. I saw a few scattered jump poles a few feet away. *He must have spooked and hit the fence.* Now I was going to catch it.

Marcelle, however, wasn't paying any attention to Jean's ministrations as she sought for a sore spot in his foreleg. All five horses in the jumping arena, Marcelle included, were far too distracted by Tiger and me. They regarded us with wide eyes and pricked ears. They couldn't have looked more astonished if their jaws had dropped open—as some of their riders' jaws had done. The other four riders had pulled up along the rail and were bunched together, watching the show Tiger and I had put on for them. No one seemed to have noticed that Marcelle had taken a bad fence, or that Jean thought he was injured.

"That was *beautiful*," Kelly told me admiringly. "If my horse took off like that I'd probably go right over his ass and hit the ground. You just sort of sprung into it."

"I couldn't do that," one of the others, Maggie or Chrissy or Melody, agreed, and there were nods.

Well, how about that.

"That was exactly what I was talking about," Jean said coldly, walking Marcelle up. The warmblood was hot despite the cool gray day, sweat foaming up on his neck, but his walk was even and smooth, without a trace of a head-bob. He hadn't hurt himself when he'd smacked the jump rails; something told me that was just Jean's theatrical way of showing everyone what a danger Tiger was to the rest of them. "You have to be able to control that horse, or I'm going to ask you nicely not to ride him when I'm schooling. I can't afford for Marcelle to go lame because your *racehorse* can't behave."

Tiger was now acting like the proverbial old sheep, of course. I felt bad that the horse had spooked, but Tiger going for a little unscheduled gallop was hardly the most alarming thing Marcelle would see at the show-grounds. HITS was a major horse show festival that drew hundreds, if not thousands, of horses to one Ocala training center, where they all stewed together in a constant foment of spooking, worrying, bolting, and shying. Their warm-up areas were downright terrifying even to me, and I'd galloped racehorses on some pretty crowded racetracks. "That was a first-time accident, and I'm sorry. But seriously? If your horse is going to spook just because another horse gallops by, something tells me he isn't ready for the show-ring after all. Some days, it's like watching a carousel of loose horses go around you."

Jean's beautiful face curdled into something fearsome to behold. "This horse has won more championships than *that* horse has won races. And I don't expect that will change any just because you think you can teach him to pop a few fences. I know why you're here, Alex. We've all heard all about you. You think you can fix your reputation by getting one of your beat-up old racehorses to a show? Not likely. And you aren't going to be welcome in the show-ring just because no one wants you at the racetrack anymore."

Of course she knows. My toes curled in my boots, but my face stayed strong. You couldn't let a bully knock you down on the very first day of school. Anyway, I was plenty mean, myself. Kerri said so. I asked Tiger to walk on, and we strolled right into that jumping arena, Tiger's eyes bright and his head high.

We moseyed right over to Jean and Marcelle. I saw her fingers tighten on her reins, as if she thought I might just keep walking and crash into her horse. I let her think so at first, but thought better of it and reined up a few feet away. I rested the reins on Tiger's neck. He stood quietly, ears waggling. *Bless you, Tiger.*

"Jean," I said lightly, "You might want to do a little fact-checking before you start quoting anything bad that's been said about me. Because it's all been disproved. My hands are clean."

Jean smirked, though her grip on the reins remained tense. "Whatever. I don't care about you and I don't care about your racetrack trash. Just don't let it get in *my* way, and we'll both be fine." She tugged at Marcelle's reins, her shiny boots deep in the arena's red clay, and then they were walking away, back to the barn. I watched them for a few strides. Marcelle's gait was still even. That was a mercy.

I looked over at the peanut gallery—four women on four geldings, all looking most impressed with the goings-on. "I really didn't intend to have so much excitement on my first day here," I dead-panned, and Kelly burst into gales of laughter. Melody, Maggie, and Chrissy paused a moment, unsure of which side they were on, and then decided to laugh along.

I grinned and waved and asked Tiger to walk on. We made our way around the arena, pausing to inspect the jumps as we went, and letting him take a look at the other horses when we met up on our travels. He was a good boy, interested in everything he saw, but not spooking or silly, and that lifted my heart—at least, in part. The part that wasn't heavy and disappointed in the way things had turned out—the scandal that wouldn't die, the mere fact that I'd had to bring him to another barn, the presence of a high school mean girl like Jean. There were very large and unpleasant flies in the ointment, and I couldn't ignore any of them.

Chapter Twenty-three

I CAME BACK TO the farm after our first ride with one determination: I *had* to avoid Jean.

Life was too complicated already, with the Archer mini-derby going on next door every morning, and Alexander preparing to enter Luna into an allowance race I had picked out for her, but would not be allowed to attend. Adding more work to the tab, a big gray colt had been sent to us from a friend with the training notation "needs serious help with the starting gate." Meanwhile, the piles of hate mail and death threats were still flooding my mailboxes, both the virtual one and the physical one that stood at the end of the driveway. Each day the mail-lady (I mean, mail carrier, of course) stuffed the big mailbox chock-full of thin white envelopes, my name scrawled upon them in a thousand different scripts.

Life was too complicated already. I couldn't take on some high school nonsense at the boarding stable, where the pretty girl didn't want me in her way.

I didn't even know why she had such a problem with me. When pressed, Kelly had shrugged and said that maybe it had something to do with my reputation as a racehorse trainer. "Not the crazy stuff that's been going around lately. The good stuff. You know, you're pretty well-known around here for doing something not a lot of women do, and doing it well." She was hosing off her big liver chestnut gelding, Payton, after a ride. It was a chilly day and the steam was rising from his back and the puddles in the wash-rack. "Jean's just getting started with her career, and she's probably afraid you'll threaten her standing with Elsie somehow."

It took me a moment to bite back a laugh. Kelly *couldn't* be serious. "If I'm well-known around here, it's a surprise to me."

"Oh, everyone knows who you are. You were in that magazine article, and then there's been this whole abuse scandal, but you've been exonerated by everyone but the real crazies, so that's not a problem. And like I said, most of the women here are like Jean and Elsie, show riders. Or like me," she added with a rueful smile. "Taking riding lessons and hoping to get a little better before we get too old to ride. You went out there and made a career for yourself. Most of us wish we'd been brave enough to do that when we were still young enough. You've got a reputation, all right, like Jean said—but it's really for being brave and taking chances, not for abusing horses."

"That's so nice of you," I said, but I hardly believed people really thought of me like that. Or that anyone thought of me at all. "But even so...I haven't shown a horse in years. If Jean thinks I want to give up my career and steal hers instead, she's just plain crazy. I never even hinted that I wanted to do anything more than retrain Tiger. For my own personal horse!"

Kelly aimed a jet of water under Payton's tail. The cold surprised him and he hunched up his back, tucking his hindquarters underneath his belly. She laughed. "Would you hand me a sweat scraper?"

I dug a rubber-bladed squeegee out of the wire bucket hanging from the wash-rack wall and handed it over, accepting the hose in return. I turned off the water spigot while she got to work squeezing the excess water from Payton's dark coat. "He's gorgeous. I wish more Thoroughbreds came in liver chestnut."

"I wish they'd call it something else," Kelly grunted. "Someone told me in Germany they call it dark fox."

"That's pretty. Let's use that instead."

The dark fox warmblood swung his sopping wet tail through the air, throwing a stream of cold water droplets over Kelly. She fixed him with an evil glare, which he ignored with aplomb. "He always does that," Kelly fumed. "I know he does it on purpose. Elsie says horses do all sorts of rude things on purpose. She says it's all in their sense of humor. Jean says they don't know they're doing it and not to give horses too many human characteristics. But I think I like Elsie's explanation better."

I happened to think Elsie's way, too. Tiger's way of shoving his head against me so that I nearly fell over, for example. He loved to see me flailing and trying to keep my balance, and there was nothing I could do, no smack I could mete out with my puny little human hands, that was going to stop him from having his laugh. "The only thing you can do is stay one step ahead of them," I suggested. "Watch." I stepped up and took Payton's thick tail in two hands, one just below the tailbone and one closer to its banged-straight tip. "You take it like this and you give it a hard *swish*—" I demonstrated, and the rest of the water in Payton's tail went arcing through the wash-rack. "There. You're safe now. It's practically dry."

Kelly, standing by Payton's head, raised her eyebrows. "I've never seen that before."

"Racetrack trick." I grinned at her. Then someone strolled up behind her, and my grin faded.

Kelly saw my face change and turned around. "Hello Jean," she said cheerfully when she saw our visitor. "That was some ride you had on Marcelle today."

"He's *fine,* thank you for asking." Jean's voice was chilly when she spoke to Kelly, but her eyes were on me. I realized I was still holding Payton's tail and dropped it. The damp hair fell to just below his fetlocks.

"We all know he's fine, Jean," Kelly pointed out. "We saw him walking up to the barn without a single head-bob. All he did was hit a few jump poles, it's not like he fell into a ditch or something. Plus...you wouldn't have ridden him today if he wasn't fine after yesterday." She resumed her work with the sweat scraper, sluicing water from Payton's dark coat, as if nothing was going on, but I could see her face was flushing. It was probably not in anyone's best interest to go against Jean. I wondered why on earth she was doing it for me.

"I'm glad he's okay," I blurted, anxious to make peace between everyone. "It was a silly mistake; Tiger thought that he knew exactly what I wanted. It's hard to make a horse understand that everything he knows is wrong." I laughed, hoping to get the same from Jean. But her face stayed hard. Only Kelly obliged me with a tinny little chuckle.

"Keep away from my rides." Jean spat out the words, her voice dripping with contempt. "We don't need you and your racetrack tricks around here."

She strode off, not bothering to stomp, not bothering to flip her pony tail, not bothering to give me one last contemptuous look over her shoulders. I could read boss-mare body language like that, no problem. She was done with me. I wasn't worth her time.

As far as she was concerned, I had been given my orders, and I would obey.

Kelly put the sweat scraper back in the wire basket and brushed hair back from her face with dirty fingers. She smiled at me weakly. "Ordinarily, I'd say, don't give in to bullies."

"But this time?"

"She's usually done riding by two, two-thirty." Kelly picked up Payton's lead shank and snapped it onto his halter, preparing to take him back to his stall. I picked up a towel to dry his feet, then set it down again; they didn't do that here. "If I were you, I'd save my rides for after that. I think I might for a while, too."

⤐⤐⤐ ⬾⬾⬾

"So it isn't going so well." I concluded my story with a sigh and a smile, and sipped a little more wine. Then a lot more wine.

Alexander considered this while he worked his way through a mouthful of eggplant lasagna. On cold nights, we pulled out the heavy stuff from the freezer. Comfort food, to warm us up after the evening chores were done and we were chilled through. Floridians had thin blood, and I was a native. Alexander had lived here so long he was nearly so. When the temperature got below seventy, I started piling on the sweaters. When the temperature got below fifty, I started making excuses to stay in bed under my feather duvet. It was supposed to freeze tonight, and I was sitting directly underneath a heating vent in response.

"It's no more than I would have expected," Alexander admitted after he'd carefully chewed and swallowed his lasagna and then taken a thoughtful sip of wine and swallowed that as well. "Those horse show people are crazy."

All that thought for a statement so obvious? *"All* horse people are crazy."

"That's so. But at least with racetrackers, you know the motivations. Money. The life they've always lived. A combination of the two. People trying to make a living jumping horses over fences and collecting satin ribbons...what's their motivation?"

I shrugged. "What was my motivation when I was a kid? I loved horses."

"Kids don't count." Alexander waved his hand, dismissing all children. "Kids aren't running the businesses or paying the bills. It's the adults that fascinate me. The sheer amount of time and money they're willing to pay for a hobby."

"It's not a hobby for Jean. She's Elsie's *rider*. The sales horses have to show and win in order to increase their value. It's her career."

"But they're hobbies to the women who buy the horses, right? For tens of thousands of dollars?"

"Probably. For the most part." I didn't really know, but I figured most professionals weren't buying horses that already had tons of show miles and the price to match. So that left the hobbyist, someone like Kelly, whose husband was a doctor and could afford her horse showing habit, to buy made horses like the ones Jean was trying to produce. "I see your point," I conceded. "Why would Jean consider me a threat though?"

"Oh, someone like Jean considers everyone young and talented a threat. Just avoid her, like this other woman said. Concentrate on Tiger. The barn politics need not concern you." Alexander went back to his eggplant lasagna with renewed determination, confident as always that all of my problems were imaginary and so easily dealt with.

I went back to my own plate as well. Let it never be said that Alex Whitehall went off her feed when she was worried. I tore off a chunk of bread from the fat loaf in the center of the table and doused it with a glutton's portion of Irish butter. Butter to soothe my feelings, butter to take my mind off the fresh collection of death threats I had retrieved from the mailbox on my way back this afternoon, butter to distract me from Jean's vitriol.

After dinner I went down to the office to look at the letters. Alexander said to throw them into the recycling without opening them, but Alexander was made of tougher stuff than I was, and less curiosity as well. I had to know what they said, who they were from, who was behind them.

So far, most of the letters had been from CASH. They must have been banking the entire future of their unknown organization on my destruction, because they had grabbed the story with their teeth and weren't letting go. The letters were signed by different names, and came from different addresses, but they were printed form letters, straight from a website or an email being passed around in the comfortable protest grounds of the Internet.

Thanks, Internet for making it so easy to hate without reason, I thought, sifting through the letters, opening the envelopes at random to let the paper slide out, the vicious words marching down the falling pages like rows of mechanical soldiers. It was so easy to spread outrage. You didn't have to do anything more than open an email, skim the contents and grow angry, and follow the simple call-to-action instructions. Copy and paste the letter below and mail it to the offending party. Control C, Control V, Control P—three commands and you were halfway there. Lick a stamp, and you were part of a movement, you were making change happen, you were the voice for the voiceless animals. Who cares if you destroyed a human life or two? *They* were the enemies here, after all!

We will not rest until you get what you deserve, you coward. Those horses deserve better than what you and the other monsters who run the horse racing industry dish out to them. These noble creatures are not your slaves, to be beaten until they run and then discarded to die when they are finished...

"Of course they aren't, you goddamn idiots," I told the letter. "And if you knew a single thing about me, you'd know that's *not me.*"

I swept the whole pile of letters towards the edge of the desk and the recycling bin. They overflowed the bin and settled across the office floor like an avalanche sliding down the precipices of a mountain.

They really *were* like snowflakes, too, almost completely alike but for the details—the slant of letters and numbers that scrawled out my name, the different stamps, the different postmarks. Proving to me that my enemies were scattered across the country, and what a relief that was, of course.

Chapter Twenty-four

"WANNA HEAR A FUN story?"

Kerri, up to her eyeballs in leaping, bucking, kicking, farting, biting baby horse, grunted in response.

I rubbed my nice quiet broodmare's star, sending a flurry of white hairs down to my black boots, and thought happy thoughts about being the boss and not the assistant. "So it turns out that Elsie's barn manager hates me and Thoroughbreds and me and Thoroughbreds but mostly me."

Kerri wedged her knee underneath the foal's furry abdomen and pinned the little monster to the wall. The foal, a vicious little filly that had me entranced with her constant fury since her birth twenty-four hours ago, squealed in outrage. "We should make her a gift of this one," Kerri panted.

"She'd feed it to the crows, and not just for those socks." I eyed the filly's four white stockings. "Flashy little snot. But I digress. She already hates me; I don't have to give her a demon filly. She thinks that I'm a piece of horse-abusing trash and I'm only gearing up Tiger for the Thoroughbred Makeover because I'm trying to save my reputation."

"Well, that's half-true."

I frowned and ran my fingers through the spiky little jungle of whiskers that grew thickly over the broodmare's muzzle. She was ignoring me, her long floppy ears fastened on her wild child in the corner of the stall. The vet was coming down the aisle, clanking along like a pack-mule with her buckets and her bottles and her needles and her syringes. Shots and bloodwork, that was how we welcomed babies into the world at my farm. Old mama Seastar here knew it well. This was her sixth foal, and every one had been just as wild as she was docile. "Were you crazy at the racetrack, mama?" I asked her softly, as Kerri cursed at the floundering filly, scrabbling her soft little hooves against the stall wall. "Is that how you won all those races, huh?"

Kerri quieted the filly again, her right hand tight on the little tail, her left hand locked around the skinny neck. "So she believes the hype from CASH and them. What about the rest of the barn? I know Elsie doesn't."

"I don't think she's well-liked. But I've only met a few of the boarders. Most of them seemed kind of scared of her. Was she riding or anything at the barn when you were riding there?"

"What's her name again?"

"Jean. Tall and blonde and thin. Young. Scary. Too scary for how young she is, really. Like it's something she has studied and mastered."

Kerri thought, then shook her head. "Don't think so. Elsie used to show all her own horses. I guess she's slowing down with age."

"Like you, huh mama?" I tickled the mare's chin again, but she kept her attention focused on her filly. Old mares knew their jobs, and they knew our jobs too. A maiden mare would have been

254 NATALIE KELLER REINERT

standing on her hind legs right now, demanding that Kerri unhand her precious little prize. Seastar knew that first comes baby, then comes the vet. And the vet, and the vet, and the vet.

She also knew that if she waited it out, she'd spend most of the next year out in the pasture, grazing with her herd. Seastar was a wise mare, and she'd teach the little runt in the corner to behave, with teeth if necessary, so that someday she'd be a wise old broodmare too. Kerri, lacking teeth big enough and sharp enough to give the filly a lesson, was simply holding her against the wall.

The vet slid the door open and came in, a syringe already between her teeth. "Oh good," she mumbled around the plastic wrapping. "Hang on tight. I know this mama's baby is always a problem." She gave Seastar an affectionate pat on the neck as she passed us.

"Your demon babies are known far and wide," I told Seastar approvingly. "You bring honor to our farm."

"Where's last year's?" Kerri asked. "The bay with the spotty ermine on her hind? She'd been weaned by the time we came back from Saratoga, but I never make it up to the yearling barn." It didn't sound like a worthwhile excuse for never walking into a barn that was just across the farm, but I knew what she meant. Working in the training barn and the broodmare barn didn't leave much room for visiting yearlings. The constant needs of mares, foals, and horses in training was a definite contrast to the yearlings, who went over to the yearling barn and its two big pastures after weaning and stayed there, grazing and growing, until, one-by-one, they were led over to the training barn to begin their careers. Last year's Seastar foal would be out there in the pasture now, still at least seven or eight months from my attention.

"Just hanging in the yearling pasture," I said with a shrug. "We should go visit, see how she's doing. She's probably leveling out nicely now." All of Seastar's babies had been exemplary in training, in contrast to the insanity of their babyhood.

"All done!" the vet announced, stepping away from the struggling filly with a vial of rich red horse blood. "I'll check the blood cell counts and make sure but...she *looks* pretty healthy."

To demonstrate her extreme good health, the filly reared up, and Kerri began illustrating her knowledge of racetrack cursing. The vet jumped out and closed the stall door, and Kerri stepped back to let the bucking, plunging little horse-demon fling herself away from the nasty stupid human. The filly did a circuit of the big foaling stall, grunting and flapping her brush of a tail, before she went in for a nose-dive straight into mama's udder. Seastar pinned her ears and lifted a hoof warningly, but her baby didn't pay her any mind. The stall filled with urgent sucking sounds from beneath the broodmare.

"Sorry mama," I told Seastar, slipping off her halter. "I'll bring you some alfalfa to make up for it."

The vet was already climbing into her truck, talking into her bluetooth. Kerri went to the hose outside the barn and gave her hands and arms a good once-over, wincing at the freezing cold spring water. It was another chilly February day, the sky ice-blue, a few traces of wispy cirrus far to the north. "That filly is going to leave me black-and-blue," she fumed. "Next one, you hold."

"Yeah, okay." I could wrangle a foal with the best of them...but none of the others would be as bad as Seastar's. I felt a momentary pang of guilt at making Kerri deal with the little bugger. *Bad boss.* But, well, she wanted to run her own farm someday...she had to be able to handle the bad as well as the good. I smiled to myself, already reassured that I'd made the right decision on passing the rotten foal off to her. I'd do it again in a few days, when the foaling heat diarrhea settled in and baby needed her bottom washed a few times a day. Ah, foaling season. A magical time. "So tell me what I'm supposed to do, Kerri."

"About what?"

"About everyone in the horse world thinking I'm evil?"

"I thought we agreed we were ignoring everyone in the horse world. I mean, we've seen evil. We've been to Otter Creek bush track and we've gone up against Mary Archer."

This was true. The little illegal racing ring we had discovered last fall was probably just as dangerous for a failing racehorse as dumping them in the swamps. "And both times we've gone up against Mary Archer we've won," I mused.

"We're unstoppable!" Kerri dead-panned. She turned off the spigot and sat down on a folding chair by the barn door. "I think you already have your game plan right. Beat them at their own game by winning the Thoroughbred Makeover. Stick to that plan. Ignore that crazy Jean person. Show up late, when she's gone. When they're all gone. And don't forget, Elsie believes you, and it's her barn. You're not going to get kicked out or anything. Concentrate on Tiger."

Chapter Twenty-five

I CONCENTRATED ON TIGER.

It wasn't easy at first. Alexander was always disappearing for two days at a time, driving down to south Florida to run a horse, staying overnight at the beach condo, then returning the next afternoon full of excitement (if there was a win) or morose grumbling and introspection (if there was a hard loss). Luckily, most of the time there were wins, or at least places and shows. My horses, who had been solid workmen at Saratoga, were turning into superstars at Gulfstream. As February began to wane and March grew larger on the horizon, Alexander and I were both thinking the same thing.

Personal Best. Three-year-old colt. The first Saturday in May. The thoughts invaded when I should have been thinking of Tiger, or when I should have been concentrating on getting that stupid gray colt into the starting gate without tearing the thing down, or when I should have been paying attention to traffic while driving to town, or when I should have been sleeping.

Of course, it was so silly, I told myself in more lucid moments. It was silly to think that our chestnut colt was *that* good. "I mean,

I love him, but the Kentucky Derby? We're just getting carried away now," I told Tiger, slipping the bit between his teeth on a blustery spring afternoon. A big cold front had blown through the day before with wind and lightning and rain, and left us gleaming blue skies, washed clean and shiny, framing a brilliant golden sun without a trace of heat in its laughing rays. The temperature was in the fifties; the wind gusts made it feel closer to forty degrees. It might as well have been a blizzard as far as I was concerned, Florida-bred and Florida-blooded. But Tiger, like most horses, thought the frigid air was a treat. He threw his head as I led him out of the stall and danced a little in the barn aisle, his steel-shod hooves ringing on the concrete.

In the office next to the tack room, a yellow light glowed through the door's window. I led Tiger right on past hoping that no one would come out and begin a conversation or start asking questions. Elsie and Jean were closeted in there, I knew; I'd seen them go inside while I was hiding in the tack room, waiting for them to go away. I had found through trial and error that Jean more often than not finished her riding by one and was usually gone after that. Then there was a quiet period until five thirty before the evening riders showed up to take out their horses or take a riding lesson.

I tried to be at the barn to ride Tiger between two and four, no earlier and no later, and managed to avoid everyone most days, even Kelly, with whom I'd gotten along so well. I missed her cheerful conversation, but I'd seen the nervousness on her face after she'd stood up to Jean for me. She knew then she was creating trouble for herself. I'd seen barn politics go too far before; boarders got thrown out, cruel tricks were played on horses. I wouldn't put it past Jean to bang a horse's tail above the hocks if she thought it would teach someone a lesson. I'd met her kind before.

Well, if Jean wanted to be Queen Bee at Roundtree, that was fine by me. I was only here for Tiger. Ninety minutes a day, six days a week, at most. Let her rule the roost all the rest of the time. I'd stay out of her way, as she'd commanded me to in that cold voice of hers. In two more months' time I needed to have Tiger ready to win the Thoroughbred Makeover, and after that, maybe I'd just bring him back to Cotswold, maybe stick him up in the half-empty stallion barn after all. Even if Alexander got his wish and turned Personal Best and Virtue and Vice into new stallions, they had years more racing to do. (He'd shut up about Kevin Wallace and wouldn't tell me if he was still trying to do business with the guy).

"I *hope* that's the case, anyway," I told Tiger as we exited the barn and his hooves quietly padded on the mulch path leading to the arenas. "I miss them, but I don't want either of them back in a hurry." Tiger flicked his ears at me, listening to my hushed tones with interest, then turned them forward again, looking out at the tossing trees, the scattering leaves, the jump standards that had been blown right over in the gusting wind.

I eyed those flattened jump standards myself. I'd been planning on riding him in the jumping arena, criss-crossing and circling around the jumps to add a little variety to his day. Tiger got bored easily, just as he had in training on the track. There, he'd acted out with sunfishes and bucking, and if he got even close to unseating me, everyone had a good laugh. Here, if anyone caught sight of his nonsense, there'd be widespread panic because Alex couldn't control that crazy racehorse. I wasn't here to perpetuate bad-racehorse stereotypes.

If we were ever going to get anywhere in the show-ring, of course, he'd have to give up that silliness for good.

The best way to stop him from acting out was to keep him from feeling the need to do it. He needed his mind occupied at all times, sorting out problems, figuring out what I wanted from him next. Endless loops around the arena while I posted trot and fiddled with his head carriage were not the answer, although it certainly seemed to be the preferred riding style for most of the boarders here. I had to get more creative if I was going to keep his interest on the job.

The voltes and figure-eights and serpentines around the colorful show jumps had proven to be a sure-fire way to keep him thinking. I was able to put my legs behind his girth and gently push him around turns, showing him how to round his body. He definitely thought about bending now—after three weeks of this, he wasn't always a tank in his turns. We were making progress. Sadly, with the jump standards toppling to the ground one after another, it looked like today would require a Plan B.

I didn't have a Plan B.

Thunk!

I started, and Tiger nearly jumped out of his skin as another winged standard hit the clay. The poles came down and went rolling across the arena, rattling and banging together. I held him together with hands and seat and cast one longing glance back at the jump-strewn arena before turning for the dressage ring. We didn't have a choice now. It was off to the boring arena.

The wind was roaring through the pine trees that lined the farm's northern boundary. Tiger went dancing into the arena, his feet slipping on the wet clay. He apparently loved the dangerous footing, because every time he slipped, he jumped around that much more.

"I refuse to wear that crap, so stay on your feet," I told him, gritting my teeth, and pushed him into a trot. The most balanced of gaits, it was the easiest one for us to get connected in. I'd put him together with some serpentines, I decided. "We don't need jumps to tell us where to go. You can figure out your body without guidelines."

For a while, he really could. Despite the wind and the occasional distant clatter as another jump fell face-first into the mud, Tiger thrived on the changes in direction and the steady nature of his own trot. He even rounded his neck once or twice and acted like a nice polite horse instead of sticking his head either between his forelegs or straight up in the air. "Figure out how to round your neck more often and you'll be less like a banana and more like a nice comfortable horse," I instructed.

He flicked his ears back to listen to me, dropped a mouthful of white foam on his chest, and rounded his neck like a Grand Prix dressage horse. I sighed in contentment. His gait floated, his hooves were not touching the ground, his back was lifting into my seat and his mouth was light as a feather. I closed my eyes.

BOOM!

The world was rocked by a deafening explosion. Bomb, I thought. The end of the world, I thought.

Ears ringing, I looked around in wild confusion, my body tense, my hands clenching the reins—

—Tiger threw himself hard to the left, and I went soaring hard to the right, the reins wrenching from my hands, and I was landing on my shoulder in the mud before I even knew what had happened. My head snapped back and hit the wet clay, which was still firm beneath its watery top layer. My jockey skullcap took the brunt of the impact, but it didn't stop me from closing my eyes against the rattle in my brain. It was a long second before I felt like lifting my head to see where my horse had ended up.

Muddy water was already seeping down the collar of my coat when I picked my head up and looked around. There was Tiger, at the end of the dressage ring, staring at something with his head high and his tail flagged. I looked in the direction of his gaze, towards the barn on its little hill, and saw what had caused the explosion.

My eyes widened, my blood turned to ice, and I scrambled up out of the mud, ignoring the protests from my shoulder and hips. I had to get to Tiger.

Just outside the barn, Jean stood with a shotgun in her hands, looking down the slope at the two of us.

❧ ❧ ❧

"It was trying to get warm in the sun." Jean had laid the gun across the desk instead of putting it away, wherever that was. I couldn't quite take my eyes off it—all that shining barrel and gleaming wood. It was a shotgun, the sort of thing that a farmer might have on hand to fend off coyotes or wild hogs. Jean had used it to kill a snake. It turned out that Barbie Doll Jean was actually a redneck at heart. Her daddy had taught her how to shoot when she was just a half-pint on the hog farm up in Alachua County. She didn't word it that way, of course, but that was how I translated her unrepentant explanation of firing the shotgun while I was riding Tiger. Now I had my suspicions about her stiff, precise speech. She was hiding something she thought might get in her way—a Southern accent. Jean was a young woman on the move.

If Jean didn't offer a single "I'm sorry," Elsie was profusely apologetic on Jean's behalf. "Alex, I'm terribly sorry. I promise you, we had no idea you were riding. Jean and I were just having a little meeting to go over show plans for next week, and then she glanced out the window and said there was a huge snake coming out of the pond. We've had a water moccasin problem before, I'm afraid. And to be quite honest, there's rarely anyone here this time of day. I'm sure Jean just assumed we were alone. This was just a terrible, terrible mistake. Are you quite sure you are not hurt?"

"I'm fine, thank you." I was covered in mud and my custom helmet cover with *Alex* embroidered on the back would have to be thrown away and replaced, but I wasn't hurt, and neither was Tiger. "I know it was all a mistake. No hard feelings, Jean."

Jean smiled sweetly, but I saw the malice in her glittering eyes. Jean was a seriously disturbing human. I wanted away from her, and quickly. I took a step back into the aisle, my hands still on Tiger's reins. "I'm just going to put my horse up and I'll get out of your hair, then," I said thinly. My hands were still shaking, and my calves were cramping inside my tight dress boots. I'd never run so fast as I had across that arena, sliding and slipping in the treacherous clay, thinking of nothing but getting to Tiger before Jean shot him. Ludicrous, of course. I could see that now. But at the time, all I'd seen was my enemy on the hillside. My enemy, with a smoking gun, looking down at us.

"Of course, but there's no need for you to go," Elsie began, but I was already walking away. Then I pulled up Tiger and turned around.

"Where's the snake?"

Jean was still smiling. "Would you like to see it? I'll leave it out for you. I was just going to cut off its head and throw it in the burn barrel."

Bluff, called. "No, that's okay. I've seen snakes."

Back in Tiger's stall, I wrapped my arms around his neck and gave his reassuring bulk a squeeze. I felt his teeth grazing my backside and picked up one heel to knock him away. "Just let me cuddle like you're a normal horse for one second, okay?" I snapped, and then I felt bad, because I'd just said he wasn't normal. That he was a racehorse, and somehow different, less well-adjusted, less *cuddly,* than a riding horse. Than a warmblood, or a quarter horse. As if you couldn't just hug a Thoroughbred.

Tiger didn't mind. He strained his neck against my hug and managed to pick up a few strands of hay without dislodging me, and that was good enough for him. I stayed there for a long time, hugging my horse just like he was normal, and after a while, I knew that he was. That no matter what Jean said, no matter her threats or her attempts to get us to leave Roundtree, Tiger was, utterly and perfectly, just another horse.

Chapter Twenty-six

M ARCH CAME TO FLORIDA with a roar of wind and lightning and flooding rains, and left us on the third day of the new month with a flooded training track, a downed tree that had stood for hundreds of years in the broodmare pasture, and three foals who came all in a rush one after another, while Kerri and Alexander and I ran from stall to stall, checking on the progress of the laboring mothers.

On the first sunny day in March I crawled back into bed after the morning training, which had consisted of riding the first set out to the track, seeing that the sweeping turns were watery lakes glinting with the first light of the coming dawn, and turning around to shed-row everyone.

Shed-rowing one set, trotting around and around the shed-row while the grooms try desperately to get the stalls cleaned without being run over, is not the worst thing in the world. It's the second, third, and fourth sets that get progressively harder, as hot horses still need to be walked somewhere. I sent the hot walkers out to walk their horses in a big loop in the grass in front of the barn, but it was muddy and water-logged out there as well, clouds of mosquitoes rising up from ground that had been steadily growing damper and soggier all through the wet winter.

The younger horses behaved exactly as one would expect when their routine was slightly changed: they cavorted and carried on like young criminals. Two babies got loose and went flying around the training barn paddocks, their lead-shanks flapping between their churning legs but miraculously never tripping them up.

I rode two babies and sat out the next two sets, watching the horses trot from the central aisle. I wheeled out my desk chair and plopped into it, instead of sitting atop Parker, but even the comfort of padded leather wasn't enough to ease my exhaustion from the mayhem of the days past. Besides, you had to sit so rigidly and pay such close attention to the horses, it was impossible to relax for a moment.

I watched the horses' gaits as they went flashing by every few seconds, keeping close watch for any trace of unevenness that might herald an unsoundness. I watched their head carriage and the way they mouthed the bits, looking for the precocious ones who had already learned how to put their heads down and brace against their riders' hands. I watched their waggling ears and their rolling eyes, waiting for the ones who concentrated on their work instead of looking for trouble at every turn. I looked for racehorses in the skins of youngsters, the slow blooming of potential in the clever ones, the confusion and distraction that characterized the silly ones. I looked for who would learn their craft first, and who would benefit from a long pasture break, the summer sun on their backs, before they got down to the serious business of racing.

In between sets, my eyelids grew heavy, and I refilled my coffee cup.

Alexander sat next to me from time to time, but this morning he spent a lot of time looking restless, roving around. He went out and watched the hots walking in their irregular circles. He stood in the middle of the shed-row and watched the horses trot away from them, studying their pistoning haunches and streaming tails. He was prowling around like a barn cat looking for mice.

I didn't ask. Alexander in his moods was more than I felt like I could handle today. Three good foals, a colt and two fillies, healthy and alive and sucking at their mother's milk within a few hours—*that* had been my focus for the past few days. Now I just wanted to get through the morning and get back to my bed, and that was exactly what I did.

I came down to the kitchen after two o'clock, my head fuzzy and my throat scratchy. All the cold air and damp from the storm, that was all it was. I wasn't going to get sick. Not now, with two more mares getting round and heavy and ready to pop. Not now, with Tiger trotting and cantering so nicely, even lowering his head from time to time. Not now, with the fuss over Market Affair finally slipping out of the mainstream, the letters beginning to lessen, my shot at returning to the track beginning to glimmer on the horizon. I would live on orange juice and echinacea, but I wouldn't stop to get sick.

Alexander was at the kitchen table, reading a racing magazine from England. A notebook and the Gulfstream condition book were nearby; he was taking a work break. He looked up and smiled. "Good nap?"

"Not bad," I croaked. "Now I need coffee."

"There's a hot pot." He went back to his magazine, thumbing through the pages, looking at pictures of hurdlers.

I poured coffee into a stately white mug emblazoned with the Gulfstream Park logo and pulled a chair alongside his so that I could look too. "It doesn't look like a horse jumping a fence at all." The horses in the photo he was gazing at were soaring over a brush fence, but without the rounded bascule so prized in the show ring. Their spines curved so little they were almost flat, a straight diagonal line from poll to tail, and their forearms were incredibly far ahead of their shoulders, their knees already unfolding at the apex of their jump, as if they were preparing to land while they were still in mid-air. All in all, if you cut out the jumps and Photoshopped in some blue skies and fluffy clouds, and a few wings sprouting from their shoulders, you'd have a photo of a herd of Pegasus, soaring through the skies.

"The jump is just an extension of an already tremendous stride," Alexander said thoughtfully. "Take an eighteen-foot stride and add five feet of altitude."

"I've never felt anything like that." Steeplechasing was unknown to me; it was uncommon in Florida. If I'd grown up in Virginia or Maryland I might have had a shot at it—there seemed to be quite a few lady jockeys in American jumps racing. In eventing I had galloped down to fences, but never actually taken them at anything like racing speed. We balanced up our horses before the fences, instead of just hurtling them at it. I tried to imagine what it felt like to point a breezing horse at a jump, but even my imaginary courage failed me.

"Nor have I." Alexander shook his head regretfully. "Too big and heavy to ride over fences like this at racing speed. Although I schooled a few, when I was a lad." He turned the page, and I saw a familiar face: a high forehead, piercing blue eyes beneath pale brows and a tow-head of perennially mussed hair. The man smiled with Alexander's jovial smile, and he held the lead-shank of a strapping bright-eyed racehorse in Alexander's big hand. "My cousin William," Alexander said tonelessly, and flipped the page again.

His family had bred National Hunt horses, I knew, although he'd come to America to flat-race when they'd downsized the farm and business. He had a brother back in England, still running a few horses, and another in Australia, managing a massive stud farm. Alexander had been successful, but he hadn't yet obtained anything like the stature his father had had as a racehorse trainer, nor the impressive stallion roster his brother had amassed down under. All those thoughtful looks he'd been giving the stallion barn...And now here he was buying English racing magazines and getting upset over a win photo with some cousin of his he'd never mentioned before...

At last, I realized what this was all about.

He wanted stallions up there to prove something to his family.

I couldn't have proved anything to my family in a million years —all my success had proven to them was that I was exactly as insane as they'd always thought I was. But for Alexander, breeding great horses was in his heritage. It was in his blood. It was the Family Business. I didn't particularly want to do it—I was happy with our quieter farm, our easier days (this past week from hell notwithstanding). But could I stand in his way if he needed to do this for himself?

I let my eyes travel over Alexander's profile as he frowned over the magazine, the strong nose and the jutting chin, and between the two, the down-curving lines of his thin lips, and I knew I couldn't stand in his way. If he had something to prove, let him prove it.

I had something to prove too.

"I'm going to go and ride Tiger," I said, sliding my chair back over to its own spot and sipping at the coffee. It burned my lips and my tongue and my throat and my stomach, but I couldn't wait, and took another sip immediately. It seared its way down, but the caffeine began fluttering its moth-wings through my nerves immediately. *Perfect*.

"I'm impressed," Alexander said absently. "I half-expected you to stay inside the rest of the day."

"It's cold enough to, so don't tempt me." I glanced outside. The broodmares were bunched near the water trough in the center of their big pasture, their tails turned towards the north to keep off the gusting wind. Hard brown leaves from the live oaks went soaring through the air, rattling against the window like hail. "But I've done so well for the past few weeks. He's been ridden every day but Mondays."

"Is he a show horse yet?" Alexander turned a page, then another, flipping past ads for supplements and lorries we couldn't buy in this country.

"He's half-not a racehorse. He goes forward with leg pressure now, instead of a kick. He reaches for the bit when I give him rein, instead of digging down and galloping against it." I considered Tiger's progress for a minute, trying to mentally ride Tiger the Racehorse and Tiger of Today, and compare the two. "He *thinks* now. I give him a command he doesn't know, and he puzzles it out and gives me a response. If it's the right response, he gets praise and

I stop asking him for a few minutes. If it's the wrong response, I bring him back and ask again. And he gets that now."

"A thinking horse, that's all a man can ask for."

"I couldn't agree more." I thought of all the racehorses I'd been on that could have done with a little bit more thinking and little bit less headlong galloping. "It's a very nice change."

"You don't *have* to ride the babies." He turned the page. "You could just ride Parker."

I could, and I preferred to, but I was afraid of losing my edge. I didn't want to be a trainer who only trained from the rail. I wanted to be able to train from the saddle. That was the only way I'd had my wins in Saratoga, I knew. But Alexander didn't agree with that philosophy; after all, he hadn't galloped a horse in decades, and he still won races. So I didn't say all that, only: "I just ride the good babies, anyway. Parker appreciates the break."

Alexander went on slowly turning the pages of his racing magazine. *Absent and grouchy,* I thought. *Better if I just head on out.* He could sort this out on his own time. I gave him a kiss on the forehead and left, bundled up against the chilly March wind.

The truth was, I could have used any excuse in the book to avoid going to ride Tiger. It had gotten downright hostile at Roundtree. Even arriving late, and riding him well after Jean had finished with her horses, had not proven to be good enough. Jean crept around corners and startled me and Tiger both. She picked at the way I treated him and the way I trained him.

"The cross-ties aren't good enough for you?" she'd sneer when she saw the way I tied him up in his stall. "Or he just can't be trusted out in the aisle?" I'd tried to explain that we didn't use cross-ties at the racetrack and since I wasn't selling Tiger, I saw no reason to change a routine that we were both comfortable with. But she just shook her head and walked away, her pony-tail swinging.

Just a few days ago, we'd received a particularly ice visit from the Snow Queen. I was out in the arena, lugging some jump poles through the clay and setting them up in little patterns. I figured Tiger could trot over them as a preliminary for jumping. Plus, he'd just plain find it entertaining.

Jean had marched out, crossed her arms across her chest, and watched me in silence. When I had finished and was brushing my palms on my jeans, she pounced. "Don't you think he's too green to go over trot poles?" Her voice was solicitous, as if she wanted to help, but in reality she wanted to poke holes in my training program.

"That's why they're not set up as cavalleti," I explained. "Just a pole here and a pole there, for him to think about while he's trotting. To make him aware of where he's putting his feet."

Jean had shaken her head scornfully. "That's not how trot poles work. They are for regulating a horse's stride, teaching him to make precise steps. You're wasting your time just throwing them on the ground here and there."

I'd gotten angry then. "No, Jean, you're wasting *your* time following me around and criticizing every move I make. Don't you have *work* to do?"

Jean had puffed up like a wet hen then, her pale skin reddening in a furious blush, but I just walked past her, up the hill and into the barn, and left her to stew. I slipped into Tiger's stall and hid there, telling myself he just needed an extra-thorough grooming session, but the truth was, I didn't want to go back out there and deal with her again. I'd been pathetically relieved when she'd gone into the office and closed the door while I tacked up Tiger. Even if she was calling Elsie and telling her to kick me out of the barn post-haste, I didn't want to deal with her another moment. I hadn't come here for hassles. I'd just come here to ride.

I'd been lucky that day. While I was riding she'd gotten into her little German car and driven away, and I hadn't seen her since.

Now, I was getting a twisting feeling in my gut as the truck went banging up the rutted driveway to the barn. She might be there now, waiting with an eviction notice, or just armed with more cutting remarks, more reminders that I was a racehorse trainer at a show barn, riding a racehorse amongst show horses, and that neither he nor I were good enough to be there. I held my breath as the end of the drive approached, the trees leaning in close to hide the barn from me until the last possible second.

The relief I felt at the empty parking lot nearly made me dizzy. No one here...

"Oh thank God," I whispered. *That* was how much I was dreading the visits here. I got *dizzy*. We had to leave here after the show. I wasn't sure what was next, but we couldn't stay here.

The barn wasn't quite deserted as it looked from the outside. I was tying Tiger up to the stall bars, my grooming kit and tack parked just outside the stall door, when Tanya peeked into the stall. She grinned. "Hiya."

"Hey Tanya." I smiled back. The working student was one of the few people here who didn't mind Tiger. I thought that was telling, considering that she was one of the few people here who actually had to *handle* Tiger. She was the one who would lead him out to the paddock at night for turn-out, and bring him in again in the morning. If he wasn't bothering her, he wasn't bothering anyone. "Tiger a good boy for you during all this weather?"

"He was a little silly in the wind this morning. Nippy when you take his rug off, but that's nothing new, half these imported wonders try to take my head off when I pull their rugs off. And he gets really persnickety about wet feet, doesn't he? Didn't want to go through the puddle in front of his gate in all that rain yesterday."

"Yeah, he's a princess." I gave the dark horse a loving pat on the neck, and he turned his head as far as the lead-rope would allow and gave my jacket sleeve a little nibble. "Never liked to run on a wet track. He'd always try to dump me in a puddle if he could."

"That's what I like about him," Tanya said thoughtfully. "He's so smart. Some of these dumb-bloods, they'd dump you if they saw a leaf go by their faces, but they wouldn't think to drop you in a puddle just because it would be funny to see you go splash."

"Careful with the dumb-bloods talk," I warned, only half-joking. "Looks like every horse in this barn is a warmblood."

"That's Jean's doing. Elsie loved Thoroughbreds, but when she stopped showing, Jean got her to stop buying them. Jean's scared of them."

Somehow that was not at all surprising. "Well, you can't bully a Thoroughbred."

Tanya smiled broadly. "And Jean's the class bully. You got that right." She reached through the bars and tickled Tiger on his nose. He obliged her by wiggling his upper lip through the bars, showing off his long yellow teeth. *My old man.* Those teeth never failed to surprise me after spending a morning in the training barn, seeing all the tiny little teeth in the babies' mouths as they opened up for the bit. "Don't let her get you down," Tanya went on. "You're doing a great job with this horse, and he behaves just fine in the barn. She's just got something against you. I don't know what it is, maybe she feels threatened or something."

"That's what Kelly said." I picked up a hard black curry comb and got busy rubbing Tiger down. The horse leaned into the brush, loving the rough treatment. "I still can't figure out why though. We've got completely different goals, we're in different sports."

Tanya shrugged. "I guess she just doesn't want anybody around who rides better than her." She gave Tiger a farewell poke in the nose. "I gotta throw down hay. Have a nice ride!"

Tanya went off down the aisle and I was alone with Tiger again. I moved the curry comb down to his belly and he stretched out his neck and nose in contentment, biting at the wall and the bars as if he was grooming another horse, standing nose to tail under an oak tree in some breezy pasture. "I'm not competition for anyone," I told him. "Unless they're at the Thoroughbred Makeover. Then, they better watch out, am I right?"

Tiger just went on biting the wall, oblivious to anything but the belly-rub he was getting. And that, I figured, was a pretty decent life strategy. I could take a few leaves out of Tiger's book, and maybe relax a little bit.

After we won.

Chapter Twenty-seven

"SO, WHAT CLASSES ARE you going to enter this horse in?"

The question took me by surprise, and I looked across the feed room at Kerri. She was slinging feed into feed buckets, her expression absorbed as she carefully aimed the scoop and let grain fly, but she managed to glance up at me between tosses. "Tiger," she continued, when all I gave her was a confused look. "Which classes are you entering him in at the show?"

I went on pulling down jars of supplements and medications that went into each broodmare's evening meal. I was helping out with feeding, letting Martina had gone home early again to deal with some school project. Having children must be seriously difficult. I really couldn't imagine it. "I haven't even thought about it," I admitted. "I guess I should look into it, right?"

"Seriously?" Kerri expertly let a scoop of sweet feed fly into a bucket from a foot away. Every single oat went into the bucket. Kerri was a feed-slinging wonder. "Don't you have to declare classes by the end of March?"

The Thoroughbred Makeover had its own peculiar prize list. Instead of entering classes when you sent in your entry fee, you were allowed to wait until one month before the show to figure out what classes you wanted to enter. That was because the horses were supposed to be so green at the beginning of the year that a trainer wouldn't really know what the horse would be best suited for until mid-spring, after they'd gotten a few months of training under their belt. "Do you think they offer Bronco Suitability?"

Kerri guffawed. "They should! He's not that bad, though. I doubt he's the worst in the ring, anyway."

"He's not doing great," I admitted.

We had suddenly regressed in our training. Tiger had been behaving so nicely about taking the reins and stretching long and low, then he had suddenly decided it was an opportunity to buck and bolt. This new game had been going on for about four days, which was enough to make me feel fairly despondent about life. This afternoon he'd nearly unseated me, and I'd heard a tinkle of laughter from the barn—a few boarders had arrived early and seen the show. Add in that Alexander was running Luna in a race in about an hour's time, and I wasn't having the best day. "I don't know how to fix this one. Every time I give him some space at the trot or canter, he gets nasty with me. Puts his head down and hops, then takes off."

"Does he look mad? Does he pin his ears?"

"Nope. Looks like he's having fun doing it."

Kerri threw the scoop back into the old freezer where we kept the sweet feed. "Is he bored again?"

"Crap. Maybe." Tiger's boredom problem was becoming an issue. "Now what? We couldn't even pull off a Training Level dressage test, and he's already bored and looking for trouble?"

"Are you going to put electrolytes in those feed buckets, or are you waiting for a higher power to do it for you?"

"Here, sorry." I handed off the tub of electrolytes and unscrewed the lid of another vitamin jar. "I'm just distracted. Luna running in an hour, Tiger showing in six weeks and he's barely rideable—"

"Jump him."

"Sorry?"

Kerri was sprinkling neon-colored salts over the sweet feed. Then, she took a jug of molasses and gave each helping a few glugs to cover it up. The mares were a picky bunch. "Just start jumping him. What's the worst that can happen? Plenty of horses go their entire jumping careers without knowing a lick of dressage."

"Not *my* horses." I threw the vitamin powder into each dark pool of molasses. What was she thinking, telling me to skip dressage? Without learning how to carry himself and round his back, riding Tiger would be just like riding a sawhorse—a plank of rigid wood perambulating around on four uncoordinated legs. He'd have his neck straight out and his nose pointed forward like a lesson horse. How was I supposed to show *that* off to a crowd of skeptics? "I've never skipped dressage. Even the long yearlings get a little dressage schooling before they go the track. Obviously I'm in the minority there, because he clearly has no idea."

Kerri put the electrolytes away and started cracking carrots in half, tossing them into the feed buckets. "I'm not saying you don't do it at all, I'm just saying that riding a flawless dressage test and scoring 78.2% is not the prerequisite for pointing him at a cross-rail and letting him fall over it a few times."

I started gathering up the feed buckets. "We skip his lay-off. We skip his dressage. You want me to start jumping a horse who was on the racetrack two months ago. Seriously?"

"Ever heard of a steeplechaser?"

I shook my head and carried my stack of buckets into the barn aisle, where I was greeted with a chorus of hungry broodmares. Morning, noon, and night, broodmares wanted to eat. Nothing else mattered. They were a simple bunch, and I loved them for it. Everything in horses seemed so straightforward...until you started riding them.

The mares were thrilled, as usual, to see their dinners parading out of the feed room. We went down the aisle with our loads of heavy buckets, sliding into stalls through barely-opened doors, pushing away the muzzles of starving mares and curious foals, and hung the buckets in their corners. The job was done in just a few minutes, since the barn was half-empty this spring.

Only one mare left to foal, and it was only mid-March—I could scarcely believe it. After all the brutal foaling seasons I had experienced, this was the first one that had seemed actually manageable. The downsizing we had done last year had resulted in a lot more sleep and lot less backbreaking work this spring. Come April, we'd have our last baby, and while the rest of Ocala was still rushing around bleary-eyed with foalings, we'd just be wrapping up our foal checks and our breed-backs.

The training barn was half-empty, too, with the client horses gone to the sales. We'd had a few buyers send us two-year-olds to prep for racing this summer, but other than that, things were quiet. If I'd known how, I'd have done a little relaxing.

Well, the light workload gave me plenty of time to worry about Tiger, anyway.

Among other things. Kevin Wallace, for example. Down in Hallandale, Alexander was still courting Wallace, hoping he would retire March Hare to stand stud at Cotswold. The horse was still at Gulfstream, where Wallace was charmingly optimistic that they'd sort out his problematic feet and get him through the summer to race in the Breeders' Cup championships this fall.

I privately doubted it would work out. The horse had rotten feet, and I didn't think they could keep him sound. Not that I wanted March Hare retiring and coming here this season, or any season. I didn't want Kevin Wallace, or anyone associated with *any* sort of dumped horse scandal, anywhere near Cotswold. Certainly not now, when the heat was starting to cool off. People had short memories, and they were always looking for new scandals. Since the Market Affair connection to me had no legs, it was still solely in the Facebook pages and badly-written blogs of the animal-rights activists.

And since Market Affair was rehabbing nicely and we'd sent his adopters a check to cover some of his vet bills, the story was becoming a tale of redemption and big-hearted humans instead. If no one else but me ever had to suffer for Market Affair's abandonment—his last trainer of record had bills of sale that showed he and the other Everglades horses had been sold to a certain Roberto L. Dominguez of Miami, and Roberto L. Dominguez had recently relocated to his home island of Puerto Rico for personal reasons—well, if he got away with it, that wasn't fair, but as long as it *ended* and I could get back to my life and my career, I'd take it.

Even if everything cleared up and the scandal disappeared, I still thought asking Kevin Wallace to be a business partner was just begging the activists to keep after me. Couldn't we just let this die a natural death, without giving them fresh fodder to chew and turn into their caustic cud?

Besides, I thought, looking down the aisle to the empty stalls at the far end, I wasn't in a big hurry to bring Cotswold back up to full capacity. I could get used to a two-month foaling season. I could get used to sending out four sets in the morning and being done by nine o'clock. As long as we had quality horses, wasn't less more?

With hours like this, I'd always have time to ride Tiger, assuming I managed to figure out his latest training issue. Even with the drama of the boarding stable, even with trying to duck Jean and her particularly malicious brand of insanity, I was enjoying riding Tiger for more than a few minutes on the training track. I was beginning to feel a closeness to him beyond what we'd felt galloping together; the way his body would mold to my seat when he lifted his back and curved his neck. It was becoming a familiar sensation, one that I couldn't wait to feel every day, anticipation speeding my fingers as I tacked him up.

Or so it had been, before this week's bucking episodes had replaced those lovely stretching sessions. I leaned against the wall at the end of the barn aisle, listening to the rattling buckets behind me, and gazed out over the pastures. Tiger, I thought. Tiger, Tiger. What I needed, I realized, was a second opinion.

"You want to ride Tiger?" I asked Kerri, who was staring into the distance herself, doing a little deep thinking of her own.

"Huh what?" Kerri blinked and looked at me. "Ride Tiger? When?"

"Tomorrow afternoon. I want to see him. I'm always on his back...maybe I can get a better idea of his progress and what he needs if I can watch him being ridden." It was the same concept as sitting on the pony watching the racehorses train. "Want to give it a shot? You never get to ride."

Kerri considered the idea, then nodded. "Sure. But if I feel like he wants to jump, can I jump him?"

"I guess." Maybe if Kerri jumped him, it wouldn't be *me* rushing to do the fun stuff instead of the hard stuff. Maybe that made it an official training session, with me on the ground, watching the horse to see his potential. Sure, I could think of it like that. "Tomorrow, two o'clock. Bring your half-chaps in the morning!"

⇒⇒⇒⟩   ⟨⇐⇐⇐

I was glad of Kerri's company the next afternoon, sitting next to me as we drove over to Roundtree. There had been bad news from south Florida last night—Luna had been a devil in the paddock, a demon in the starting gate, and a dud on the racetrack. Alexander was starting to think it was time to bring her home. "She can be your next show horse," he said jokingly, and I hung up on him.

I called him back a few minutes later, and we argued back and forth about what Luna needed—more training from home, I said; more retirement or claiming races, Alexander said—and finally I was so riled up that I told him I was perfectly fine with retraining every single one of our failed horses, as long as *he* was the one who had failed them, and then *he* hung up on *me*...basically it was a bad evening. Things did not go well.

Luckily, we did manage to apologize to one another before midnight and grab a few hours of sleep—he called me, knowing it was his turn as he'd hung up last. I woke up at five o'clock feeling hungover from all the arguing, and the feeling had hung around, low in my stomach, all day long.

Kerri, sensitive as always to my bad moods, had drawn back from her usual jokes and was sitting quietly in the passenger seat of the truck, watching the pastures flash by. So quietly, in fact, that I thought she might be a bit nervous. "When's the last time you rode a horse?"

"Like, properly ride? With a purpose?"

"Yeah. Not on one of the broodmares in the pasture." Alexander and I had both seen her climb onto open mares a few different times, although she rarely did anything more than sit on them bareback while they grazed.

"Oh...a year or two."

"What? Why so long?" Kerri was around horses literally all the time. How could she just not ride?

Kerri shrugged. "I prefer taking care of horses to riding them, I guess."

"Did something happen?" I persisted. A bad accident, a nasty injury, the loss of a horse—lots of emotional reasons for someone to stop riding came to mind, and I didn't want to stir anything up by putting her on Tiger unless she was absolutely ready.

"Not really. There's just a lot of variables. You trust a horse, he does something stupid, you start thinking, 'Man, I could actually die without any warning at all,' and I decided it wasn't a thing I wanted to do. I just prefer it on the ground."

I considered this as we turned off the road and went down the oak-shadowed barn lane. "It sounds like you had your mortality wake-up call a lot earlier than most people. I'm pretty sure I haven't had mine yet."

Kerri laughed. "I'm positive you haven't had yours yet. And I bet you never will."

She was probably right, considering the falls that I'd taken and the fact that I kept putting my boot in the stirrup every day anyway. "Well, Tiger isn't dangerous. He's just an asshole."

"I know," Kerri said. "He's always been that way. And that's why we love him."

The barn was blissfully empty, dark despite the sun's attempt to shine through the ceiling panels, and when I flipped on the aisle lights there was a general rumble of nickers from dozing horses. They mainly stayed in during the day and went out at night, even in winter when the schedule was flipped at most barns, because Jean liked to keep their shimmering coats from being sunburned. Each stall's blanket bar had an impressive pile of thermal gear slung over it, made even messier today by the balmy spring-like weather. It was nearly eighty degrees, and the sun's rays had real heat in them.

I glanced into Tiger's stall. He was in the patch of sunlight streaming in his stall window, eyes half-closed. "Hey man," I called, and he flicked an ear in my direction. "That's all I'm getting?"

Tiger shifted his weight from one hind leg to the other and sighed.

"Big and tough, I see," Kerri said. "Ready to wake up and jump some fences like a real horse?"

Tiger turned and looked at her, blinking as he started to wake up, and Kerri burst into laughter. "What did I tell you?" she asked, elbowing me in the ribs. "Let's grab his tack and get this party started. I'm ready to teach this monster what fun is."

Whatever trepidation she might have had about riding again seemed to be gone. Okay then. I led her to the tack room and we got busy.

⤜⤜⤜ ⤛⤛⤛

Kerri rode with an easy grace that instantly made me jealous. She sat a little too forward, true, but if her posture was not perfect, her balance certainly was. Her hands floated elegantly above Tiger's withers, dropping to either side of his shoulders when she wanted him to stretch into the bit. Her thighs hugged the saddle, her knees rested against the padding, her toes pointed forward, and no part of her calf touched Tiger's side unless she wanted it to.

They trotted around the jumping arena harmoniously, weaving in and out of jumps while she encouraged Tiger to stretch. His head would come up; her hands would drop; his head would follow. For a few strides he would move with an elongated, reaching stride, his nose tipping towards the earth, reaching down as if searching for a blade of grass to pluck while he was in motion, before he'd lose the strength he needed to hold the position and his head came up again. It was the dance of the green dressage horse, and Kerri had clearly danced it before.

It was after they had done a little canter work that the rot started in. By now Tiger had a sheen of sweat on his neck, and Kerri didn't have gloves. I could see the wet reins start to slip in her fingers, and when Tiger tugged the reins from her instead of gracefully stretching his neck, she ended up with nothing but the buckle in her hands. Tiger hunched his back and I winced—here came the buck, and she didn't have any hold on his mouth to stop it from coming.

Kerri was quicker than I had given her credit for. With her heels shoved home in the stirrup and well ahead of her body, she flung her hands out to either side, the reins zipping through her fingers until they were taut again. Then, she hauled Tiger hard to the left, not bothering to be careful with his mouth this time. Tiger grunted with displeasure, but he went where she commanded, his head coming up, and then his eyes locked on the target she had placed him in front of.

Just a half-dozen strides away, a tiny cross rail was waiting. His ears pricked and his stride became forward and eager again. Meanwhile, Kerri quietly readjusted her reins to the proper length. She posted easily, keeping him as balanced and even as she could, and didn't look a bit worried when Tiger darted into a canter just before the fence, and scrambled over the two little poles with all the grace of a baby learning to walk.

He stumbled and nearly fell flat on his face on the other side, but Kerri was standing in the stirrups, independent of all his clumsiness, and let him figure out his balance without jabbing him in the mouth or falling on his neck.

She pulled him up to a walk and rode him over to the fence where I was standing.

"You've got some seat, missie," I called as she neared. "Who trained you, George Morris?"

Kerri just grinned. It wasn't until she pulled up along the fence that I saw how tired she was. She was red in the face and panting. "I'm out of shape," she gasped. "I don't think I can do anything else with him. But it's a good stopping place anyway. He tried to be bad, he jumped a fence, he liked it. End of day."

She was right—Tiger was bright-eyed and happy despite his sweat-damp coat and flaring nostrils. He side-stepped and snorted, clearly ready to go give that cross-rail another try. I could see Kerri didn't have it in her, though. If he did anything naughty around the fence, she'd have to just keep schooling him—and riding that well after taking a year-long break meant that her muscles had to be screaming. "Sounds good," I agreed. "Let's take him in."

I went over to the in-gate and swung it open so that Kerri didn't have to lean down from the saddle to do it—always a struggle with Tiger, who wasn't exactly understanding about side-passing. A trail horse, he was not. We started up the slope to the barn together, my hand brushing against Tiger's warm neck, and I didn't even notice that Jean had showed up until we reached the barn entrance and saw her there, leaning against the wall, looking like a particularly beautiful and insane thunder-cloud.

⟫⟫⟩ ⟨⟨⟨

I tugged Tiger's reins as soon as Kerri had vaulted out of the saddle, trying to drag the horse into the barn and past Jean before she could say anything. I didn't know what difference that would make—it wasn't as if she couldn't follow us down the aisle, shout at us, do whatever it was she was planning if we were in motion, walking away from her. I had an instinct to get away from her that I just couldn't ignore. Jean had proven dangerous once before, when she'd fired the shotgun while we were riding. Being alone on the farm with her, even with Kerri there as a witness, wasn't exactly my first choice.

Sure enough, she came marching right after us. Tiger dragged his hooves along the concrete aisle, making a scraping sound that I'd always found irritating, but that was quickly drowned out by Jean's querulous voice, sounding more southern than usual. "What the hell do you think you're doing out there? These are Elsie's fences, and I need them for my training. I can't have you out there wrecking our property because you want to play jumper with your reject racehorse. Now I'm going to march out there and inspect those jump poles, and if there's so much as a scratch in the paint from his deformed hooves, I'm going to tell Elsie to write up a bill and send it to you. You can add it to your last month's board, because if that fence is damaged you are going to have to find someplace else to keep that Godawful piece of crap horse—"

Kerri, who had been in lockstep with me since we entered the barn, suddenly disappeared. I turned my head and saw her marching up to Jean, who had quit her bellowing as Kerri jutted her chin at her.

"You're a nasty piece of work, you know that?" Kerri said quietly. "You got a lot of nerve, acting like you've never had a horse drag a toe across a jump pole. The funny thing is," I stopped Tiger so that I could hear what she was saying, utterly impressed with her nerve, "the funny thing is, I haven't ever heard your name before. Even though I know half the jumper people in this town and my cousin is the secretary for the North Florida Show Jumping Alliance. So you want to tell me what you've done that makes you so important? You want to tell me about all the jumper shows you've been double-clear in? Maybe you're showing under a different name? I'm willing to give you the benefit of the doubt on this one. I'm sure you have a good answer."

Jean actually leaned back a little from Kerri's squared jaw, as if she was finally intimated by someone else's bravado. I resisted the urge to applaud.

Tiger nudged my arm, eager to get back to his stall and start ripping apart his flake of hay like a wild animal, but I tugged at the reins to straighten him out. I needed to see the rest of the show.

"Your cousin is Tilda Howell?" Jean asked after a moment of fish-faced silence, her mouth seeming to have forgotten how to make sounds for a while.

"Who's Tilda Howell?" I whispered to Tiger, who had commenced chewing on the reins he'd somehow slurped into his mouth. "Never mind, you don't know."

"That's right," Kerri said genially. "And when Alex told me that Elsie had a rider named Jean Martin who was as beautiful and nasty as an ice queen, I made sure I mentioned her the next time I had coffee with Tilda. And she said, Jean who? And so I'm saying it to you now: Jean Who? As in, Jean Who The Hell Do You Think You Are?"

Jean took a step backwards. Kerri looked very frightening. I was ten kinds of proud of her right now. Tiger, gnawing blissfully on his cheap reins, was lost to the world, or I'm sure he would have approved as well.

"I haven't shown very much on the A-circuit," Jean admitted, her southern twang still showing through the voice she usually controlled so carefully. "This is my first big season of HITS."

"And how many classes have you won?"

Jean looked mutinous. She worked her jaw for a moment before she spat, *"None."*

"So you've pulled a few rails in your time?" Kerri nodded. "That's what I thought. Now you better apologize to Alex for the nasty things you said, or we're going to have to let Elsie know how bad you are at customer service, Miss Barn Manager."

Jean looked at me with hatred in her flinty blue eyes. I waved a hand at her. "Nah," I said. "I'm good. Just don't do it again, okay?"

She gave me a little shake of her head and then stormed away, her elegant boots clicking on the concrete with every stride. There was a little bang when the office door closed, and then I allowed myself to look at Kerri.

She was grinning at me like an idiot. I burst out laughing and covered my mouth with my free hand as quickly as I could, but I was afraid Jean had heard me. When *Kerri* started laughing uproariously, making no attempt to cover it up, I knew we'd be heard. I supposed it didn't matter. Jean already hated me, and even if Kerri had just insured that it was a hate that would burn forever, outlasting the very fires of the sun, at least it probably wouldn't make things any worse.

It might even make life at Roundtree a little better. After all, I wasn't looking for a friend. I was looking for some peace and quiet for six more weeks, to get Tiger ready to win the Thoroughbred Makeover.

"So for classes," I said, when we'd managed to stop laughing. "What if we just do Versatility?"

"Which one's Versatility?"

"Two different riders in two different classes. Same horse. Kind of a cool idea. So I will do Dressage Suitability for the Versatility class, and you do Jumping. It's just cross-rails. Then, we can score in the dressage, jumping, *and* get an overall score for Versatility. Three chances to win."

"Hedging your bets?" Kerri grinned.

"Can you blame me? Look at this racetrack reject!" Tiger, who still had his reins in his mouth and was now dripping a mixture of green slobber and foamy saliva onto the barn aisle, ignored us as we laughed at him. Who could blame him? He was gorgeous and he knew it.

Chapter Twenty-eight

"EVERYTHING IS REALLY COMING together," I was telling Alexander. I flopped back on the couch and stuck my feet in the air, sitting upside-down the way I used to when I was a kid, the way that made my father so annoyed. "Sit right," he'd tell me, and I'd argue "there's no right way to sit," and then my mother would overrule us both and say that I could sit on the floor however I liked, but not on the furniture.

So now, ostensibly an adult, I had developed a weird habit of sitting upside-down on the couch, just to prove that I could do what I liked. It came in handy when life was just a bit over-the-top. Like right now, while I listened to Alexander enumerate all the ways in which things were not, in fact, coming together. With his dispatch from the races, life was suddenly feeling *very* over-the-top.

"He's been an absolute terror, that's not too strong a word for it. Bolting with his rider, refusing to come off the track after a work, leaping about at the gap until the outriders have to get involved. It's an embarrassment. I'm this close to sending him back to the farm and forgetting this whole Derby nonsense."

I sat up again, the blood rushing through my face and roaring through my ears. He wasn't seriously going back on our plans for Personal Best—oh no sir, he better think again. "You can't do that! We agreed, we had a plan—he has to run in the Bahia Honda, he *has* to or he won't have the points to go to Kentucky." The Bahia Honda Stakes was on the same day as the Thoroughbred Makeover, which meant that I wouldn't be there to run him— something I didn't like to think about—but it was the best placed race to get Personal Best the points he needed to go to Churchill Downs in May.

Just the fact that we were already to March and Kentucky was still on the table was a fact I could barely take in. Even if it seemed like a million-to-one shot, I wasn't about to throw in the towel yet. Look how close we had come! Crazy dreams are just as hard to give up as the regular kind.

"Alex, he's not *ready* for the Bahia Honda, so he's clearly not going to be ready for Kentucky." Alexander's tone was grim. "He's gotten sour and needs a break. He can't do it all—take a break, run the Bahia, take a break, be fit for Kentucky. It's all or nothing now. And he'd prefer nothing, I can assure you. You've never seen such a bastard. Gary won't ride him anymore, so we had to find a new rider, and he's been having them off one after another like some sort of circus horse. It's been a shambles. I don't want to take him out there with my name on him again until he's been sorted out. This is my reputation on the line here."

And yours is already sullied enough, I silently added for him. He might not have said it, but you can bet he was thinking it. Cotswold Farm was looking a bit like Loserville these days. No stallions, no stakes horses, and two trainers who couldn't seem to keep their names out of the gossip columns.

Still, I had an awful time believing that Personal Best would be so suddenly soured on racing. He loved living at the track, he loved the hustle and bustle of the training center, the training track full of horses each morning, the brief interlude in his little paddock each afternoon, the other horses along the shed-row looking up and down as they worked through their hay-nets and listened to the radio left on by the grooms. He was a social horse, chatty and neighborly as they came; racetrack life suited him. And of course, he was a racehorse through and through. He loved to go to the track in the afternoon, his blood high and his head higher, waiting to be led out to the track like a child's pony, kept in check by taut hands on the lead-shank, until he could burst from the starting gate and show the others his heels.

It was what he did. It was what he lived for. Why would that suddenly change now?

It had changed for Tiger. But then, Tiger was a different horse, with a different personality, a different soul. Tiger lived to be in charge, to have his head, to make his own decisions about everything. That was what made the jump this afternoon such an unexpected head-turner for him. He had been making up his own mind, and Kerri had surprised him *and* shown him a good time. If I could keep surprising Tiger, he'd stay fresh and excited about work. It worked for him, but I didn't think it was what P.B. needed.

I just didn't know what he needed. Still...

"A few more days," I pleaded. "I'm not ready to give this up. Just put him out in his paddock every day. He doesn't need to go to the track. He's fit enough. Find something for him and drop him in, let him race himself fit instead of working out."

"So let's say we turn him out and then find a race for him in a week, ten days. Okay, fine, but what kind of prep do we give him for *this* race? We send him out two days before the race? I can't blow him out if he isn't in work. That's hell on his legs."

"Just jog him," I said resolutely, feeling more confident since Alexander was actually asking my opinion. Including me in the conversation again, instead of telling me—thank goodness for that. "A good long jog to loosen all his muscles. And a short one again the day before the race. If he doesn't want to run, we'll know then." *We'll.*

Alexander considered this. "He *is* fit enough for a few days off. Bursting out of his skin, as a matter of fact."

"Dying for a race," I said. I tipped myself over on the couch again, letting my ponytail hang behind me to pool on the floor. I rested my feet on the back of the couch and wiggled my toes against the cool wall. Upside-down could be a good way to think. "Give him a race and he'll be ready for the Bahia without dealing with training track nonsense. He thinks the work-outs are boring. He wants a race, not a work-out."

"And you," Alexander said gruffly.

"What's that?"

"He's used to you coming to see him. And you running him. I think he misses you."

My head slid down to the carpet with a thump, and I slowly rolled off the couch. "You really think that?"

Alexander sighed. Emotional attachments were not his favorite thing, especially when it was something as sentimental as a horse and a human with a social bond. *Gross*, he'd be thinking, every time someone tried to sell him some story of their miraculous relationship with their soul-mate horse. Horses, he had declared more than once, do not care about human souls.

Despite all that, though, he couldn't say a word against deep friendships with horses. He'd had them as much as I had.

"Let me come down," I said urgently.

"Not yet."

"But Alexander—"

"Not. Yet."

I subsided. He was taking my training advice. That was really more than I could reasonably ask for, anyway. The invitation to return would come in time. Then, I could get back down to the business of training racehorses. I loved my Tiger, but bless him, he was going to have to stay a fun hobby. Nothing stirred my blood like a galloping racehorse.

Chapter Twenty-nine

MAYBE IT WAS THE training chat with Alexander the night before, but when I went out to the training barn in the morning, I took a look at the whiteboard and decided that I would ride a work this morning. I'd left before Alexander, so there was no one around to hem and haw, looking for a good reason to tell me no. It was now or never; he'd be down any minute. "Juan?" I called, and the rider ducked his head into the tack room.

"Yeah boss!" He grinned. Apparently the kerfuffle in January was long forgiven and I was no longer considered to be on the verge of some sort of breakdown that was endangering the entire farm, because everyone had been very nice to me for the past few weeks. That, or they'd decided I was a ticking time bomb who should be humored and kept as cheerful as possible. Either way, the atmosphere around the training barn was much improved. I'd take it.

"I want to do a fast work on the Miss Frosty colt. We have the Surfside colt marked for one, too. You want to go do this with me right now?" It was still pretty dark out, but the track would be ideal first thing in the morning, before the other horses went out and tore up the neat furrows that had been plowed into it yesterday afternoon.

Juan had been a jockey in Puerto Rico and was always game for a fast gallop, so we shouted to the grooms to get the tack out for the two colts and set about zipping ourselves into our half-chaps (leggings, everyone called them but me, because old habits die hard) and safety vests. Once our hard hats were on and the harnesses snapped, we were ready to go. I tossed Juan a stick and he snatched it out of the air—a neat trick I just couldn't master, no matter how many times I had tried.

The morning was warm and damp, the air smelling of mildew and soil and the manure pile. I breathed it deep as we went walking down to the training track. The two-year-olds, free from the disapproving nanny-gaze of Parker and Betsy, felt frisky and naughty. My colt, a long-legged dark bay without a splash of white anywhere on him, squealed and kicked out at Juan's, but he wasn't actually trying to strike him—just childish high spirits. I straightened him out, chiding him with a motherly voice, and Juan laughed when his own colt humped his back and gave a warning hop.

These were our two oldest colts, well past their actual second birthdays, which had come in late January, and they were the closest to the racetrack. Both had done two fast works already, learning the difference between a workmanlike gallop and a few furlongs at racing speed. I loved the way they discovered the rivalry inherent in a paired work, when you finally shook out the reins and told them to go.

"You mean I can go faster, I can try to beat this guy?"

"Yes, that's the idea."

"Oh, *awesome!*"

We jogged around the track the wrong way, listening to the wings of early-rising mourning doves as they fluttered up from the long grass along the rail. In the pine grove at the north end of the track, a whip-poor-will was still awake, whistling out into the dawn. "Time for bed, silly bird," I called as we jogged past, and I heard his little chuckling chirp that followed every call of *whip-poor-will,* as if he was laughing at me for trying to tell him what to do.

The track was clear, but there was fog settling along the pasture next door, where Mary's makeshift training track was furrowed and ready for the day's works. There were ridges in it, and bumps where harder ground was standing out from the settling sand. We still saw her horses out there from time to time, whenever our sets went out at the same time by coincidence, but there seemed to be fewer of them. I wasn't surprised. There was no way they were staying sound, galloping over that uneven ground. She was ruining her own chances. "Self-destructive," I murmured, and Juan looked at me questioningly, but I just shook my head. I had to forget about Mary once and for all, worry about my horses and nothing else.

Luckily, a nice fast breeze was the very thing to knock every other care out of your head.

We opted for a short work from the three-eighths pole, and turning our horses about at the center of the stretch, we galloped along easily the way we had just come. The gray sky was brightening, the whip-poor-will was silent at last, and all that I heard now was the rumble of our horses' hooves on the good ground, the sound of their breathing as they exhaled every time their fore-hooves hit the ground, the jingle of buckles on the training yokes around their necks.

And it was good, good, good.

At the three-eighths pole we both shook out our reins and shouted. Juan showed his horse the stick when the colt hesitated, a little wave in the air to convince him that yes, this was really what we wanted, and I swear I could see the delight in the horse's eyes as he comprehended *it's time to go fast!* Their strides built and built, a slow roar like a growing wave rather than a rocket launch of instant acceleration, and that was fine too—they would learn, they would get stronger, they would come to anticipate this and burst forward at the signal with a fierce intensity.

By the time we sailed around the short turn and were thundering down the homestretch, the horses had discovered just how much they wanted to beat the other, and then it was a game of noses—first my colt shoved a nose in front, then Juan's colt. We let them see-saw this way, each horse experiencing the thrill of winning and the challenge of falling behind, until we had swept past the final pole and it was time to stand up in the stirrups and bring them down to a slow gallop.

Just as I did so, my colt shaking his head against my lifting hands, I saw a horse to my right. I looked—there was a rider there, wearing a cowboy hat and sitting a paint pony, reined up in the makeshift training track.

Mary.

I shouted to Juan and nodded in her direction, then as the horses slowed to a jog in the turn, I reined the colt around so that I could go back and talk to her. I wanted to know what she wanted from me, I wanted to know how we could end this bad blood. The only thing I knew for sure was that I was ready to move on. I didn't need a nemesis, or an arch-rival. We weren't children any more, or high school students telling tales on one another at the boarding stable. We were adults, and we were trainers, and we were committed to putting our horses and our sport first in all things. Racing had enough trouble without us tearing it down from within. We had to put up a united front, do the right things for our horses, build up our sport's reputation and integrity. Our livelihood was at stake.

I was ready to say all these things to her.

But, she was already gone.

Juan grinned at me. "She wouldn't listen to you anyway. She crazy."

I figured he was right.

⇒⇒⇒⇒ ⇐⇐⇐⇐

It turned out that slow rides and fast rides could be equally exhilarating, though in different ways.

Kerri couldn't come with me to Roundtree that afternoon; she had vet visits to deal with. I decided to play with the jumps again, although not quite the same way that she had done it yesterday. I just wasn't sure if the element of surprise was the right way to teach him to jump. If I kept pulling stunts like that on a regular basis, he'd eventually take a hard stumble and get hurt—

—Or put a scratch on one of those damn poles. Sure, Jean had been bluffing when she threatened to check the jump poles for damage and send me a bill, but there was no reason to prove her right by actually damaging them. I wanted to concentrate on helping Tiger get *over* the poles in as comfortable a way as possible, not trick him into scrambling over them in a desperate effort not to hurt himself. Let's do this thing with a little bit of grace, shall we?

Kelly was at the barn when I arrived, Payton in the cross-ties while she was settling a saddle on his back. She waved hello as I walked in. "Oh good, a riding buddy! I took the chance you'd be here this time of day. I heard you gave it to Jean yesterday."

I was dying to ask exactly what she'd heard, but I remembered the sense of peace I'd felt galloping this morning. If it had inspired me to try to work things out with Mary, then I could use it to work towards peace at Roundtree, as well. I needed to let all of this conflict roll off my back, like water from a duck. "It wasn't anything too big, not really," I said instead. "I'm glad you're here too! Tiger could use a work partner."

We rode in pairs around the jumping arena for a while, an exercise which taxed Tiger's self-control no end. He tugged at the reins whenever Payton pulled a little ahead of him, his strides lengthening as he tried to make sure he was in front. However, he didn't flatten his ears or try to reach over and bite the warmblood, which was a significant improvement over his previous behavior with ponies. "This is incredibly good for him," I said after a while, panting a little from all the posting trot. "He doesn't usually like other horses around."

"He's mellowing out," Kelly laughed. "He just figured out what *retired* means, and he likes it."

"Hah! I wish." Tiger snorted and tried to spook away from a palm frond lying on the ground. "See? We're having a nice time and he's getting bored and looking for trouble."

"Oh, I know what he needs," Kelly said authoritatively. "I hear you started jumping him."

I guess that came with the Jean story. "Not exactly. He stumbled over that little x over there." I nodded at the tiny cross-rail he'd fallen over yesterday.

"Let's play follow-the-leader, then. You come along a few strides behind me, and let him follow Payton over fences. He'll have to concentrate on where he's putting his feet, so instead of wanting to race Payton, he'll be watching him to see what to do."

"That's actually a really good idea." I looked around at the other jumps. None were higher than two-six. There had been a kid's lesson over the weekend and no one had lifted the jumps since. "Maybe after the x we can do some of the little fences, too."

"I'll even drop a few to eighteen inches." Kelly looked delighted. "Wait here while I fix a fence for us." She trotted Payton briskly over to a plain little oxer, hopped off, and started moving the rails around. Tiger watched with pricked ears, his head high for a better view, and jumped a little when one fell from its cup with a loud bang.

"You're going to jump over that," I told him. "You'll love it." He ignored me.

"All set!" Kelly slapped the dirt from her hands, led Payton over to the roll top, and used it as a mounting block. "Ready?"

"Let's do this!" I gathered the reins again while Tiger watched Payton come back to join us, fluttering his nostrils a little. I shook my head. Half an hour and Tiger had a boy-crush on his new German friend. At least he was starting to act like a normal horse again. Maybe he could start going out with a buddy, the way he used to with Parker.

"Let's go!" Kelly trotted around us. "Follow along!"

I nudged Tiger into a jog. He pulled at the reins eagerly, ready to get back into lockstep with Payton. Then, Payton did something Tiger was not ready for. Payton jumped over two little cross-poles, his knees tight and pretty although the fence was no higher than six inches off the ground. His fetlocks looked handcuffed together as he neatly cleared the fence.

Tiger stopped dead, his entire body registering alarm, and stared at Payton as if the horse had come from another planet. Evidently he did not associate his falling-over-the-fence achievement yesterday with the smart little jump that his new friend had just displayed.

I burst out laughing. Kelly pulled up Payton and turned around. "What happened? Why aren't you coming?"

"Tiger was so horrified by Payton jumping that he just stopped!" I shook my head. "Maybe he's not a jumper after all."

"You *have* to do it now!" Kelly insisted, turning her horse back towards us and trotting over. "Now it's a refusal."

We were still about ten strides away from the fence, which was hardly enough to be considered a presentation to the jump. Still, though, I saw what she meant. "You jump it a couple more times," I suggested. "And then we'll follow you over." Maybe if he saw Payton hop over the jump a few more times, he would realize it was part of the game, and not a flight from danger. "He probably thought Payton was spooking or escaping something scary on the ground."

Kelly nodded. Her face was bright and excited, as if this was the most fun she'd had all day. "Take him over and let him look at the jump too," she said. "We probably should have done that first."

Probably. "Duh," I said. "What were we even thinking?"

Naturally, Tiger now refused to go anywhere near the jump—or any of the other jumps in the arena. He balked and stamped and spun and pinned his ears and swatted his tail, firmly in opposition to any plan to get him near those dangerous horse-eating fences. "Damn," I panted, circling him for the tenth or eleventh time to try to get him to walk *near* the jump. "I think I might have screwed him up this time."

"No, no, we'll get him over it," Kelly said determinedly. "We just need to be patient."

"Ladies?" We turned, and when I saw Elsie watching us I felt a twinge of guilt, as if I was a kid doing something my riding instructor had firmly warned me against. "Is everything all right?"

"Fine!" Kelly announced, her face alight with joy. "Everything is great!"

Elsie looked at me.

"Fine," I said, with less conviction. "We're doing just fine."

Elsie cocked her head for a moment, no doubt assessing my sweating horse, his flattened ears, his swishing tail, the tiny cross-rail. Then she nodded and waved. "Let me know if I can help." She turned for the barn. I looked back at Kelly.

"That was embarrassing."

"Now we *really* have to get him over it," Kelly said, grinning. "Let's do pairs. Next to each other. He'll walk next to Payton." She rode her horse over to us and lined up with me, boot to boot, facing the scary jump. Tiger immediately leaned over and gave Payton a love-nip on the neck. Payton squealed and shook his head. "You guys are so gross," Kelly chided. "Quit making out and let's get our work done."

Payton started forward and Tiger went with him in lock-step, keeping one ear on his friend and one on the jump. Which left no ears for me, but that was fine. He'd already proven that he didn't care what I had to say on this subject. Hopefully his crush on the handsome Payton would be more convincing than our long-term relationship was proving to be.

We were within two strides of the fence before Tiger started getting *really* concerned. His head came up, he sucked back, and his strides felt sticky. I put my heels to his sides, but I was prepared for a stop. Prepared for failure, you might say. I just didn't want to hit the dirt if he dropped his shoulder and ran. Elsie might still be watching from the barn.

Luckily for our future jumping career, Kelly wasn't having any of it. Just as Tiger's forward motion started to peter out, she leaned over and shrieked "*Yeeeeee-haaaaaaaaa!*" in Tiger's pricked ears.

Tiger leapt like a deer, leaving me sitting in the middle of his back like a beginner.

I was apologizing to his poor spine and his poor mouth as soon as he landed, but Kelly was already turning Payton towards us, pushing us in a circle. "Again, again!" she yelped. "Let the lesson sink in!"

Kelly was crazy, I realized. She was bonafide crazy horse-people.

But I went with her.

By the fourth time jumping the cross-rail, Tiger wasn't leaping six feet in the air and Kelly wasn't yelling like a banshee at him. We were just trotting up, taking a snorty look, and hopping over the rails. It was the first time I had jumped a horse in years, and it was so, *so* fun.

Just about as fun as working a fast horse, in fact.

I thought I'd tell Alexander so, just to annoy him.

Chapter Thirty

D AYS TURNED INTO WEEKS, winter turned into summer (or so it felt like some days, as the "spring" sun heat the days up into the eighties), and Tiger turned into a quieter, gentler version of himself. Well, at times. He still did mad Tiger things like attack his hay, and bite the frame of his stall door when he thought dinner was late, or that I was dawdling in the aisle chit-chatting with Kelly or Kerri instead of getting him out and riding him. He still thought digging down on the bit and bursting into a short, choppy gallop was an excellent boredom-release mechanism. He still went over fences with more gusto than skill, and I was hard-pressed to regulate his canter stride well enough to bring him to a jump at the correct moment. His long legs would suddenly lengthen the stride from collection to full gallop in a matter of seconds, and he'd ruin the perfect presentation I'd been laboring over and find himself either having to jump from a ludicrously long spot or from an eyeball-popping short spot.

"But it's not the worst problem in the world," Elsie said gently after we had somehow toppled over a small upright fence looking like we were involved in desperate last-ditch cavalry charge down a rocky mountainside. "Right now, the jumps are to keep him interested. As you grow more skilled and consistent in his flatwork, you'll be able to add gymnastics in order to teach him that he must be careful about where he puts his feet, or he simply won't be able to get over the fences."

Gymnastics—I knew what that meant. A series of fences in a straight line, mostly bounces or one-strides, with a few longer distances scattered within, to keep a horse sharp and focused. They'd been the scourge of my hunter/jumper childhood, riding a school pony up to a gymnastic, holding my breath, hoping for the best...

What Elsie considered a simple gymnastic could be a terrifying thing indeed. I'd watched some of her students leap through the gymnastics she set up—one had been seven fences long and involved nothing more spacious than two strides between fences. If you muddled up the first jump, you muddled up the entire series of jumps—that made for a lot of messy spots, rattled poles, and scary moments.

I was thankful she didn't think we were ready for gymnastics yet, or that they were even necessary at the moment. I wanted to keep things as light and fun as possible. Elsie had become our unofficial trainer, though. I was waiting for the day she pointed to an impossible series of bounces and said, "Go trot over those."

Elsie, who had evidently heard that Jean and I had finally had our ultimate fight, had started contriving to be at the barn whenever I was, saying "Why don't I just walk down to the ring with you," as I led Tiger out of the barn. It had become pretty obvious that she had decided to use Tiger and I to show Jean who was still boss of the barn, but I was perfectly happy to be used in such a manner. The coaching Elsie gave was invaluable, and the good rides we were starting to achieve had given me my old confidence back. I was remembering how to ride off-track Thoroughbreds, turning them from racehorses into show horses. It wasn't exactly a reversal of the work I did at the training track each morning, but I guessed it was pretty close.

After a ride, we would sit in the barn office and drink coffee and I'd listen while Elsie told me about the Thoroughbreds she'd had in the past. "The bravest and noblest of breeds," she'd say, nodding gravely. "And still bred to compete. Sometimes I think what I like best about Thoroughbreds, is that they aren't bred for temperament."

"What?" That was a bombshell of a statement. Breeding nasty horses to nasty horses because they were both athletic was one of my primary pet peeves in life. "But don't you think breeding bad tempers becomes a problem genetically?"

"If you don't have the riders to ride them, it does," Elsie conceded. "But if you're breeding kind, giving horses to kind, giving horses and don't leave in the fire, where is the horse's competitiveness going to come from? Where's that last burst of energy that gets a horse through when he thinks his reserves are all used up? That 'look of eagles' the old horsemen used to talk about, that didn't come from being a gentle old sheep. That came from pride, and power, and a rejoicing in one's own strength. Puppy dogs are lovely, but they don't have that spark. The allure of the Thoroughbred, now, that was always his fire. Your job is to harness that fire, show the horse that he should trust you, and make sure he'll do anything for you."

I sipped at cold, bitter coffee and thought about the truth in her words. I had never for a moment thought of it like that, but all the things that made my beloved horses so singular to me, whether it was Tiger or Luna or Personal Best, was surely wrapped up in their faults just as much as their attributes. Perhaps more so. Wasn't that the damnedest thing, I thought.

"But not everyone can ride that sort of horse," Elsie sighed. "Now more than ever. When you lack horsemen, you lack the capability to ride a horse with a mind of its own. Then you need the gentle old sheep."

"There aren't enough riders for Thoroughbreds, you mean."

"That's a fact. Look at my barn now. Nice, comfortable warmbloods, for nice, comfortable part-time riders who lack the seat and the skill and the desire to stick to a Thoroughbred who gets an idea in his brain. Good horses, sweet horses, kind horses. Sheep." Elsie shook her head. "Even *my* horse is a warmblood these days. But I'm too old to get into a fight and fall off. That's another story altogether. And he's a very nice horse. I couldn't help but fall in love with him, and he's taken care of me ever since."

I nodded. I understood *that*. I'd had plenty of days where I hadn't expected a fight, but the horse had brought me one anyway. There would be a limit to how much of that I could physically handle some day...but that day wasn't here yet. I could still devote years yet to riding Thoroughbreds. "I guess I never realized the problem is so multi-faceted."

"What problem is that?"

"The retirement problem. Making sure the horse is retired sound is one thing. Making sure he's trained well in a new discipline, another thing. But making sure there are enough riders to be able to want them and ride them...that's a whole other thing, isn't it?"

Elsie nodded. "We have to make more *horsemen*, but what we are making the most of, is part-time riders." She reached over and patted my hands. "You worry about your end of the business, and I'll worry about mine. That Jean...I should put her on a few Thoroughbreds, teach her that not everything is as dangerous as her aunt's horses. Jean has had a few bad experiences. The Thoroughbreds she rode as a child were made dangerous through poor handling and unsoundness. But they were free, and she loved horses so much, she couldn't help herself. She kept getting on, and she kept getting hurt. By the time she could get a job as a working student, she'd sworn off racehorses. I could never get her on one. But she does well with my students, she runs my barn well, she has picked some good sales horses...I've let her run a little wild with the place, I suppose."

"It's a shame about her...her aunt's horses, did you say? Her aunt had racehorses?"

Elsie smiled sadly. "Her aunt *has* racehorses. Her aunt is your friend Mary Archer."

I sat back in the folding chair so hard that it nearly tipped over backwards. "You're kidding!"

"Just a funny coincidence...but imagine if you had to try to learn to ride on one of Mary's poor, beat-up horses."

Ugh. Poor Jean. Now I was feeling sympathy for Jean. Elsie was some kind of wizard-trainer, for both horses and humans. Well, if anyone could fix Jean's anti-OTTB hysteria, it had to be Elsie. "If you want a good Thoroughbred, I can connect you with my friend

Lucy," I said. "She has to have something that you could use for a lesson horse...or that Jean could turn into a show jumper."

"Maybe we'll do that. And maybe we'll come down to your Thoroughbred Makeover so that she can see what you have done with Tiger. You need a cheering section, don't you?"

I grinned. "Well, cheering might not be the greatest idea if we want Tiger to hold it together in one piece. But...yes, I'd love for you to come."

Elsie smiled happily. "We need more retired racehorse advocates —I'll see who else in the barn I can get to come. You've reminded me, dear—you've reminded me that Thoroughbreds need people who are willing to stand up and *shout* about what wonderful horses they are. We have to create demand for them—and that's *my* job, as a riding instructor. It's your job to retire them safe and sound, and get them to the right trainers, so that they are ready for their new careers."

I nodded, my face serious again. That was my job. If Elsie was going to be an advocate, I was going to have to be an advocate, too.

Chapter Thirty-one

J UST LIKE THAT, THE horse show weekend was upon us.
There was the familiar cramping in my stomach, the familiar
nerves keeping me awake at night, the familiar nightmares about
arriving at the show-grounds completely naked. We've all had that
nightmare, haven't we?

Alexander wasn't really making things easier for me, though not
through any malicious forethought. He was having a devil of a
time with the Gulfstream horses, although he didn't want to admit
it, and so he spent a lot of his time at the farm muttering and
making phone calls to the assistant at the training center, and
sketching out training strategies in a weekly planner and scratching
them out again, and thumbing through the condition book, its
pages grown tattered with abuse, trying to find the right spots.

Not just the right spots—Alexander had to look for the most
advantageous spots. Where could he place Virtue to get him into
the right company to prep for a stakes race? What race would come
up at the right time to match Luna's work schedule? He had
sharpened her up with some fast works in company, and he
thought he had her blood up for a fight now. I listened, and looked

over his shoulder, but somehow it only made me feel more removed from the training process. I found I had a hard time concentrating on racing.

Instead, I was spending my days thinking about Tiger, and his progression as a riding horse. I walked through the Roundtree tack room, paused by the horse show calendar, and found myself placing my finger against shows in late May, shows I thought that I could take Tiger to once he had successfully competed in the Thoroughbred Makeover. I had the feeling that I was losing my focus, and that if I wasn't at the racetrack for much longer, I'd find myself shopping for a new hunt jacket and a fancy new hard hat.

The thing was, I didn't know if that was so terrible.

Maybe, just maybe, I was capable of doing both.

Not this time, as it happened.

I came into the kitchen as Alexander was finishing up a phone conversation. "That's right," he was saying, "And I'll need you in the paddock as well."

I pursed my lips, uncomfortably certain what he was talking about.

He finished the call and turned around. "Luz is going to come down for the Bahia Honda and help us run Personal Best. She's got the calmest nature of any groom I've ever met, so I think she can help him settle."

I nodded and dropped my eyes. Maybe I could show and race, huh? Silly me. Still, I persisted in the fantasy. "I'm going to try and get there," I promised. "I've been looking at the ride times, and I think I can do it."

Alexander shook his head dismissively. "There's no need to worry about all that. Concentrate on Tiger, let us worry about P.

B. I don't want you to miss your chance at this show because you're busy fussing over us."

How was I supposed to concentrate on a horse show while Personal Best was running the biggest race of his career? Clearly, Alexander was insane. "Okay," I agreed, but in my mind, I was still calculating the fastest route to Gulfstream from the show-grounds. I still figured I could make it, if no cops caught me on the way there.

Kerri and I decided to take Tiger down to south Florida a few days before the show, just so that he wouldn't think he was going to a race the minute he stepped out of the trailer. With his history of shipping to Tampa for races, I could only assume what his state of anticipation would be when we wrapped his legs and loaded him up. The last thing we needed was for him to come leaping out of the trailer on show morning and start bounding about like a gazelle, ready to go to the post, maybe taking out a few well-meaning ponies along the way.

"Although he wouldn't be the only horse there acting like that," Kerri said reasonably. "Since they're all supposed to be green Thoroughbreds."

"Well, then, we'll have an advantage over the rest," I countered, and sent off the email confirming that we'd like a stall at the equestrian center neighboring the county show-grounds for four nights before the show. This was really happening now.

Just like preparing for a horse show back when I was a teenager, there was a mountain of prep work to be done. There would be leather that needed to be cleaned, buckles that needed to be polished. The problem was, I really didn't have any English show tack to clean. My saddle was up to the task, but my nylon racing bridle, already a source of derision at Roundtree, was not going to do the job. I was considering going to Winning Edge and dropping several hundred dollars on a new bridle, but worried about how to break it in and make it comfortable enough for Tiger.

Kerri saved the day. She arrived one morning with a tack trunk wedged into her little car's backseat. Once we had coaxed it out of the car without doing too much damage to the seats and the doorframe, she nearly clapped her hands with excitement as I opened it up.

Myself, I was too overcome to speak. I just gazed into the treasure chest she had brought me, not even knowing where to begin. Kerri might not ride anymore, but she had certainly invested in some very nice tack before she gave it up.

Finally, I reached inside and lifted the topmost item from the trunk, a self-padded dark brown eventing bridle, its brass buckles gleaming dully in the midday sun. I ran my fingers along the butter-soft reins. "This is beautiful," I sighed.

"They don't make them like this anymore," Kerri said. "Like, literally, that saddlery closed down. I bought it when I was twelve. I had to mow a lot of lawns to get this bridle."

I touched the matching martingale and the sheepskin-lined jumping boots nestled in the box. The tack trunk was jam-packed with show gear—everything from bell-boots to saddle pads, spur straps to rein stops. "I think the sheepskin would be too hot on his legs," I said regretfully, stroking the furry padding. "But those are gorgeous boots."

"Dress lightly," Kerri said sensibly. "He goes in a saddle and bridle and neck strap. Why change?"

"I'll be leaving off the neck strap. But otherwise, you're right. This bridle, Kerri! I'm obsessed with it."

"That's awesome," Kerri said. "Because I don't want to polish the brass. You love it so much, you can do that part."

Chapter Thirty-two

M UCH TO MY OWN surprise, as well as everyone else's, Tiger was a gentleman at the new equestrian center.

Sure, he came out of the trailer on his toes; sure, there were a few gasps from the boarders nearby as he reared straight up in the air and waved his legs around like a bay version of The Black Stallion. That should surprise no one.

Happily, though, once he had hay in his face, he was fine. Kerri helped me cart in the tack trunk and set it up in front of his stall, but Tiger never seemed to notice our comings and goings. He was too busy tearing up the sweet orchard grass we'd brought along from home.

Tacking him up the next morning was no different than back at Roundtree, either. I looped his lead around the stall bars—why did all show barns have stall bars, I wondered. Why not build extra wide aisles and let your horses poke their heads out, the way we did at the races? It seemed silly—and I saddled and bridled him without any fuss at all. I mounted up in the barn aisle, racetrack style, because I felt contrary.

Kerri had been holding him for me. She dropped the reins, stepped back, and waved. "Happy ride!"

I took him down the driveway at first, between the empty rows of paddocks, their green grasses winking at us under the brilliant Florida sun. It was odd to see such glorious grass gone uneaten, but the horses here only went out first thing in the morning, and then only until lunch-time. I'd asked the barn manager, Amy, about that last night. They could not be left out overnight, Amy explained, for fear that they'd be stolen. There was a terrible problem with horse thieves in South Florida, and all of the owners were terrified their horses were next. Nor could they be left out all afternoon, she had continued, for fear the sun would bleach their show coats.

"And of course the bugs are always terrible," she'd sighed, and peered out west as if she could see the Everglades and wanted the swamps to know she was watching them. The wet, flat land sizzled with heat, a mosquito's paradise. "So many of these northern horses develop skin allergies and have to shipped back north. That's why part of the barn is screened." She pointed back at the west end of the center-aisle barn, where screening had been installed over about half the barn, stalls, aisle, and all. "Those are my allergy boarders down there. We get people who move to Florida, bring their horses, and then find the horses can't take it. They don't want to send them away, so we try the screens first. I do pretty decent business in allergy boarding. It's the new frontier of horse care, I think."

I couldn't help but think about my hardy broodmares, tails swishing, sweating through the summer sun while they grazed through the hottest part of the day without complaint, but I just nodded and said the screens were a fine idea. Privately, I wondered if horses ever needed gluten-free diets. She could expand into that next.

Amy had sighed again and looked a little sad. "We're losing one next week. He's going back to upstate New York. His owner is thinking of moving back to be with him."

Apparently even keeping horses walled off from the outside world wasn't always enough. Maybe you had to be born to the swamp life. It made the Everglades horses even sadder to think about. At least Market Affair had been a Florida-bred. He was born to the mosquitoes and the biting flies that rose up from the wetlands in buzzing clouds.

Then again, Tiger did pretty well himself, despite coming from New York. He never got anything more than a bump or two from mosquito bites.

"You don't mind staying in all afternoon though, do you?" I patted Tiger on his hot, hard neck. He flicked his ears back at me and then pricked them again, intent on the horses grazing in the pasture across the street. They evidently did not have such sensitive skins or coats as the horses in Amy's barn. He was keen to see what they were up to, but there was no nonsense in his step, no dancing underneath me. His razor-edge nerves were finally mellowing out. Enough slow mornings grazing and slow afternoons jogging around a sandbox of an arena will do that for a horse. Enough timothy in the hayrack will do wonders to add a bit of a belly and slow down the metabolism, as well. "You're almost a regular old horse again," I told him, not unkindly. "Pretty soon we'll be going on trail rides and falling asleep in the sun between our classes at horse shows. Doesn't that sound idyllic?"

Tiger took the opportunity to snort and blow at a passing mockingbird. I shook my head at him and made sure my heels were down. You never knew with this horse. Bored with the driveway already.

"You want to do something hard, huh?" I asked him, turning him back towards the barn. Despite my long inside leg and my guiding inside rein, he could still be a bit of a tank in his turns, somehow managing to negotiate a turn without bending one vertebra in the long line from poll to tail. It was one of those million things you didn't notice on the track, because they just plain didn't matter, but which blew up into glaring absences of education once you were concentrating on the little things. "Let's go find something hard," I suggested.

We started off for the arenas.

The dressage arena and jumping arena were side-by-side, glittering expanses of white sand and clay that were hard on the eyes on a sunny day. In the jumping arena three different riders were posting their way in and out of the show jumps, making circles and transitions and looking as if they were working very hard indeed.

In the dressage ring Amy was standing in the center of the ring and shouting commands at a female rider, who was being tugged around a semblance of a twenty-meter circle by a very eager and full of himself warmblood. "You're not in control, are you Charlotte?" Amy asked, and Charlotte sounded near tears when she replied, "No!"

Poor girl, I thought. Better stay out of the dressage arena, then. That looked like a disaster waiting to happen. I glanced back at the jumping arena. The three horse-and-rider teams in there all looked fairly together. One was cantering in a taut collected gait, the horse's neck curved elegantly and his well-conditioned muscles rippling in the sunlight. His rider turned him towards a small vertical fence and the horse bounced over it with no noticeable adjustment to his gait.

Tiger looked very, very interested. "Wanna go see?" I asked him, and he practically dragged me to the jumping arena. "Okay then," I said. "But please don't embarrass me."

We went through the little gate, which had a second fence in front of it to discourage horses from running away and right out the gate, and he shuffled his hooves a little in the sandy footing, testing it after walking on the firm driveway. Tiger, like so many racehorses, was a connoisseur of footing, adjusting and altering his movement and stride to every new surface he came into contact. Now, he danced a little, shuffling his hooves in a jig, and then settled into a long, head-bobbing walk, his ears pricked and watching the other horses.

The woman who had been cantering brought her horse down to a prancing halt and then walked over in our direction. Her horse, an elegant light bay, was hardly sweating. She, on the other hand, was beet-red and completely winded. Despite the impending heat exhaustion, her face was friendly and interested. Tiger and I watched them approach, and Tiger was *almost* composed when she brought her horse alongside to walk with us, stride for stride. I jiggled the bit and sat deep, asking him to remain demure and not reach over to take a chunk out of his new companion, and he complied, though his ears were tilted and carefully watching the bay horse.

"Well, *he's* very pretty," the woman announced, smiling as she looked Tiger over. "I haven't seen this little guy before. What sort of horse is he? He's so small."

Tiger was a sixteen-two hand horse, no small potatoes, but the light bay, though slender by warmblood standards, was a monster. He towered at least a hand taller than Tiger. I had to look up to meet his rider's eyes when I answered her. "He's a Thoroughbred," I began patiently, ready to start leaping into a spiel every time I talked to anyone about Tiger. *Breed advocate.* "He was one of my racehorses, and now that I've retired him, I'm retraining him to be a riding horse. We're here for the Thoroughbred Makeover this weekend."

"But he's been a racehorse?" The woman looked excited. She was much like the others I'd seen at the equestrian center— somewhere near middle-aged, relatively decent shape, sweating through her make-up. (Why did people wear make-up to the barn? It must be habit.) A brunette pony-tail swung from the lower rim of her gorgeous Charles Owen hard hat. "Well *that's* pretty exciting. I've never seen a racehorse in person before!"

"Really? That's too bad. You should come to Gulfstream and see them run sometime. It's not far from here. We have horses running there all the time." A good breed advocate would show them every side of the Thoroughbred breed, right?

"I've been to the mall there," she said thoughtfully. "I like the shopping. I don't know if I'd like the races. They're always getting hurt, aren't they? Has he ever gotten hurt?"

I bit my lip to stop from saying something I'd regret. Maybe I didn't really have the temperament to be the ambassador for the horse racing industry, especially after my attempts to do just that had bit me so hard in the ass. Ah, but what choice did I have? Breed. Advocate. "This guy? Just little things here and there," I said evenly, pressing down a surge of impatience. "A nick. A strain. The same as any sport-horse. We're very careful with our horses. Although accidents do happen. He's very tough."

"I've heard they get hurt all the time." The woman sighed, reflecting on the stories she had heard, the articles she had read. For a moment, she looked downcast, then she shook her head and smiled brightly at me. "But I could be wrong! I'm Jessica," she added. "And this is Cosmos." She patted the bay on the neck and he dipped his fine-boned head, snorting. "He's a Hanoverian."

More like half-Thoroughbred, half-Hanoverian. How many Thoroughbred mares had been approved into the registry that called this athletic beast a Hanoverian? He was no cart-horse from the villages of Germany, that was for sure. Would a breed advocate burst into a speech on the Thoroughbred's contribution to the modern-day warmblood horse? Probably not on the first date. "He's lovely," I said instead. "I'm Alex, and this is Tiger."

"Tiger! Oh, you big scary thing you!" And she growled at him.

That's how I made friends with Jessica, who might not have been entirely living in the same realm of reality as most folks, but who was awfully nice anyway. We rode off together, Tiger swishing his tail to declare his displeasure with being so close to another horse and yet not allowed to gallop past him, and talked about everyday equestrian things: hoof-picks, pulling manes, barn politics. No one could have looked at us and seen that Jessica and I occupied two different worlds in the horse business. We were both sitting on horses in the same sort of tack, and suddenly we had a common language. It wouldn't have been so simple, I knew, if we had met in a restaurant, or even in a shed-row. Now, it was easy, and it was nice. I wasn't a girl to have too many friends, but a riding buddy—that wasn't so bad.

"Ride tomorrow morning?" Jessica asked as we led our horses into the wash-racks. Kerri ran up to hold Tiger, while Jessica merely slid a halter onto Cosmos and clipped him into the cross-ties. If she found my reluctance to use cross-ties weird, she didn't say anything. Already getting used to racetrackers, I thought. See, it can be done! We can live in harmony!

"I might be out later than this." Kerri looked at me questioningly. "Well, since we're here," I explained to her, "I'm going to see if I can blow out P.B. tomorrow morning."

"Blow out? P.B.?" Jessica looked mystified.

Kerri laughed and started unbuckling Tiger's bridle. Tiger, tired and hot, leaned into her and started rubbing. Scary racehorse, I thought. "P.B. is Personal Best," I explained. "One of my racehorses. He's entered in a big race Saturday, and I want to give him a fast workout tomorrow morning. It's called a blow out."

"But today's Tuesday! Why do you want to wear him out just a few days before the race? Shouldn't he have time off?"

"That's not how it works. I want to build up his blood, and I want his attitude sharpened. He'll associate the work with a race, so it's good for him mentally and physically."

Jessica shook her head. "Rocket science. I have no idea what you're talking about. Sounds completely different from showing. If I were showing on Saturday, then Wednesday I'd probably do a few little jumps, Thursday I'd do some flatwork, and Friday he'd have off."

"That's not so different. He'll just jog Thursday and Friday."

"Jog? Is that like, a slow canter?"

"No, it's a trot." I shoved Kerri, who was laughing openly now. "*Jog* is trot, *gallop* is anything from a canter to a full gallop. A breeze is a fast timed work, racing speed."

"Why?"

"Why is it breeze?"

"Yes, why is it breeze?"

I considered this for a moment before conceding the point. "Jessica, I have no idea."

"Well," Jessica chuckled, stripping the tack off of Cosmos while he leaned against the cross-ties, working his jaw like a silly racehorse himself, "you have fun with that, then. And wait—isn't your horse show on Saturday? The same day as your horse race?"

"It sure is," I sighed, and turned back to the job of untacking Tiger. "It sure is."

"Well, what are you going to do?"

"I have to show Tiger," I said. "That's first and foremost. Alexander can run Personal Best" —even if it killed me— "But I tell you what I'm going to do...I'm going to head over to the training center this afternoon and give him a big kiss. Even if Alexander doesn't want me to ride him in the morning, I'm still going to make sure I see him before his run."

Jessica, hidden behind her horse, sounded muffled when she said "That's so nice," but I was turning back to Tiger, who was in desperate need of a cool shower, and didn't answer. Kerri just smiled at me, because she knew I couldn't resist going to see my horses, and said she was going to the beach all afternoon, so I was free to wander wherever I wanted alone.

Chapter Thirty-three

I T DIDN'T TAKE AS much pleading as I had expected. Alexander seemed almost...eager? Relieved? Desperate?...for me to come out and do the honors of blowing out P.B. The horse had been a nightmare for the past month, by all accounts. Although he'd romped in the little race Alexander had dropped him into a few weeks ago (at *my* suggestion, I reminded myself proudly, meaning that *I* was still training my colt), he'd remained a pill on the training track and even in the shed-row. The only time he seemed happy was when he was out in his tiny paddock, and on the day he'd gone to the race.

"But he was a monster in the paddock," Alexander had warned ominously. "If he goes on acting out like this, we're going to have a real problem in the Bahia. And I want you to ride him with an abundance of caution in the morning. I don't need you getting hurt on your first time back out."

As if I had a history of getting hurt. I agreed demurely that I would ride Personal Best with all the delicacy of a nuclear scientist disarming a bomb, and silently cheered that tomorrow morning I was going to get to ride my baby. Even if I was going to have to miss the Bahia Honda Stakes in order to show Tiger, if I could settle his nerves and get his brain into a workmanlike place before the race, I'd be doing right by *both* my favorite boys.

And Alexander, besides. I had a feeling it had been hard on him, taking all this on while I sat at home and played with Tiger. (And managed the two-year-olds, and dealt with the breeding and foaling, and managed the yearlings...but mostly, he would see it, playing with Tiger.) It wasn't that he wasn't capable of training alone—it was that for the past few years, with a few exceptions, we had done it together. Dissolving a happy and successful partnership for no good reason at all rarely made the job more fun or satisfying.

Well, all of that was over now. Once the Thoroughbred Makeover was out of the way, I was renewing the partnership. I was taking horses to races again. I was standing beside Alexander along the rail again, waiting with a halter and a lead shank for our horse to come galloping home. CASH or no CASH. Protestors or no protestors. This nonsense had gone on long enough. I wasn't willing to be punished for trying to do the right thing any longer.

"I'm not your poster girl anymore," I told my reflection in the rear-view mirror. "Find someone else to blame. I'll be busy making a difference."

First things first, say hello to my horses that *weren't* retired yet.

I called up the training center and let them know I was coming. The security guard said that would be fine, and then he paused. "Alex, something you ought to know..." His southern drawl added an extra measure of fatherly concern to his tone. "We have a few protestors out here today."

"Protestors?" Alexander had said that was over. "I thought—not for *me?*"

"I guess someone got wind you was in town. Don't know. They showed up a few hours ago, after training hours. Almost like they knew you was comin' over here."

My heart sank. I'd only told one person besides Kerri that I was going to visit.

⊷⋙⋙〉 〈⋘⋘⊷

There were fewer of them than I had expected.

I had been fearing a shouting crowd of hundreds, waving signs with my face and a big red *x* over it, but maybe I was just flattering myself if I thought I was worth so much attention. I'd never been a big-shot in this game—if I was a celebrity animal abuser, it was just amongst the lunatic fringe in CASH.

When I finally got to the training center, cursing at south Florida's ridiculous traffic the entire way, the front gates were closed tight as usual, but the security guard sitting in his car, parked just inside of them, was a change.

So were the fifteen or twenty women milling about on the manicured St. Augustine lawn in front of the training center sign. Sunburned and disheveled, the pack of ladies were evidently taking a break from protesting. A few were sitting on their cardboard signs, backs against the ram-rod straight sabal palms that shaded the driveway, and one woman had taken off her flip flops and dipped her feet into the sparkling reflecting pool beneath the burnished lettering of the farm sign.

Classy, I thought.

Most of them were wearing flip flops, shorts, and tank tops, in fact, but that really didn't mean much in this part of the world. Most of the time, it was too hot to wear anything else. There was every chance that these ladies were high-powered members of the equestrian community or, failing that, the Keep Everything Family-Friendly community. Soccer moms, PTA power brokers, Pony Club volunteers—anything was possible in an anti-racing protest. You didn't have to be a member of anything in particular to hate horse racing, unfortunately. You didn't have to fit any demographic at all. My sport had more enemies than friends these days, most of them deserved—but I was trying to do things *right*.

I flung the truck into park and hopped out, ready to do battle.

The women had been organizing the minute they saw a visitor pulling up to the gates—jumping up, gathering their signs, readying their rallying cries. The little hive had burst into a frenzy of motion, but when I slammed the truck door and faced them down, every last one of them froze in place.

I looked down at myself and hid a little smile. Polo shirt, riding breeches, dress boots—from head to toe I was dressed in the uniform of the English equestrian. I bet that was the last thing these ladies had expected. I gave them a moment to enjoy their discomfiture. *That's right, girls. I look just like you. Assuming any of you ride.* The really militant ones probably just let their horses graze, because riding would be cruel. Maybe they didn't even own horses, because owning horses was cruel. Horses should be wild and free. Where wild and free was, I didn't exactly know, but I doubted it included the sweet feed, alfalfa, and peppermints that a horse like Tiger considered requirements for life.

332   NATALIE KELLER REINERT

"Ladies," I said expectantly, looking around the motley little group. "You have something you wanted to say to me?"

There was a general murmur of confusion, heads tilting to whisper amongst themselves. It wasn't hard to figure out that these uninformed rabble didn't even know who I was. It was no wonder —my picture didn't show up in the industry rags often, but when it did I was usually looking a bit more dapper and polished in my race-day attire, leading a horse from the paddock or standing at his hindquarters in the win photo. A far cry from the sweat-soaked, horse-stained, real-life version of myself standing in front of my detractors now.

Then Jessica, whom I had somehow missed, stepped forward. She was wearing a t-shirt with a jumping horse on it and holding a homemade sign that announced "Horse Racing Kills Horses!" in large capital letters. The letters were very straight and even, I noticed. She had worked hard on it. More than I could say for a few of the other women holding signs today. Her face was flushed nervously. She opened her mouth to talk, but no sound came out.

I shook my head at her. "Shame on you, Jessica," I chided, as if she were a bad horse. "Acting like you were my friend."

She flinched and her eyes dropped to the ground. "Horse racing is cruel," she muttered. "You can't change the facts."

"You don't *know* the facts, Jessica. You literally said that to me. You've never even been to the races, let alone see how the horses are cared for or trained. How dare you call me cruel to horses, after riding with me? You think I'm cruel to Tiger?"

Before she could answer, not that she was *going* to answer, a redhead with positively demonic flashing green eyes shoved her aside. Her pony-tail was coming loose and she shoved loose strands behind her ears impatiently. "Are you Alex Whitehall?" she demanded. "Because we have a few things we'd like to say to you. If you are. Alex Whitehall."

I grinned. I'd recognize that accent and that stilted speech pattern anywhere. "I am *Alex* Whitehall, as a matter of fact. And I have a feeling you're Cassidy Lehigh. Glad you figured out my first name this time." I leaned back against the truck and affected a casual pose. My heart was racing and I was willing my face not to flush, but the truth was that despite the jangling nerves inherent in facing an angry mob that hates you, I was feeling pretty great. I'd dealt with some pretty shady characters in my time, after all. I'd put up with some real pieces of work, day after day, in Saratoga. Yet, here I stood, the trainer of stakes horses and the co-manager of an Ocala breeding farm. No one had been able to take my triumphs away from me yet. This rag-tag little bunch of sunburned suburbanites wasn't going to, either. "You say what you have to say, and then I'll tell you why you're mistaken, and then you can all go home."

"You're a horse-killer!" someone shouted, and there was a chorus of *shush's* and *yeah's,* mixed about evenly, from the group.

Cassidy didn't say anything at all. She just waited until her acolytes were quiet again, and then she spoke.

"We're here about the matter of Market Affair, the horse that you bred who was found abandoned in the Everglades," she announced, her voice ringing out as if she was addressing a stadium full of people. "You paint yourself as some sort of—"

"You okay, ma'am?" It was the security guard, who had evidently been taking a nap or something. He leaned out of his car window. "Everything okay out here?"

"We're fine," I said. "Thank you." I turned back Cassidy. "Do go on. You were about to tell me about the kind of person I pretend to be."

I'd absorbed a fair amount of English disdain in my years with Alexander.

Cassidy flushed, but forged ahead with her airing of grievances against me. "You give your little interviews talking up your retirement programs, and all along this horse was being passed around from owner to owner, being run to death, and then tossed out in the swamp like trash. You're a hypocrite, just like everyone else in this business."

"Assuming this were actually true, what would you want from me?" I was genuinely curious. Did they want a public apology? A large cash donation to a charity? My head on a pike?

"So you don't deny it?" There was a lot of hissing from the ladies. Pack of snakes, indeed.

"Of course I deny it, because it isn't true. I had nothing to do with this horse, although I'm heartbroken at what happened to him." I shook my head. "He was a good colt, he was a beautiful colt, but he wasn't *my* colt. Not for one second." I found it amusing that I didn't even need to mention Sunny Virtue. Cassidy must have done her homework on that one. You couldn't pin too many false accusations on one person, or someone might notice how much lying you were doing. Just the one horse, though, was enough to get everyone riled up.

"He was your colt!" someone else shouted. "Your farm bred him!"

I held up a finger. "One," I stated. "I wasn't part of farm management then." I put up another finger. Let's make it easy for these kids to understand. "Two. He was a client's horse. He wasn't the farm's. Whether I was ever his owner or not, if the horse doesn't belong to me, I can't control his care. He's someone else's property. And," I went on, talking over Cassidy's sputtering protests, "It is now a farm policy to track all of our horses to the best of our abilities and provide retirement assistance, but we still can't force an owner to sell or change training policies. As I told the interviewer from *New Equestrian*. Which I assume is what you were talking about when you mentioned 'all my interviews.' I gave *one*. Now, if only Cassidy was as forthcoming with information, you all could be doing something else with your afternoon. Because she already knows *all* of this. She's had this conversation with me before. Cassidy, notice that my story hasn't changed in all these months? That's because it's true."

Cassidy squared her jaw and glared at me. I got the feeling that if she showed up at her neighbor's house with Girl Scout Cookies, her neighbor bought those damn cookies just as fast as he could. She was a woman who liked being in charge, liked getting her own way.

Funny, so was I.

"If you have a problem with property rights and how owning things works, which I think is what is confusing Cassidy right now, you're going to have to address that separately from any problems you have with horse racing," I said. "Now why don't you get on out of here and go ride your own horses."

Her eyebrow twitched. "We're not going anywhere until the public knows that you're no better than the rest of them."

I cocked my head. "The rest of who?"

She smiled thinly, and it was so malevolent that I was immediately reminded of Mary Archer. Mary Archer...so pleased with herself when she broke the news back in Tampa. So obviously at the bottom of this whole mess. My dear lovely nemesis-next-door.

"The rest of the *racetrackers,*" Cassidy hissed, her green eyes narrow and dangerous as a snake's. "We're tired of cleaning up your messes. We're rescuers and we're horsewomen, and we've been nursing your wrecks back to health and putting down your disasters for too many years now. You spit out horses year after year like machines producing cheap toys, and when you break them you toss them out like trash. But they're not trash—they're alive, and you're going to be forced to take responsibility for them. All of you. This isn't over."

"So let's do it."

"What?" Cassidy cocked her head like a confused border collie.

"Let's *do it.* Of course this business needs cleaned up. Of course we need to fix these holes horses slip through and get rid of these fake horsemen who do things like dump horses, or run them until they break. Of *course we do!* What do you think, I like the way these people act?" I shook my head. "Stop lumping us all together. This is just like politics. You know how nothing changes because of who holds the power, who holds the purse-strings? We're playing the same nothing-changes game here. It's all politics. It's regulations. It's who has the money to push things through.

"Remember," I held up a finger—I was warming to my lecture, I was a *breed advocate* and that didn't just mean selling Thoroughbreds as show horses—"Remember that racing is regulated by the individual states. The gaming boards. That's where the change has to come from. So who here is a lawyer? Who is going to donate time to start putting together proposals, and taking delegations to Tallahassee, and changing the rules?"

There was a silence in the group. A few signs came down, tired arms giving in to the dull reality. Cassidy's wasn't one of them, but she was starting to look like a lone psycho in a crowd slowly coming to their senses.

A crowd that was realizing that standing here, yelling at me, wasn't going to change a thing.

Then, a woman in the middle of the pack spoke up. She was wearing a shirt with a rescue logo on the chest, a horse-head and a heart intertwined. Her bronzed skin was the result of years out in the Florida sun. She could have been a farmer, a rancher, a horsewoman her whole life.

"I'm a lawyer," she said, and I smiled. A person can be both. That was one of the great things about being a horsewoman— anyone from any walk of life could do it. All you needed was a love of horses and enough grit to work endlessly for them. "I can start this," she went on. "We can get this ball rolling if we work together."

Cassidy turned and sought out her face in the crowd. "You sure, Danielle? You have a full farm right now. How're you going to take this on? Don't let this liar turn your life upside-down."

Danielle smiled a tired smile. "I can do it with all of your help, I guess. If we can gather together for a few hours to make a protest, we can gather at my kitchen table and look through some laws, start writing some new ones. It'll take time, but...I mean..." She shrugged. "So does this. I could be riding right now, you know?"

Jessica spoke up. "Alex is right. There are good people in racing—I've ridden with her and I've seen that she's a horsewoman. If she says that it can be fixed, well...then we have to try to fix it. I can help."

I couldn't believe it. This was happening. I'd given a speech like some sort of freedom fighter and the masses had stopped waving signs and started to listen. I had misjudged them, just as they had misjudged me. Now I had their attention. A little more engagement, and maybe I could have their loyalty. These women weren't just the lunatic fringe, after all. These were horse-people who were desperate to help horses, so desperate they were willing to pay attention to anyone who told them they could make a change. It was just a sad truth that the people most likely to stand up and lead them were the people with the least amount of true integrity.

"I can help," I said. "I'm not a lawyer, but I'm a trainer. I'm a breeder. I'm an owner. And I'm here to do what's right for the horses."

Then, because I'd seen too many movies, I suppose, or because I was just so damn excited, I started clapping my hands. Slowly, then all at once, the crowd followed suit. They were dropping their signs and we were all clapping in unison outside of the gates of a training center, while the security guard peered at us from the air-conditioned comfort of his car, and the trucks drove by on the county road as if nothing was happening.

But something was happening. Something was starting. Change was starting.

Cassidy Lehigh left.

Chapter Thirty-four

I PULLED THE GIRTH tight with trembling fingers, ignoring Tiger's tail as it slapped as close to my face as he could get it. *Let him complain in the barn. If he behaves under saddle, that's all I can ask for.* It was nearly time for our spot in the jumping class, the only class we were entered in since the versatility had been cancelled due to lack of entries. We had to go into the arena, put in a short dressage-type test as a warm-up, and then trot or canter a tiny course of tiny fences—the course was rider's choice. It would be no different than any other ride, I kept telling myself —and Tiger. The only difference was that it would be in front of an audience, in an arena we'd never been in before, and I could only hope that Tiger wouldn't take one look and think that he was in a strange new kind of racetrack.

No pressure there.

"Be a good boy," I told Tiger, voice cajoling, and he turned his head to look at me. His eyes were bright and his nostrils flared wide, but he wasn't trembling or pawing or pinning his ears at me, and for now that was all I could ask for. "It's not a race," I reminded him. "This is just another ride, in another boarding stable arena. Your third one! You're some globe-trotter now!"

The loudspeaker in the barn aisle crackled and hummed, preparing to make some announcement. My hands froze on the saddle's billet, waiting. Tiger jumped as if it was the call to post he'd been waiting for, but instead of the blaring tones of a trumpet, he heard only the static-roughened voice of the show announcer. The thin skin on his shoulder shook.

"Next rider on deck, Arlene Bowen on Splashtastic."

Only a call to the arena, for a rider well ahead of me. The breath I didn't know I'd been holding rushed out of me, and I finished buckling the girth. Now all I needed was my hard hat and bridle. I opened the stall door a crack and reached through, grasping blindly where I thought the bridle hook ought to be. My hand closed on empty air. I shoved the stall door a bit wider, its ungreased wheels groaning in protest, and stuck my head out inquiringly.

There was nothing there. The hook was empty. The beautiful padded bridle that Kerri had brought out of retirement was nowhere to be seen.

"No," I whispered, and threw a quick glance behind me; Tiger was standing quietly, one hind leg cocked, his ears pricked as he watched me do the hokey-pokey with his stall door. "You stand," I commanded in a firm tone. His ears waggled in response. *Good enough.*

I slipped out of the stall and slid the door closed again, then looked up and down the aisle. A few other riders were bustling about in front of their own stalls, polishing tack or rolling bandages, but most of them were either already on their horses in the warm-up arena, or had finished their rides and joined the spectators in the arena bleachers, watching the final rides of the competition. The barn wasn't quite deserted, but it would have been fairly easy for someone to just lift a bridle without being noticed. Someone who would be in and out constantly, like the organizer, maybe? *Cassidy, you nightmare.* I'd bested her yesterday and stolen away her acolytes. Now she wanted to make sure I wasn't going to ruin her horse show by winning it, too.

What the hell was I going to do now? There was no point in searching for it—this wasn't a scavenger hunt. If someone had taken my bridle, it was as good as gone forever.

I was just going to have to find another bridle.

There was a *bang* from within the stall. I whirled around and peered through the bars. Tiger rolled his eye at me and flung his head up and down, then casually lifted a long foreleg and rapped his hoof against the wall board again. *Bang!*

"You knock that off," I snapped. "Shame on you!"

Bang, bang, bang!

"Son of a..." I stopped myself from saying another word, lest disapproving ears catch me calling my horse names and call the local papers. I started off down the barn aisle, heading in the direction of the nearest human. Maybe someone would *lend* me a bridle. Fighting back a bright red blush, I made the rounds, begging for tack.

"I only have one with me, sorry."

"Oh no! I didn't bring a spare bridle. I really should have."

"Wait, you said yours went missing?"

"Who would take your bridle?"

I had tried to be discreet, making inquiries quietly and with a great deal of humility, rather than drama and urgency, but it only takes one loud voice, and suddenly half-a-dozen other women were grouping around me, brushes and bandages in their hands. "Nora, someone took this lady's bridle!" one of them shouted, and a head popped out of a stall door.

"You're *kidding!*"

I bit my lip. "Look, I don't want to start a big fuss over nothing. I'm sure someone just took my bridle by mistake. And we all have to compete today, so I don't want to distract any of you from getting your horses ready—"

"Are you kidding?" the one named Nora shouted, sliding her horse's stall door shut and marching down the aisle. She was tall and thin and had a jutting chin that gave her a commanding appearance, and everyone seemed perfectly willing to stop chattering and let Nora take charge. "This is clearly an attack by another competitor. Someone doesn't want you to win. Is there anyone here that you've had a disagreement with? Bad business deal? Come on, we've all been there. We all have our enemies."

There was a lot of solemn nodding at this. As horse trainers, every one of them knew that using the word "enemy" was not an exaggeration. This business was not for the faint of heart.

I choked back a rueful laugh. "I wouldn't know where to start," I admitted. "I'm Alex Whitehall."

The solemn nods turned to dropped jaws. Not the greatest reaction, but at least no one turned on their heel and walked away from me.

"I can see that my reputation precedes me," I said, and attempted a smile.

A rider who didn't look much older than sixteen gave me a careful boots-to-baseball cap assessment before she spoke. "They say you dumped that horse in the Everglades because he was always coming up lame and you didn't think he'd be more than a pasture pet if you retired him."

"Define *'they,'* because that's the first I've heard of that particular twist on the story." Behind me, I heard Tiger kick the wall again, and I wished they'd hurry up and decide whether they were going to help me or run me out of the barn with a pitchfork. None of this mattered if Tiger lamed himself. I set out to explain myself yet again. I should have this story printed up on business cards. I could just walk around distributing them. *Before you say anything...just read this.* "The thing is, I never owned that horse. And the guy that did own him left the country. There's no one here to take the blame, but a lot of people think I should do it." I shrugged. What did it matter anymore? "I'm just trying to do the right thing, one horse at a time. They're going to say whatever they want. Talk is cheap. Training, making change happen—that takes a little more effort."

There were a few nods of approval. I bit back a hopeful smile. If I could win over these ladies, these retired racehorse devotees, I'd be amongst friends at last.

"It was CASH, wasn't it?" another rider asked. This woman was older, stouter, and more skeptical looking. The voice of reason, I hoped. "Those bastards at CASH are a pack of liars. And the groups they work with are worse. Some of those people think all horses ought to be set free on the plains to run wild, didja know that? They're against all of us, not just horse racing."

"That's true," another woman said. "Those animal rights activists are all tarred with the same brush. They say it's about drugs and racing two-year-olds, and it's really about anyone who shows horses. They hate us all the same. It's a slippery slope. I won't let my students have anything to do with them."

I wondered what would happen if I announced that the show's organizer was also behind CASH. I wondered if anyone actually knew. I bit my lip.

"So what happened to the horse, then?" The young girl looked annoyed, as if she'd rather not be proved wrong quite so publicly. Well, it was hard being the youngest one in the group. I understood that.

"He's at a farm somewhere, Indiantown, maybe? Getting better. We sent money for his vet bills, because it was the right thing to do. But of course then people said it was an admission of guilt. I can't help that. I can't help what people say, or what they think. Fact is, I was just an exercise rider when he was at the farm, and he was a boarder. That's the only connection I have with the horse."

His winsome face, with that thick black forelock blowing across his tiny white star; his pricked ears watching me as I entered his stall to get him saddled for the day. The spring in his step every time he saw a beloved mud puddle in his path...There was *that* connection, too. That had been a real connection, even if it wasn't on paper, wasn't legally binding, and could never truly be explained to anyone. I took a deep breath, let it out, steadied myself. "He was a good boy," I told them. "I won't say I didn't care about him. He was special." I took another shaky breath, thinking of the two-year-olds we'd had this spring. The ones who had gone on to sales, the ones who had been mine, the ones who had never been mine, the ones who I had complained about and the ones who had made me thrill and the ones who had never, really, done much for me at all—but I remembered all of them.

"They all have something that makes them special," I realized aloud. "And they're all perfect for someone."

There was quiet for a moment.

Nora crossed her arms across her chest, looking like a large judgmental grasshopper, and pointed her chin at me for a long, weighty moment. I met her gaze and waited. Then she gave me a half-smile and turned to the others, fixing her eyes on them one at a time. "We've all heard the stories. But I gotta be honest with you, Citizens Against Slave Horses doesn't seem like the most reputable source. I almost didn't come to this whole show because I know Cassidy's got mixed up with them. But I think she only did it to go after Alex here."

The stout woman nodded emphatically. "You know I agree, Nora. But she was wrong to do it. You can't wipe out years of responsible behavior with the accusation of one fringe group. That's what I say, anyway. I read that interview you did in the fall," she added, turning towards me. "I agreed with every word you said. And that's why I'm here. The Thoroughbred is the single greatest resource we have as sport horse trainers. Strong, versatile, and smart. And there are thousands of them just waiting for a new career. We have to stick together if we're going to bring this breed back to the top."

I could have kissed her. Those were my words, right off the pages of *New Equestrian*. The ones that had been overshadowed these past four months by the words of Mary Archer, as translated by CASH and their press releases and their mass e-mails. It was all I could do to remember the girl I'd been when I'd said them, so confident in their simple truth. I had never expected them to get me into trouble.

Nora spoke up again. "I'm with Marla on this one. I read that interview too, and I remember thinking, 'Hey, this girl is one of us.' I still think she is. And if we let these radical animal rights activists get their way, it won't be long before they'll be coming after our show horses. I think we *have* to give Alex a fair shot in competition. And that means finding a bridle for her. Does anyone have anything, anywhere? In your trailer maybe? In your tack trunk? Let's do some scouting. We can put together some spare parts if we have to."

The crowd scattered, half a dozen women of every age and size and shape, all wearing breeches and boots, united in the common cause of finding me a bridle. I was so grateful, I nearly burst into tears. Maybe I would have, too, but Tiger started kicking again, and I excused myself to go tell that wretch that he was just going to have to wait like a gentleman, or he'd have to answer to me in a round pen.

Chapter Thirty-five

"*A*LEX WHITEHALL, RIDING THE Tiger Prince.*"
My name was still echoing around the lofty rafters when I trotted Tiger into the arena. I couldn't help but glance at the crowds in the bleachers as we made our first round of the arena, and I could see the round eyes, the turned heads as people whispered.

Alex Whitehall, Horse Murderer, I thought glumly. *My name precedes me.* Tiger stuck his head out, neck stiff, and that's when I realized that I had to ignore them and ride as we had done back at the farm, or all of my discomfort would show in the gaits of my horse.

One more glance, and there they were—Elsie, and Jean, and Kelly, and a few other ladies from Roundtree—they had all driven all the way down here from Ocala to be our cheering section! Elsie was smiling at me, looking encouraging; Jean looked grim, as if she was certain that Tiger was going to go on a rampage worthy of his name—perhaps he would kill me, kill the judge, and then kill everyone in the bleachers.

I had to convince her that she was wrong.

Breed advocates, that was what we all were today. We had to be breed advocates, taking every opportunity to show off the gorgeous moves and incomparable nature of the Thoroughbred horse. Tiger's flashing good looks were one thing; now I needed him to show that he was a competitive, but tractable, partner in the show-ring. With that attitude, maybe Jean would be one step closer to giving Thoroughbreds another shot. And hey, maybe we'd win the class while we were at it.

After all, we were here to win. Would I have left Personal Best for anything less than first place?

Resolved, I fixed my gaze between Tiger's two pricked ears, softened my hands, and relaxed my shoulders. I let my legs hang as long as they could reach, and I felt him come back to me; his mouth elastic on the bit, his back rising to meet my seat, his gait springing forward with the cat-like grace I knew so well. As we trotted in a big figure-eight with panache, I thought that the arena grew quiet, the whispers silenced. Perhaps I was just so caught up in the ride, the distractions around us disappeared.

We cantered twice, one time around on each lead, with lovely round twenty-meter circles to show that he was beginning to grow aware of bending on the turn. Tiger stuck his nose out and grew stiff on the right lead, and still couldn't quite bend in that direction, but at least he picked up the lead correctly at the first asking. I rode him down the center line and asked for a little leg-yield to soften his jaw and relax his top line again, and Tiger complied, the foam dripping from his mouth and sweat darkening his poll as he thought hard about each request.

Then, it was time for the fences.

He'd already seen them, five little jumps at the far end of the arena. Two cross-rails, two verticals, a nicely stepped oxer. Nothing higher than two-foot-three, as advertised. They were baby novice jumps, designed for the advanced beginner, but they were still thrilling to a young horse who had just found out about jumping.

Earlier in the competition, I'd overheard, the jumps had caused some excitement. There had been a lot of rushing, a little bolting, a few subsequent crashes. No one had gotten hurt, and nothing had really been out of the norm for a new jumper, but still—if I wanted to win this, I had to keep Tiger calm, calm, calm. There could be no repeats of the mistakes we had made back at the farm.

I breathed deep and tried to release the tension I could feel creeping back through my back and shoulders. Tiger shook his head and blew hard through his nostrils, and I loosened my fingers in response, giving him the space he needed to stretch his neck without catching him in the mouth. He moved forward lightly and tucked his nose in a gentlemanly approximation of a horse on the bit, and I gave him a little leg, just the slightest bit, for more impulsion. We wound through the jumps, his ears following the standards of each one as we circled them, and his steps picked up a bit. I closed my fingers in response and felt his mouth harden a bit. "Easy, son," I muttered. "One step at a time."

When he seemed more settled and relaxed, I took him in a big loop around the fences, and then turned him towards a cross-rail. We were still about ten strides away, plenty of time for him to judge the fence and decide what pace he needed for his approach. Tiger judged the fence and decided that it was going to require maximum velocity. He stuck out his nose and proceeded to charge at a huge sloppy trot, his entire body sloping forward onto his

350 NATALIE KELLER REINERT

forehand. I felt like he was going to trip on his own toes and tumble head-over-heels, taking me with him. If he thought he was going to gain a canter with this sort of gait, he was sadly mistaken. *This isn't it, Tiger.*

I dropped my hands to either side of his withers and stretched them far apart, wiggling the bit just a little with my ring fingers to remind him—*soft, calm, relaxed.* He flicked an ear back towards me, as if to acknowledge that yes, yes, he knew I was there, but there was this *jump* thing ahead, and it needed to be dealt with before he could give me what I wanted. Which of us was more determined? I set my jaw and sat down in the saddle, letting my legs slip ahead of me in a chair seat well removed from his sides, and pushed my seat bones into his spine with everything I had.

Tiger nearly skidded into a crashing halt, responding immediately to the pressure of my seat. His head came up, his hindquarters came under him, and I immediately brought my legs back beneath me and lightly touched his ribs.

Spring! Tiger's motion poured upwards and he was floating forward in a correct trot once more, his mouth finding my firm hands and softening to them.

We trotted like a pair of dressage queens up to the cross-rail. Tiger popped over the cross-rail, trotted away, and, when I asked, halted with all the aplomb of a veteran school horse. Fence number one, complete. Now to trot through five more with the same gravity and presence of mind.

There was a ripple of applause around the arena when we completed the course, the soft polite claps of equestrians who do not wish to disturb a green horse, especially when said green horse has just given the performance of life.

I should have saluted the judge, but instead, I fell forward on Tiger's neck and gave him a hug, tears pricking at my eyes. There were some things more important than protocol.

Chapter Thirty-six

K ERRI MET ME AT the in-gate, her eyes huge. "I saw," she said before I could ask. "He did everything right."

"I have to go now. Can you untack him?" I was already slipping from the saddle, bunching the reins to pull over his neck and hand off to her.

"You can't," Kerri breathed. "There's going to be a tie-breaker. You have the same score as Cassidy Lehigh."

I didn't notice the name. I was running through my timeline in my head. Did I have time for the tie-breaker? It wouldn't take long —just like a jump-off in a regular show-jumping competition, but this would be a little more simple for the green off-track Thoroughbreds. Another, slightly more elaborate dressage-style test, plus a half-volte, backing five strides, and a little triple combination added to a short jumping course. I'd studied the course tacked up in the stables just as avidly as everyone else who dreamed of winning the Thoroughbred Makeover. I took a long look at my watch, counting off the hour in ten-minute blocks, then shook my head sadly; there wasn't time now. "I have to go run Personal Best. I have an hour—I can just make it if I leave right now."

Kerri took Tiger's reins, but her face was unbelieving. "Did you hear me? It's *Cassidy Lehigh*. You can't just let her win. There's literally no one else here you need to beat, and this is your only shot."

My heart sank to my toes. "Who else is leading?"

Kerri pointed at the scoreboard behind me, where the top five horse and rider teams were illuminated in shining lights. I turned and looked. With 72.5 points each, Cassidy Lehigh and I were three points ahead of the next rider in line.

It was her or it was me, to win the Thoroughbred Makeover.

But Personal Best...

"You have to win this," Kerri insisted. "Beating Cassidy is everything. It's why you came! To prove her wrong, to prove all of them wrong—"

"It was," I admitted. I put a hand on Tiger's warm neck; he was sweating gently, hot in the humid south Florida air, but not distressed. He was fit enough to handle the heat and then some. Perhaps he wasn't racing fit anymore, but he was fit enough to go out and jump a course of fences, to trot and canter through a dressage test, to show the world that he was more than some one-trick pony. So was I. So were all of us, the horsewomen and horsemen who had devoted ourselves to all horses, not just racehorses, not just show horses, but every single horse on the earth who deserved a home and deserved a job and deserved a life.

We'd done good things today, but he wasn't the only horse who deserved a shot at being the best. As far as I was concerned, Tiger had already done that, tie-breaker or no tie-breaker.

But this afternoon was Personal Best's last chance.

"I have to go the track," I said. "Personal Best has to run his race, and he won't do that unless I'm there to hold his bridle." I looked into Kerri's eyes, willing her to understand. "I'm not abandoning what we did here today, or all the work we've put into this. I've put it out there that every horse matters, and now I'm going to go prove that."

Kerri worked Tiger's reins in her hands, taking them into the perfect butterfly loop she'd been shown by some riding instructor years ago, taking the lead-rope of a pony in her soft little hands and learning how to hold the cotton lead so that it never looped around her hand, in case the pony should spook or run away. The horses changed, but the basics stayed the same. She nodded slowly. "Okay. I'll cool him out." She smiled tremulously. "Show Personal Best the way home."

I gave Tiger one last hug, his wet neck hot on my cheek, and then I was speed-walking from the warm-up area while onlookers gawked and pointed at the runaway competitor. By the time the announcer was calling for me to appear at the in-gate, my name echoing from the loudspeakers, I was in the parking lot, running across the gravel, my dress boots scuffing through white shells.

Personal Best was waiting.

Chapter Thirty-seven

H E WAS STANDING UP in the paddock, standing on his two hind legs and reaching for the heavens with his forelegs, pawing at the air like a wild stallion, like a calendar photo, like a child's idea of what a racehorse should look like. But I was a trainer, and I knew better than that—a racehorse waving his legs in the air was a racehorse distressed and wasting precious energy.

Alexander, looking dashing in gray coat and cerulean tie, was at the end of the lead-shank, his gnarled hand against the knot in the end, waiting for Personal Best to come down. As I hurried across the green grass of the paddock's center, I admired his quiet, the way he stood patiently and gave Personal Best all the time he needed. Others might shout and berate, upsetting the colt's high-strung nerves and sending him into a frenzy from which he would not recover, but not Alexander—he would wait all day, if he needed to, while Personal Best hung up there in the atmosphere, daring all and sundry to try and make him come down again.

As I got closer, though, the gravity of the situation grew more apparent—the looks of despair on the faces of Luz and Hector, the pallor beneath Alexander's deep tan. Personal Best had been playing up for some time. This wasn't his first time in the air.

Luz saw me first, and gave Hector a punch. The groom rubbed his shoulder and scowled at her, then followed the direction of her finger as she pointed at me. His face burst into a relieved smile. "Ai, Alex, you get here at last!" he shouted across the paddock.

Everyone turned then: the grooms with a neighboring colt, who was watching Personal Best's antics with some interest, the nearby trainers and owners, even Personal Best. Only Alexander did not turn, his attention firm on the rearing colt, who seemed to have been in the heavens forever.

"Personal Best, you get down!" I shouted.

Right on cue, the colt's swiveling ears found me, and he came back to the earth.

Alexander slid a cautious hand up the lead and took Personal Best by the bridle, then laid his other hand on the colt's neck. "Settling down, there, lad?" he asked gently. He then turned to me. "Alex," he said, none too warmly. "You gave up on the other then." He wasn't so worried about P.B. that he couldn't find some time to be annoyed with me. "You should have finished what you started."

"I *won* the other," I snapped. "Or close enough. I told you I'd be here." I put my own hand on Personal Best's hot neck, just below Alexander's. The colt rumbled a welcoming whicker from deep within his chest, and turned his head to nip at my sleeve. Alexander's hand fell away from his bridle at the quick motion; he was always careful not to jerk on the colt's head for any purpose. I slid my other hand up under his forelock and rubbed the white blaze, bringing away a flurry of snowy hairs. "You're going bald, man," I laughed. "We better win you a race before you get old on us."

"He glad you here," Hector said approvingly. "Luz, you get the bucket and we go. It's almost time for the call, man."

"Talk to the rider," I told Alexander, who was still trying to decide if he was angry with me or proud of me. It was probably a constant struggle for him. I didn't mind. "I'll walk him."

He nodded and turned away. Across the paddock, I saw a little man in our green silks break away from a circle of media and raise a hand to Alexander. I fixed my attention back on Personal Best. Alexander could tell the jock how to ride this race. It was my job to settle the horse and put his mind on his race. *It feels good to know what your job is,* I thought suddenly, rubbing Personal Best between his fuzzy-tipped ears. *No wonder Tiger has settled down so much now that he knows what he's supposed to be doing. We all just want a job we're good at.*

To be part of the team, that was my job. Not Alex the trainer, not Alex the boss, not Alex the underling either. Alex and Alexander, the team.

I let him go at the gate, although in that moment I wished I had a pony, that I was on the smiling, laughing crew out there on the track, that I could take him out to the gate myself. In the ten minutes since I'd arrived, Personal Best had gone from wild mustang to professional racehorse, stepping up to the pony with the quite aplomb of a horse with many successful races under his girth strap. For Personal Best, it hadn't been long enough. He'd been without me for so long, causing trouble and terrorizing grooms and dumping riders while I had been wrapped up in retraining Tiger. Was it going to be enough that I was here by his side before a race? Would it make a difference to him that I shown up for his race? Or would he go back to his old criminal ways by the time he made it to the starting gate? "Hang in there, P.B.," I muttered, bellying up to the railing by the winner's circle where I'd wait for him to come galloping home. "Be cool, be cool."

"Maybe he should stay hot," Alexander suggested, coming up to join me. He had loosened his bright blue tie and unbuttoned his white shirt collar; his sleeves were rolled up. The south Florida sun was brutally hot this afternoon. It had seemed cooler than this back at the show-grounds, but the covered arena had surely helped. Sometimes I daydreamed about a covered racetrack. Why did the show horses get to work in the shade while we toiled in the blazing sun? It was a pleasant fantasy. "Cool him down too much and he'll be one of your nice quiet show horses."

I sighed. Would he *never* stop?

Alexander put a hand on my elbow. "I was only joking," he said contritely. "It's just become a habit, that joke."

I nodded stiffly, though I appreciated the apology more than I was willing to let on. At the moment, my nerves were strung far too tight to deal with anything approaching emotions. I had to stay stone-faced and stoic to see this thing through. "Let's see how he does, and then we'll joke about show horses."

The starting gate was on the far side of the infield, and I squinted across the heat waves shimmering above the baking hot track, across the glittering lake with its population of egrets wading through the reeds, across the tight turns of the turf course. Far, far away, beneath the towering sentinels of oceanfront condominiums, my chestnut colt from Ocala was loading into the starting gate.

"Just look, you can see on the screen, there—" Alexander pointed to the tote board off to our left, but I shook my head. I didn't want an HD picture on an enormous screen. I didn't want anything to be so crystal-clear. I just wanted it to be over.

Luz and Hector came strolling over, buckets and halter and chain rattling together. Hector gave me a resounding slap on the back that had horseplayers and owners nearby staring. "I put money on him," Hector stage-whispered, a grin playing on his lips. "Today, P.B. and J win his race! Right Luz?"

"Oh, *si,*" Luz sighed, taking in my white face and set lips. She shoved Hector out of her way and put her arm around my shoulders, squeezing me tight. I bore it because she meant well. "He do just fine," Luz proclaimed. "And tomorrow I bring you my grandmother's flan. She make for you. It'll build you up after all this worry."

I managed a sickly smile. Suddenly, the bell rang and the starting gate doors flew back, and I forgot about everything but Personal Best.

Chapter Thirty-eight

K ERRI WAVING THE BLUE ribbon in my face didn't make things any more clear to me.

"What did you *do?*"

She laughed and hugged me instead of answering. I've never been big on human contact, but in this case her enthusiasm was contagious, and I found my arms wrapping around her back, squeezing her tight, although I didn't have any idea what was going on.

Finally she pulled back and grinned at me. "I rode," she announced proudly. "And helped Tiger win it for you."

"What?" I sat down on a handy straw bale and gaped up at her. *"What* now?"

Alexander looked over from his perch against Personal Best's stall, where he'd been watching the big horse work at his hay-net. He was still feeling fresh after his third-place finish in the race. I supposed we all were. We weren't going to Kentucky—at least, not for the Kentucky Derby—but he'd run a good race and he'd come back sound and happy. That was all any of us could ever hope for.

Alexander looked stern. "Kerri, you didn't cheat, I hope."

"Only a little." Kerri winked. "I just counted on the judges not knowing what you looked like—remember how we were looking them up and saw they were from every business *but* racing? And two of them were from big cattle ranches. I figured they weren't paying any attention to CASH either—cowboys and cowgirls don't have time for all that animal rights crap, they're too busy taking actual care of their actual *animals*, you know? But my show gear was in the trailer from when I brought out the tack trunk. So...I just ran back to the trailer, pulled out my jacket and hat from the tack room, and mounted up. I rode back to the ring, told the steward I was ready, they said 'The Tiger Prince is next in the arena,' and in I went." She shook her head as if she couldn't believe she'd gotten away with it. Neither could I. "It was really too easy," she admitted. "Everyone from Roundtree were quiet as mice. Even Jean."

"But at the end—someone must have known something. What about Cassidy? She knows me well enough."

"Well, Cassidy did give the game away," Kerri admitted, and she held out the ribbon flat against her palm so that I could read the gold letters printed on the blue satin. *Thoroughbred Makeover ~ Versatility.* "So it's not the whole competition. But we were the only ones who put two different riders on a horse, and remember that was the versatility category they cancelled?"

"What happened to versatility?" Alexander demanded.

"They cut it out of the program because everyone complained they couldn't get an off-track horse to go so nicely for two different riders with only a few weeks of training," I recalled, rolling my eyes.

"Which is nonsense," Alexander replied, his gaze never leaving Personal Best, "considering how many different riders a racehorse is used to carrying."

"Right," Kerri agreed. "And we were *going* to try it—"

"We were going to try it, until everyone thought it was a bad idea, because it would give us an extra chance to win a division. But apparently you can't put more than one person on a Thoroughbred?"

"Even though I'd ridden him twice with no problems at all," Kerri confirmed. "But we'd already entered it, and we were the only ones with two riders, so...they gave us the first place ribbon. And said not to do it again." She laughed.

Now I reached out and she put the satin ribbon in my hand. It wasn't a huge ribbon, as the rosette awarded to Cassidy had no doubt been. But it was something. It was a blue ribbon for Tiger, and not just any blue ribbon, but one that no one else could have won. No one else believed that their horse was good enough for that phase of competition. Three months ago, I didn't even think Tiger would be ready for any of it, let alone a class so scary to trainers they protested its very offering. Tiger had proved everyone wrong...including me.

"I'm a terrible mother," I sighed, putting the ribbon back in Kerri's hands. "I didn't believe in my own child."

"Children love proving their parents wrong," Kerri said cheerfully. "Does this mean I can start calling you *Mom?*"

I kicked shed-row dirt onto her already-smudged show breeches for that one. "I meant my *horse.*"

"Whom you should probably go visit," Alexander interjected. "I have a feeling he's waiting for you and a bag of mints."

"What about P.B.?"

Personal Best shoved at his hay-net with his white-tipped nose and then snorted all over Alexander's beige blazer. Alexander jumped backwards into the shed-row, but the damage was done. "I think this one is done with our company for the night," he said ruefully, looking down at the black specks that had rained over his jacket. "And I am ready to head home for a hot shower and a change of clothes, besides."

"Oh, you have to come with me." I stood up and took Alexander's hands in mine. "You have to see him too."

"I'm no horse show dad, Alex." He grinned at me, his eyes laughing. "Don't think you can convert me just because you've fallen back in love with horse showing. I will have all I can do to hold down the racing string while you and Tiger are out jumping colored poles."

"Oh, don't be silly." I stood on my toes and planted a kiss on his tanned cheek. "I can do both. I've done both this long, I can keep it up. And I think we have a few more races to look forward to with this big bad child of ours."

We both turned back to Personal Best then, and the colt threw his head up and down, his forelock obscuring his eyes, and showed us his little yellow teeth, still baby teeth despite all of his accomplishments on the racetrack. He had a long career ahead of him, our Personal Best, and things were only just heating up.

Personal Best was going to have a different story from Tiger's, or Market Affair's. By the time he was as long in the tooth as Tiger, he would be retired to the stallion barn. He was having the story we wished for all of our racehorses, from the moment their noses poked into the world atop their feathery little foals' hooves. But

Tiger's story wasn't bad either, I reflected. As for Market Affair—all I could do was work like the devil to make sure that stories like his were told differently in the future.

I wasn't sure what that it was going to look like, yet. All I knew was that there were people out there now who believed in change, and they believed that I was going to help bring it about. Whatever happened with Personal Best, with the farm, with Alexander's dreams of standing big stallions there—I was going to be involved on the other end of the business, with retirement, just as heavily as I was with bringing new racehorses into the world.

It seemed like a good balance.

The End

Afterword

Thank you so much for reading the Alex & Alexander Series. I truly hope you enjoyed it. The writing of these books spans a decade and so I know there are some inconsistencies in there, but the heart of it all is what's most important: horses, and what they mean to us.

Alex's story doesn't end here. She appears consistently throughout The Eventing Series as a guest character, and you can also find her as a star of the new for 2022 series, Briar Hill Farm. Be sure to visit my site at nataliekreinert.com to learn more about this exciting equestrian fiction series, which includes lead characters from The Eventing Series, *Show Barn Blues, Grabbing Mane,* and *The Project Horse.*

Acknowledgments

The Thoroughbred Makeover wasn't my idea.

That honor goes to The Retired Racehorse Project, an organization of trainers, riders, and other dedicated equestrians who have been putting together Thoroughbred retirement and retraining events since 2010. The Retired Racehorse Project's training challenges, which have included the Trainer Challenge, the 100 Day Thoroughbred Challenge, and the Thoroughbred Makeover and National Symposium, have been an incredible asset to the racehorse retraining community. Using national conferences and social media, they bring the stories of retired racehorses, along with the training challenges and triumphs that come along with these amazing horses, right into people's homes.

If you haven't visited Retired Racehorse Project's wonderful website yet, please do so. You'll find resources on training retired racehorses, along with some great YouTube channels full of all the Thoroughbred videos you need to get through a rainy afternoon. You'll leave inspired and that much more knowledgeable about the amazing athlete that is the Thoroughbred horse. Go to retiredracehorseproject.org for more information.

I hope they'll forgive my lifting the title "Thoroughbred Makeover" for the purpose of my little book about the challenges facing racehorses and retirement!

I'd also like to mention some of the Thoroughbred rehoming organizations I've been privileged to work with.

Hidden Acres Rescue for Thoroughbreds, in Cocoa, Florida, has been kind enough to put a lead-rope in my hand and put me to work with their wonderful horses. They always have a beautiful selection of horses available for adoption—visit their website at hartforhorses.org.

Thoroughbred Retirement of Tampa (T.R.O.T.) offers retirement, training, and adoption services to horses from Tampa Bay Downs, a racetrack that appears in several of my books. I'll always appreciate T.R.O.T. for helping me put together my very first author event. Their website is at tampatrot.org.

Way back when, before any of these stories were written, I decided to find myself a Thoroughbred fresh off the track and retrain him, blogging about him at retiredracehorseblog.wordpress.com. Final Call went from racehorse to winning hunter pace horse in less than six months. Thanks, Final Call. You're a one-in-a-million horse, and you helped make all of these stories possible.

And finally, going back to my teenage years, thanks to Amarillo Elbert. You had a silly racehorse name, but you were the best hunter/jumper - dressage - eventer - trail horse - school horse - best friend a girl could ask for. You made sure the motto of my life would be "It's all about the Thoroughbreds."

There are hundreds of organizations and thousands of dedicated people across the country working to ensure safe and happy retirements for racehorses, both within the racing industry and without. There's probably someone in your neighborhood. Reach out, see what you can do to promote Thoroughbreds with them. Together, we can be breed advocates, creating awareness about the true value of these incredible athletes.

About the Author

Like many of my characters, I live in Florida, where I write fiction and freelance for a variety of publications. In the past I've worked professionally in many aspects of the equestrian world, including grooming for top event riders, training off-track Thoroughbreds, galloping racehorses, patrolling Central Park on horseback, working on breeding farms, and more! I use all of this experience to inform the equestrian scenes in my novels. They say that truth is stranger than fiction, and those of us in the horse business will certainly agree!

Visit my website at nataliekreinert.com to keep up with the latest news and read occasional blog posts and book reviews. For previews, installments of upcoming fiction, and exclusive stories, visit my Patreon page at patreon.com/nataliekreinert and learn how you can become one of my team members.

For more, find me on social media:

- Facebook: facebook.com/nataliekellerreinert

- Group: facebook.com/groups/societyofweirdhorsegirls

- Bookbub: bookbub.com/profile/natalie-keller-reinert

- Twitter: twitter.com/nataliegallops

- Instagram: instagram.com/nataliekreinert

- Email: natalie@nataliekreinert.com

Printed in Great Britain
by Amazon

52887864R00211